Pusan Perimeter

The Forgotten War

Book 1

Matt Jackson

Matt Jackson Books

Dedicated to those who served and were never appreciated for their service.

Introduction

The "police action," as declared by then-president Truman in 1950, has frequently been referred to as the Forgotten War. By those that served, it is referred to as the Korean War and is anything but forgotten. There were 36,634 US personnel killed in action, and another 7,400 are still listed as missing in action to this day. Wounded amounted to 92,134 US personnel and 4,439 prisoners of war. Most MIA are believed to be in North Korea. Over 2 million civilians, North and South, were killed in this "police action." Estimates place the number of Chinese killed between 180,000 and 400,000 and North Korean soldiers killed at about 500,000. South Korean forces suffered 313,000 killed. Financial cost to the US over the course of the war was $144.5 million, a paltry number compared to the costs of war today. At the conclusion of the war in 1953, an armistice was signed but a peace treaty was not, and so technically the war is not over yet.

To the Western world in the mid-twentieth century, Korea was generally a forgotten land. To the Chinese, Japanese and Russians, it was always of interest and had at various times throughout its history been occupied by one of the three. The Japanese occupied Korea for forty years before and during the Second World War and declared it a province of Japan, attempting to replace the Korean culture, language and institutions with its own. The successes of the Japanese during the

First Sino-Japanese War in 1894–1895 ended China's ambitions for Korea. The Russo-Japanese War of 1904 saw Japan gain total dominance over Korea and rule there until 1945. At the Potsdam Conference, the Allies agreed that Korea would be divided, with the Soviet Union supervising above the 38th parallel and the US supervising south of the 38th parallel. Many felt this arrangement prevented the Soviets from gaining a larger footprint on the Japanese islands. The stated US position of a blue-water defense ignored Korea but included Japan, Ryukyus, Formosa, Philippines, the East Indies, Indonesia and Malaysia.

Korea is a peninsula spanning from the 34th parallel to the 43rd parallel, 600 miles in length and ninety to 200 miles wide with 5,600 miles of coastline and 85,000 square miles. The Yalu River forms a common border with China for 500 miles and flows northeast into the Yellow Sea. The center of the peninsula consists of craggy ridges generally running north to south and is unfit for farming. Few roads were paved at the time, and one rail line ran from Seoul to Pusan. The southern portion of Korea was primarily agricultural along the coastlines, while the north was noted for mining and hydroelectric production. Population distribution was approximately 9 million north of the 38th parallel and 21 million south of the 38th parallel.

Soviet forces moved into Korea in August of 1945. It was September of that year before any US forces reached Seoul. In the years between 1945 and 1950, elections to unify the two Koreas were attempted and repeatedly stopped by the Soviets. In 1948, North Korea refused to allow a UN commission to enter the country. Eventually, South Korea held elections and Syngman Rhee became the first president of South Korea.

The US position on armament for the South Korean military was seen as a minimal amount. The US viewed the South Korean military as a police force to put down communist guerrillas as opposed to being a full-fledged army, and thus it was equipped with only small arms and light machine guns. The State Department also feared that with too strong of an army, Syngman Rhee would attempt to invade North Korea. Thus, the US provided South Korea with no tanks or antitank guns, and the only artillery given to them was 105 howitzers. The South Korean Army had 95,000 soldiers organized into eight divisions, while the South Korean Air Force consisted of twelve L-2 observation aircraft and ten T-6 Texans, single-engine piston trainers. There was no navy but a coast guard of 6,000 sailors with the mission of preventing smuggling. Everything was Second World War vintage. The US provided 500 advisors to support the rebuilding of the South Korean military.

The Soviet position, on the other hand, was much different. The Soviets equipped the North Korean Army with tanks, artillery, mortars and fighter aircraft. They also provided over 3,500 advisors to train the North Koreans. Many of the North Koreans had fought with the communist Chinese forces during the Second World War. The North Korean Army could field eight fully manned and equipped divisions plus two independent regiments and five reserve regiments. The armored brigade had 120 T-34 tanks. The air force had forty Yak fighters and seventy ground-attack aircraft. Leading the North Korean forces was Kim Il Sung, who had served in the Soviet Red Army in Manchuria.

Kim was determined to unify Korea under communist rule. He wanted the communist world to recognize Korea and acknowledge him as a leader in the communist movement. He was as fervent a supporter of communism as Rhee was of democracy. Add to this the ego and ambitions of General MacArthur, and the stage was set to drag the world's two superpowers into a global conflict.

In conducting my research for this series, I was surprised at the similarities between the US Army of then and the US Army of today. In both cases, the Army had just come out of a major conflict, World War II back then and twenty years in Iraq and Afghanistan today. In both cases, recruiting young men to fill the ranks was a problem. Funding was lacking and therefore the acquisition of new weapons was reduced. Funding also affected the ability to conduct realistic training. To make the service more appealing, physical fitness standards were lowered and more time was spent in lectures and off-duty hours. The service was also disrupted by social changes, desegregation in the late

Introduction

1940s and the demise of "Don't Ask, Don't Tell" in the twenty-first century.

This historical novel is my attempt to pay tribute to those Americans that fought in this "police action." I have researched and attempted to recreate the events as they happened and when possible used the names of those that fought in these battles. In most cases, conversations are what I believe would have been said under the circumstances. Where I was able to find and use actual quotes, I have footnoted them.

Chapter 1
Prelude to War

17 JUNE 1950
Alexandria, Virginia

"EXCUSE ME, gentlemen, but I need someone that can mix a martini," Patricia Godbold, the hostess, announced as she walked into the kitchen, where all the men had migrated, leaving their wives in the living room. Military wives all knew when the men clustered in the kitchen it was to talk shop. Patricia was married to Lieutenant Colonel Bryghte D. Godbold, USMC, a rising star in the Pentagon.[1] Working in the five-sided puzzle palace had its drawbacks but also its perks. One of the perks was meeting the right people, and Bryghte was meeting the right people in his position as an aide in the SecDef office. He had joined the Marine Corps after graduating from Auburn University with an electrical engineering degree in 1936. He'd sat out the Second World War in a Japanese POW camp, having been captured on Wake Island when it fell in December of 1941. This was his going-away party as he would be leaving in the morning for a choice assignment as

---

1. Lt. Col. Bryghte D. Godbold retired from the USMC in 1958 as a brigadier general. He passed away in 2013 at the age of 99.

assistant to the chief of staff for the 1st Marine Division in Camp Pendleton, California. Patricia would follow on after she got the house sold.

"I believe I can make that happen, dear," Bryghte said, reaching for the martini shaker. "I'll bring it to you as soon as it's ready." What Patricia heard was *We're talking shop and it's not for your ears.*

"Thank you, kind sir, but don't take too long. I'm thirsty," Patricia said with a coy smile and returned to the ladies.

"I'm telling you Louis Johnson is going to destroy the military. If he isn't removed, we won't be able to fight our way out of a paper bag," Lieutenant Colonel Bob Shields said. Bob worked in the SecDef office and absolutely hated the job. "Hell, Roosevelt fired him when he was assistant secretary of war during the Second World War."

"Bob, he's doing the president's bidding, isn't he? Truman made him SecDef and the guy has no military background. He was, what, a lawyer in Truman's campaign and a big fundraiser," Lieutenant Colonel Jim Johnson injected. Jim worked as a liaison officer to the newly formed Central Intelligence Agency. "Undersecretary Army Draper is no help. He says that Korea is of no strategic interest to the US and we need to be emphasizing Europe. There's no money in the Army budget to maintain a substantial US force anywhere but Europe. There are, what, three or four hundred military advisors in Korea, and they don't even work for DoD."

"Who the hell do they work for? KMAG is a military organization under MacArthur, isn't it?" Lieutenant Colonel Stew Wilson asked. Stew was from the Office of Logistic Management.

"No, they work for the State Department. They report to the ambassador. Far East Command only provides logistical and administrative support," said Lieutenant Colonel Bob Atwell, who worked in the Army Chief of Staff office.

"Truman is the problem, I'm telling you. He was only a captain in World War I—artillery, I believe. He was a farmer before the war and had a clothing store after the war. That went under when he went into politics. He hates the service chiefs, calling them 'dumb spendthrifts,' and doesn't hold back on letting everyone know it.

Thinks he's militarily smarter than Bradley and the others. He's a fiscal conservative penny pincher. Our budget for the entire military this year is thirteen billion dollars—thirteen billion. That's it. Hell, divisions are at only two-thirds of authorized strength and we don't have any ammo stockpiled," Stew said. "The new Air Force claims they can stop any war with their atomic bombs, and Secretary Johnson believes that bull. General Vandenberg, the new Air Force chief of staff, says we probably don't need a navy any longer because his bombers can destroy any fleet that opposes us. Says the Navy and Marine Corps shouldn't have their own air forces. It all should be under the Air Force. You would think that the Revolt of the Admirals last year would have turned things around, but it hasn't."

"I can tell you that the Army chief of staff is saying that it's time to do away with the Marine Corps as amphibious operations are a thing of the past. General Eisenhower thought the Marine Corps should be reduced to only ceremonial duties here in Washington and at embassies," Bryghte informed the group as Patricia entered the doorway and stopped.

"What does a lady have to do to get a drink around here?"

"Sorry, babe, I'll get right on it," Bryghte said, grabbing a fresh martini glass.

"See that you do or I'll start calling you sailor," she said with a cocked eyebrow and departed.

"Hey, I understand that General Farrell is leaving us and heading to Korea to take over Korean Military Advisor Group in July. Wonder who he pissed off to get that assignment?" Jim Johnson asked.

"He didn't piss anyone off," Lieutenant Colonel Bob Atwell said. "I was in the chief's office when Major General Keating, who was slated to take the position when Roberts retired, decided at the last minute that he was going to retire as well. General Collins hit the ceiling and Farrell made the mistake of being the next appointment on the chief's calendar. Roberts left last week and the chief gave Farrell until the twenty-fifth of July to get over there. Right now the KMAG chief of staff, Colonel Wright, is in temporary command. Bad for

Farrell is that Wright departs there just about the time Farrell gets there," Atwell explained.

"Has Farrell ever worked for the Emperor before?" Bryghte asked.

"The Emperor?" Stew asked with a questioning look.

"Yeah, the Emperor, General MacArthur. If he hasn't, then he's in for a rude awakening even if he is working for the ambassador. He'll still have to play nice with the Emperor. MacArthur has surrounded himself with guys that served with him in the Pacific and they're all yes-men in my opinion. Now if Louis Johnson would fire MacArthur, then I would think a little better of him," Bryghte indicated.

"I can tell you the CIA wouldn't mind seeing MacArthur taken down a notch," Jim Johnson said. "He won't allow the CIA to operate in Japan or anywhere in his empire. We've been trying to find out what Mao in China is up to and he's shut the door on us. Same with looking at North Korea. He has General Willoughby, who in my opinion tells MacArthur exactly what he wants to hear, regardless of the facts."[2]

"Who's Willoughby?" Stew asked.

"He's MacArthur's chief of intelligence and is intelligent only in title," Johnson offered.

"I understand that Dean Acheson is over in Asia right now.[3] Has anyone heard how his trip is going and what he's being told?" Bob Atwell asked.

"He's getting the usual glad-handing from MacArthur, my source says. He made a speech at the National Press Club back in January that detailed the blue-water strategy for the containment of communism and left Korea out of it. Some people are pissed that this was a mistake. MacArthur wants to turn Chiang Kai-shek loose on mainland China and is trying to get Acheson to go along with his plan. He published a State Department white paper on China–US relations that has some people really upset. They blame him for the fall of Chiang. He says it

---

2. Major General Charles A. Willoughby was considered by many to be the worst chief of intelligence ever. Franz-Stefan Gady, "Is This the Worst Intelligence Chief in the US Army's History?," *The Diplomat*, January 27, 2019, https://thediplomat.com/2019/01/is-this-the-worst-intelligence-chief-in-the-us-armys-history/.
3. Dean G. Acheson was the fifty-first secretary of state at the time.

would be a mistake for the US to get involved in mainland China," Bryghte said.

"Well, I can tell you we shouldn't get involved anywhere with the condition of the Army right now. There's no money for training, so the troops sit and listen to lectures about the evils of venereal disease and communism. When they're not in lectures, they're in education classes. Hell, they should be on the rifle ranges, working in the motor pools, in the field on maneuvers—but there's no money for that stuff. The result is we have untrained, unmotivated, out-of-shape troops," Atwell said.

"Okay, I've waited long enough," Patricia said. No one had noticed that she had entered the kitchen area. "You men march your butts into the living room with the ladies and stop this shop talk. You get to do that five days a week for ten hours a day. Not having it here tonight. Now march. And you"—she pointed at Bryghte—"had best have my drink in your hand when you get there." Everyone recognized who wore the pants in this house and complied immediately.

Chapter 2
It Begins

24 June 1950
KMAG Officers' Mess
Seoul, South Korea

THE DAY HAD BEEN one of festivities. The Republic of Korea Army Headquarters in Seoul was celebrating the opening of its first Officers' Club. They had invited the Korean Military Advisor Group (KMAG) to attend the celebration as well as members of the embassy staff. In addition, ROK headquarters had extended leave to thousands of soldiers who had been positioned along the border with North Korea as a reward for the previous months of false alarms, which resulted in units having to respond to possible threats. As festivities at the ROK Officers' Club were winding down, Lieutenant Colonel Carl Sturies, the acting commander for KMAG, invited Major General Chae Byong Duk, the chief of staff for the ROK Army, to join the KMAG officers at the KMAG Officers' Mess. Korean officers were never noted for turning down an invitation to attend a party, especially with Jack Daniel's being served, and General Chae quickly accepted.[1]

"Okay, everybody, listen up. We're moving over to the Officers' Mess, and our Korean friends have agreed to join us. It's 1600 hours now, so let's meet at 1830 at the mess. That should give you time to change into appropriate attire. Ambassador Muccio, I hope you and your staff will join us as well," Sturies said.

General Roberts was the commander of KMAG but had departed ten days prior in order to return to the United States. Colonel W. H. Wright was the chief of staff and was slated to attend the Industrial College of the Armed Forces but was being delayed until Brigadier General Farrell could arrive on 25 July.[2] Wright was not present as he was in Japan, putting his family on a ship to precede him to Washington. Sturies was the senior US officer at KMAG in Seoul, and so the honors of hosting the festivities at the Officers' Mess fell upon him. The KMAG Officers' Club hosted a dance every Saturday night— Class A uniform or coat and tie required.

In the past sixteen months, the KMAG had been expanded from ninety-two officers and one hundred and forty-eight enlisted men to its present size of four hundred and eighty personnel with one hundred and eighty-four officers, four warrant officers and three hundred and nine enlisted men. The growing pains in such a short period had been taxing on the senior staff. Along with the additional people came expanded responsibilities. Advisors were now being introduced to the battalion levels in the divisions as well as managing a schools program for the Korean officers. Besides pains from the rapid growth, other problems had to be overcome. Language, for one, as the Korean language didn't have words to describe modern technology or even many military terms, so US advisors had to write a Korean–English dictionary.

---

1. Korean names place the family name first. In this case, he will be referred to as General Chae throughout.

2. Colonel W. H. Wright retired at the rank of lieutenant general in 1965 and died in 2009. He was a national equestrian champion, winning the International Military Equestrian Championship in 1946.

Another area that had to be resolved was who KMAG worked for. KMAG was a Department of the Army organization, but the State Department, through Ambassador Muccio, had operational control of KMAG. The Far East Command under General MacArthur had responsibility for the logistic support of KMAG and the emergency evacuation of US personnel if the need arose. A close relationship with Far East Command was imperative. They also had to work with the Joint Administrative Services (JAS), which was a government organization responsible for maintaining facilities such as barracks, family housing, utilities, and mess halls. Facilities management included the Sobinggo Housing Area with one hundred and nine Western-style homes, dispensary, chapel, officers' mess and EM barracks and a DoD school for children. Yongdungpo Housing area seven miles south of Seoul had thirty-seven housing units, and the ASCOM City housing area had sixty housing units, all for military dependents. Dependents were allowed to live in Taejon, Taegu, Pusan and Kwangju as well. Most of KMAG personnel were stationed in the vicinity of Seoul, but others were located in eighteen locations around Korea.

At 1800 hours, people began arriving at the Officers' Mess. Advisors would seek out their counterparts and attempt to include them in conversations, but as few advisors spoke Korean and few Koreans spoke English, it was a challenge. Generally after an hour or so, Americans would tend to gather together and Korean officers would do the same. None objected or felt slighted by this.

"Sir, I'm telling you we have got to get better intelligence from our counterparts," Captain Reed, the G-2 advisor, said. "Tokyo isn't telling us anything except the sky is blue, and yet our contacts are telling me different. They're saying there's been a lot of movement along the border." Unfortunately, Captain Reed had been saying the same thing for some time, to the point that senior officers were tired of hearing it as there was nothing they could do about it and Tokyo wasn't confirming any of the information.

"Look, General Roberts felt confident that the South Koreans could handle anything the North Koreans would throw at them. He told that *Time* magazine reporter just the other day that South Korea has the best army outside the US. He pointed out to them that tanks can't operate in Korea because of the terrain with narrow roads and boggy rice paddies. They have an army of a hundred and forty-five thousand troops with eight divisions, and they're well equipped with M1 rifles, bazookas and 105 howitzers," Lieutenant Colonel Thomas McPhail, senior advisor to the 6th ROK Infantry Division, replied.

"Sir, I can say that your division is probably one of the better-equipped divisions, but the others are not. We've supplied them with enough equipment for a constabulary of sixty-five thousand men. They're at about one hundred thousand now. They've drained their stocks of ammunition and spare parts. They don't have the supply and maintenance systems in place yet to service their equipment. In June last year, we sent them fifty-one million rounds of ammunition of all types. Last week I looked into what they have now…only nineteen million rounds left," indicated Major Geist, the G-4 advisor, who had been monitoring the conversation. Like Captain Reed, he had been voicing his concerns, though with somewhat more tact.

"Sir, the ROKs don't have a single long-range howitzer, no fighter aircraft, no heavy mortars and no recoilless rifles. The M1 rifle is too big for them considering their physical size. They'd be better served with the M1 carbine or Thompson submachine guns," Captain James Hausman, LNO to Major General Chae, indicated.[3]

"Let me ask, Captain," McPhail said, "is that your opinion or the sniveling of General Chae looking for more equipment?"

"What's this about General Chae?" Ambassador Muccio asked. No one had noticed him walking up behind them. John Muccio was Italian-born and had graduated from George Washington University and served faithfully in the State Department before being appointed ambassador to South Korea in 1949 by President Truman. "Personally, I think General Chae's sniveling has merit, as I testified before

---

3. Many, to include President Rhee, considered Captain James H. Hausman the father of the Korean Army. He retired as a lieutenant colonel. Allan R. Millett, "Captain James H. Hausman and the Formation of the Korean Army, 1945–1950," *Armed Forces & Society* 23, no. 4 (Summer 1997): 503–39, https://doi.org/10.1177/0095327x9702300401.

Congress last month. The South Koreans need additional military support and equipment."[4]

"We were just asking Captain Hausman about serving as the liaison officer for General Roberts to General Chae," McPhail answered quickly.

The evening festivities continued for several more hours as the next day was Sunday and an off-duty day for almost everyone.

"Sir, may I ask what's probably a stupid question?" Captain Reed asked, looking at Ambassador Muccio. Ambassador Muccio was a bespectacled man and generally wore a bow tie, which was fashionable in 1950.

"The only stupid questions, Captain, are the questions not asked. What is your question?" Muccio said.

"Sir, why is KMAG under the State Department and not Far East Command?" Captain Reed asked.

"The powers in Washington in 1944 formed a committee to oversee political-military issues in the occupied Axis countries. They were fearful that under Rhee, South Korea would take off and attack North Korea. This committee, known as the State-War-Navy Coordinating Committee, or SWNCC, was composed of the secretaries of the services so that they could hammer out common problems. One problem was the question of Korea. The US really didn't want to have an occupation force here but recognized the need to bring the South Korean government and military up to speed. Remember, Japan ran everything in this country for the past forty years—the military, the police, city and government administration, industry, the economy. The Koreans were virtual slaves and left on their own would quickly fall under the communists. We had to do something to get South Korea on its feet. So the decision was made to create KMAG but put it under the control of State to coordinate the activities involved. I think we're doing a good job of achieving that goal," Muccio said.

---

4. Howard W. French, "John J. Muccio, 89; Was U.S. Diplomat in Several Countries," *New York Times*, May 22, 1989, https://www.nytimes.com/1989/05/22/obituaries/john-j-muccio-89-was-us-diplomat-in-several-countries.html.

"Sir, how was Mr. Acheson's visit?" Colonel McPhail asked. Dean Acheson had been touring Korea and had left earlier that day.

"I think it went well. General Chae was gracious and answered all the questions with the right answers. Mr. Acheson flew out this afternoon and is now General MacArthur's problem." Muccio's comment brought a chuckle from the group.

Chapter 3
First Thunder

25 June 1950
    12th Regiment
    Kaesong, South Korea

CAPTAIN JOSEPH DARRIGO, advisor to the 12th Regiment, was snuggled down in his bed, lost in a dream. Darrigo had served in World War II, assaulting across Utah Beach on 6 June 1944, and later that year was awarded the Silver Star for his actions. His roommate, Lieutenant William Hamilton, was attending the festivities in Seoul and had departed the day before. Darrigo was just enjoying the solitude for a change. The soft rain had been pelting the tin roof all night and Darrigo found it comforting. The sound of thunder, however, jarred him from his sleep at 0400 hours. *That's the first thunder I've heard with this front passing through,* he thought. As he lay there listening and becoming more awake, it dawned on him that it wasn't thunder caused by the weather front but thunder caused by artillery, and a lot of artillery at that. The Kaesong sector had been under frequent artillery bombardment for the past month.

When the first round impacted a hundred yards from his billet, he knew whose artillery it was and immediately jumped up, pulled on his pants and sprinted outside. In the night sky to the north, he could see the muzzle flashes of countless guns firing and now heard the distinct sound of small-arms fire. Returning to his room, he frantically got his boots on, retrieved his shirt and helmet and raced out to his jeep. His houseboy was already in the jeep, waiting for him.

"We go, we go now," the houseboy yelled as Darrigo came out the door.

Driving as fast as possible, he headed for the closest town, Kaesong, which was northwest of Seoul and housed the 1st ROK Division headquarters. Before he reached the headquarters, bullets were pockmarking the walls of buildings. Reaching the headquarters, Darrigo ran inside and found Colonel Paik Sun Yup, the division commander. Yup was on the radio, contacting his units in the vicinity of Seoul and ordering them to move up. Most of the regiments of the four divisions positioned along the 38th Parallel had their regiments billeted well south of the border. Grabbing an available phone, he called Captain Reed at his quarters.

"Reed, Darrigo here. Can you hear me?"

"At this ungodly hour of the morning, yeah, I hear you and you sound like a bad dream. What the hell do you want?"

"I told you these assholes were going to launch an attack, and it's started. We're getting the crap shelled out of us and we have troops in contact. Hell, they have troops in Kaesong right now in street-to-street fighting. Yup has ordered up his regiments from Seoul, but I don't know if they'll get here before we're overrun," Darrigo explained as calmly as he could. Reed had become more alert the more Darrigo talked and was wide awake now.

"Let me call Colonel Sturies and I'll get back to you," Reed said, hanging up on Darrigo and dialing Colonel Sturies, who answered on the third ring. Carl Sturies was a graduate of the US Military Academy, West Point, and had seen action in World War II as a signal corps officer. He was forty-eight years old.[1]

"Colonel Sturies here," a groggy voice said.

---

1. He retired at the rank of colonel and died in 1978 at the age of 75.

"Sir, Captain Reed here. Darrigo just called me. They're under a full-blown attack in his sector."

"What! How does he know that?" Sturies said, sitting up in bed and throwing the covers off.

"Sir, he was taking artillery fire and small-arms fire at the 1st ROK Division headquarters. I could hear the small arms in the background when I was talking to him. Yup is calling his regiments forward according to Darrigo," Reed explained.

"Execute the alert roster. Call the duty officer and have him do it. Everyone in my office in one hour," he ordered, and the phone line went dead.

MAJOR GERALD LARSEN, the senior advisor to the 8th Division, was asleep in his quarters in Kangnung on the eastern coast of Korea when a pounding on the door woke him up. Two ROK officers were standing outside with very anxious looks on their faces. One handed Larsen a note. As Larsen opened it, one of the officers blurted out, "North Korea attack."

The note read, *North Korean attack on 10th Regiment along 38th Parallel.* Larsen immediately got dressed and headed over to the 8th Division command post. As he did so, he could hear small-arms fire coming from the north. Reaching the headquarters, he picked up a telephone and called Major George Kessler at Samch'ok.

"George, Gerald here. Hey, I just got a report that the North Koreans have hit the 10th Regiment along the 38th. What's your status?" Larsen asked. George Kessler was about thirty miles south of Kangnung.

"Appears to be all quiet down here. Let me get—hold on, someone's knocking at my door. Be right back," he told Larsen and set the receiver down. Opening the door, he found two police officers standing there and fidgeting.

"You come, come quick. We have boats offloading people. You come," one said in broken English.

Kessler got back on the telephone. "Hey, Gerald, I have two cops here and they're saying that there are boats offloading people north and south of my location. Let me look into this and get back to you."

"Okay, but be careful."

Kessler finished getting dressed and drove north of the town to a bluff overlooking the northern beach. *Damn*, he thought at the sight he saw. Below on the beach was a large group of men, with more offloading from boats. Out to sea, other boats were standing by to come in and offload the men on their decks. From the distance, he thought they might be guerrilla forces. They were in no military formation, just milling around on the beach. Satisfied, he pulled back and drove south of the town. The same scene was unfolding there as well. More boats with men on decks and offloading. *This is not good*, he thought as he drove back to the 21st Regimental headquarters.

When he ran inside, it was obvious that the regiment had been alerted. Kessler immediately grabbed the regimental operations officer and explained to him the situation on the beaches, which he was not aware of. Quickly he issued orders, and while he led one group north, Kessler led the second group south. Both groups were well armed with machine guns and recoilless rifles. Kessler watched as the ROK commander positioned his forces overlooking the beach and then gave the command to open fire. The combination of machine guns and recoilless rifles was devastating to the enemy below. The recoilless rifles focused on the boats that were shuttling soldiers ashore, sinking several and setting others on fire. As this was going on, Kessler noted that the mother ships further out began to withdraw. He drove back to the regimental headquarters and called Larsen after he checked to verify the situation on the north side of town.

"Gerald, we caught the two parties on the beach and hit them hard. The mother ships are withdrawing over the horizon. The landing craft have been sunk. The regiment is deployed along the coast at this time. We still have contact on the north side," George reported.

"Okay, I'll keep you posted on the situation and you do the same. Talk more later," Larsen said and hung up.

BY 0800 HOURS, most of the KMAG personnel had been alerted and were beginning to realize the gravity of the situation. Lieutenant Colonel Sturies contacted Colonel Wright in Tokyo. Colonel Wright was attending Mass with his family when a sergeant tapped him on the shoulder and handed him a note.

From: KMAG Headquarters, Seoul
TO: Commander, KMAG Headquarters Seoul. Colonel Wright.
Subject: INVASION
Comments: Call office LTC Sturies immediately.

Wright excused himself and left the Mass to find the chaplain's office and a telephone. After a few brief comments to the military operator about priority calls, he was put through to KMAG head-quarters.

"Carl," Wright said, "what the hell is going on?"

"Sir, the North Koreans have launched an attack across the 38th," Sturies reported.

"Where?" Wright asked in surprise.

"Across the entire front. Ongjin, Kaesong, Tongduch'on-ni, P'och'on, Ch'unch'on and amphibious landings at Kangnung and Samch'ok. Every division on the front is committed and engaged. The only one not committed right now is the Capital Division, but the 17th Regiment is in a fight on the peninsula. The 1st Division has already called for the reserve regiment to come forward," Sturies outlined.

"What's Chae doing?" Wright asked with concern.

"He's called a meeting and is assembling his staff."

"Recommend that he initiate the defensive plan we developed three months ago with him. For now, tell our people to stay with their coun-terparts. I'll see about getting a flight out of here and get there as soon as I can. You probably should talk to the ambassador about initiating the evacuation plan for the dependents and nonessential personnel. I'll swing by MacArthur's headquarters and see what they're looking at," Wright stated.

"Sir, I talked to Chae…they need ammo badly. Major Geist said they only have about nineteen million rounds in the system. Can Tokyo send more and fast?"

"I'll request it as soon as I get over there. Do we know what units are attacking?"

"On Ongjin it started with the North Korean Constabulary Unit, but reports now indicate the 6th Division is leading the attack against that regiment. It looks like two divisions are hitting each of our forward divisions supported by tanks. Details are a bit sketchy at this point."

"But you're sure that this is a full-blown invasion and not just a harassment?" Wilson asked.

"Oh yes, sir. This is way more than the usual harassment, I'm sure of that," Sturies said.

"Okay, let me get over to MacArthur's headquarters and see what I can generate. I'll call you later."

AMBASSADOR MUCCIO RECEIVED the call from President Rhee at 0800 hours. Rhee explained the situation and requested that additional ammo be sent immediately to Korea, which Muccio forwarded to Tokyo. His major concern at the moment was not for more ammo but for the nonessential embassy personnel and the dependents of both embassy and military personnel.

"Get me Commander Seifert," Muccio said to his secretary as he passed by her desk en route to his office. Commander John P. Seifert, USN, was the naval attaché at the embassy.[2] Moments later, Commander Seifert was in the ambassador's office.

"You wished to see me, sir?" Seifert asked.

"Yes, I may be enacting the evacuation plan Cruller Highball," Ambassador Muccio indicated. The overall evacuation plan was code-

____

2. For his actions, he was awarded the Legion of Merit.

named Cruller. There were three levels. The lowest level carried just the code word Cruller, which indicated civil disturbances, such as student demonstrations or workers' strikes. The second level was code word Fireside. Transmitted in the clear over the embassy radio network, this code word alerted all civilian and military personnel to report for duty and all other civilians and dependents to return to their respective quarters. The third level was code word Highball. On this level, everyone in the Seoul area would move to ASCOM City and the evacuation would commence. Those outside of Seoul would move to Pusan for evacuation.

"Commander, I want you to get over to Inchon and find usable ships for us to place evacuees aboard and get them to Japan if necessary. I've spoken with the embassy in Tokyo and with General MacArthur's headquarters. They're making preparations to receive them once we issue the order. Get back to me as soon as you can on the status of a ship there. I anticipate we'll also have to fly some out of Kimpo Airfield, but that won't handle a lot. The ship is our best bet," the ambassador outlined.

"Sir, how many people are we talking about?" Seifert asked.

"Considering wives and children alone, we're looking at over seven hundred just from Seoul. That includes military dependents and embassy staff personnel," Muccio said.

"Sir, it's probably not going to be a cruise ship," Seifert warned.

"I don't care what kind of a ship it is and neither will they, as long as it floats and can make it to Japan."

"I'll leave immediately, sir," Seifert said and departed.

MAJOR GENERAL CHAE had assembled his staff along with their advisors. An air strike by North Korean aircraft had already hit Seoul earlier in the day and the result was panic in the streets caused by the strike and the number of refugees moving south from the frontier. There was no doubt in anyone's mind that this was a full-blown invasion.

"Gentlemen, let's review our defensive plan. General Park, please discuss what we know of the enemy situation at this time." General Park was the chief of intelligence and had been attempting to determine the size and identification of the North Korean units. General Park spoke very good English, and with the advisors present, the decision was to use English for the presentation.

"At this time, we have several types of units and a few of the unit designations. On the Ongjin Peninsula, action was started by the North Korean Constabulary Brigade, occupying a position that overlook our side of the 38th Parallel. The 14th Regiment of the 6th North Korean Infantry Division replace them and made the crossing of 38th Parallel," Park said and pointed to a map with both friendly and enemy units indicated. "Against 1st Infantry Division at Kaesong is remainder of 6th Division, with tanks from the 105 Armored Regiment. Another division following the 6th." Again Park pointed at the map. "Now 7th Division being attacked on two avenues. One division with tanks moves south from Yonch'on towards Tongduch'on'ni, and a second division from Kumhwa south towards P'osh'on. I believe these units fall under the First North Korean Corps." Park paused to let the audience grasp the situation.

"In the east, the Second North Korean Corps directs the assaults. Our 6th Division, located at Ch'unch'on, has an infantry division coming from Hwoch'on and another infantry division coming from Inje. Two amphibious landings have cut the road at Kangnung, and the 10th is engaging. The 21st Infantry Regiment is holding the beach against one of the amphibious forces at Samch'ok," Park concluded, laying his pointer down. "I should expect continued air strikes and long-range artillery fire for the remainder of the day. If no questions, General Jung will discuss the current disposition of our forces." General Park sat down and General Jung came forward, picking up the pointer.

"Gentlemen, the disposition of our forces is as indicated," he said, pointing at a map. "Seventeenth Regiment of the Capital Division in Ongjin is slowly being pushed back to the southern end of the peninsula. One LST standing by to extract them if necessary and two more en route currently to assist if it becomes necessary. One regiment of the 1st Division at Kaesong. Two regiments left their barracks north of Seoul, moving north to join the division headquarters. Two regiments of the 7th Division moving north to join the one regiment of the 7th astride the two roads. The 6th Division has one regiment in Ch'unch'on. A second regiment is in Hongch'on and a third regiment is in Hoengsong. The 10th Regiment of the 8th Division is north of Kangnung, and the 21st Regiment is located at Samch'ok," General Jung outlined.

"So you're telling me that we really are facing this threat with just four regiments initially," General Chae said in a bit of a shock.

"Yes, General. Many soldiers were granted long weekend passes and were not at their assigned posts when the invasion commenced this morning," Jung explained. "We have issued orders to 2nd Division at Taejon to reinforce and they are boarding trains now. The 5th Regiment being the first. The 5th Division has also been alerted and should be on the way by 1800 hours today," he concluded.

"What about the 3rd Infantry Division? Have they been alerted?" Chae asked.

"Sir, Colonel Yu Sung Yuk is in conference in Chinju. We have left word at his headquarters in Taegu, which told us he's on the road driving back to Taegu. They are attempting to contact him," Jung stated.

"General Chae, I have instructed all advisors to remain with the units for the time being," Sturies said. "I'm awaiting orders and instructions from Tokyo on what we're to do. It seems that clear instructions on what to do in the event of an invasion were never given to KMAG. I've spoken with the ambassador and he couldn't even give us clear guidance on what to do. The alternatives are one, we could take up arms and fight alongside our counterparts; two, we could continue as advisors without actively engaging the enemy; and three, we could pack up and go home. A fourth alternative was offered by the ambassador, and that's for us to move into the embassy and claim diplomatic immunity status. We've expressed that the fourth, as far as the advisors are concerned, is not an option, and option three is only if we're ordered out by Tokyo. We'll continue to offer advice for the time being."

"Thank you. We look forward to continue working together," Chae said and turned to General Jung. "General Jung, review our general defensive plan. See where we can give up ground and redeploy forces."

Jung stood and moved back to the map. "Area A is the Ongjin Peninsula. If we give it up, we move 17th Regiment back to support the Capital Division in Seoul," he said.

Chae quickly turned to Park. "General Park, what are the capabilities of the North to move forces from Ongjin to attack Inchon?"

"Sir, very difficult. Require flat-bottom boats for the most part. The tides extreme, and ships can only enter the channel during high tide, which occurs every twelve hours. I don't think they have the capability to launch an amphibious assault there," General Park said.

General Chae turned back to General Jung. "Be prepared to extract the 17th from Ongjin in the morning. Notify the 17th Regimental commander and the Capital Division commander," he ordered in Korean. "Please continue, General Jung," he went on, switching back to English.

"Sir, Area B covers thirty-five air miles across the Ch'ongdan area from Haeju Bay to Yesong River. It is mountainous terrain along the 38th Parallel. Low hills, flatlands between there and coast. Good lateral roads in this area. Six fair roads north and south. There bridge for rail and a separate bridge for highway over the Yesong River. The 1st Infantry Division is located in this area as well as Area C," General Jung said and was acknowledged by General Chae.

"Area C stretches from the Yesong River to Imjin River, with a major road running north to south. This is center of the 1st Infantry Division's sector. Terrain is similar to Ch'ongdan area. Suitable for armor. There are three fair north–south roads. One good lateral road south of the parallel, with large numbers of footpaths and ox trails crisscrossing the area. The primary railroad link between North and South Korea passes through here. If held by enemy, zone would provide excellent tactical base to launch an assault into Seoul district. Such assault would be difficult by the Imjin River. Successful attack must include capture of two large single-lane railway bridges. One has been converted for the use of wheeled and light tracked vehicles," General Jung outlined and paused to check his notes.

"Area D, called the Uijongbu area, is from Imjin River eastward, to include north–south valley running between Seoul and Wonsan. Wonsan is east coast seaport and rail center for North Korea. This ancient invasion route with road and railroad connecting the lowlands around Seoul with the flatlands in the vicinity of Wonsan. Not first-class condition, corridor is best approach to Seoul from the north, militarily important. There good observation both north and south of the parallel in this zone. One poor lateral road and numerous mountain trails led east toward Ch'unch'on."

"Excuse me, General Jung," Lieutenant Colonel Sturies interrupted. "That's the 7th Infantry Division's sector, is it not?"

"Yes, it is," Jung replied.

"Thank you, sir," Lieutenant Colonel Sturies replied as he wrote down a note.

General Jung continued, "Area E runs from Seoul-Wonsan corridor approximately thirty-six air miles to the eastern limitation of Hongch'on River valley where it crosses 38th parallel at Pup'yong-ni. Terrain mountainous lends itself favorably to guerrilla action. On each flank of zone, minor valleys run north and south along Choyang and Pukhan Rivers, which converge at Ch'unch'on to become tributary of Han River. Although highway and railroad run over mountains from Ch'unch'on to Seoul, good roads in zone are few. There is improved airstrip in the valley containing Ch'unch'on. Laterally, road winds through the mountains toward Kangnung, on east coast." Again, Jung stopped to check his notes.

"Last defensive zone is Area F. It is twenty-nine miles and most rugged country along 38th parallel. Except for few miles of coastal plain, terrain is wild and completely mountainous. One good road along the coast; other roads in the zone hazardous and practically impassable during the winter months. Railroad bed along the coast by Japanese, but no tracks or bridges. But they build tunnels and concrete abutments. Coastal road follow roadbed. Second-class seaport at

Chumunjin, one airstrip at Kangnung are only strategic targets. Tactically, this zone only guerrilla warfare," Jung concluded. There was silence for a long minute as everyone absorbed what had been briefed.

General Chae turned to Lieutenant Colonel Sturies and asked, "So, Colonel, what do you advise?"

Sturies had reviewed the general plan and terrain just the previous month with General Roberts before he'd departed as Roberts wanted to ensure his replacement would have a sound plan. Sturies didn't hesitate to respond.

"General, I—and General Roberts—believe that any thrust by the North will be through zones B, C, and D as those offer the high-speed routes to Seoul. The Uijongbu area is the key to the city of Seoul. We believed it would be concentrated there. I recommended a series of strong outpost positions blocking probable avenues of approach as the best defense. I suggest moving the 2nd and 3rd Infantry Divisions to reinforce the 7th and 6th Divisions," Sturies stated. ROK officers present in the room nodded in approval as well.

THE ROAD from Chinju to Taegu was not a superhighway but a two-lane road in need of maintenance. Colonel Yu Sung Yul and Lieutenant Colonel Rollins S. Emmerich were riding back from a conference that Yul had attended with several province chiefs and police commissioners to discuss the insurgency situation in the area.[3] Taegu was the center of communist guerrilla activity in South Korea. They were riding in a Chevrolet staff car left over from the Second World War and driven by a Korean soldier. Colonel Emmerich felt the car decelerate and wondered what the problem was as the police roadblock to their front came into view. *Wonder what this is about,* Emmerich was

---

3. Lieutenant Colonel Rollins S. Emmerich would retire as a colonel. After his retirement, it came to light that he had initially disapproved actions by Colonel Kim Chong-won, the regimental commander at the time, in the executions of 3,400 "communists" but then later agreed and photographed the executions. "Bodo League Massacre," Wikipedia, October 25, 2024, https://en.wikipedia.org/wiki/Bodo_League_massacre.

thinking as the driver came to a stop. Quick words were exchanged in Korean that Emmerich couldn't understand. Then the police ran back to their cars and, with lights and sirens, led the staff car down the road.

"Colonel Yul, what is going on?" Emmerich asked.

"North Koreans have crossed 38th Parallel. Headquarters in Seoul is trying to contact me. Police say 22nd Regiment, Engineer Battalion, Antitank Company ordered to Seoul by General Chae. They left with advisors. Advisor families go to Pusan with Korean police. We have meeting with Taegu mayor and police chief at 1800 hours. Major Guillory is waiting for you to explain," Colonel Yul stated, in a bit of a shock.

"Kirby Guillory is a good man and a good advisor. He'll have all the facts for us when we arrive," Emmerich said, hoping his family was on their way to Pusan.

PRESIDENT TRUMAN WAS at his home in Missouri when his naval aide, Captain Robert L. Dennison, approached him in his study.[4] "Excuse me, Mr. President," Dennison said, getting the president's attention.

"Yes, Captain Dennison. By the look on your face and the hour, I take it this isn't good news," Truman said. "Just give it to me straight."

"Mr. President, I've just been informed by Washington that the North Koreans have launched a full-blown invasion into South Korea with possibly six divisions. The fighting on the 38th Parallel is intense," Dennison said.

"I guess we best be getting back to Washington. Have my plane ready," Truman said, standing and walking out of the room.

---

4. Captain Robert L. Dennison retired from the US Navy in 1963 at the rank of admiral.

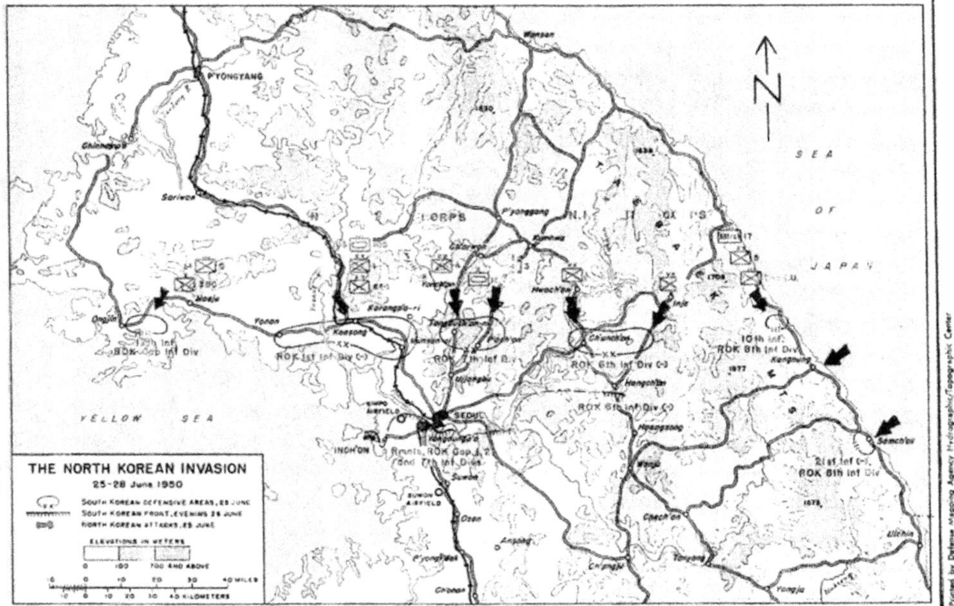

SEA OF JAPAN
YELLOW SEA
P'YONGYANG
Chinnampo
Sariwon
Onjin
Haeju
Yonan
Kaesong
Kumchon
Uijongbu
Munson
SIMPO AIRFIELD
INCH'ON
SUWON AIRFIELD
Suwon
Osan
P'yongdaek
Chonan
Haengju
SEOUL
Kumch'on
Korangpo-ri
Tongduch'on-ni
Pochon
Wonsan
P'yonggang
Kumhwa
Chorwon
Hwach'on
Inje
Ch'unch'on
Hongch'on
Hoengsong
Wonju
Ch'ech'on
Ch'ongju
Tanyang
Yongju
Kangnung
Samch'ok
Uljhin
ROK 17th Inf
ROK Cap Inf Div
ROK 1st Inf Div (-)
ROK 7th Inf Div
ROK 6th Inf Div (-)
ROK 6th Inf Div (-)
10th Inf
ROK 8th Inf Div
21st Inf (-)
ROK 8th Inf Div
Rmnts ROK Cap & 2d and 7th Inf Divs
I CORPS
N. K. II CORPS

THE NORTH KOREAN INVASION
25–28 June 1950
SOUTH KOREAN DEFENSIVE AREAS, 25 JUNE
SOUTH KOREAN FRONT, EVENING 28 JUNE
NORTH KOREAN ATTACKS, 25 JUNE
ELEVATIONS IN METERS
0   100   700 AND ABOVE
0   10   20   30   40 MILES
10   0   10   20   30   40 KILOMETERS

Printed by Defense Mapping Agency Hydrographic/Topographic Center

Chapter 4
Battle for Ch'unch'on

25 June 1950
   7th Regiment, 6th ROK Division
   Ch'unch'on, South Korea

Lieutenant Colonel Thomas McPhail had attended the party at KMAG headquarters the night before. His quarters in Camp Sobinggo were only a block from the Officers' Mess, and getting home after an evening of alcohol consumption was fairly easy. The pounding noise, however, was not helping his headache.

"What the hell is that noise?" he asked his wife, who was moving around the bedroom.

"Tom, you need to get up. There's a sergeant outside that needs to speak to you, he says," Mrs. McPhail said, handing her husband a cup of coffee. "Here, you might need this."

Getting out of bed and accepting the cup of coffee, Colonel McPhail headed for the door in his skivvies.

"Don't you think you should put some pants on?" his wife asked.

"The sergeant is a male, right? Nothing he hasn't seen before," McPhail said, reaching for the doorknob. Opening the door, he came face-to-face with a young sergeant with three stripes on his sleeve and a bad case of acne.

"Okay, Sergeant, what's so important that you can't let me sleep?" McPhail asked, raising his cup to his lips.

"Sir, the North Koreans are attacking across the 38th! Colonel Wright said to have you get up to the 6th ROK Division and tell him what the situation is," the sergeant said. "I have a vehicle here to take you, and sidearms."

McPhail nearly spat his coffee out and just looked at the sergeant for an instant, attempting to determine if this was a gag some of his fellow lieutenant colonels had put the sergeant up to or if it was on the level. He quickly reached the conclusion that this was not a joke.

"I'll be right out as soon as I dress," McPhail said, leaving the door standing wide open. Tossing on his fatigue uniform, he barely had his boots on when he went out the door, figuring he could lace them up in the jeep. As he passed his wife in the doorway, he gave her a kiss and left her with some final guidance.

"Keep the radio on, and don't leave the house. Start packing just what you and the kids need as well as the important papers. Just the things we discussed. Love you."

With that, McPhail was out the door and into the jeep. The drive from Seoul to Wonju, where the 6th ROK Division was located, was against a flow of refugees fleeing south and an increasing sound of artillery fire. Wonju sat forty-five miles south of the 38th parallel and held the division reserve regiment. The 7th Regiment was at Ch'unch'on, and the 3rd Regiment was east of Ch'unch'on at Hoengsong.

Entering the command post, McPhail immediately got with the division operations officer, Colonel Park.

"So what's the situation, sir?" McPhail asked, respectful of the operations officer's rank.

"They attack at 0600 hours with artillery followed by ground attack. It appears that 7th Regiment is holding. It seems that the 2nd North Korean Division has attacked with two regiments, the 6th and

4th. One is attacking along the river road with the other coming over the mountains north of the city," Colonel Park outlined.

"What was our strength this morning?" McPhail asked.

"We are at full strength. No one was on leave or pass," Park responded.

"That's good news. Okay, I'll head up to Ch'unch'on and see what I can do. Have any of the passes been seized?" McPhail asked.

"No, we still control all the passes."

"I'll call you when I get up there," McPhail said as he headed for the door and got back in his jeep. The forty-five-mile drive took two hours due to the condition of the road and the increasing number of refugees moving south. Arriving, he found the situation as Park had described it. The 7th Regiment was holding the enemy from well-prepared defensive positions that had been stockpiled for some time with extra ammunition and supplies. He reported to the command post of the 7th Regiment.

"Colonel McPhail, nice you join us," Colonel Lee said with a smile. "We hold now." Colonel Lee was the regimental commander for the 7th and had worked well with McPhail.

"I heard you were having a live-fire exercise up here today, Colonel, and thought I'd come up and have a look," McPhail joked to release the tension.

"You funny man," Colonel Lee replied with amusement. "We are holding them. Our defensive positions are strong and they have not penetrated anywhere on the line."

"What about tanks?" McPhail asked, concerned that these would be able to destroy the concrete bunkers of the 7th.

"We see no tanks. No tanks," Colonel Lee stated, surprised by the question.

"No tanks, that's good. How is your artillery support?" McPhail asked.

"Good artillery support. Artillery observers do good. Hurt enemy badly." McPhail was feeling better about the situation already when Lee was handed a message, which he read.

"What's wrong?" McPhail asked, almost dreading the answer.

Lee looked up with a smile. "Nothing wrong. Reserve from Wonju is coming."

Chapter 5
United Nations Steps Up

25 June 1950
UN Security Council
New York City, New York

THE WEATHER HAD RAPIDLY WARMED up from the morning low of a pleasant seventy-one degrees. By time the Security Council was called into session by the Secretary-General, Trygve Lie, the temperature had risen to ninety-one degrees and only the air-conditioning system was keeping the council chamber tolerable, but it was doing nothing to cool the anger of the members. The four permanent members arrived earlier than the 1400 hours meeting time to discuss the situation in Korea. Only the Soviet Union representative was absent as they were boycotting the UN due to communist China not being seated on the permanent council and replacing Taiwan. The US representative, Ernest A. Gross, took his seat and waited for the Secretary-General to open the meeting.

Trygve Lie was from Norway and had been installed as the Secretary-General in 1946. To say he was upset at the challenge to the UN that North Korea was ignoring would be an understatement. He had already spoken to the other permanent members and they felt as he did.

"Gentlemen, let us begin to decide on the matter before us," Mr. Lie began. "I have here the communication from our representative in Korea, and Mr. Gross has provided a communication from the American ambassador in Korea. One supports the other. We are all aware that this morning, North Korean forces initiated a surprise and unprovoked attack across the 38th parallel. As we speak, the North Korean forces are driving deeper in an attempt to capture Seoul, which is being evacuated at this time. South Korean forces are putting up a gallant effort, but they are unable to hold the tide of North Korean armor and airpower. The actions of North Korea are a direct challenge to this organization of nations and shouldn't be tolerated." Although not a member of the Security Council, the UN representative from South Korea was present at the invitation of Mr. Gross. He showed no emotion but sat humbly staring at Mr. Lie.

"Mr. Secretary-General," the representative for Yugoslavia, Mr. Edvard Kardelj, interrupted.

"You have a question, Mr. Kardelj?" Lie asked.

"Mr. Secretary, the representative from South Korea is present at the invitation of the American representative. I would like to invite a representative from North Korea to be present as well," Kardelj said. The other members all looked to Mr. Lie to see his reaction.

"Mr. Kardelj, North Korea is not a member of this organization and has no representative and therefore will not have a seat at this meeting. South Korea is a member, and as this discussion focuses on the actions in Korea today, it is appropriate for him to be here," Lie said. Mr. Kardelj didn't press the point. After a brief pause, Mr. Lie continued, "Gentlemen, before you is a proposed resolution. This was drafted by myself along with the permanent members for your consideration. Please take a moment to read it and then we will discuss it."

Each member opened the folder in front of them and read the document. It had been prepared by a staff that had translated every document into the languages of the sixty members. When Lie saw that each member was done reading the document, he asked if there were any questions. He knew Mr. Kardelj would have something to say.

"Mr. Kardelj, you have the floor."

"Thank you, Mr. Secretary. I believe this should be tabled until the representative of the Soviet Union is present. We, the Yugoslavian delegation, believe, as the Soviet delegation believes, that China should be represented. That is, China should be represented by its real government—" Kardelj didn't finish before the representative from Taiwan interrupted him.

"China is represented by the real government, Dr. T.F. Tsiang—" the representative from Taiwan almost yelled.

"Gentlemen," Mr. Lie said. "Mr. Kardelj, we are not here to discuss the China question but the event unfolding in Korea. At this time, China is represented in this organization. Now do you have anything else to add to the discussion before us?" Lie asked.

"The events in Korea are a result of political division within the country. Yugoslavia feels that there's a question of whether they constitute aggression by one nation against another or if this is simply a civil war. We consider this more of a civil war than an act of foreign aggression. The Korean people have our sympathy for the years that they were enslaved by foreign powers. Their wish is to live with independence and unity—to be able to settle their affairs without outside influence. Unification is the will of the Korean people under a democratically elected government. The present policy of North Korea does not promote independence and unity, nor peace. The policy of North Korea will weigh on the people of Korea in this civil war.

"Our delegation believes that a quick and peaceful solution must be found in the best interest of the Korean people and world peace. This body must find a quick and honorable solution to this issue which will result in the termination of hostilities, reestablishing the former boundaries and work towards unification of Korea through a democratic process," Kardelj concluded.[1] Everyone remained silent. Finally the Secretary-General adjusted his microphone.

"Gentlemen, you have before you a prepared draft of Resolution

---

1. For the more thorough statement that was actually made by the Yugoslavian delegation, see United Nations General Assembly Fifth Session Official Records for the 282nd Plenary Meeting, September 25, 1950, https://documents.un.org/doc/undoc/gen/nl5/012/54/pdf/nl501254.pdf.

82. It will be read into the record after some discussion if necessary. Basically it reaffirms the right of the Republic of Korea to exercise control over that portion of Korea south of the 38th Parallel. It notes the grave incursion by the North Korean forces, which constitutes a breach of peace, and demands a cessation of hostilities with the withdrawal of North Korean Forces to the 38th Parallel. We are requesting the United Nations Commission to observe the withdrawal and keep us informed. We ask all member states not to render any aid to the North Korean state."[2]

As he finished, he looked around the room at the faces of the delegates. They had all heard his summation in their native language and had been provided a written copy of the resolution, also translated into their respective languages. There was no doubt in his mind that each member fully understood the resolution before them. As the last member looked up, Lie began.

"Gentlemen, you have all had a chance to read the resolution and hear my summation. I now ask for a vote to approve the resolution as written." He waited as the vote was taken. It was almost unanimous, with Yugoslavia abstaining. He had expected that.

"Gentlemen, Resolution 82 passes. I thank you, and the people of South Korea do as well. This meeting is adjourned."

---

2. A verbatim copy of the resolution can be found in Appendix A of this book.

Chapter 6
Counterattack

25 June 1950
ROK HQ
Seoul, South Korea

Captain James W. Hausman had been the liaison officer between Colonel Wright and General Chae, and where Chae went, Hausman was sure to follow. Hausman was fluent in Korean. After the morning brief, Chae decided that he wanted to see for himself what the situation was, and the most dangerous and traditional avenue of approach from the north to Seoul was the Uijongbu Corridor. Accompanying Chae up to the corridor, Hausman listened to Chae as he developed a counterattack plan.

"I need 7th Division attack on the left using the Tongduch'on-ni Road. We can have the 2nd Division attack on the right along the P'och'on Road. We must issue the order to move the 2nd Division up," Chae said, thinking out loud.

"Sir, it's going to take time to bring the 2nd Division up. They can't get here until well after nightfall coming from Taejon. That's ninety miles away. They will need time to assemble, move, reassemble and prepare to attack," Captain Hausman pointed out. Chae didn't seem to hear him, or he ignored his points.

Returning to Seoul headquarters, Chae was on the phone with Brigadier General Lee Hyung Koon, the 2nd ROK Division commander, outlining his plan.

"General Chae, I have some difficulty with this plan. First I will have to commit my division in a piecemeal fashion as I cannot get everything up there by dawn tomorrow. Why not take the Capital Division and use them for the counterattack?" General Lee asked.

"The Capital Division is for securing the city of Seoul. They have no artillery and their cavalry regiment is a palace guard. They are not a tactical unit. I need your division and I need it now," Chae stated emphatically.

General Lee acknowledged the order and hung up, turning to one of his advisors. "We must move. I will give the order to load the trains, but this will not be a wise move. I wish you to accompany me. We will send the headquarters and the 1st and 2nd Battalions of the 5th Regiment right away," he said.

"Where are we going?" the advisor, Lieutenant Colonel James Gallagher, asked.

"Uijongbu. We establish blocking positions two miles northeast of Uijongbu covering the P'och'on Road," General Lee said.

"General, with just two battalions, how are we going to stop a major attack?"

"We will hold with two battalions and counterattack when the remainder division arrives. We cannot conduct counterattack with just two battalions and no artillery support," General Lee explained.

The trip up to their assembly area south of Uijongbu was long and made longer by the refugees flowing south as well as inadequate rail support. Arriving in the assembly area, General Lee moved his small force north and took up positions as planned. He reported to General Chae that he was in position with only two battalions. Chae didn't inform General Yu Jai Hyong, commander of the 7th Division, that the entire 2nd Division was not in place. General Yu had moved to the forward positions to observe as his division launched its counterattack, ignorant of the size of the 2nd Division. Initial success was rewarding but short-lived as the 2nd Division couldn't offer much in the way of reinforcements. When he called for reinforcements, only a paltry force was available and the counterattack came to a halt.

Chapter 7
Situation Deteriorates

26 June 1950
 US Embassy
 Seoul, South Korea

"Mr. Ambassador, would you like a cup of coffee? You look like you could use one," the ambassador's secretary asked. It was midnight, and Ambassador Muccio had been in the office all evening, coordinating with the staffs of President Rhee and General MacArthur for an emergency resupply of ammo and an evacuation of nonessential personnel.

"I'll take you up on that, thank you. Also, will you get me Mr. Everett on the phone, please?"

"Yes, sir, he's in charge of the Embassy Radio Network, correct?"

"That's correct. They're located in the Embassy Hotel. You call the desk and they'll put you through to him."

"Yes, sir."

A few minutes later, Ambassador Muccio's phone rang. "Hello, Mr. Everett. Cruller Highball."

"Mr. Ambassador, did I understand you correctly? Cruller Highball?" Mr. Everett asked.

"You've heard me correctly, Mr. Everett...Cruller Highball."

"Yes, sir, I'll get that on the air immediately," Mr. Everett said as the ambassador hung up.

LIEUTENANT COLONEL STURIES'S wife had several of the KMAG wives at her home in Camp Sobinggo. All had been listening to the embassy broadcasts on WVTP radio throughout the day. The wives found some comfort in all being together while their husbands were at work. Children were asleep in the bedrooms, where mattresses and box springs had been laid on the floor. The coffeepot had been refilled several times that night. Some of the wives were sleeping on the floor of the living room and others on the couch. Betty Sturies was in the kitchen next to the radio, which was playing soft music.

"When is the next broadcast?" Joanne Geist asked.

"It should be any minute now. It's almost three a.m.," Betty responded, fine-tuning the volume up a bit. Then she heard the announcer.

"We interrupt this broadcast for an important announcement. Cruller Highball. I say again, Cruller Highball. Please proceed immediately to your designated locations."

Betty and Joanne turned to each other with looks of dread, which were quickly replaced with determination. They both moved into the living room and started waking the other ladies up. They all knew what had to be done and began getting the sleeping children up. Each person had a small suitcase with them as they filed out the door. Betty was the last to leave, not knowing if her personal belongings would be here when and if she came back. Besides her clothes, she carried only the family photo album. Outside in the darkness, she could see other mothers and children walking in the same direction towards the Camp Sobinggo motor pool, where they would be told where to go and how they were going to get there. She was sure she wouldn't be coming back here anytime soon.

Upon entering the motor pool, Betty saw lines were forming in front of five field desks. Each desk had a sign above it with letters. A sergeant with a bullhorn was asking the ladies to line up in front of the desk marked with the first letter of their last name. She recognized a couple of the soldiers from KMAG that were checking people's names off a list. She fell in the line under the S, and when it was her turn she gave her name and the names of her two children.

"Mrs. Sturies…," the soldier repeated as he went down the list. "Yes, ma'am, I have you here. Will you proceed to bus number six outside, please? It'll take you and the children to Inchon, where you'll board a ship for Japan. Here's your boarding pass," he said, handing her a tag that she was instructed to pin on her shirt and one for each of the kids.

Commander Seifert had returned to Inchon after having informed Ambassador Muccio that he had found a ship and negotiated its use with the captain. The ship had been hauling fertilizer, but of the two ships in port it was in the best condition. Normally, the *Reinholt*, a Norwegian-flagged ship, only carried twelve passengers. The captain and crew were now being asked to take seven hundred aboard. When Seifert returned to the ship before the first of the buses arrived, he was amazed at the condition of the ship. It was obvious that the crew had worked all day and into the night cleaning and preparing the ship to receive the families.

COLONEL WRIGHT ARRIVED at Kimpo Airfield on a C-47 transport plane that was coming to take dependents and embassy staff to Japan. Ambassador Muccio had spoken to MacArthur about air support to carry out those who couldn't get to Inchon. The ambassador wanted to get all nonessential embassy staff out of Korea. Arriving at KMAG headquarters, Wright gathered the staff to review the events in the past twenty-four hours. He was especially pleased and relieved that the evacuation of dependents was going smoothly in Inchon and that the US Air Force had fighter aircraft overhead providing protection to the *Reinholt*.

"Carl, good update. Glad to see that the evacuation plan worked as well as it did," Colonel Wright said.

"Sir, the dependents were great. When they got the word Fireside, they responded quickly and got prepared. When Highball went out just after midnight, the processing centers were filled almost immediately. It's working better than we expected," Sturies said.[1]

"Well, the UN Security Council has declared North Korea as the aggressor and is asking for a cessation of hostilities. I don't think the North is going to pay them much attention. They're discussing whether or not they should have member nations boycott the North and provide military assistance to South Korea. I understand the president is going to attend that session of the UN. He'll be making a public statement later today, I think," Wilson said.

"Well, sir, what do we do for right now?" Sturies asked.

"I think for right now we continue to advise our counterparts until I hear something different. We also should be thinking about displacing to the south as Seoul may not be able to remain in the South's hands much longer," Wright indicated. "Let's look at either Suwon or Pusan for an alternate location, and I think we should have all nonessential personnel head to either location of evacuation. I want all our personnel records to go with them as well. I'll keep thirty-three officers and communications enlisted men here, and let's get everyone else loaded up and on the road. I'll have a list of names for you in an hour."

"Okay, sir. I'll get the personnel people going on boxing records and lining vehicles up for the road trip," Sturies said, heading for the door.

"FLIGHT OPS, CAPTAIN OLIVER, SIR."

Captain Oliver was the duty officer this morning for the 374th Troop Carrier Wing located at Tachikawa Air Base, Japan. The wing

---

1. The evacuation plan was the model for the evacuation of US dependents from Vietnam in 1965.

had only arrived in Japan sixteen months before, having been formed and serving in Guam. He had come on duty at 1700 hours the previous evening and had been warned that he might be getting a call due to a crisis in Korea.

"Oliver, this is Major General Partridge. Activate the alert rosters for the mission. Flight briefing will be at 0430 hours. Any questions?"

"No, sir, I'll start alerting them right now," Oliver said and motioned for the staff duty NCO to start calling people on the other phone.

"Be sure and let maintenance know that those aircraft best be ready to fly at first light. Have your CO call me when he comes in. I have the 51st Fighter-Interceptor Wing providing cover for you. That's all." And Major General Partridge hung up.

Oliver returned the receiver to its cradle and opened the contingency instructions for events such as this. All day they had been listening to Armed Forces Radio and following the events in Korea. Now it appeared they would be executing the plan that had been hammered out earlier in the day. Picking up the phone, he dialed the maintenance shop.

"Captain Blake," a voice answered.

"Marty, Pete here. They activated the mission for 0600 in the morning or thereabouts. General Partridge just called me, and we're alerting the crews. He told me to tell you those aircraft had best be ready to fly."

"I didn't figure he'd want to drive them to Korea. Of course they'll fly. Give me the count again so I can be sure I have the right number and a few backups just in case," Blake requested.

"Let's see…they want seven C-54s, four C-46s and ten C-47s," Oliver read off.

"Yeah, the C-54s are right here and the C-46s too. The C-47s are coming from all over Japan and they've been arriving all afternoon and evening. We're going over them as soon as they land and making sure they'll be ready in the morning. Not going to be the most comfortable ride in some of those aircraft as people will be sitting on the floors, but we'll attempt to get seats in as many as we can," Blake said.

"I don't think people are going to mind as long as they're getting out of Korea."

THE 51ST FIGHTER-INTERCEPTOR Wing was alerted and at first light had aircraft over Kimpo Airfield and the port of Inchon. Word of the air strikes the day before on Seoul had gotten everyone's attention, and the unit was put into action. Aircraft from the 51st Fighter-Interceptor Wing arrived over Seoul late in the afternoon. Two La-7 North Korean fighters appeared to attempt to engage the F-82s that were on station but broke off when the F-82s turned on them. They didn't engage.

"What do you mean they didn't engage!" General Partridge said over the phone.

"Sir," Colonel Gabreski explained, "they didn't engage because the La-7s never got close to either Kimpo or the harbor. The pilots said they weren't sure of the rules of engagement as it hasn't been defined as to what those rules are."

"Well, why the hell have they not been defined?" Partridge asked, almost coming out of his chair.

"Sir, Far East Command headquarters didn't send any rules with the mission order." Gabreski cringed as he realized he'd just dropped a dime on General Partridge's own staff.

"You have got to be…" He didn't finish, but his message was clear. "I'll get this cleared up right now and get the rules of engagement out to you. Briefly, I can tell you they will be 'if you see a North Korean aircraft, shoot it down.' Is that plain enough?" Partridge said.

"Yes, sir, that is and I'll pass that to the pilots," Gabreski said, and the line went dead.

"COLONEL WRIGHT, General Almond here. Can you hear me okay?"

Almond asked.[2] Major General Ned Almond was the chief of staff to General MacArthur and generally spoke with the authority of General MacArthur, or so he liked to think.

"Yes, sir, I hear you fine," Wright responded.

"We just got word from the State Department that they want the KMAG liaison officers to remain with the Korean counterparts. The ammunition that President Rhee requested will be coming on the aircraft that will be extracting nonessential personnel. The ambassador has requested that we fly out his nonessential personnel as well, so they'll coordinate with you for processing at Kimpo or Suwon. Those planes should start arriving tomorrow morning. Any questions?" Almond asked.

"No, sir, no questions," Wright replied, only to hear the sound of a phone being hung up.

GENERAL MACARTHUR HUNG up the phone after talking to the ambassador. *The man does get excited easily. I suppose I should get someone over there to look at the situation. Korea isn't my responsibility, but serving the ambassador is, so...*, he was thinking when General "Ned" Almond walked in.

"Ned, Ambassador Muccio was just on the line and is a bit excited over an incursion by North Korean forces over the 38th. Let's get an advance party over there to see what's going on," MacArthur said.

"Anyone in particular you want to send?" Ned Almond asked.

"It should be a small group to show the ambassador our concern, but nothing monumental. I'm thinking that this is a molehill that the ambassador has turned into a mountain. Send General Church from the 24th over with some people from the staff that haven't been over there. Give them a chance to get out of Japan for a few days and get in some

---

2. Lieutenant General Edward "Ned" M. Almond served in World War I, World War II and Korea; he retired in 1953.

pheasant shooting," MacArthur directed with all the urgency of eating an ice cream cone.

Chapter 8
Seoul Evacuated

27 June 1950
KMAG Headquarters
Seoul, South Korea

THE RAIN from the day before continued off and on in the early-morning hours. The streets were jammed with refugees fleeing south as the fighting to the north of the city intensified. The sounds of artillery could be heard throughout the night, but small-arms fire also sounded in the distance. The only comforting sounds were those of US jets overhead.

"Colonel, excuse me, but Ambassador Muccio is on the phone for you," Major Geist said, standing in the doorway to Colonel Wright's office. Wright glanced at his wall clock as he reached for the phone. It read 0800 hours. *God, I'm tired,* Wright thought as he picked up the receiver. He hadn't slept but for a catnap during the night since he'd arrived back from Japan.

"Mr. Ambassador, Colonel Wright here."

"Colonel, I've decided to close the embassy and move my staff to Suwon or Pusan. I just wanted you to know we'll be leaving in an hour and shutting down the radio station. I've already informed General MacArthur's headquarters and the embassy in Tokyo."

"I appreciate you letting me know, Mr. Ambassador. I've heard nothing from Tokyo, so we'll remain here with our counterparts and assist them in any way we can. I did order my nonessential personnel out yesterday along with everyone's personnel records. They're at Kimpo now, loading planes. Good luck to you," Wright offered.

"Thank you, Colonel, and to you and your staff as well. Goodbye."

"Goodbye, sir." Wright hung up after he heard the line go dead. *I best see what the latest developments are over at ROK headquarters*, he was thinking when Major Geist came back into his office.

"Hey, sir, want you to know that we're starting to get planeloads of ammunition coming into Kimpo. They're unloading it and hauling it out as fast as they can and have trucks standing by to haul more out," Geist said.

"Is it a mixture of artillery and small-arms?" Wright asked.

"Yes, sir, it's just what the Koreans are asking for," Geist said.

"Good, keep me posted," Wright said.

CAPTAIN HAUSMAN HAD BEEN at ROK headquarters since the first reports had come in. As the KMAG liaison officer to Major General Chae, Hausman was expected to keep Colonel Wright informed of what Chae was thinking and requesting. As Captain Hausman sat in his office just down the hall from General Chae's office, he noticed an increase in activity in the hall. Finally, curiosity got to him and he walked out to observe. What he saw alarmed him.

"Colonel Wright, Captain Hausman here," Wright heard over the telephone line.

"What is it, Captain?" Wright asked.

"Sir, I think the ROK headquarters is bugging out. They've been loading trucks, jeeps and POVs with files and it appears that they're going to be leaving shortly. They're talking about moving south to

Sihung—I believe that's halfway between Seoul and Suwon if I'm not mistaken, sir."

"You're not, and has something happened to generate this move?" Wright asked with some concern.

"Nothing that I can determine. It appears that Chae or the defense minister, Duk, ordered the move."

"You stay with Chae. Keep me abreast of the situation. I'll try and head off Duk and talk some sense into him," Wright said and hung up.

"Sturies!" he yelled for his deputy. A moment later, Colonel Sturies came into Wright's office. Wright was grabbing a map and his hat.

"What's up, sir?"

"Chae and the entire ROK headquarters are bugging out. Hausman just called and said they were loading out and heading for Sihung. Let's get the staff loaded up and see if we can catch them and get them turned around. His bugging out is going to leave the units north of the Han River in dire straits. Damn," Wright said as Sturies did a quick about-face and raced off to get the staff loaded up, which went fairly quickly as all nonessential personnel and records had already flown out.

As the KMAG convoy entered the streets of Seoul, the departure of the ROK headquarters was already noted as more and more civilians were leaving their homes and heading south. Crossing the Han River Bridge, the communications deuce-and-a-half truck with the SCR-399 radio beeped its horn. This was the signal that an important message had been received from MacArthur. As soon as the convoy stopped, the communications sergeant ran up and handed Colonel Wright a message. The staff had gathered around Colonel Wright's vehicle as he read it.

Looking up from the paper and gazing at the anxious faces, Wright said, "Well, gentlemen, it appears that the Joint Chiefs of Staff have directed General MacArthur to assume operational control of all US military activities in Korea, to include us. He's sending over a team designated as the General Headquarters Advance Command and Liaison Group under Brigadier General Church. Appears that US ground forces may be en route." Wright paused for a moment. "Okay, let's mount up and catch up to Duk and see if we can turn them around." Everyone immediately returned to their respective vehicles and resumed the race to catch the ROK headquarters.

Arriving in Sihung, Colonel Wright went immediately to the building that the ROK headquarters was entering. He quickly located Chae.

"General Chae, I have a message here from General MacArthur for you to read," Wright said, handing the message to Chae. Chae slowly read the message and then looked at Wright.

"Is this accurate?" Chae asked.

"Yes, sir. We received that as we were driving down here. We received a second message that General MacArthur encourages us that major decisions are pending. Based on that, I'm recalling any KMAG personnel that are at Suwon waiting to catch a flight out. We're going back to Seoul. Sir, your departure from Seoul has left your units north of the Han River without communications with your headquarters or support from your headquarters. Sir, I cannot stress strong enough that you and your headquarters should return to Seoul," Wright said as tactfully as he possibly could.

Chae looked at him for a moment and reread MacArthur's message. "Yes, we will return to Seoul. Our departure was premature. Thank you, Colonel Wright," Chae said and immediately issued the order to head back to Seoul. Wright was relieved that Chae had accepted his advice but didn't look forward to the ride back as he knew it would be slower with the number of refugees on the road, all flowing south. It was after 1800 hours when the KMAG staff arrived back at their offices.

"Carl, can you handle things here for tonight? I haven't slept since I left Japan and really need to get some sleep. You can call me if anything comes up," Wright said. Colonel Sturies could see that Wright was physically exhausted and in need of some downtime.

"Sure, sir, I got this. I'll set up a shift roster tonight and we'll start getting everyone some sleep. I'll call you if anything comes up."

"Thanks. I'm going to head home and sack out for a while." And with that, Colonel Wright left the building. His quarters were located at Camp Sobinggo, a few hundred yards from his office. *Bed never felt so good*, he thought as he slipped between the cool sheets and immediately fell off to sleep.

Chapter 9
Air War Begins

27 JUNE 1950
  51st Fighter-Interceptor Wing
  Seoul, South Korea

EVERYONE FELT tired but happy that their families had departed the previous afternoon at 1600 hours. The *Reinholt* sailed under the protection of the 51st Fighter-Interceptor Wing, which had chalked up its first kills. First Lieutenant Charles B. Morgan, 68th Fighter Squadron, was orbiting over Kimpo at four thousand feet when he was jumped by North Korean aircraft in a swift pass that damaged his aircraft.

"Lancer Three-Five, Lancer Two-One, I'm hit. Bandits at my six," Morgan transmitted.

Four thousand feet above him, First Lieutenant William Hudson and his radar operator, Lieutenant Carl Fraser, spotted the enemy Yak-11 aircraft.

"Lancer Two-One, I have him and am in pursuit," Lieutenant Hudson transmitted as he wheeled the F-82 Twin Mustang around and dropped into a steep dive.

"Roger, I'm going after his wingman," Morgan transmitted and executed a tight turn to get behind the second aircraft.

Both Yak-11s knew they were in trouble as they couldn't outrun the F-82s. Pulling behind the Yak-11, Hudson began firing. His hits were effective as the wing on the Yak-11 caught fire. The Korean pilot climbed out on the wing and appeared to be talking to his observer. Either the observer was wounded or he was afraid to jump, but either way, he didn't move. Hudson backed off a bit, knowing that the Yak was going to go down and crash or explode in midair. Finally the pilot activated his parachute while standing on the wing and allowed the plane to dive into the ground with the observer on board. Morgan got behind his target and drove him into the ground in a hail of machine-gun fire.[1]

"Lancer Two-One, Lancer Three-Five."

"Go ahead, Three-Five."

"What's the status of your aircraft? Over."

"Oh, I have a hole or two in the tail but nothing to write home about. We should be relieved shortly by the boys from the Three-Five," Lieutenant Morgan transmitted. Almost immediately he received a call.

"Lancer Two-One, Circus Three-Seven, over."

"Circus Three-Seven, Lancer Two-One, good day," Morgan transmitted, scanning the sky to see the F-80 jets of the 35th Fighter Squadron. The 35th had been flying the P-51 Mustangs up until a few months ago but had transitioned into the new F-80 jets.

"Lancer Two-One, Circus Three-Seven, we're coming on station and are ready to relieve you. How have things been? Over," Captain Raymond Schillereff asked.

"Circus Three-Seven, we were visited by two Yak-11s and we bagged two Yak-11s. They came in at four thousand and were hiding in the clouds. Over."

"Roger, nice to know. We have it now," Schillereff said.

"Roger, good hunting, Lancer Two-One out," Morgan said as he executed a wingover, followed by Hudson.

---

1. First Lieutenant William Hudson was credited with the first aerial kill of the Korean War. William T. Y'Blood, *MiG Alley: The Fight for Air Superiority* (Washington, D.C.: Air Force History and Museums Program, 2000), 3.

The F-80 Shooting Star fighter was the first jet fighter of the US Air Force and had been in operation since 1944. Captain Schillereff had been one of the first in the squadron to qualify in the aircraft and was very comfortable flying the single-seat fighter. His wingmen for the day were First Lieutenant Robert E. Wayne and First Lieutenant Robert H. Dewald, forming a flight of three in a right-echelon formation. Orbiting at eight thousand feet over Kimpo Airfield, they weren't noticed by the eight IL-10 ground-attack fighters on a run at the airfield.

"Circus Three-Five, Three-Six, do you see what I see?" Schillereff asked."Tally-ho, Three-Seven" was heard over the radio as Schillereff lowered his aircraft into a steep banking diving turn, followed by his two wingmen. While they closed on the unsuspecting IL-10 aircraft, each F-80 picked a target. As the distance rapidly closed, the IL-10s were just completing their initial attack on the airfield. They had been effective, destroying seven ROKAF aircraft that were on the tarmac. But while rejoicing at their victory, they hadn't checked their six and were only aware of the danger when Lieutenant Wayne destroyed two aircraft almost immediately. Not to be embarrassed, Schillereff and Dewald each downed an enemy aircraft. The first jet kills of the war had been made. Many more would follow.

Chapter 10
President's Address to the Nation

27 June 1950
WTOP-TV
Washington, D.C.

THE NEWSROOM HAD ONLY BEEN ALERTED an hour before that the president wanted to address the nation. What about, they weren't sure as the coordination between the television studios, the correspondent covering the story and the White House press secretary was still a bit new, and some of those involved weren't familiar with the procedures for television. The previous president had used the power of the radio to hold his Fireside Chats with the nation, but the use of television broadcasts was still in its fledgling stages. Many homes in America were without a television at this time, but it was becoming a hot consumer item. Many saw it as a replacement for the radio, and Mr. Truman was taking advantage of it. He would be broadcasting on both in a few minutes.

Walter Cronkite had been a rising star in the broadcast world. He was noted as a war correspondent during World War II but had recently joined the CBS family and was working out of the Washington, D.C.

station, WTOP-TV. He watched the director flash his fingers in the countdown to broadcast. Then the director pointed right at him.

"Ladies and gentlemen, we bring you an important announcement from the president of these United States," Cronkite said straight into the camera before it suddenly cut away and the president came on the screen.

"In Korea, the government forces, which were armed to prevent border raids and to preserve internal security, were attacked by invading forces from North Korea. The Security Council of the United Nations called upon the invading troops to cease hostilities and to withdraw to the 38th parallel. This they have not done, but on the contrary have pressed the attack. The Security Council called upon all members of the United Nations to render every assistance to the United Nation in the execution of this resolution. In these circumstances I have ordered United States air and sea forces to give the Korean government troops cover and support.

"The attack upon Korea makes it plain beyond all doubt that communism has passed beyond the use of subversion to conquer independent nations and will now use armed invasion and war. It defied the orders of the Security Council of the United Nations issued to preserve international peace and security. In these circumstances the occupation of Formosa by communist forces would be a direct threat to the security of the Pacific area and to United States forces performing their lawful and necessary functions in that area.

"Accordingly I have ordered the 7th Fleet to prevent any attack on Formosa. As a corollary of this action, I'm calling upon the Chinese government on Formosa to cease all air and sea operations against the mainland. The 7th Fleet will see that this is done. The determination of the future status of Formosa must await the restoration of security in the Pacific, a peace settlement with Japan or consideration by the United Nations.

"I have also directed that United States forces in the Philippines be strengthened and that military assistance to the Philippine government be accelerated. I have similarly directed acceleration in the furnishing of military assistance to the forces of France and the Associated States in Indochina and the dispatch of a military mission to provide close working relations with those forces.

"I know that all members of the United Nations will consider carefully the consequences of this latest aggression in Korea in defiance of the Charter of the United Nations. A return to the rule of force in international affairs would have far-reaching effects. The United States will continue to uphold the rule of law.

"I've instructed Ambassador Austin, as the representative of the United States to the Security Council, to report these steps to the council."

The camera quickly flipped back to the announcer. "Ladies and gentlemen, you have just heard from the president of the United States. We will now return to our normal scheduled broadcast."[1]

Lieutenant Colonel Bryghte Godbold was in the outer office of the SecDef with Lieutenant Colonel Shields and had listened to the president's address. "What do you think, Bob?" Godbold asked.

"What do I think? I think we're screwed and not ready to take on anyone. The entire defense budget is only fourteen point two billion dollars. Our equipment is obsolete, we have no repair parts, we have no ammunition, or what we have is so old it may not fire. Truman and Johnson have gutted the military and now commit us," Shields said in disgust.

"Well, at least he didn't say how much of a commitment we're going to make. I understand that the chiefs are over at the White House right now talking to the president about what we can do. I'm sure the Air Force is smiling and warming their hands up. They have all the new toys and can't wait to use them," Godbold stated.

---

1. Press Release, Statement by the President; 6/27/1950; June 1950; White House Press Releases, 4/1945—1/1953; Collection HST-WHPRF: White House Press Release Files (Truman Administration); Harry S. Truman Library, Independence, Missouri.

"I'm sure they're—" Shields started to say when his secretary interrupted.

"Excuse me, Colonel Godbold, there's a call for you on line one," she said, motioning to a telephone on a side table.

"Thank you," he said, moving to the phone and answering, "Colonel Godbold." After a moment, he responded, "Yes, sir, I understand, sir....Right away, sir." He glanced at Shields. "Tomorrow morning, sir. Goodbye." Godbold hung up the phone.

"What was that all about?" Shields asked.

"That was the chief of staff for the 1st Marine Division. I'm to report no later than the day after tomorrow for duty. I best get a plane ticket for tomorrow. Talk later," Godbold said, grabbing his hat and heading out the door.

Chapter 11
3rd ROK Division Advisor's Confusion

27 June 1970
3rd Division KMAG Advisors
Taegu, South Korea

ALL NIGHT, Lieutenant Colonel Rollins Emmerich and his staff had been up monitoring the situation. All the families had departed the previous evening under a military escort for Pusan except for two, and they were on the road very early with an MP escort to catch the train to Pusan.

"Sir, you have a call from Ambassador Muccio," the sergeant said, approaching Colonel Emmerich with a phone.

"Sir, Emmerich here."

"Colonel Emmerich, Colonel Wright has evacuated Seoul along with the ROK headquarters. I want you to get your people out of Taegu and get to Pusan," Muccio directed. Now Emmerich was confused. Did he take orders from the ambassador or the senior KMAG officer?

"Sir, is Colonel Wright aware of this order?" Emmerich asked.

"I'll take care of that, Colonel. You just get your people out of there and down to Pusan. You should go to the Hialeah compound. You'll get further instructions when you arrive," Muccio stated.

Emmerich was still uncomfortable with the order, but it was from the ambassador, who had always had operational control over KMAG.

"Yes, sir. I'll get my people loaded up and moving," Emmerich said less than enthusiastically.

When everyone was assembled, Emmerich issued instructions. "Okay, the ambassador has ordered us to proceed to Pusan. We have eleven military vehicles and one civilian car. I want everyone to have one of the Special Services shotguns along with your personal sidearm.[1] If we hit any roadblocks or ambushes, we drive through. Crash the roadblocks if we can, and that's why the deuce-and-a-half will be the lead vehicle. Stay together. If a vehicle breaks down, lay on your horn and we all stop as each vehicle hears the horn—they in turn lay on their horn until we all stop. The Koreans will be clogging the roads with refugees. We cannot be taking them with us. If they climb on your vehicle, knock them off. If you let one on, you'll be swamped. If you have to fire your gun to get their attention, do so. Korean police will be escorting us, so that should help. Put extra fuel on the vehicles and food. Be sure and have your foul-weather gear. Any questions?" Emmerich asked.

"Sir, what about our personal property?" a young sergeant asked.

"Take only what you can wear and put in a backpack. There will be no room for anything else," Emmerich said. There were no more questions, and people separated to get their belongings and load the vehicles.

Leaving the compound, the Korean police to which Major Gillmore had been an advisor took the lead in escorting the convoy. Even with the police escort, travel was slow. As the convoy wound through the narrow streets of Taegu, Korean citizens attempted to climb on the vehicles and begged for the soldiers to take them to Pusan. Korean mothers offered money for the Americans to take their children. Emotionally, it was difficult for the advisors as they slowly moved out

---

1. Special Service shotguns were sporting pump shotguns issued to members when they wanted to go hunting for pheasant, which were plentiful in Korea.

of the city. As night fell, so did the rain, turning the road into a quagmire of mud.

Reaching Pusan, the convoy made its way to Hialeah Housing area. They were appalled at what greeted them. Hundreds of Koreans were surrounding the high wire fence, which had been breached in several places. Those Koreans inside the compound were carrying out everything that evacuated families had left behind, to include kitchen sinks, toilets and furniture. Some were pushing private vehicles towards the main gate. The commissary had been looted, with individuals carrying armloads of groceries out of the store and throwing cases of food over the fence. The mass of Koreans blocked the main gate, resulting in Emmerich ordering his men to fire the shotguns above their heads to disperse the crowd. The question for Emmerich was whether there were any Americans left in the compound.

Entering, the advisors began inspecting and searching the buildings. At the Flamingo Club, a servicemen's club, they found several civil service individuals, led by Mr. Thomas Reiner. They were enjoying a morning beer as well as listening to a small ham radio that they had. Communications with Tokyo headquarters had been established.

"Mr. Reiner, I'm Colonel Emmerich, senior advisor to the 3rd ROK Division in Taegu," Emmerich said, approaching Mr. Reiner with an extended hand.

"Glad to meet you, Colonel. Your families passed through here yesterday all safe and sound," Reiner said.

"How do you know that?" Emmerich asked, a bit skeptical.

"Because we helped Captain Putnam process them and put them on the ship."

"Who's Captain Putnam?" Emmerich asked.

"Sir, Captain Gerald Putnam is the senior American officer here at Hialeah. He's gone to his quarters and is probably asleep as the poor devil had been awake for almost thirty hours straight processing dependents on the ship. It sailed yesterday for Japan. There's another ship, the *Letitia Lykes*, in the harbor with AMIK and KMAG personnel on board ready to sail for Japan when we feel we have everyone on board that's coming to Pusan," Reiner explained.

"Have you got comms with Tokyo on that ham radio?" Emmerich asked.

"No, sir, but I do have a telephone line to Tokyo. You're welcome to use it if you like. It's back in my office," Reiner said, pointing to the door in the back of the club.

"Thanks, I'll do that. You haven't heard anything from Seoul, have you?" Emmerich asked as he moved past Reiner and opened the door to Reiner's office.

"No, sir, not a word from them," Reiner explained.

Reaching Reiner's desk, Emmerich found a list of phone numbers in Tokyo. Not sure which to choose, he picked a number from the list and dialed.

After a second ring, he heard, "General Back speaking. Who's this?" Brigadier General George I. Back was the GHQ chief signal officer.

"Oh, excuse me, sir. This is Colonel Emmerich, senior advisor to the 3rd ROK Infantry Division. I—" Emmerich didn't get a chance to finish his sentence.

"Colonel, what the hell is going on over there? We're hearing very little here. What's the situation in Seoul? Have you had any indication of the battle around Seoul?" Back asked.

"No, sir, I've had no contact with KMAG headquarters and was ordered by the ambassador to move my people to Pusan. All the dependents got out yesterday, and what KMAG and civil service people are here are aboard a ship ready to depart as well," Emmerich explained.

"Okay, hold the line while I get the Ops people on the line," Back said.

Moments later, another voice was heard. "Hello, is this Colonel Emmerich?"

"Yes, sir."

"Colonel, this is Major General Willoughby, G-2. What can you tell me of the situation there?"

Emmerich again explained that he could only tell him what was going on in his sector and had no knowledge of what was happening around Seoul.

"Okay, Colonel, I understand. I want you to keep this line open. I ask that you phone in daily weather reports. As you get any intelligence updates, please call us immediately. You're to stay in Pusan for as long as possible. Those KMAG and civilians on that ship are to remain in Pusan and assist you in establishing a headquarters in Pusan. It'll be a provisional KMAG headquarters until such time as KMAG headquarters from Seoul links up with you. Understood?"

"Yes, sir, understood," Emmerich said as the call ended. Turning to Reiner, he asked, "Where can I find Captain Putnam?"

"Sir, he's in his quarters. I'll take you there if you like," Reiner said.

"No, would you go over there and get him? Tell him to get to the ship and have everyone disembark and get back here. We're reestablishing the KMAG headquarters," Emmerich explained.

"I'll get him moving right away," Reiner replied with a cocked smile. "So we aren't running, Colonel?"

"No, Mr. Reiner, we're staying."

Chapter 12

Flee Seoul

28 June 1950
KMAG Headquarters
Camp Sobinggo, South Korea

THE POUNDING noise on the front door finally awakened Colonel Wright. As he climbed out of bed, he glanced at the clock: 2:00 a.m. *Oh, this really can't be good*, he thought. Opening the door only confirmed his suspicions. There stood Colonel Vieman, the G-4 advisor.

"Sir, you best come back to the HQ. The forward divisions are retreating back into Seoul and the ROK headquarters is vacating their headquarters and heading back to Sihung. General Chae left about an hour ago," Colonel Vieman said.

"Damn. Okay, let me get dressed and I'll be right over. Have our people all assembled and ready to roll. If the ROK headquarters left, we might as well too," Wright ordered.

"Yes, sir. We'll be waiting for you," Vieman said and turned to walk back to the headquarters building.

It took Wright only a few moments to climb into a clean uniform and head out the door. As he briskly walked across the compound, the southern sky suddenly lit up, followed by the sound of an explosion. *Holy hell, something big just blew up. Hope that wasn't an ammo dump,* he thought as he picked up his pace. As he reached the headquarters, the first officer he saw was Captain Reed.

"Captain, any idea what caused that explosion?" Wright asked.

"No, sir, it appears to be down by the Han River Bridge," Reed responded.

Wright had other things on his mind right now, so he didn't think any more about it. Entering the headquarters, he approached Sturies.

"What's the status at the ROK headquarters?" Wright asked.

"Confusion. Chae pulled out an hour ago and right now those that are there are standing around sucking their thumbs. Not sure if anyone's in charge. We do have some of the 1st Division pulling back to the north side of the river and reports of the 6th and 7th still holding but heavily engaged," Sturies said.

"Okay, I'm going to run over there and see if I can make heads or tails out of things. You get everyone ready to pull out of here when I get back," Wright directed and departed, leaving his very capable deputy in charge.

When he arrived at the ROK headquarters, he found Major General Chang Chang Kuk, the G-3 operations officer for ROK Headquarters, in charge. "General Chang, what's going on?" Wright asked as if he didn't know.

"General Chae has departed and we displace headquarters to Suwon again. The minister of defense, Sihn Sung Mo, he go too. We will leave in one hour," Chang said.

"Alright, sir, I'll displace my headquarters within the hour as well and meet you in Suwon. Do you know what the explosion earlier was?" Wright asked before he left.

"We not know but hear as well" was all Chang could answer.

Returning to the KMAG headquarters, Wright found fifty vehicles loaded and in a line to depart. Artillery rounds were beginning to impact in the housing area. Finding Colonel Sturies, Wright asked, "We ready to roll?"

"Yes, sir. We've loaded extra fuel, food and some clothing, and everyone is armed as well. We set fire to all the files that were in the offices, so that should be burning pretty good shortly. Everyone is loaded up and ready," Sturies reported.

"Okay, let's move out. We'll head out the East Gate and head over the Han Bridge," Wright said, climbing into his jeep.

Surrounded by refugees, the convoy slowly moved through the East Gate and headed for the Han Bridge. As they approached, the crowds became thicker and finally the convoy was stopped by Korean soldiers with military police armbands. A Korean captain approached Colonel Wright.

"What's the problem, Captain?" Wright asked.

"You no cross. Bridge is gone. Bridge blow up. Many dead and hurt. Must go back," the captain said in his broken English. Wright wasn't sure he'd heard him correctly and asked him to repeat, which he did.

The Han River Bridge was a four-lane concrete bridge spanning the river. It had been rigged with demolitions the day before by Korean engineers supervised by KMAG advisors. It was supposed to be blown only after all South Korean forces were south of the river. Now four divisions were trapped north of the river. At the time of the explosion, a thousand people and cars had been on the bridge. The river was now covered in broken and dead bodies.

While part of the convoy turned around and returned to Sobinggo, a small reconnaissance was conducted to see if the destroyed bridge could be crossed by foot. The Korean engineers had performed their duties too well. The situation appeared bleak when reconnaissance revealed that a second bridge eight miles east of the city had also been destroyed.

As Colonel Wright and staff were discussing their next course of action back at KMAG headquarters, Colonel Lee Chi Up, ROK, came into the KMAG headquarters.

"Colonel Wright," Lee said, getting everyone's attention.

"Colonel Lee, what can we do for you?" Wright asked.

"Colonel, it what can I do you. I know way across Han River," Lee said, and everyone exchanged looks of surprise and relief.

"What happened at the Han River Bridge?" Wright asked.

"I ashamed, but either General Chae or Minister Sihn I think ordered bridge destroyed after they crossed. My opinion only, please. Soldiers there tell me it blew from south side shortly after they cross," Lee said with some embarrassment. "Come, we must go."

Everyone followed Lee out to the waiting trucks and mounted up. Slowly the convoy moved through the crowds of frightened civilians and a few soldiers and made its way to a dike across the Han. Boats of all sizes were transporting people across the river, but few were large enough to take military vehicles. Colonel Lee spotted a large raftlike vessel in the river and called out to the vessel. A conversation began between Lee and what many believed to be the captain of the vessel and turned heated. Finally, Colonel Lee had had enough. He drew his sidearm and shot the man. A brief conversation commenced with another crew member and the vessel came to shore.

Only one vehicle was really important to Colonel Wright and that was the deuce-and-a-half that carried the radio and the only connection to MacArthur's headquarters. Wright sent everyone on that vessel except two officers and three enlisted men with him to get the deuce-and-a-half on another large vessel. The first vessel had no problems delivering everyone to the south side. The second vessel approached the dike and waited. The difficult part was getting the deuce-and-a-half down the face of the dike and onto the vessel, but they were finally able to do it and moved to the south side as daylight was dawning along with North Korean artillery.

Once across, Colonel Wright and his small party spent the day driving down back roads crowded with refugees. The remainder of the KMAG personnel began walking to Suwon. Colonel Lee came to the rescue again, commandeering vehicles to pick up the American advisors and transport them to Suwon. As they moved south, their spirits lifted slightly when US Air Force aircraft streaked overhead and were seen making bombing and strafing runs on Seoul.

Chapter 13
Exercise Initiative

28 JUNE 1950
USMC HQ
Arlington, Virginia

GENERAL CLIFTON B. CATES, Commandant, United States Marine Corps, carefully listened to the president's speech. There was no doubt in his mind that the nation was headed for a full-scale conflict, regardless of what the politicians called it. To him, it only seemed right that Marines should lead the fight. This meeting with Admiral Forrest P. Sherman, CNO, and Francis P. Matthews, Secretary of the Navy, was the critical first step to make that happen.[1]

"Thank you, Mr. Secretary, for this meeting, and to you, Admiral, for joining us," Cates started. The Marine Corps was still subservient to the Navy at this time, something that Cates hoped would change in the near future. "I followed the decisions of the UN Security Council yesterday and the president's speech. It's clear to me that we're about to be engaged in a conflict in Korea. I feel that the US Marine Corps should be the first in this fight until the Army can arrive. Aside from

---

1. CNO stands for Chief of Naval Operations.

the 82nd Airborne Division, which is focused on Europe, I believe that our preparedness puts us in the best shape to lead this mission," Cates outlined.

"General, no specific orders or decisions have been made yet. General MacArthur is the theater commander in the Far East, and it's his responsibility to assess the situation and decide what force level he needs to accomplish the mission and stop the invasion. He has, what, the 1st Cavalry Division, the 24th Infantry Division, the 7th Infantry Division, and—oh hell, what's the other division that's in Japan?" Matthews asked.

"That would be the 25th Infantry Division, sir," Admiral Sherman answered.

"Yes, the 25th Division. He should have sufficient combat strength to turn back the North Koreans," Matthews said.

"Sir, if those divisions have been manned and equipped as the rest of the military has been for the past five years under Secretary of Defense Johnson, they're probably at three-quarters strength, lack equipment, and have grown fat sitting around with no training areas or training dollars. We've been in a similar boat, but we've maintained a high level of physical conditioning and have conducted training in Camp Pendleton, Twentynine Palms and Camp Lejeune. With our assigned air wings, we've conducted close-air support exercises, which I'm sure the guys in Japan haven't done. This police action, or whatever you're going to call it, is going to require close naval gunfire support, which the guys in Japan haven't done, have they, Admiral?" Cates asked, putting Admiral Sherman on the spot.

"I can't say that they have. We now have gunnery ranges in Japan on which naval gunfire can be employed. We've done some gunfire training in the Philippines, but not in conjunction with the Army," the admiral admitted.

"Let me ask this, Admiral, how difficult is it going to be to ship a Marine Force to the Far East?" Matthews asked.

"Sir, we have to assemble a fleet to do it. Transport ships from the Military Sealift Transportation Service are available in the Pacific but will have to be assembled in California, and that'll take some time to pull them back to load. We'll need fleet auxiliary ships for the cargo and heavy equipment. Again, it's a matter of assembly. Maybe a week. Loading will be a weeklong process and two weeks to sail. Probably have a force there in thirty days once told to move. And that's if the Army isn't competing for the same ships. If MacArthur decides to move forces from Japan, he'll be insisting on some of the shipping capabilities that we'd use for the Marines. Priorities will be competing," Admiral Sherman explained.

"Well, right now we have no marching orders, so let's see what the president and Mr. Johnson have in mind before we get people excited," Matthews said. Cates couldn't believe what he'd just heard.

"But, sir, shouldn't we be at least anticipate that the president is going to order action on the part of the military as he stated in his speech?" Cates said as politely as possible, glancing at Sherman for support. Sherman just sat and avoided eye contact.

"Well, the ball is in General MacArthur's court, and we'll wait to see what he requests from us. Until that time, let's not be getting everyone excited. Now if you gentlemen will excuse me, I have a meeting with Mr. Johnson that I need to prepare for. Seems the Air Force wants a bit more of our budget," Matthews said, indicating that the meeting was over.

Sherman and Cates stood to leave together, but Sherman paused and turned back to Matthews. "Excuse me, sir, do you have a minute for me to talk to you about the contract for that new carrier?" Sherman asked.

"Just a minute, no more," Matthews said.

Cates knew that this was a ploy on the part of Sherman to avoid having to go into the hall with him to discuss the Korea situation. He left and walked down the hall to his office. The walk was a time of contemplation, and the longer he walked, the faster his pace increased. As he entered his outer office, his secretary and aide were surprised by his speed.

"Sir, is something wrong?" Colonel Bledsoe asked as Cates came through the door.

"Get me General Weaver now!" General Weaver was the chief of operations, G-3, for the US Marine Corps.

"Yes, sir," Colonel Bledsoe responded and was immediately dialing a number. Moments later, General Weaver entered Cates's office.

"Sir, you wanted to see me?" Weaver asked.

"Yes. Issue a warning order to the 1st Marine Division to be prepared to deploy to Korea within forty-eight hours," Cates said to the shock of both General Weaver and Colonel Bledsoe.

"Sir, has the president ordered this?" Weaver asked.

"Not yet, but he will shortly—I'm sure of it. The 1st Marine Division is manned at what level currently?"

"Sir, the 1st is manned at about eleven thousand to include the air wing," Weaver said.

"So in reality it's about the size of a regimental combat team at full strength, right?" Cates asked.

"That's about right, sir," Weaver responded, glancing at Bledsoe.

"Good, it'll be easy to move them rapidly. I want them designated as the 1st Provisional Marine Brigade, and put Brigadier General Edward Craig in command. He's the assistant division commander for operations, and that'll free up General Smith, the division commander, to bring the rest of the division over once it's up to full strength. Get that warning order out today." This was Cates's final word on the matter.

ADMIRAL SHERMAN LEFT Secretary Matthews's office and started the long walk down the Pentagon corridor. As he walked, he considered Cates's comments. *If we do get the nod from the president and if MacArthur does ask for troops, I wonder just how long it'll take. Were my estimates accurate considering the current state of the Navy? Could we move a Marine division that fast with the current assets we have? The man with those answers will be Admiral Radford. I think I need to talk to him,* Sherman concluded as he entered his outer office. Admiral

Arthur W. Radford was the Commander in Chief, Pacific Fleet, located in Honolulu, Hawaii.

"Get me Admiral Radford on the phone if you will, please," Sherman said.

A few minutes later, Sherman's phone lit up, indicating that his call had gone through.

"Arthur, Forrest here. How you doing? Hope I didn't wake you."

"You didn't. The ringing phone woke me. I had to get up anyway. What's on your mind?" Radford asked. He knew this wasn't a social call.

"Question—how long will it take to ship out a Marine regimental combat team from California?" Sherman asked.

"We sending the boys someplace?" Radford asked, sitting up a bit straighter in bed.

"Hypothetical—Korea, maybe," Sherman responded.

"Take six days to load and sail in ten, but let me crunch some numbers and get back to you," Radford replied. "It may be a day or two to get hard numbers."

"That'll be fine. Appreciate the information when you have it. Now go back to bed," Sherman ordered.

"Roger, sir, like I can sleep now. Have a good day, Forrest."

"You too, Arthur. Best to the family."

Radford rolled out of bed, attempting not to wake his wife. From under the sheets, a muffled voice asked, "Should I put on a pot of coffee?"

"Go back to sleep. One of the house boys can take care of it. I suspect the phone woke one up and he's already in the kitchen making a pot," Radford said, pulling on his bathrobe and slippers.

As he reached the top of the stairs and started down to the main level, the kitchen light was on and he could hear movement. *These kids are the best. Never have to ask—they always anticipate what I need*, he was thinking when Petty Officer First Class Akino came though the doorway with a steaming cup of coffee in hand.

"Admiral, the way you like it," Akino said, handing the cup over.

"Captain Bower is holding on line one for you. I thought you would probably want to talk to him."

"Thank you, Petty Officer," Radford said with a chuckle. "Anytime you want to take over my job, you just let me know."

"Oh, no, thank you, sir. Too many late-night phone calls, but I'd be happy to take your paycheck," Akino responded with a smile. It was part of a running joke between the two.

Going into his study, Radford picked up the phone. "Captain Bower," he stated.

"Yes, sir. What do you need?" Bower answered. Captain Bower was the assistant operations officer for the Pacific Fleet.

"I need you to give me an estimate of what it'll take to move a Marine combat brigade, men and equipment with basic load of ammo, from California to Japan. Dust off some of the old files from World War II campaigns and see what you come up with," Radford ordered.

"Yes, sir. Are we talking an air wing with this brigade?" Bower asked.

"Yeah, let's include that as well. If not, at least we'll have an idea. If they drop out of the package, it's easier to drop that shipping than it is to scramble to get it at the last minute. When can you have those numbers to me?" Radford asked, and Bower realized this wasn't some mind game.

"Sir, I'll have those to you buy COB today, if that's satisfactory."

"That will be good, Captain. I'll clear my calendar for you late this afternoon—say 1800 work for you?"

"That'll be fine, sir. I'll get my staff on that first thing," Bower said, knowing that something big was brewing.

Chapter 14
Army Aviation Enters the Fray

29 June 1950
24th Aviation Section
Brady Field, Japan

Captain James C. Goode, US Army, field artillery officer, was sitting in his office enjoying that first cup of morning office coffee. Few people were in the hangar at this early hour and most would come by to get a cup as well. Goode was from Clementsville, Kentucky, so getting excited early in the morning was not his style even though he had seen action in World War II. Although he was an artillery officer, his assignment was as a pilot assigned to the 13th Field Artillery Battalion, 24th Infantry Division. Because of a memorandum of understanding from when the US Air Force was created, the US Army wasn't allowed to have an aviation branch, so all officers that were pilots were assigned to other units and attached to the division aviation section, which in many cases fell under the transportation battalion, artillery battalion, communications battalion or intelligence battalion. Army pilots were really the bastard children of the family. To get ahead, they would do a flying assignment and then rotate back to their basic branch for an assignment before rotating to another flying assignment.[1]

Captain Goode had heard about the crisis in Korea. Rumors at such times were plentiful as to who was going and who was staying in Japan. Master Sergeant Ronald Miller was the aviation section NCOIC and walked in not long after Goode. Goode suspected that the master sergeant deliberately waited until he was sure Goode made the coffee before entering each morning.

"Morning, sir," Miller said, approaching the coffeepot. "Oh good, you already made the coffee. I would have done it, sir. Thanks." A sly smile crawled across his face.

"Good morning to you, Master Sergeant. What's the status on the aircraft?" Goode asked. The aviation section had roughly seven flyable L-4H aircraft. The L-4H was a beefed-up version of the Piper J-3 Cub airplane. The 65-horsepower engine would allow the aircraft to fly at a maximum speed of ninety-five miles per hour. The service ceiling was twelve thousand feet and it could cruise for two hundred and fifty miles. It was a canvas-covered airframe with tandem seating and dual controls. It had an extensive array of instruments: compass, airspeed indicator, rpm gauge, fuel gauge and oil pressure gauge. What more would a pilot need?

"Sir, we have one bird down for periodic maintenance. One is waiting on parts, which should be coming this week. Have we heard anything about which units are going over to Korea?" Miller asked as he took a sip of coffee.

"It's considered a police action. One battalion is going over, but I doubt if it will be much more than that. Hell, the North Koreans are a ragtag bunch left with old Japanese equipment. I suspect that the unit that does go over will be back within two weeks," Goode said as the phone on his desk rang. Setting down his coffee cup, he picked up the receiver.

---

1. This policy remained in effect until 1983, when the US Army Aviation Branch was created and officers no longer had to bounce between aviation and their parent branch but were given the opportunity to decide between their original branch and the aviation branch.

"Captain Goode speaking....Oh, good morning, sir," Miller heard. *Hmm, someone that outranks the captain...could be interesting.* "Sir, I have five flyable aircraft this morning and five pilots on standby." Now this really started to pique Miller's interest. "Sir, that's a long way for an L-4," Goode said, motioning Miller to get him something to write with. "Sir, we could try putting the gas tanks from a jeep in the back for the trip and that would almost double the range.... Yes, sir, we did that in North Africa in the last war. Worked pretty good." Now Miller was really interested. *Where the hell am I going to get gas tanks from jeeps?* He frantically wrote a note, slipping it to Goode. "Okay, sir, when they get here, we'll start installing them. When we're ready, I'll call you back.... Yes, sir, I should be able to have one flyable this afternoon and make the trip.... Yes, sir."

"Okay, sir, what is this about putting jeep gas tanks in the back of the planes? And where am I to get the gas tanks and everything needed to jury-rig this? And is this an authorized Army modification? Are you trying to get me court-martialed, sir?"

Still writing, Goode began to answer questions. "The G-4 is sending over the jeep gas tanks and they should be here within an hour along with everything you need to jury-rig them. Put them in the back seat. It's an easy connection, we did it in North Africa. Second, get me Lieutenant Bolton and have him get weather reports for here and Korea."

"Are you nuts? Are you going to fly a bird to Korea?" Miller stammered.

"I'm going to fly one this afternoon and we're flying all of them just as soon as you have them ready. Start working and then start packing," Goode yelled as he ran out the door. "I'll be back when I find some maps of Korea. You ever heard of a place called Taegu?" He didn't hear Miller's response. If he had, he wouldn't have been so eager.

By 1200 hours, an L-4H aircraft was ready. Everyone was on the field to see this takeoff. None had flown across open water to Korea before. Goode was loaded down with Mae West, parachute, sidearm, coffee thermos, sack lunch, carts and frequency book. It seemed that everyone had taped a good-luck note to the inside of the aircraft. His housemate had even given him a small pouch that fit in his shirt pocket. It was traditional in Japan for every soldier to go into combat with this embroidered silk pouch to protect him. His wife was crying when he kissed her and left the house with a small bag of clean clothes.

The small plane with a full load of fuel in two tanks had no problem getting off the runway and turning onto the course that would take him over the Korean Straits and Taegu. The weather forecast, on the other hand, was not a good one, and the closer he got to the coast, the lower he was flying. At five hundred feet, he realized that he was not going to make landfall in this weather and made the wise decision to return to Brady Field. The planes had no instruments for flying in clouds. He would successfully try the next day.

Chapter 15
24th Division Alert

30 JUNE 1950
24th Division Headquarters
Camp Wood
Kyushu, Japan

"GENERAL DEAN, there's a call for you from General Almond's office," General Dean's secretary said, standing in the doorway.

"Which line?" Dean asked, reaching for his phone.

"Line two, sir," the secretary stated.

"General Dean speaking," Dean said, picking up the receiver and holding it to his ear.

"Walter, Ned here. Prepare your division for deployment to Pusan, Korea. Send an advance battalion to Pusan by air as soon as possible. The rest of the division will follow by ship. The advance battalion should head to Taejon when it arrives and contact General Church for further instructions. They're going to be establishing a blocking position north of Taejon. Who are you going to send?" General Almond asked.

"It'll be a battalion from the 21st Infantry Regiment, probably the

1st Battalion under Colonel Brad Smith. We'll call it Task Force Smith."

"How soon can they be ready to fly over?" Almond asked.

"I'll have them ready to fly over by 1 July. I'll follow on the third to set up a forward headquarters, colocate with John Church and take General George Barth. I'll get back with you as our plan progresses," Dean concluded and hung up. Brigadier General John Church was the assistant division commander and had been sent over on June 26. Brigadier General George Barth was the division artillery commander in the 25th Division but had been in Japan for a conference with the 24th Division. Both would be an asset as the division flowed into Pusan and deployed north.

"Miss Hill," Dean said into the intercom, "please get Colonel Stephens of the 21st Regiment on the line, and Colonel Lovless after that call." Moments later, the intercom buzzed and Dean picked up the phone. "Colonel Stephens, General Dean here."

"Yes, sir. What can I do?" Colonel Stephens asked.

"You can have the 1st Battalion put on alert for an immediate deployment to Pusan, Korea, by aircraft. Have your staff coordinate with mine for any assistance or information we can provide. The rest of your regiment will follow by ship when we have the shipping information from higher. When the 1st Battalion arrives in Pusan, they're to make their way to Taejon. Brad Smith is to link up with General Church, who's already there with an advance command post. Brad should take his orders from Church. I'll be flying over on the third and establishing our division command post alongside Church. My staff will be getting out further instructions, orders and deployment schedule to you in short order," Dean said.

"I understand, sir, and will get the 1st Battalion moving. I'll probably shift people from the other battalions to bring Brad up to strength, but he's still going to be short one rifle company. He'll deploy with his two rifle companies and headquarters company," Stephens said.

"That should be fine. I don't expect them to be over there very long. It appears that the North Koreans are pretty much a ragtag outfit. How the hell they've gotten so far only shows that we're wasting our time with advisors over there training the South Koreans," Dean said with a level of disgust in his voice. "Let me know if you run into any roadblocks with my staff. I need to talk to Lovless now. Goodbye."

Shortly after Dean hung up, the phone rang again and he knew it was Colonel Lovless. Colonel Lovless had only been in command of the 34th Regiment for a month. The previous regimental commander had been relieved for cause and the regiment was really not trained for combat.

"Colonel Lovless, Dean here. Consider this an alert order. Prepare your regiment for deployment to Pusan, Korea. The 21st is sending an advance battalion by air in the next forty-eight hours. You will deploy next by ship, followed by the 21st. My staff will be sending your deployment orders and schedule as soon as they have it together. Any questions?"

"Sir, only a million, but I need to organize my thoughts and will get with the staff," Lovless said.

"Well, you can ask those questions when you get to Korea as I'm leaving in the morning with the advance command post. See you there, Colonel," Dean said and hung up the phone.

"Lieutenant Clarke," he called out, knowing his aide was seated right outside his door at his desk. Moments later the eager beaver lieutenant stuck his head in the doorway.

"Yes, sir?" Clarke said.

"Lieutenant, pack your bag. You're going to Korea and link up with General Church. You're going to be our liaison officer with his advance headquarters until I or someone from the G-3 staff gets there and relieves you. Let me know when you're ready and I'll tell the G3 to lay on a flight for you to get you there ASAP. I want a rep on the ground to protect our interest. If something doesn't sound right, you call me and let me know what's going on. Before you leave, I want you to go over to the 21st Regiment and deliver some instructions to Colonel Stephens," General Dean said, standing and looking Clarke in the eyes. Dean and Clarke were both tall men of equal height and had a lively competition during workouts at the base gym.

"Sir, it'll take me an hour to pack and I'll be ready," Clarke said with some enthusiasm. Clarke had joined the Army out of West Point, graduating in 1945 just after V-E Day. He hadn't seen action in the Pacific before the war ended but, like most young men, he yearned for the excitement of combat, especially as this appeared to be just a short skirmish.

"Well, go have some fun, but don't get yourself killed…and that's an order, Lieutenant," Dean joked.

Chapter 16
TF Smith

30 June 1950
1st Battalion, 21st Infantry Regiment, 24th Infantry Division
Camp Wood
Kyushu, Japan

THE NIGHT WAS clear and still, a bit unseasonably warm for Japan. The hot months would be August through September, and then the household fans would be working overtime. People went to the movie theater to sit in air-conditioned comfort. For now, open screened windows would do, both in quarters and in the barracks, which were less than full. Most of the soldiers rented apartments in the local villages as they could afford to do that. Soldiers' pay didn't go far in the States in the early 1950s, but in occupied Japan, young soldiers found they could afford to live off base. Normally they had small two-room apartments with a young lady who would take care of all their needs. All the soldier was required to do was provide food and a roof over their heads. Laundry, boot shining and housekeeping were provided, along with other services.

The barracks were partially empty because of the number of soldiers living "on the economy," as it was called, but also because the unit, like all units in 1950, was so undermanned. The battalion was supposed to have three rifle companies and it did, on paper. In truth, it had enough soldiers to man two reinforced rifle companies. The 1st Battalion, 21st Infantry Regiment, 24th Infantry Division, had the mission to close with and destroy the enemy. To accomplish that, it was organized with a headquarters company, three rifle companies and a heavy weapons company. The rifle companies were supposed to have six officers and one hundred and ninety-seven soldiers. The heavy weapons company was organized with five officers and one hundred fifty-five enlisted men while the headquarters company had eleven officers and one hundred sixty-six enlisted soldiers for a battalion total strength of nine hundred and forty-five men—in theory. The current battalion strength was under six hundred men.

Corporal William "Bill" Dowd had just arrived that day in Japan following a two-week leave at home in Queens, New York, after his previous assignment, serving on the Fort Benning baseball team. Reporting to the battalion headquarters on a Sunday afternoon, he noticed everything was quiet with few people around. Upon entering, he was immediately confronted by a staff sergeant wearing an armband that had the letters SDNCOIC.

"What'cha need, Corporal?" Staff Sergeant Wilson asked from behind his desk. An oscillating desk fan blew a slight breeze across him.

"Reporting for duty, Staff Sergeant," Dowd said, handing over a brown manila envelope with his military files.

"Corporal, welcome to the 1st Battalion, 21st Infantry Regiment," Staff Sergeant Wilson said, taking the envelope and tossing it in a box marked "IN." Wilson had served in the Army for almost ten years and had seen action in the Pacific in World War II. Wilson was considered a "lifer" by the young men in the unit but respected for his military experience and bearing. He was not married. The scars on his face indicated he might have gotten too close to an exploding grenade. "Give me a minute and when the runner gets back, he'll take you to the barracks. It's 1700, so drop your stuff, get some chow, and in the morning come back and they'll have you assigned to a platoon. For tonight you're restricted to the base. Any questions?"

"Why am I restricted to the base? Did I do something wrong?" Dowd said, almost terrified that he'd screwed up.

"One, you don't know Japan. Out there on your first night with no escort, the gals will have your pockets picked clean by the morning. You'll declare you're in love and probably find yourself sleeping it off in the street. Once you get a platoon, then you can go into town like everyone else. Two, there's a rumor that we may get called out for a police action in Korea and if you're out and about we have no way of contacting you. And third, you're restricted because I said you were and that's the end of discussion," Wilson said firmly. "Anxious to see the sights, are you?"

"That and I played semipro baseball and played against a team from Japan one year. Wanted to see if they have a team here that I could play on," Dowd said.

"Wait one…you played semipro baseball back in the States?" Wilson asked, sitting up straighter in his chair.

"Yeah, it was a farm team for the Yankees. I played for one year as a pitcher. Then my draft number came up. I was a pitcher for the base team at Fort Benning in my last assignment. Now I'm here," Dowd informed the staff sergeant.

"What's your MOS?" Wilson asked.

"Infantry, Staff Sergeant."

"You're probably going to be assigned to Headquarters Company. Captain Adams is our pitcher, and a hell of a pitcher too. We have a ball team and if you're good enough, you'll be assigned to that platoon. They travel around Japan playing exhibition games with the Japanese and against other divisions. How does that sound?"

"Sounds fine by me. Do we have a lot of infantry training between games?" Dowd asked.

"Boy, we're an occupation force. The war was over five years ago and nuclear bombs pretty much make war obsolete. Nothing's out there that's going to get us back into the infantry mode. You play ball, enjoy Japan and in two years, you'll be back in the States and well trained to play pro ball. Now, get out of my office. See you in the morning," Wilson said, dismissing Dowd as the runner, a private, came in.

LIEUTENANT COLONEL CHARLES B. "BRAD" Smith commanded the 1st Battalion, 21st Infantry Regiment, 24th Infantry Division. A 1940 graduate of West Point, Smith had spent his entire career serving in the Pacific Theater in World War II and was only out of theater to attend service schools. Life at Camp Wood on Kyushu, Japan, was relaxing for everyone. Occupation duty was considered "cushy" as there was little space for infantry training. Weekends were occupied with cocktail parties, barbecue outings and Sunday church followed by brunch at the Officers' Club.

All afternoon, Smith and his wife had listened to the reports on Armed Forces Network radio about an incursion across the 38th parallel in Korea. Reports on the local Armed Forces Network Japan radio were sketchy at best. At 2100 hours the phone in his quarters rang and his wife answered.

"Brad, it's for you. It's Colonel Stephens,"[1] Betty said with the knowing look an experienced Army wife gives when she understands the situation without being told.

Rising up off his sofa, he reached for the phone. "This couldn't be good," he whispered to his wife as he accepted the receiver. "Good evening, sir," he said as cheerfully as possible.

"Brad, Stephens here. Get to my headquarters ASAP. Call your company commanders and master sergeant and have them meet you at your headquarters in an hour," Colonel Stephens, the commander for the 21st Infantry Regiment, 24th Infantry Division, ordered.

"Yes, sir, I'll be there in ten minutes," Smith answered, only to hear the line go dead. Placing the receiver in the cradle, he turned to his

---

1. Colonel Richard W. Stephens retired from the US Army at the rank of major general. He received three Silver Stars over the course of his career, as well as the Distinguished Service Cross for his actions in Korea. He died in 1977.

wife. "Best get my laundry done tonight. I'll be packing it in the morning. I have to go," he said, and he picked up his car keys and headed out the door.

Within ten minutes, he pulled up in front of the 21st Regiment headquarters building. Immediately he noticed the parking lot was full and all the lights were on. In fact, the lights were on in all the barracks as well as his headquarters building. He could see people moving around past the windows. Walking through the front door, he collided with a young officer heading outside.

"Oh, damn. Sorry, sir," First Lieutenant Arthur Clarke apologized. Smith knew Lieutenant Clarke. Clarke was a West Point graduate and Ranger-qualified along with having completed airborne school. Tall, he had a slender build and a confident demeanor. Perfect picture for a general's aide.

"It's okay there, Lieutenant. What brings General Dean's aide to our humble domain?" Smith asked.

"Oh, sir, General Dean wanted me to get some final instructions to Colonel Stephens before he departs," Clarke said.

"Colonel Stephens going someplace?" Smith asked, fishing for information.

"Sir, we're all going someplace," Clarke said, pausing for a moment as he realized he may have said too much. "Sir, I have to go. Have a good evening, sir."

Before Smith could ask a follow-on question, the young lieutenant was out the door. Turning, Smith spotted Colonel Stephens heading for the regiment conference room and pointing for Smith to get in there. Entering, he saw that he was the last person to arrive. The other battalion commanders, along with the company commanders for the medical company, tank company, mortar company, headquarters company and service company, were already standing behind their respective chairs, and numerous staff officers were positioned along the walls.

"Sit down, gentlemen," Stephens said as he came through the door and closed it. Once everyone was seated, he began, "I've received a warning order from division. We're to be prepared to deploy from here to Pusan, Korea, with further deployment to the interior of Korea to engage and repel the invasion by the North Korean Army into South Korea and drive them back to the 38th parallel. We'll fly from here to Pusan. Our heavy equipment will follow on ships and join us in Pusan. The S-3 will provide you with deployment times and the S-4 will get with your staffs on the deployment for heavy equipment and vehicles. Right now I want you to alert your people and have them pack their gear."

"Excuse me, sir, but when are we looking at deploying?" asked the 3rd Battalion commander, Lieutenant Colonel Carl G. Jensen.[2]

"The first planes leave in forty-eight hours and I suspect the first battalion will close on Pusan in seventy-two hours," Stephens said to some very sober faces.

"Sir, what is the order of deployment?" Lieutenant Colonel Smith asked.

"It's 1st Battalion, followed by 3rd. Brad, you have the least amount of time, so I would get on it right away. You'll deploy with Baker and Charlie Companies. Leave Able and Dog Companies to follow on. Gentlemen, that's all I have for you. As we get more information and deployment orders, I'll get it to you. You're dismissed, except you, Brad. I need to talk to you," Stephens said.[3]

Everyone stood and filed out of the room. They all knew it was going to be a long night. Once the room cleared, Stephens motioned for Colonel Smith to sit down. Broad-shouldered and with a stocky build, he looked as if he could still play the line on a football team.

"Brad, when you arrive in Pusan, there's no telling what you're going to find. I understand the refugees are flooding the place. When you get there, I'm hoping someone is going to meet you. MacArthur has sent Brigadier General John H. Church, head of General Headquarters Advance Command and Liaison Group, located at Taejon. He'll

---

2. Lieutenant Colonel Carl G. Jensen received the Distinguished Service Cross and was KIA on 12 July 1950.

3. Normally, infantry regiment had three infantry battalions. However, with the personnel shortages, the 2nd Battalion had now been stood up.

give you your orders when he sees you. Until such time as the division gets there, he's your boss. Understood?"

"Yes, sir."

"Now, you will draw ammo for your people here. One hundred rounds per man should be sufficient. Not sure what ammo is there waiting for you, but Church will give you what you need for the mortars and the bazookas," Stephens explained. "What do you need from me?"

"Sir, I'm short people. Charlie Company is manned at ninety percent, but Baker Company is an entire platoon short," Smith explained.

"I'll alert 3rd Battalion to provide you fillers. The best platoon leader over there is Second Lieutenant Carl Bernard, and he has a pretty good platoon," Stephens said, pausing momentarily. "Be sure that you pack your Class A uniforms for the parade in Seoul."

Lieutenant Colonel Smith wasn't sure he'd heard correctly. "Sir, parade in Seoul?" he asked with a question mark all over his face.

"Look, Brad, these North Koreans aren't much but a ragtag bunch. They run up against you, they're going to turn tail and run for the hills. They probably didn't think we would come over to save the South Koreans, but we are. I'll bet we may not even get the full regiment over there before you're kicking ass and taking names all the way back to the 38th parallel," Stephens said, standing up and extending his hand.

"Make us proud, Brad, and good hunting," he added, heading for the door but then turning back around. "Oh, one last thing. Your unit designation will be Task Force Smith as you will be picking up other units when you arrive over there, I suspect."

Brad Smith walked back to his headquarters building, leaving his car at the regiment headquarters as he wanted time to think about what he was going to tell the company commanders. When he entered the building, a soldier at the door sounded off with a loud "Attention!" and everyone froze in place.

Smith quickly responded, "As you were," and people got back to work. To say that chaos was afoot would have been an understatement.

He stopped by his office and was met by the senior master sergeant, Gent. Master Sergeant Gent was old-school. "If the Army wanted you to have a wife, they would have issued you one," he was fond of saying when someone complained about not seeing their wife often enough, which didn't happen very much in Japan. He had joined the Army in the early 1930s and served through the lean years of the Depression. On December 7, 1941, he was serving at Schofield Barracks, Hawaii, as the Japanese attacked, and he'd spent the rest of the war in the 25th Division, slugging it out across the Pacific. He liked duty in occupied Japan.

"So, sir, are we really heading for Korea?" Gent asked, not convinced the rumor mill was accurate.

"Afraid so, Master Sergeant. We fly out in forty-eight hours minus Able and Dog Companies. We're going to get fillers from 3rd Battalion, a platoon from Love Company. A Lieutenant Bernard is the platoon leader and a former Marine. Has combat experience in the Pacific and got a commission a year ago in the Army. Parachute-qualified as well," Smith said, grabbing a notepad off his desk. "Let's get into the conference room and brief the commanders. Are the unit first sergeants in there too?"

"Yes, sir, and I'll have a meeting with them when you're done with the company commanders. I'm sure that the Able and Dog commanders are going to be pissed. It's going to be a long night," Gent said. "I have people out right now rounding up those that live off post. Be interesting to see who shows up. If they don't, then they can just move back into the barracks when we get back—if we get back."

"What makes you say that? This should be a pretty easy operation according to Colonel Stephens," Smith asked as he walked past Gent.

"Sir, I served in China in the mid-1930s. These communist guys are tough, hard-core people. They can go on almost no food in the worst of weather conditions and move as silently as a snake. They will not be easy to take," Gent said.

"Sergeant, we're going to be kicking the North Koreans out, not the Chinese. The North Koreans are a bunch of peasants who got some ancient equipment from the Russians. When they see us, they'll think twice and head back north. I don't think we have too much to worry about. Let's think positive and brief the commanders and get people moving." Gent's face showed no emotion, but his thoughts were laughing.

"Why are we being called out to go…where are we going?" Private Norman Fosness asked as he stuffed his duffle bag. He'd been in town drinking when the MPs had dragged him and his buddies out of a bar.

"The sergeant said we were going to Korea. Where the hell is that, and why?" Private Vincent Vastano questioned as he attempted to find all his field gear.

Standing next to him and looking forlorn was Private First Class Charles Hendricks, also in Fosness and Vastano's squad. "Wish I would have written to my mom this week. Not sure I'll be able to get a letter off to her before we go."

"We'll be back by the end of next week. Hell, I'm going to leave my money here in my wall locker so I don't lose it," Corporal Robert Fountain said as he walked past. Fountain was nineteen and a farm boy. "Oh, and Korea is that peninsula across the Sea of Japan. This is no big deal."

Chapter 17
A Miserable Trip

1 JULY 1950
Task Force Smith
Pusan, South Korea

THE DEPLOYMENT HAD NOT GONE AS SMOOTHLY or as quickly as everyone had wished for. The soldiers had boarded trucks at 0300 hours for the eighty-mile trip to the nearest airfield. The downpour made for a cold, wet ride to the airfield. Upon arriving, Lieutenant Colonel Smith was approached by Major General Dean, the division commander. Dean was not a West Point officer but came to the active Army through the California National Guard in 1923. He served as commander of the 44th Infantry Division in Germany at the close of the Second World War. After the war, he served as military governor of Korea with a follow-on assignment as division commander of the 7th Division in Japan. Commanding the 24th Division would be his third division command.

"Colonel Smith, when you get to Pusan, head for Taejon. We want to stop the North Koreans as far from Pusan as we can. Block the main road as far north as possible. Contact General Church. If you can't locate him, go to Taejon and beyond if you can. Sorry I can't give you more information. That's all I've got. Good luck to you, and God bless you and your men."[1]

"Thank you, sir. We certainly will do our best," Smith said, coming to attention and rendering a smart salute. *Hope the hell someone is going to meet me at the airport and have transportation arranged,* he thought as Dean walked away.

Smith was aboard the first C-54 aircraft, which took off at 0800 hours. He had been awake for the past twenty-four hours, making sure everything and everyone was ready for the deployment. Upon arrival at the K-1 Airfield in Pusan, they couldn't land due to the bad weather and had to return to Japan. Finally, accompanied by five other C-54 cargo planes, he had arrived with part of his battalion. The remainder of those flying in would arrive during the night or the next day.

"Colonel, welcome to Korea. Are we damn glad to see you," Lieutenant Colonel Emmerich from KMAG said as Colonel Smith stepped off the plane with his first load of soldiers. "I've organized a hundred trucks of various types to take your soldiers to the train station seventeen miles from here. There you'll board a train that will take you to Taejon, where you'll be met by Lieutenant Colonel LeRoy Lutes. He'll take you to General Church."

"Sounds good. We're ready to start loading the trucks," Colonel Smith said as the noncommissioned officers took charge and began the loading process. A cheering crowd greeted the battalion, and to the soldiers all was very festive.

The train ride drive to Taejon was uneventful but tedious. Colonel Smith noticed out the window the oxcarts, bikes, overloaded buses and refugees all moving south towards Pusan. The ride took longer than Colonel Smith felt it should have. As they drove through Taejon, he became more concerned with the flood of refugees he was seeing, with the North Korean forces pushing them south. As he studied the refugees, he noticed a woman approaching, but something looked odd

---

1. Roy E. Appleman, *United States Army in the Korean War: South to the Naktong, North to the Yalu (June–November 1950)* (Washington, D.C.: United States Army Center of Military History, 1992), 60.

about her appearance. Then he realized why. Her blouse was open and she was carrying a baby under each arm. The babies were nursing at her breasts as she walked.[2]

Arriving at the headquarters building, Colonel Smith was quickly ushered in to see Brigadier General John H. Church, head of General Headquarters Advance Command and Liaison Group (short title: GHQ ADCOM). General Church was an elderly gentleman and probably past his prime, Colonel Smith was thinking when introduced to the general. Originally Church's headquarters had been located at Suwon, much further north, but as the North Koreans had moved south, he had displaced the headquarters to Taejon. *Damn, he looks tired. I hope he can hang in there long enough,* Colonel Smith thought as he approached the general.

"Lieutenant Colonel Smith, we're damn glad to see you've arrived. I got word that your airflow is going smoothly and a train is standing by to haul your people up here. Sit down," Church said, pointing at a straight-backed chair. "Want some coffee?"

"Yes, sir, that would be great," Colonel Smith replied. The lack of sleep in the past twenty-four hours was beginning to catch up with him. Without being told, General Church's aide departed to retrieve the coffee.

"Let me give you a quick rundown of what's happened. North Korean forces crossed the 38th parallel in force on the twenty-fifth. They swept through Seoul and crossed the Han River on three fronts from what I've been told thus far. Intel is pretty sketchy at this point. The Republic of Korea forces initially held out, and then panic set in. The result is that they've been folding all along the front. The main attack by the NKPA is coming down this road from Yongsan to Osan. Osan is six-two miles north of here. If they get through Osan, they have a clear road to here, Taejon and on to Pusan. We cannot let that happen," Church said, pausing for a moment to see if what he'd just said registered with Colonel Smith. "I really think that once you arrive, that'll raise the spirits of the ROK soldiers and they'll get this panic

---

2. True story as related to me by a soldier in TF Smith.

settled. All we need is someone who won't run at the first sight of a tank."

"I understand, sir."

"Good. What I want you to do is move your unit north to Ansong by train. Trucks will be waiting there to take you north to Osan. You're to select defensible terrain to control the road north of Osan and prevent any force you encounter from progressing to Osan," Church said, pointing at the map as he spoke. Realizing Colonel Smith didn't have a map, he directed his aide to get him one. When Colonel Smith opened it, he saw that everything on it was written in Japanese. Before he could say anything, Church had read his mind.

"Colonel, we don't have any good US topographic maps. Seems no one ever thought we would be fighting in this place and so there was no need for them. We're using maps left over from the Japanese occupation," Church explained.

"This should work, sir. My units will be close together, so we can make do with these. I am concerned, however, about being able to communicate information with supporting artillery," Colonel Smith said.

"No need to worry about that. The 52nd Field Artillery Battalion has arrived with one battery of artillery, 105-millimeter howitzers. Battalion commander is Lieutenant Colonel Miller Perry and he will meet you in P'yongt'aek. Do you know him?" Church asked.[3]

"I know the name as his unit was also at Camp Wood, but we haven't trained together. Not much space there for training. Certainly no live-fire exercises above company level," Smith offered.

"Do you have any questions for me?" Church asked.

"No, sir, I understand my mission. I'll need transportation for the troops. I'll have four hundred and six total when they arrive—"

"Four hundred and six...that's all you have?" Church said, a bit surprised.

---

3. A 1931 graduate of West Point, Lieutenant Colonel William Perry retired at the rank of brigadier general in 1961. For his actions in Korea, he received a Distinguished Service Cross. He passed away in 2010.

"Yes, sir. We're short one rifle company, as are all the units. I've put together two reinforced rifle companies. We have 75-millimeter recoilless rifles and 2.36-inch bazookas as well as our light machine guns and four 60-millimeter mortars," Smith explained.

"Well, that's going to have to do. I'll arrange for transportation to get your people up to Osan by truck from Ansong. Good luck," Church said, extending his hand. Smith stood, accepted the handshake and departed, intent on conducting a recon of the terrain north of Osan before his soldiers arrived. *I've just been handed a shit sandwich*, he thought.

He climbed into the front seat next to his driver. Corporal Dowd. As Corporal Dowd was new to the battalion, it was decided that he would be the colonel's driver. Major Hopkins, the battalion operations officer, jumped into the back seat.

"Okay, Dowd, we're going to P'yongt'aek. You know where that is?" Smith asked.

"Sir, I have no earthly idea," Corporal Dowd said, looking at the colonel, who had a map spread out on his lap.

Colonel Smith chuckled. "Okay, get us out of this compound and head north on that road we were on earlier," he instructed. As Dowd maneuvered the jeep back onto the road heading north, the situation with refugees was no different. They were streaming past them, all going south. Smith did begin to notice ROK troops with no weapons or equipment traveling south in no orderly fashion as well.

Rolling into P'yongt'aek, Smith spotted a US Army jeep and directed Dowd to pull over next to it. "Are you my artillery support?" he asked as another lieutenant colonel stepped out of the parked jeep.

"Ah, the king of battle is here to save the day. Miller Perry, 52nd Field Artillery Battalion, at your service," Perry said, extending his hand.

"Just remember, the queen of battle tells the king where to put his balls," Colonel Smith joked in reply. "Brad Smith, 1st Battalion, 21st Infantry. Glad to meet you. What have you got to support me with?"

"Well, I have six 105 howitzers with vehicles and we're ready to move out when you give the word," Perry stated. "Troop strength is one hundred and eight."

"What is your ammo situation?" Colonel Smith asked.

"I have twelve hundred rounds of HE."

"What about antitank rounds?"

"That's a problem. I only have six rounds of HEAT."[4]

"Damn. Well, it's going to have to do. I'm heading up to Osan to conduct a recon before the troops get there. They're on a train heading for Ansong and will take trucks from there to Osan. Why don't you accompany me and we'll look the ground over together?" Smith offered.

"Sounds good," Perry said, returning to his jeep.

Passing through the town of Osan, Smith decided that it didn't offer much in the way of good defensive positions. The surrounding hills dominated the town, and the structures were mostly wood and would be subject to easy destruction. Slowly, the two jeeps rolled north, stopping occasionally to study the terrain. Three miles north of Osan, Smith had Dowd pull over to the side of the road. Perry pulled in behind him and approached.

"I think this may be a good location," Smith said, looking to his right and left. The road cut between two hills that had a commanding view of the road for about three miles. The two hills offered good vegetation for cover and concealment of his position. Smith and his operations officer, Major Hopkins, began to walk the hill on the left side of the road first with Perry.

"Sir, I think we could put a platoon up here nicely with good fields of fire, a commanding view of the road and elevated above the road where it cuts between this hill and the hill to the right. A position here and one on that hill on the right will have mutual support for each other," Hopkins pointed out.

"Position my forward observers up here and they can pretty much cover the road north for three miles," Perry suggested.

"I think you're right. Let's look at the hill on the right," Smith said

---

4. High-explosive anti-tank rounds.

as he started off in that direction. Reaching the adjacent hill, the three officers stood in silence for a moment, surveying the terrain.

"You know, from here and that hill on the left, my FOs will have a clear field of vision to observe any force coming down from the north either on the road or following the railroad tracks over there on the right," Perry observed.

"I like this as we have mutual support with the unit on the left and can have another unit to the right overlooking the railroad line and curl back of flank security on the right side," Hopkins pointed out.

After a few moments of thought, Smith made his decision. "Okay, it's settled. We'll set up a blocking position on these two hills. Hopkins, I want Baker Company on the left and Charlie on the right. Have Baker place a platoon on that hill to the left of the road and the remainder on this hill on the right side of the road. Position Charlie to the right of Baker and have it curl back to protect the flank on the right side. Once the vehicles have dropped off the troops, they can park along the road behind these positions. Mortars will be behind and between Baker and Charlie Company. Our CP will be behind Baker. The aid station should also be behind Baker and centrally located. Tell the XO to hold the field trains back in Osan. Any questions?"

"No, sir, sounds good to me," Hopkins said.

"Now what about positioning the artillery?" Smith asked, turning to Perry.

"I saw a place that I think will work just fine about two thousand meters back on the left side of the road. I'll place five tubes there and one tube with the HEAT rounds one thousand meters behind your unit on the left side of the road. That way if a tank gets through your kill zone, my guys will engage it at one thousand meters and that should be enough," Perry said.

"Okay, then, it's settled. Let's get back to Ansong and bring the troops forward," Smith said, moving back towards the awaiting jeeps.

Arriving back at Ansong, Smith noted the refugee situation was no better. The train station was packed with refugees and some soldiers, all attempting to go to Pusan.

"Do you understand anything that's being said?" Smith asked Perry.

"Not a word. I was concentrating on learning Japanese, not Korean," Perry replied. "We probably should see if we can find someone that speaks English."

"I have just the ticket. Dowd!" Colonel Smith called out. He didn't realize that Dowd was standing right behind him.

"Yes, sir," Dowd responded, surprising Smith.

"Oh, there you are. Dowd, find me someone who speaks English," Colonel Smith directed.

"Okay, sir, but how much are you willing to pay them? They're going to want some pay and I can't afford to do it," Dowd pointed out.

"Hell, two dollars US a day and food. I don't know what the going rate is. Negotiate," Smith directed.

"Okay, sir," Dowd said, turning around and moving into the middle of the crowd. At the top of his lungs, he yelled, "Anyone here speak English and want to make a buck?" Several people pushed through the crowd and in various degrees of proficiency spoke to Dowd, all at once. A few minutes later, Dowd approached Smith with a young man in tow.

"Sir, this is Jung and I think he'll do. Jung, this is Colonel Smith," Dowd said. Smith initially didn't say anything but turned and looked over the man standing before him. Jung was a typical-looking young Korean man, dark hair cut short, thin-framed glasses and short stature.

"Jung, why are you not in the army?" Colonel Smith asked, out of curiosity but also to test the young man's English.

"Sir, I was student at medical university in Seoul when the North Koreans attacked the city. I go Pusan to join the army as a medic or doctor's assistant," Jung said in pretty good English.

"Where did you learn your English?" Smith asked.

"I learn from the missionaries. I attend missionary school long time," Jung said.

"Okay, you're hired. How much you want?" Smith asked.

Jung pointed at Dowd. "He say one dollar a day, food and transportation to Pusan when you go there."

Smith looked at Dowd, who just shrugged. Looking back at Jung, he said, "Okay, we have a deal. You stay close to me. You're my interpreter. You hear anything you think I should know, you tell me. Understood?"

"Okay," Jung responded with a broad smile.

Smith had to wait for the train to finally arrive with his soldiers on the morning of the Fourth of July. The train platform at the station was packed with cheering refugees as the train pulled into the station. The soldiers on board were overwhelmed with the display of enthusiasm for their arrival.

"I'm really surprised at the enthusiastic welcome the people are giving my soldiers," Smith said to Perry. "Jung, what are the people saying?"

"People very happy. They cheer that train has arrived. Now they can go Pusan," Jung said, knowing he had just deflated Smith's bubble.

The streets were lined with buses and trucks to take the soldiers north towards Suwon. As the soldiers loaded the trucks and buses, the drivers suddenly refused to move.

"Okay, Jung, what is their problem?" Colonel Smith asked, frustrated and anxious to get moving. Jung pointed out an individual that appeared to be in charge of the drivers, and he and Smith approached him. Jung struck up a conversation, which became heated very quickly, as demonstrated by the elevation of voices and the flapping of arms.

Jung turned to Colonel Smith. "He say drivers no drive north, only south. He say North Koreans coming south. Drivers want to go Pusan."

"I have to get my soldiers north so the North Koreans can't go to Pusan. Tell him that," the colonel directed. Jung turned and had another conversation with the man, but it became obvious quickly that the drivers were not going to go north. Now Colonel Smith was becoming upset.

He called Master Sergeant Gent over. "Master Sergeant, toss every damn driver out of their vehicles and find soldiers that can drive these vehicles. Don't shoot any of the drivers, but no need to handle them gently if they won't move. Understood?"

"Yes, sir," Master Sergeant Gent said, and he went about finding drivers and removing Korean drivers. Finally, soldiers capable of driving the buses and trucks were found and the vehicles were commandeered by the soldiers.

The convoy departed for the long drive to Osan and passed through P'yongt'ack just after midnight. The crowded roads with refugees flowing south made for slow progress going north. At 0300 hours on the morning of 5 July, they arrived at the intended location to establish the blocking position. The soldiers dismounted and moved to their respective positions. The buses and trucks were parked along the side of the road to the south of the positions. Colonel Perry moved his guns into position and then parked his trucks in concealed positions off the road.

Chapter 18

Arrive Pusan

1 JULY 1950
  34th Regiment, 24th Infantry Division
  Sasabo Naval Base
  Sasabo, Japan

COLONEL LOVLESS STOOD on the dock at the Sasabo Naval Base and watched as soldiers of the 34th Regiment filed aboard the ship for the twenty-four-hour passage to Pusan. For most of the soldiers, this would be their first time at sea. Old salts that had fought in the Second World War would be sufficient to get the new men settled on board. Many of the NCOs had combat experience, as did the company and battalion commanders. Most of the junior officers, however, did not as they were recently commissioned officers from West Point or ROTC.

He looked across the dock, where two LSTs or "landing ships, tank" were loading the vehicles and heavy equipment of the 34th. They would follow the troop ships and were scheduled to arrive on July 3. LSTs weren't noted for their speed. Because they were so slow, sailors referred to them as Large Slow Targets. They were also miserable to be aboard in heavy seas as they were flat-bottom vessels and rolled easily in turbulent waters. Seasickness was common aboard these vessels.

The flat bottom allowed them to sail right up to the beach and disgorge their vehicles right onto the sand. These same ships would offload the 34th and return to Sasabo to pick up the 21st Regiment, depositing it at Pusan as well. Lovless was in no hurry and waited to be the last member to board. He was met at the rail by the ship's captain, Lieutenant Jack Bridges. Bridges had been a senior chief petty officer when he was offered a commission to lieutenant junior grade. He had recently been promoted to full lieutenant and given command.

"Welcome aboard the USS *Walworth County*, 1164, Colonel. If you'll follow me, I'll escort you to your cabin," Bridges said.

"Thank you, Captain. How soon will we sail?" Although Bridges was only a lieutenant, all officers commanding a vessel are referred to as captain when aboard.

"Just as soon as I show you your cabin, I'll be getting underway. I was told to get you to Pusan as quickly as possible," Lieutenant Bridges explained as he led Lovless through the ship.

Pausing in front of an open door, he remarked, "This is the officers' wardroom. I'd like you and your senior officers to join me for dinner here. Unfortunately on an LST the wardroom isn't big enough to accommodate all your officers."

"Not a problem, Captain, and we'll be glad to join you."

Moving down the passageway, Commander Bridges paused in front of a closed door. "Sir, this is your quarters, which you may share with three others as it has four bunks. I'll leave it up to you who you wish to share with. Now if you'll excuse me, I want to get on the bridge and get underway," Lieutenant Bridges said, excusing himself.

Entering his quarters, Lovless found a small cabin with two bunk beds and a small sink. Lieutenant Bridges had pointed out the officers' latrine when he was in the passageway. Choosing a bottom bunk, Lovless went to find the battalion commanders. Wandering the ship, he felt the vibrations of the engines as the USS *Walworth County* started to get underway.

"Hey, sir," someone called out from down the passageway. Lovless turned to see Lieutenant Colonel David H. Smith coming down the passageway with his duffle bags.

"Sir, sailor said I was to bunk with you tonight and to find you here," Smith said, not sure if he'd been set up.

"Yeah, this is our cabin and I've already staked out a bottom bunk. You can have the other bottom bunk," Lovless joked. "Let's get settled in and then check the troops."

"GENERAL DEAN, SIR," a soft voice said, pulling Dean out of a pleasant dream. Dean was catching a few hours of sleep on the couch in his office. Too much was going on to sleep at home.

"Yeah, I'm awake, what is it?" Dean asked, sitting up and turning a light on next to the couch. Captain Bodine, an assistant operations officer, was standing there holding a piece of paper.

"Sir, we've received the formal order for this operation," Captain Bodine said, holding the message out for Dean to read.

"What's it say?" Dean asked.

"Sir, it states that the division will immediately deploy a delaying force of two rifle companies reinforced with 4.2-inch mortars and 75-millimeter recoilless rifles. Second, the division headquarters with one battalion will depart immediately to Pusan by air," the aide read.

"Looks like we're leaving for Korea today. I understand that General MacArthur flew over there the day before yesterday and Yak fighters strafed the airfield at Suwon while he was there," Dean said, standing and looking around for his shirt.

"Did he get hit, sir?" Bodine asked in surprise.

"No. He was off at the headquarters with General Church and his plane had returned to Japan to refuel. When it came back, it brought a fighter escort and then he flew up to Seoul to observe the shit show up there. All he saw was refugees and retreating ROK soldiers. I understand after he left the air-defense detachment at Suwon, they got to engage some enemy aircraft, downing one and damaging another," Dean said. "We best get with the G-3 and see about our transportation to Korea. Got a feeling it's going to be a long day."[1]

COLONEL JOHN W. Childs sat in his office, which he thoroughly enjoyed. He'd been the chief of staff for the 25th Infantry Division for the past year and a half—almost all the authority of the division commander with none of the responsibility. That suited him just fine. He had hoped for a star promotion, as most colonels wish for but few achieve. Retiring as a full colonel was okay in his mind. When the door of his office swung open unexpectedly, it destroyed his thoughts of pheasant shooting on the island of Chejedo off the coast of Korea.

"Jesus, Colonel, don't you know how to knock?" Childs said with a start as Lieutenant Colonel Charles Berrman, the assistant chief of staff for operations, burst into his office.

"Sir, you're not going to believe the message I just got. Police action my ass," Berrman said, handing a written communication to Childs. "Sir, we have to prepare to receive and process over one thousand civilians and dependents being evacuated from Korea. In addition, we have to deploy one regiment to Kyushu to relieve the 24th of administrative and logistical responsibilities up there by the fifth of this month," Berrman said hurriedly.

"Slow down, let me read this," Childs said, leafing through the multipage document. "Jesus, we've already sent General Barth over there. What's next after this? Well, who do we recommend to send to Kyushu?"

"Sir, I'd recommend the 35th Regiment. Colonel Fisher is pretty squared away and relates well to the Japanese leadership. I think his easygoing manner will go far with them," Berrman offered.

"Okay, I'll recommend that to the general. Go ahead and prepare a warning order for the 35th, and I'll go in and see the old man. Don't issue the order until you hear back from me, however," Childs said,

---

1. Detachment X, 507th Anti-Aircraft Artillery Battalion, with four M-55 machine guns.

standing and gathering up the order and a pencil to take notes. *This is probably just the start. Police action my ass*, he was thinking.

Chapter 19
MacArthur Gets an Offer

2 JULY 1950
Pentagon
Arlington, Virginia

ADMIRAL SHERMAN SAT in his office, reading the latest reports from Far East Pacific Fleet Command. The reports were not encouraging. North Korean forces were moving steadily down the peninsula, having captured Seoul, and were moving towards Pusan. General Walton Walker, commander of the Eighth Army, was experiencing difficulties with the "peacetime" Army forces that had arrived thus far in Korea. Across the board, the Peacetime Occupation Army was not prepared for this fight, lacking the physical stamina, mental discipline or proper equipment to take on the North Korean Army at this time. Something had to be done, and quickly in Sherman's opinion.

He pressed the intercom button for his secretary. "Have General Cates come and see me, please."

Moments later, General Cates came through the door. "You wanted to see me, Admiral?"

"Yes, sit down. I want to run something by you," Sherman said, taking a seat in an overstuffed chair while Cates chose the couch. "I've been reading over the latest situation reports from Korea. Things don't appear to be going well over there for General Walker," Sherman said.

"You must be reading the same reports as I am. Walker is slowly being pushed back to Pusan, and if this keeps up, he'll be pushed off the peninsula by the end of next month," Cates observed.

"I was thinking the same thing. MacArthur needs help and fast. I'm thinking of offering him the 1st Marine Division and wanted your thoughts on the matter," Sherman stated.

"My thoughts are we should have done that on the twenty-sixth of June. However, the 1st Marine Division, like every other division in the United States, is at sixty-two percent strength. The air wing is no bigger than an air group in manpower and aircraft," Cates outlined.

"So, how big of a force could you put together and send over there quickly?"

"A regimental combat team built around the 5th Marine Regiment. Give me the word and we'll be out of here in less than two weeks, depending on the sea transport," Cates offered.

"Thank you. I'll get back to you as soon as I know something," Sherman said, standing. That signaled the meeting was over, but not the work. As soon as Cates left the room, Sherman began writing a message for Admiral Turner Joy, commander of the Far East Fleet.

TO: Commander Far East Fleet
FROM: Chief of Naval Operations
SUBJECT: GENERAL MACARTHUR EYES ONLY

A Regimental Combat Team USMC could be available for service in the Far East Theater in two weeks at the earliest if so desired. Request for use must be submitted to Chief of Naval Operations for approval by Joint Chiefs of Staff. Advise accordingly.

Sherman read it over twice before calling his secretary into the office. "Chief, get this out ASAP if you would, please."

"Aye-aye, sir. I'll personally walk this over to communications," the chief said, glancing at the note. "I don't mind saying, sir, I was wondering when we were going to get the boys there."

Chapter 20
Help Is on the Way

3 July 1950
> **Far East Command**
> **Tokyo, Japan**

Admiral Turner was asleep at 0130 hours when the knock on the bedroom door woke him. His wife stirred next to him, so he knew it wasn't her wandering around. This could only be one other person, his aide. As not to wake his wife, the admiral gently got out of bed and walked quietly to the door, opening it slowly. "This can't be good, now can it?" Admiral Joy said to his aide in a whisper as he stepped into the hallway.

"Sir, it's a message for MacArthur's eyes only, addressed to you," the aide said, handing the message to the admiral, who stepped into the hall and closed the bedroom door. *This is an eyes-only to MacArthur, but someone's putting me in the middle. Someone wants me to take the salvo if this blows up on the Emperor,* Admiral Joy was thinking when he opened the message and read it. *Oh hell, this should make the old boy happy* flashed through his mind.

"Call General MacArthur's office and get me an appointment, preferably first thing in the morning— the earlier the better. This is going to make him happy," Admiral Joy said as he returned to bed for another four hours of fitful sleep. His mind was racing with thoughts. Finally getting up and dressing, he headed for MacArthur's office.

"Good morning, General," Admiral Joy said, attempting to sound as positive as possible considering all the bad news that had been swirling around the headquarters in the past week.

"Good morning, Admiral, I understand you needed to see me right away today," MacArthur said in his typical superior tone.

"Yes, sir, I received a message last night, early this morning, actually. It's for your eyes only," Admiral Joy said, handing the message to the general, who quickly took it and scanned it.

MacArthur looked up at Admiral Joy. "I'll have an immediate response sent in the affirmative. Thank you very much," he said, handing his message to General Almond, his chief of staff. "Get a message to the JCS requesting a Marine division be dispatched as soon as possible and a regimental combat team immediately. Make preparations for receiving them here in Japan," MacArthur ordered.

"Yes, sir," Almond replied, his usual response to General MacArthur's orders. Almond pictured himself wearing General MacArthur's stars. People had to wonder sometimes if he was speaking for General MacArthur or himself. He was a self-centered individual with his nose firmly planted in MacArthur's rear end, many thought. His usual manner was to speak condescendingly and arrogantly to all those but MacArthur.

Born in Virginia at the end of the nineteenth century, he had grown up listening to tales of his grandfather's battles in the Confederate Army. Serving in World War I and remaining in the Army, he had risen to command the 92nd Infantry Division, a division of predominantly black soldiers, in World War II. Many attributed his promotions to his close relationship with General George C. Marshall, a fellow VMI graduate. To say that he would be considered a racist bigot would be an understatement. He admitted to many that he had been given the 92nd Infantry Division because his southern upbringing had taught him how to handle the culture of the black soldier. To close friends, he acknowledged that command of the 92nd Infantry Division had cheated him out of promotions to higher levels. "No white man wants to be accused of leaving the battle line. The Negro doesn't care…people think being from the South, we don't like Negroes. Not at all, but we understand his capabilities. And we don't want to sit at the table with them," he'd once said.[1]

Almond read the note that was for MacArthur's eyes only and left the room. In his office, he wrote the request for a Marine regimental combat team and had it transmitted immediately. He had his own ideas about how this division could be employed.

2100 Hours
Washington, D.C.

"GENTLEMEN, I just got a request from General MacArthur for a Marine division as soon as possible and/or a regimental combat team immediately," Secretary of Defense Louis Johnson said to the assembled officers. General Cates, although not part of the Joint Chiefs of Staff, was asked to sit in on this discussion since it did involve the Marine Corps. General Omar Bradley, General Dwight Eisenhower, General Hoyt Vandenberg and Admiral Forrest Sherman were all present. As Johnson laid out MacArthur's request and requirements, all listened patiently. None had the fortitude at this time to buck up against MacArthur, and blanket approvals were generally given for his requests. When he was done, all eyes turned to General Cates.

Without waiting for a question, Cates said, "Mr. Secretary, we can have a regimental combat team en route to Korea or Japan in eleven days, if I have the ships to move them."

"That's a bold statement, General, don't you think?" Omar Bradley asked.

---

1. "Edward Almond," Wikipedia, November 2, 2024, https://en.wikipedia.org/wiki/Edward_Almond.

"No, sir. We're prepared to move and have always been," Cates said with a straight face.

"Gentlemen, do I hear any objections to sending a regimental combat team immediately to General MacArthur?" Johnson asked. There were no objections.

"I'll run this by the president, but consider the order issued, General Cates. And God be with your boys," Johnson said in closing.

Chapter 21
TF Smith Meets the Enemy

5 July 1950
TF Smith
Osan, South Korea

LIEUTENANT BERNARD WAS POSITIONED on the left flank of Baker Company, thus becoming the left flank unit of the task force. He and his platoon sergeant walked the line and designated the position of each foxhole, ensuring that they had interlocking fires. From his position, he couldn't see much to the north due to the darkness and the rain. Before he finished, both he and the platoon sergeant as well as every soldier were soaked because of the downpour. Some soldiers had rain ponchos, but most didn't as they couldn't find all their field gear before they left Japan. Throughout the rest of the night and into the early-morning hours, soldiers worked on digging foxholes and preparing their positions in a steady drizzle of rain.

"Sergeant, let's get the foxholes dug at least four feet deep," Bernard directed. "I want to position our bazookas along the road shoulder. The CO is positioning the recoilless rifles on the right side of the road. Our bazookas will support them from this side."

"Good, sir. I'll place the machine guns on each of our flanks with interlocking fires across our front," Staff Sergeant Donald indicated.

"Be sure we can tie our right flank gun in with the left flank gun for the platoon on our right flank, although I doubt if it will be necessary," Bernard said. "I'll get with the platoon leader over there and make sure we're tied in."

Colonel Perry's soldiers offloaded ammunition, test-fired their machine guns and registered the howitzers. The proficiency of the gunners was so good it only took three rounds to register the base howitzer. Civilians were moving south on the road through the American lines. Jung had been on the road talking to some as they moved through.

After the artillery had registered, Perry came up to Smith's CP. "Hey, Brad, the guns are registered and the FSO is working up a target list for us. Commo is crap with the radios because they're soaked, so I have my guy laying wire to your CP and to each of the FO positions with the line companies by field phones. Now for some good news," Perry said.

"I thought that was good news, but I'll always take more," Smith said, eager to hear this next piece.

"I have some eager beavers that want to volunteer to man four .50-caliber machine guns and four bazooka teams if you want them. I told them I would check with you first. What do you say?" Perry asked.

"Hell yeah. Send them up and I'll put them with Baker Company to reinforce his platoons along the road and a couple of the .50-cals with Charlie Company to reinforce him," Smith said.

"Good, I'll tell them to get their asses up here and report to your CP," Perry indicated as Jung walked up.

"Sir, people say large force about ten miles to north moving this way. They afraid of them. They say enemy stealing everything, shooting anyone that resists," Jung said, looking northward.

"Did they say anything about tanks?" Colonel Smith asked.

"They not say, but not sure they would know what one is. They peasants from the local countryside. Most of earlier refugees from

Seoul and north. These are the holdouts," Jung said, pointing at the stream on the road.

The night was quiet, but the rain that had pelted the soldiers the day before was still present, though not as intense as it had been. The sky was still overcast with low cloud cover. As Smith sipped a strong cup of coffee that Dowd had made, he looked skyward and knew there would be no close-air support on this day. His attention then turned to the young soldiers he was commanding. They were a new breed of soldier. Many were draftees who really didn't grasp why they'd been drafted when the World War had ended five years before. In turn, the Army had attempted to appease them by making Army life as much like home as it could. To do that, physical training standards had been lowered and off-duty time had been increased, resulting in less training time. A dissatisfied soldier's complaint to a congressman had become a monumental headache for a commander. The overall result was a lack of discipline and a definite lack of a warrior spirit. Colonel Smith was thankful to the handful of noncommissioned officers he had that were experienced World War II servicemen. A couple of his lieutenants had seen action in the Second World War as enlisted men and then had returned to college and received ROTC or Officer Candidate School commissions.

Finishing his coffee, Colonel Smith decided to walk the line and talk with the soldiers. He wanted a sense of their level of anxiety. He thought he would start with a few of the soldiers that he had interacted with before in one way or another. He spotted a soldier with a BAR and recognized the young man.

"Fosness, how you doing?" Smith asked.

"Morning, sir," Fosness responded with water dripping off his helmet. "Sir, when are the reinforcements going to arrive?" he asked. His question caught Smith by surprise.

"Who told you we had reinforcements coming?" Smith inquired.

"Sir, that's the scuttlebutt," Fosness replied.

"Well, let's not worry about that. They'll get here when they get here," Smith said, moving to the next foxhole, where PFC Vincent Vastano was digging.

"Vastano, how you doing this morning?" Vastano was noted throughout Baker Company and the battalion for his sense of humor. It was immediately noted by Colonel Smith that the sense of humor was probably still in Japan.

"I'm okay, sir," Vincent responded with the look of a wet cat. As Smith continued to move along, he was sensing that morale was as low as he had ever seen it in the battalion. Ninety-six hours of no sleep, no hot chow, only cold C rations, rain soaking through their summer-weight uniforms and the fear of the unknown were beginning to take its toll.

Smith was about to cross the road when he checked his watch— 0700 hours. He then looked north up the road just as he would crossing a busy boulevard. The long column of tanks driving south towards his positions appeared out of the morning mist two thousand meters north of his position.

He turned to Dowd and Jung, who had been following him. "We have company, gentlemen."

Sergeant Loren Chambers yelled to his platoon leader, Second Lieutenant Phillip Day. "Hey, sir, look over there."

"What the hell is that?" Day responded, not sure what he was seeing.

"Sir, those are T-34 Russian tanks and they're headed straight for us." At this point everyone was aware of what was coming and started preparing themselves. Smith ran back to his command post and cranked on the field telephone to Perry.

"Perry, we have tanks approaching from the north. I count four at this time but few infantry," Smith reported.

"Brad, I don't have commo with my FOs. The damn things are soaked in this rain. We'll have to keep this landline open so I can talk to them for adjustments."

"Roger, I'll stay off and coordinate your fires through them," Smith said and hung up.

Shortly afterwards, the first sounds of outgoing artillery could be heard. Looking through his field glasses, Smith could see that the artillery fire was on target but having little effect. Even direct hits with the HE shell weren't stopping the tanks, only causing them to button up. As the first tank came within seven hundred meters of Baker Company's positions, one of the 75-millimeter recoilless guns opened fire. Perfect hit, but little damage to the tank as it continued to move forward and in doing so began to engage the Baker Company positions.

Perry had moved forward to be with the forward 105 howitzer with the HEAT rounds. As the first tank passed between the two forward positions of Baker Company, Perry told the gun crew to engage. The 105 howitzer position opened fire with an HEAT round at two hundred meters. The shot was perfect and severely damaged the tank, which did manage to pull off the road. The tank stopped and a white flag appeared out the top hatch.

"Boys, we just captured a tank. Let's go," Perry said, jumping up and running towards the tank. The driver's hatch opened and a North Korean began climbing out as another clambered out of the top hatch. Before those two could dismount from the tank, a third soldier rose from the top hatch and immediately opened fire with a burp gun, hitting Perry in the leg.

"Shit, I'm hit," Perry yelled as he spun and collapsed. Perry's soldiers took no prisoners, engaging not only the Korean on the tank but the two that had climbed down.

"Sir, are you hurt bad?" Sergeant Abrams asked, handing his M1 carbine to another soldier as he dug out his first aid kit.

"No, it went through my calf muscle, but no bones broken. Damn, that hurts," Perry whined a bit.

"Hey, sir, be thankful it didn't hit you in the ass or crotch," Abrams joked, cutting Perry's pant leg and wrapping a compress on the wound.

As a second tank appeared, the gun crew fired again and destroyed that tank, but it didn't block the road. That was when the casing on the fired round jammed in the chamber, putting the gun out of action until the crew could extract the casing. Perry watched as the third tank rolled between Baker Company's positions and the infantry opened fire with the 2.36-inch bazookas. The round bounced off the tanks, causing no damage. Each tank turned its attention to the parked trucks and buses along the side of the road behind the infantry positions. Those trucks and buses made great targets for the tanks. The third and fourth tanks continued to roll past Perry's positions and into Osan three miles behind, leaving a trail of broken, burning vehicles.

Colonel Smith watched in total frustration that his antitank weapons, holdovers from World War II, had no effect on the T-34 tanks. After the last tank had passed, Smith called for casualty reports and was pleased that there were relatively few serious casualties. About thirty minutes later, four more tanks were spotted approaching from the north.

"Okay, enough of this bullshit," Second Lieutenant Carl Bernard mumbled and grabbed one of the bazookas. Bernard was a nerdy, bookish, glasses-wearing guy,[1] not an inspiring figure, but to his soldiers he was a confident warrior. He had served in the Marine Corps in 1944 in the Pacific and in the interim years transferred to the Army, gaining a commission in 1949. He possessed something most lieutenants didn't have—combat experience.

"What the hell are you going to do, sir?" PFC Lopez asked.

"I'm going to kill a tank, that's what I'm going to do. Wanna help?" Bernard replied.

"Yes, sir," Lopez replied enthusiastically.

The two crawled out to a ditch on the west side of the road. Soon across the road, they were joined by Second Lieutenant Jansen Cox and his gunner, who had a bag of bazooka rockets.[2] Above Lieutenant Cox on the hill, they spotted Second Lieutenant Ollie Connor setting

---

1. It was his son, Joel Bernard, who offered this description of his father. Bernard would retire from the Army in 1978 at the rank of full colonel after having served in Laos and Vietnam. He was awarded the Distinguished Service Cross for his actions in Korea. He felt his greatest accomplishment was reestablishing the ROTC program at the University of California, Berkeley in 1972. He passed in 2008. "Col. Carl Franklin Bernard," Military Hall of Honor, n.d., https://www.militaryhallofhonor.com/honoree-record.php?id=309299.

2. First Lieutenant Jansen Cox would be taken prisoner in this action and sent to a POW camp along the Yalu River. He died in captivity in December 1950 of illness. His remains were never recovered. "1st Lt. Jansen Calvin Cox, Service Member Personnel Profile," Defense POW/MIA Accounting Agency, n.d., https://dpaa-mil.sites.crmforce.mil/dpaaProfile?id=a0Jt000000x894YEAQ.

up on the hill overlooking the road cut.[3] Although they weren't from the same battalion, with Bernard coming from Love Company in the 3rd Battalion, the three quickly formed a bond. As the first tanks approached, they allowed the first two to go through. The third tank was hit multiple times in the rear by the three lieutenants but just kept on rolling. When the fourth tank rolled through, again the lieutenants opened fire. Some of the rounds hit, resulting in no damage.

"Damnit, this one is going to kill that bastard," Bernard said in frustration as he took a kneeling position. When the tank was about thirty feet away, Bernard sighted in on the engine deck and slowly squeezed the trigger. The round immediately fired and exploded as it left the bazooka.

"Oh, shit," Bernard yelled, falling to the ground. PFC Lopez was beside him immediately and was also wounded but not as severely as Bernard.

"Sir, sir, are you okay?" Lopez yelled.

"Would I be yelling my head off and rolling around on the ground if I was okay? No, I'm not okay. Shit, that hurts," Bernard said, turning to face Lopez. "Are you okay?" Lieutenant Bernard's face was cut and burned from the round exploding as soon as it left the launcher.

"I will be, sir. Just a couple of pieces of shrapnel. Let's not fire any more of these things. They really are worthless," Lopez said.

For the next hour things appeared to be quiet for the 1st Battalion. The only bad news was delivered by the battalion executive officer, Major Floyd Martin, who told Smith that the tanks had pretty much destroyed all the buses and trucks that were parked along the road. If they pulled out, it would be on foot. Finally the main body of the enemy came into view.

---

3. Second Lieutenant Ollie Connor was awarded a Silver Star for his actions.

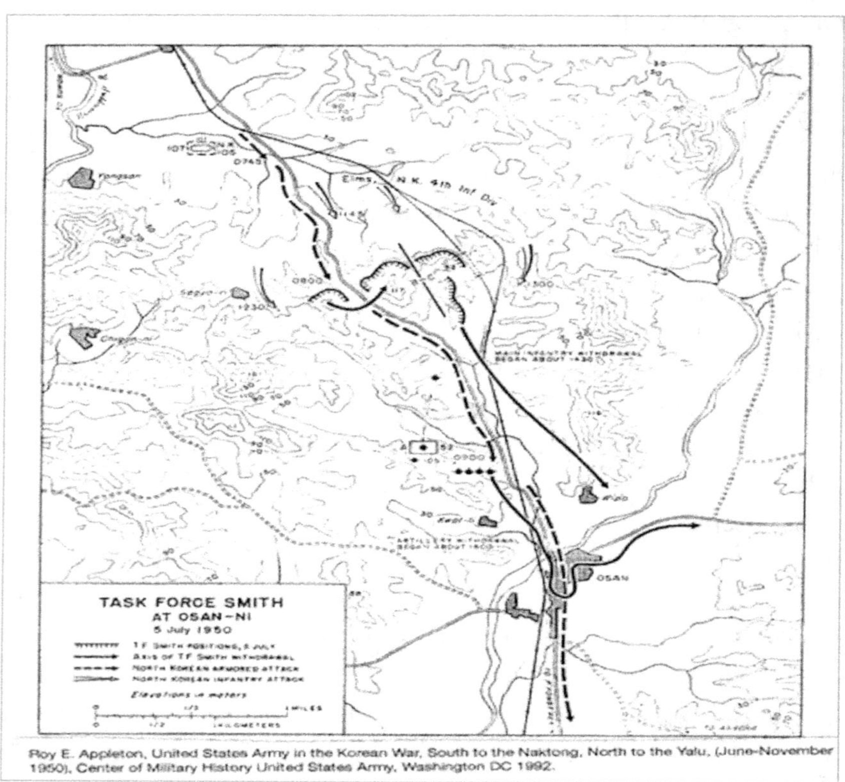

Roy E. Appleton, United States Army in the Korean War, South to the Naktong, North to the Yalu, (June–November 1950), Center of Military History United States Army, Washington DC 1992.

"Sir, we have company," PFC William Thornton said to his platoon leader, Second Lieutenant Cox. Grabbing his field glasses, Cox focused on where Thornton was pointing. There were thirty tanks approaching down the road, followed by infantry four abreast as far up the road as Cox could see.

"Oh, shit" was all Cox said as he grabbed the field telephone and called the battalion command post. As the tanks approached, two 75mm recoilless rifles opened fire and expended every recoilless round. All six bazooka teams expended every rocket that they had, to no avail. The tanks remained in single file and rolled down the road towards Osan despite numerous hits on each tank. As the last tank passed the positions, the North Korean infantry began to leave the road and deploy into combat formations outside of small-arms range.

Lieutenant Colonel Perry's soldiers grabbed up two bazookas and headed for the road ditch. Perry grabbed a third launcher and rockets and headed out to join them. Moving across a rice paddy, the third tank spotted Perry and opened fire with its machine gun. Slowly the turret turned in Perry's direction. The 85mm cannon fired, knocking over a telephone pole. One of Perry's 105 howitzers zeroed in on the tank and knocked the track off. Two Koreans jumped out of the tank and went into a culvert under the road. Perry's troops killed them both. Unfortunately, this tank had gotten a bit close to Perry's guns, and several gun crew members had departed in unauthorized and great haste. Officers had to start unloading ammo and feeding the guns. Embarrassed and ashamed, the soldiers returned to manning the guns.

Colonel Smith and Major Martin sat in a position between Baker and Charlie Company and watched the North Koreans deploy. Smith quickly surmised that they were not going to attempt a frontal attack against his prepared positions but attempt to flank their positions and get behind them to cut off any possible escape. As he watched them, he realized that his four-hundred-man force was facing an infantry force of about four thousand soldiers. The odds were not in his favor at this point. Initially he saw the enemy approaching to the east of the road on two avenues, one towards Baker Company and one towards Charlie Company. When the enemy was one thousand meters away, mortar rounds, artillery and borrowed .50-cal machine guns from the artillery swept the massed formation. As soon as the infantry came within range, small-arms fire from the defending infantry soldiers commenced. The effectiveness of the defensive firing, however, demonstrated that not enough time had been spent on the rifle ranges in Japan.

Second Lieutenant John Dooley was in charge of the battalion's 4.2-inch mortars, of which only two had been brought over on the plane. Each round weighed about forty pounds. The gun crews were firing as fast as they could but were quickly tiring from lifting the round head high to drop them down the tube. As Dooley observed, he realized that they would probably be out of ammo before the soldiers were too tired to lift another round.

PFC Thornton suddenly found himself in the role of squad leader at the ripe old age of twenty. He was an excellent marksman, being from the woods of Louisiana, and had been shooting off guns since he was eight and hunting squirrels with his dad. He was carefully placing his shots at the approaching enemy infantry, but there were just too many of them and not enough ammo for him.

"Aim your shots, damnit!" he yelled to his squad. "Don't just be blasting away."

Suddenly three North Koreans burst over the crest of the hill in front of him and opened fire with burp guns that struck his M1 rifle, rendering it inoperative. Knowing he was about to die, he closed his eyes and waited. The roar of small arms was all around him, so he didn't recognize the sound of a US Thompson submachine gun firing over his head, killing the three enemy soldiers. Startled when someone jumped into his foxhole, he opened his eyes and grabbed the individual.

"Hey, Thornton, this is the way you thank someone that just saved your bacon?" Private Hernandez said, slapping another magazine into the Thompson.

Captain Ross, Baker Company commander, ran across the company frontage to Colonel Smith's position and approached Smith in a low crouch. "Sir, commo is down. Bernard reports that they're attempting to flank his position and is requesting to pull back and join us on this side of the road. I know he wouldn't request that if he thought he could hold out. Do I have your permission to pull him in, sir?" Ross asked.

It took Colonel Smith all of thirty seconds to make a decision. "Pull him in now. Put him behind your forward platoons and we'll use him as battalion reserve," he directed. Lieutenant Bernard didn't need to be told twice to move his platoon. As the order was given, the left side began pulling back to the east across the road until the entire platoon was across the road and in position as the battalion reserve. As he counted heads to make sure everyone was across the road, he scanned his previous positions. Movement caught his eye.

"Son of a bitch," he mumbled as he observed three soldiers running not to join the unit but heading south to Osan.

"Hey," Bernard yelled at the three. They looked in his direction but kept moving south. "I swear to God Almighty that I will put you three up before a firing squad when we get back. Fucking cowards!"

Sergeant Donald was standing next to Bernard. "Sir, just let me shoot them and save us the trouble."

"Don't tempt me. We need to save the ammo. I know who they are," Bernard said with disgust dripping from every word.

As the morning wore on, so did the heat. The previous rain now raised the humidity. Drinking water was becoming a problem along with ammo.

Major Hopkins approached Colonel Smith. "Sir, Charlie Company reports an enemy column to the east is moving to envelop them, besides the small force that had been engaging them to their front. They hadn't seen this second column until it began to cross the railroad tracks to the east as they were masked behind the hills."

Colonel Smith and Major Hopkins started assessing their situation with the enemy now closing in on three sides. Something had to be done and done quickly, with more casualties falling to enemy fire, ammo running out and lack of support.

"It's 1400 hours. Send a runner to notify Baker and Charlie to pull back to Osan. Bounding overwatch with Charlie pulling out first, followed by the medics, battalion CP and Baker last. Tell mortars to destroy the tubes as well as the recoilless rifles. They cannot carry those weapons. We'll regroup at Osan," he said to Hopkins. "Dowd, you're with me. We're walking out of here. Hopkins, you fall back with Charlie and I'll fall back with Baker. Let me know when you're in position to cover Baker," Smith said with a look of disgust.

"Got it. I'll send a couple of runners to notify the units," Hopkins said. Moments later, Hopkins grabbed two soldiers from the commo platoon. "You two are my runners. Jameson, you go to Charlie Company. Brown, you head over to Baker Company. Tell Baker to hold until we send word that Charlie is ready for them to pull out and pass through. Jameson, you tell Charlie Company to pull back to that next ridgeline and hold until Baker passes through. You got it?" Hopkins asked.

"Yes, sir," both responded, departing at a run.

But the runners sent by Major Hopkins didn't relay the message to the company commanders as ordered, instead running along the front-line positions and shouting, "Retreat! Retreat to Osan!"

Before any of the chain of command could organize an orderly withdrawal, soldiers were out of their positions and running to the rear under heavy machine-gun fire from the flanks.

Lieutenant Bernard heard the runners but didn't believe the order. He attempted to contact his company commander on the field telephone, but there was no answer. He sent a runner to find that the company was gone. Gathering his platoon around him, he issued his orders. "We're heading south to Osan. Take only your weapons and any ammo you have. Destroy the bazookas and leave everything else. We move out in two minutes."

"Sir, what about our wounded?" one of the soldiers asked.

"We take as many as we can. Walking wounded certainly. Litter cases we take too. We do not leave anyone behind," Bernard said, but he knew in his heart that the litter patients would probably not make it.

As they moved out, machine-gun fire at close range killed many of the litter patients and those carrying them.

PFC Thornton was wounded in the arm before the order to fall back was given. As he came out of his foxhole, he was nearly run over by two other soldiers fleeing in the same direction, causing him to fall. Lying on the ground, he saw the first of the enemy cresting the hill over the position next to his. The enemy didn't hesitate to shoot the soldier attempting to surrender there. Wounded soldiers were treated in a similar manner. The entire withdrawal disintegrated into a panicked stampede. All command and control was lost. Stragglers were still reaching friendly lines five and six days after the retreat order was given.

Lieutenant Colonel Smith made his way with remnants of Baker Company down the ridge parallel to the railroad tracks. Dowd and Jung were right beside him. Dowd had already proven that he could use the M1 rifle he was carrying and was very capable at throwing a grenade with accuracy. When Smith decided he was east of Colonel Perry's location, he turned west and went looking for Perry, whom he found.

"They've pushed us off the hills. There's just too many. I estimate a force of maybe four thousand. We can't do any more here," Smith said.

"Get in. I'll give you a ride," Perry said, motioning for Smith, Dowd and Jung to climb in the back of the jeep.

The artillery soldiers had seen Smith come into their area and knew it was time to get out of there. The artillerymen removed breech blocks and sights from the tubes and set out on foot to recover their vehicles, which were on the outskirts of Osan. Perry and Smith got in Perry's jeep along with Perry's driver, Dowd and Jung, and they started out through Osan, only to run into three T-34 tanks parked in the middle of the street with the crews smoking and joking next to them. A fast U-turn was executed and the dirt road that led to Ansong was taken.

Along the way, soldiers from the 1st Battalion were picked up by the artillerymen, thus saving about one hundred infantry soldiers. Over the course of the next couple of days, more soldiers reached friendly lines. All told, two hundred and fifty soldiers of the four hundred and sixty in the 1st Battalion reached friendly lines. Lieutenant Bernard and twelve men from his platoon reached Ch'onan two days later. The deserters he threatened to place before a firing squad were never seen again. Of the five officers and ten enlisted men from the artillery for the forward observers, machine guns, and bazooka groups with the infantry, none survived. Colonel Perry lost five officers and twenty-six enlisted men. US forces had encountered the enemy for the first time and met defeat. It would not be the last time.[4]

---

4. Both Lieutenant Colonel Charles "Brad" Smith and Lieutenant Colonel Miller Osborne Perry received the Distinguished Service Cross for their actions. Both retired from the US Army at the rank of brigadier general. "Charles Bradford Smith," Wikipedia, July 9, 2024, https://en.wikipedia.org/wiki/Charles_Bradford_Smith; Military Times, "Miller Perry," Hall of Valor: Medal of Honor, Silver Star, U.S. Military Awards, https://valor.militarytimes.com/hero/7062.

Chapter 22

34th Moves into Position

5 July 1950
34th Regiment, 24th Division
Taejon, South Korea

As TF Smith was fighting for its life, it took three days before all of the 34th Regiment was ready to leave Pusan. The regimental executive officer, Lieutenant Colonel Robert Wadlington, supervised the unloading of the vehicles and heavy equipment off the LSTs, while Colonel Jay B. Lovless, with his operations officer, Major Dunn, drove north to Taejon to meet with General Dean. Lovless found Dean in the division command post.[1] Word of the debacle at Osan was just coming in when he arrived. Everyone was a bit depressed at the news.

"Colonel Lovless, good to see you," General Dean said as Lovless walked into the division command post with Major Dunn and Lieutenant Colonel David Smith, the 3rd Battalion commander, in tow. "Come over here and meet your new 1st Battalion commander, Lieutenant Colonel Ayres," Dean introduced. Lieutenant Colonel Harold

---

1. Colonel Jay B. Lovless retired at the rank of colonel and was a recipient of the Distinguished Service Cross for actions in World War II.

"Red" Ayres had flown in from Japan that morning with the 1st Battalion. Ayres was an experienced combat commander, having served in Italy in World War II. After the introductions were completed, General Dean had all four officers join him at the wall map showing enemy dispositions as they understood them as well as friendly locations as they thought they were. Brigadier General George B. Barth joined them and started explaining what had happened at Osan to Task Force Smith. Barth was the artillery commander for the 25th Infantry Division and had come to Korea as part of the 25th advance party. He'd observed what had happened to TF Smith. Within the 24th Division, he had no authority. When Barth was finished, General Dean gave his guidance to Colonel Lovless.

"Here's what I want you to do. I want the 1st Battalion to establish a position at P'yongt'aek. I want the 3rd Battalion to do the same at Ansong. The division headquarters will move up to Songhwan-ni," Dean outlined. "Holding P'yongt'aek is paramount as if they get through there, it's a straight shot into Taejon. Understood?" Dean asked and continued talking. "The Yellow Sea will protect your left flank and the mountains will do the same on the right."

"Yes, sir," Lovless answered, and Ayres and Smith simply nodded their heads in understanding.

"Sir, a couple of questions if I may?" Lovless asked.

"What are they?" Dean replied.

"Who is our artillery support? Do we have any tank support?" Lovless asked.

"There's no tank support and no artillery support as it hasn't arrived as yet. As soon as it does, I'll move them up to support you," Dean said.

"Sir, you're expecting us to defend against an infantry force supported by tanks with no artillery support or tank support, even after you and I've discussed the state of training in the regiment," Lovless said with some surprise and disgust. The month prior, Lovless had taken command of the 34th Regiment as the previous commander had been relieved because of the poor condition of the regiment. Dean and

Lovless had discussed the status of the regiment right after the change of command.

"Colonel, you have your orders. I suggest you carry them out," Dean responded in a terse manner.

"Yes, sir," Lovless said, rendering a salute and departing with the battalion commanders behind him.

Barth stopped the trio outside. "Gentlemen, from what I observed at Osan, the enemy is going to come at you leading with tanks—T-34 tanks. I'd recommend you send bazooka teams out front to initiate delay action," General Barth advised.

"Roger, sir, sounds good. If there's nothing else, we'll head out and conduct a recon of the areas before the troops arrive," Lovless said, not wanting to waste time and assuming that General Barth was working for General Dean.

Leaving the division command post, Ayres and Lovless headed for P'yongt'aek as Dean had indicated this was the most important place that had to be held. Smith drove off to Ansong, which was about seven miles due east of P'yongt'aek.

After Colonel Lovless departed, General Barth returned to the CP, where General Dean was studying the map. "George, I want to make you my task force commander for the 34th. I'll give you two artillery battalions when they get here to round out your task force. Okay?" Dean asked.

"Sounds good to me, General. Rather be doing something than sitting here twiddling my thumbs," Barth responded.

"Good. Now I want Ayres and Lovless to occupy successive delaying positions when they withdraw from P'yongt'aek. Lovless had every right to ask about support, but I want him to make a determined stand, only withdrawing when necessary," Dean directed.

"I best be getting up there, then. I'll move to the CP for the 34th if you need to talk to me," Barth said, rendering a salute and departing.

SOUTH OF P'YONGT'AEK, the landscape flattened out for forty-five miles with road networks permitting an enemy force to outflank any force on the Seoul-Taegu Road. The landscape was mountainous coming close to the eastern side of the town of Ansong. Good defensive terrain was located on this side. Both towns were important transportation hubs with two major roads passing through them from the Yellow Sea to the central mountains. An enemy penetration of these towns would make it more difficult to stop an advancing enemy force.

As Ayres placed his companies in defensive positions two miles north of P'youngt'aek, he instructed his intelligence and reconnaissance platoon to move forward with bazookas and find tanks. He also instructed an engineer platoon that was attached to prepare for demolition a bridge that supported the road forward of his position. Lieutenant Charles Payne drove north across the bridge, looking for signs of tanks. Reaching the village of Sojorg, he saw tank tracks in the dirt road and cautiously began to follow them. At the railroad station, Payne saw five tanks, just sitting there. Easing back to his small force, he gathered the leadership for a conference.

"Okay, we have five tanks parked around the train station. Let's break down into five teams with two bazookas per team. I want a fire team covering each antitank team. Two bazooka rounds per weapon. When we're in position, I'll fire the first round and you all fire on my first shot. Two rounds per tank and then back to the assembly area and get the hell out of here, understood?" Payne asked.

"Sir, did you see any supporting infantry around those tanks?" Sergeant Roy F. Collins asked.

"I didn't, but I'm sure the supporting infantry is close by, so two shots and haul ass. Got it?" Payne emphasized.

"Yes, sir" was heard from everyone in a whisper.

"Alright, let's move out, slow and quiet," Payne instructed. The teams dispersed as they moved forward behind concealment offered by the vegetation in approaching the parked tanks. When Payne could see that everyone was in position, he slowly stood with his bazooka on his shoulder and fired. The round flew straight and slammed into the turret of the tank he was aiming at. Private Hamilton immediately loaded his weapon with the second round as Sergeant Collins, standing next to Payne, launched his first round at the same tank. Payne and Collins were too busy to notice the rounds from the other teams hitting their respective tanks, but all the tanks were taking hits from the 2.36 bazookas. In less than twenty seconds, all the rounds had been fired and everyone was hightailing it back to the vehicles. Before Payne could make an assessment of the damage inflicted, intense small-arms fire was received, chasing his small force back down the road to their awaiting vehicles. The North Korean infantry had been in hide positions and hadn't seen Payne's party until after they'd fired. *Damn, I've just kicked over a hornet's nest*, Payne was thinking.

As he sprinted to his vehicle, a voice yelled out, "Shadrick is hit!"[2]

Payne responded, "Get him in a vehicle!" The force sped back to P'yongt'aek, where Payne immediately reported to Colonel Ayres.

"Sir, there were five tanks at the railroad station and we engaged, but then the small-arms fire was so intense we got out of there as quick as we could. We lost Private Kenneth Shadrick, however. His body is over at the aid station," Payne reported.

"How big of a force do you estimate?" Ayres asked.

"Sir, there were five tanks that we saw. The small-arms fire was at least a company-size force. I would say—"

"Excuse me, sir," a sergeant from operations interrupted, "but A Company just reported that he has tanks approaching from the north."

"Order A Company to blow the bridge, *now!*" Ayres ordered. Moments later, the explosion of the bridge could be heard, creating an amazing sight for those close enough to see it destroyed. The engineers had done their job well. Ayres left the battalion command post and moved forward to observe the situation. As the bridge was destroyed, General Barth arrived and surveyed the situation.

"General Barth," Ayres said, surprised to see the general.

---

2. Private Kenneth Shadrick died from his wounds.

"Colonel Ayres, did you just blow the bridge?" Barth asked before he was in a position to see it.

"Yes, sir. My reconnaissance team located five tanks and engaged them. Before they could make a damage assessment, they were engaged by what we believe to be at least a company-sized infantry force and maybe larger. We lost one soldier in the engagement. We do know that each of the five tanks was hit with two rounds, but we don't know the damage. Now we have a combined infantry and tank force approaching the bridge, so I ordered it blown," Ayres explained.

"Good. Colonel Ayres, I don't want you to be another Task Force Smith. Hold for as long as you can, but don't let them get behind you," General Barth said. "We'll leave it up to you to decide if and when you pull out. Understood?"

"Yes, sir. We'll hold for as long as possible but not allow ourselves to be outflanked and surrounded," Ayres indicated.

"Good. I'm going to head back and talk to Colonel Lovless. Any questions?"

"Just one, sir. If I give the word to pull back, where are we to go?" Ayres asked.

"Ch'onui, and I'll meet you there with a new defensive position location," Barth said.[3] "See you later and hold for as long as you can." Barth headed for his jeep and departed to see Colonel Lovless at the 34th Regimental command post.

Finding Colonel Lovless, General Barth provided new instructions. "Colonel, you need to conduct a delaying action position and consolidate the regiment in the vicinity of Ch'onui. The 3rd Battalion should move to Ch'onui with one company providing a rear guard," General Barth directed. Lovless didn't question the new instructions as General Barth was acting on behalf of the division commander, General Dean, or so Colonel Lovless thought, and so Lovless issued the orders to the 3rd Battalion to move.[4]

---

3. Korean maps indicate the spelling as shown. Other sources indicate that the spelling is Ch'onan. I elected to use the Korean map spelling.

4. There was confusion in Barth's role and command authority. Lovless and Ayres did not know that Dean had appointed Barth as a task force commander. As the artillery

commander, even one assigned to the division—which Barth was not as he was instead assigned to the 25th Infantry Division—he would not have been in the regimental commander's chain of command, Lovless was clear about Dean's intent, but the order from Barth had him withdraw and move right to Ch'onui. Barth, not Lovless, ordered the 3rd Battalion to move from Ansong to Ch'onui.

Chapter 23
Retrograde to Ch'onui

6 July 1950
  34th Regiment
  Ch'onui, South Korea

THE EVENING BROUGHT thick fog and rain, which continued into the morning hours. Thankfully, the night before had been quiet as far as enemy probing was concerned. Soldiers of the 1st Battalion sat in the mud on the edge of their water-filled foxholes, eating cold C rations. *Nothing like rain, mud and cold C rations to lower morale in the morning hours. At least it isn't a cold rain,* Colonel Ayres was thinking as he made the rounds at daybreak, moving from one foxhole to another and offering words of encouragement to the soldiers. Many complained about missing their quarters in Japan and hoping they would be going back there in the coming week. Ayres was talking to Captain Leroy Osburn, Company A commander, when Sergeant First Class Roy Collins let out a yell.[1]

"Tanks!" Collins said, pointing at the blown bridge. The tanks had stopped but the accompanying infantry had not and were moving past

---

1. Captain Leroy Osburn retired as a lieutenant colonel.

the tanks and entering the river. Almost immediately, the 4.2-inch mortars of the battalion opened fire and were impacting around the river-crossing site. Serious damage from the mortars was being inflicted on the enemy infantry but not the tanks, which commenced firing. Riflemen in the 1st Battalion engaged with long-range rifle fire, but their lack of training became apparent very quickly as they weren't hitting the enemy with any accuracy. Fifteen minutes into the battle, a tank round slammed into the forward observer's position for the mortars and no one replaced him. The accuracy of the mortars dropped off quickly.

As the enemy infantry crossed the river, they fanned out to the right. Ayres quickly determined that they were attempting to flank A Company. The same was happening forward of B Company as well. *Just as General Barth indicated they would. Lead with tanks and then flank our positions*, Ayres was thinking. Then he recalled Barth's other words: *Do not become a Task Force Smith.*

"Captain Osburn," Ayres said, turning to the A Company commander. "They're going to attempt to flank you. I want you to leave one platoon here as a screening force and withdraw the rest of the company."

Ayres attempted to contact regimental headquarters, but communications were horrible. Radios were inefficient in operating over the long distances in the mountainous terrain, and they were soaking wet with old batteries. Landlines were in place and repeatedly cut by refugees who took the wires to make harnesses to carry their belongings. Messenger traffic was the most reliable but slowest means of communications. Returning to the battalion command post, Ayres contacted B Company and ordered the same for them. "Withdraw leaving a screening force to cover your withdrawal." Next he was able to contact Major Dunn, the regimental S-3.

"Dunn, we're being hit hard. They're attempting to outflank us. We're pulling back. Moving to—" The line went dead before Ayres could finish.

Dunn immediately contacted Colonel Lovless, and together they surveyed a map. "Major, tell Ayres I want him to pull back to here next, to Ch'onui. Have we heard from 3rd Battalion?" Lovless asked.

"No, sir. Commo is pretty bad in this terrain and with these distances," Dunn responded.

"Alright, take a jeep and get to Ayres's CP. Show him where General Barth wants us to fall back to around Ch'onui. See if he can contact 3rd Battalion and pass the order on to him. Be careful. I don't want to lose a good S-3," Lovless said sincerely.

"Nor would I want you to lose a good S-3, sir," Dunn said with some humor and departed to head to Colonel Ayres's location. The drive was slow due to the flow of refugees coming south. Finally arriving at Colonel Ayres's command post, Major Dunn approached the commander, who was observing the action. He was occupying a foxhole between A and B Companies.

"Sir, Major Dunn. I have a location that General Barth wants your battalion to move to when it reaches Ch'onan," Dunn said, pulling out his map and spreading it out. The sounds of small-arms fire and the distinctive sound of the North Korean burp guns were clear.[2]

"I'll get my people moving immediately," Ayres said and passed new orders to Companies A and B for the move. By late afternoon, the battalion elements were arriving at the new location in a disorganized fashion along with discarded equipment along the road to Ch'onui. Company A was the last element to arrive after dark.

"WHAT OUTFIT IS THIS?" General Barth asked a young captain who was just getting off a train that had arrived in Ch'onui that morning.

"Sir, A Company, D Company and part of Headquarters Company, 1st Battalion, 21st Infantry, Lieutenant Colonel Smith commanding," Captain Osburn said.

---

2. North Korean M49 PPSh-41 submachine guns were commonly referred to as burp guns and were very plentiful in the North Korean Army. They fired a 7.62-caliber round and had a thirty-five-round box magazine or a seventy-one-round drum magazine. The effective range was two hundred meters.

"Well, Captain Osburn, are you the senior officer with this bunch?" Barth asked.

"Ah, yes, sir," Captain Osburn said, unsure of where this was going.

"Good, now I want you to form these people up and move them to a location I'm going to take you to. Do you have a map of the area?" Barth asked.

"No, sir," Osburn answered.

"Well, you can have mine when we get there. Let's go," Barth said, leading the way to a point two miles south of Ch'onan. Osburn returned to the train station and brought the elements of the 1st Battalion, 21st Infantry, up to the new location and the two companies began to prepare defensive positions. As the first elements of the 1st Battalion, 34th, arrived, they joined the two companies from the 21st Infantry. Lieutenant Colonel Ayres now had a reinforced battalion with the two additional companies and the headquarters company.

"Smith, General Barth here. Can you hear me okay?" General Barth asked over the field telephone.

"Yes, sir," Lieutenant Colonel Dave Smith replied.

"Do you have any contact with the enemy?"

"No, sir. Has something happened?"

"First Bat is being pushed back. I want you to fall back to Ch'onan before you're cut off. Leave one company behind to provide a rear guard and screening force. When you get to Ch'onan, I'll put you into position. Any questions?" Barth asked.

"No, sir, I'll get my people moving."

"Good, try to stay in contact with my headquarters," Barth said and hung up.

Turning to his S-3, Smith said, "Get the company commanders up here now!"

When the company commanders arrived, Smith outlined the plan for withdrawal. "Love Company will be last in the order of march and serve as a rear guard," Smith said. No mention was made of a company serving as a screening force.

Chapter 24
Fight for Ch'onui

6 July 1950
  34th Regiment
  Ch'onui, South Korea

ALL THROUGH THE afternoon the town was choked with people passing through from north to south. Americans were streaming in not in military formations but in gaggles of ten to fifteen, some on foot and others in vehicles. As they entered, they streamed off to a location two miles south of town. Civilian refugees were a mixed bag of children, young men with wives, and single females with babies. Old men with thinning beards and conical hats carried all their earthly possessions on their backs. ROK soldiers, some with military equipment and most with nothing but their uniforms, were in the mix of refugees. Most didn't smile at the soldiers of the 34th as they viewed foreign soldiers with disdain. For centuries, Korea had been fought over, first by the Chinese, then the Russians and then the Japanese. Now here were the Americans, and to the refugees, regardless of their purpose in Korea, they were just another foreign invader. They knew that, as in the past, their homes would be destroyed, their worldly possessions stolen and their loved ones probably killed. In the mind of a Korean, there wasn't much to look forward to at this time.

As the 1st and 3rd Battalions of the 34th Regiment arrived, they took up positions south of Ch'onan. Colonel Lovless moved his CP to the vicinity and began to confer with the battalion commanders when General Dean and General Barth arrived. It was obvious from the start that General Dean was upset.

"Who the hell told you to pull out of P'yongt'aek?" Dean started off, approaching Colonel Lovless. "Did I not make it clear how important it was to retain our position there as well as the position at Ansong?" Everyone was a bit surprised at this tirade. No one said anything for a long moment.

"Well, Colonel, I'm waiting for an answer," Dean said, appearing to be a bit angrier if that was possible.

Finally Colonel Ayres spoke up. "Sir, it was my decision to pull out of P'yongt'aek. The enemy was maneuvering to outflank and encircle my force, and I felt it was best under the circumstances to withdraw after delaying him for approximately six hours," he said. No one said anything else, not even the man who'd given the order to pull out, General Barth.

That's right, stand there with your mouth shut and act stupid, Ayres was thinking as he stared at General Barth, who avoided looking at him.

"Well, Colonel, I'm tempted to tell you to march your regiment right back up there. If it wasn't getting so close to dark, I would. If I did, you'd probably get into a night ambush and blame it on me. No, but tomorrow morning at first light I want you to send a company back towards P'yongt'aek until they make contact with the enemy. Do you understand me?" Dean said, moving closer to Lovless.

"Yes, sir, completely," Lovless replied, but he had not backed up as Dean entered his personal space.

"See that it gets done and done right this time," Dean said, turning on his heel and storming out of the command post with Barth in tow. That was the last that anyone saw of General Barth as he returned to Pusan to meet his division.

The next morning, Love Company got the mission to head north to P'yongt'aek until he gained contact with the enemy forces. He was reinforced by the regiment's reconnaissance platoon taking point. They moved out at 0800. For the next two hours, everyone in the 34th Regimental CP was glued to the radio, listening for a report of any kind, but the radio remained silent.

Colonel Robert R. Martin had arrived from the States the day before and was taken directly to General Dean. He and Dean had served together in Europe. Dean thought very highly of Martin and had requested him when he found that Martin was coming to the Far East Command. As soon as Martin arrived, Dean sent him north to join and observe the 34th. Martin was still in low-quarter shoes and khaki uniform with no weapon or field gear. What he did have was a message from General Dean, which he presented to Major Dunn when he arrived. Two and a half hours later, Major Dunn handed Colonel Lovless a message.

"Excuse me, sir," Major Dunn said, and Colonel Lovless turned to see Dunn and another officer in khaki uniform. "Sir, this is Colonel Martin and he was sent by General Dean—"

"How do you do? Bob Martin," Martin said, cutting off Major Dunn in midsentence and extending his hand. "General Dean sent me up here to observe and learn. I hope you don't mind. It caught me by surprise, I can tell you. I only arrived in-country yesterday," Martin said with sincerity.

"Glad to meet you. You're welcome to come along. Give me a minute to read this," Lovless said, opening the folded message.

TO: CO, 34TH RGT
FROM: CG, 24TH DIV
TIME: 1024, 7 JULY 1950
MOVE ONE BN FWD WITH MINIMUM TRANSPORTATION.
GAIN CONTACT AND BE PREPARED TO FIGHT DELAY
ACTION BACK TO RECENT POSITION. PD AIR REPORTS NO
ENEMY ARMOR SOUTH OF RIVER.

Colonel Lovless understood the order but questioned the pilot report.

"Major Dunn, contact 3rd Bat and tell them to be prepared to follow L Company. They should move out as soon as possible," Lovless directed. "We'll move a TAC CP right behind 3rd Bat."[1]

"Very good, sir, I'll get the TAC ready to move as soon as I contact 3rd Bat," Major Dunn said and went to find the senior NCO for the CP. An hour later, the battalion with the regimental TAC CP following was moving up the road to P'yongt'aek. As they did so, Colonel Lovless noticed some soldiers on the adjacent ridgeline moving in the opposite direction from his route of march.

"Sergeant Kong," Lovless called to his interpreter, pointing at the ridgeline. "Do they look like South Korean or North Korean forces?" He handed Sergeant Kong his field glasses and turned to Colonel Martin. "The North Koreans have been putting their armor on the roads, but their infantry stays on the high ground and attempts to flank our positions, cutting them off from withdrawing," he explained.

After a moment, Kong said, "I think South Korean." He handed the field glasses back to Lovless. No one thought anything more of the incident, and the 3rd Battalion and TAC CP continued moving north. Lovless and Martin continued a conversation about fighting in Korea and the tactics that Lovless had learned about the way the North Koreans fought and maneuvered. Refugees moved south past them as well as ROK soldiers in no type of formation but as individuals, some with weapons and equipment but most without.

"Did I just hear an explosion?" Lovless asked, cocking his head to one side. Major Dunn was on the radio talking to someone.

"Sir, Love Company reports small-arms contact and is receiving incoming mortar rounds," Dunn said. Quickly Lovless, Dunn and Martin began studying a map and the disposition of Love Company

------

1. TAC CP stands for tactical command post. It is a smaller, more mobile command post with a reduced staff and positioned closer to the front lines than the main command post. Depending on the unit type, it usually consists of a couple of vehicles with powerful radios, perhaps a general-purpose small tent, and eight to ten staff officers and soldiers.

and the 3rd Battalion. Their conversation was interrupted by the sound of an L-3 observation plane making a low and slow pass over their location and a message being dropped. One of the soldiers from the TAC CP retrieved the message and brought it to Major Dunn, who in turn handed it to Colonel Lovless.

TO: CO 34TH RGT
FROM: CG, 24TH DIV
1600 7 JULY
PROCEED WITH GREAT CAUTION. LARGE NUMBER OF
TROOPS ON YOUR EAST AND WEST FLANKS. NEAR ANSONG
LOTS OF TANKS (40–50) AND TRUCKS. MYANG MYON LARGE
CONCENTRATION OF TROOPS/ SONGHWAN-NI LARGE
CONCENTRATION OF TROOPS TRYING TO FLANK YOUR
UNIT.
SGND DEAN.

Lovless and Martin read the message and returned to the map, plotting the locations of the enemy concentrations.

"Major Dunn," Lovless said, "tell 3rd Bat to hold in place. Do not advance further. Have Love Company withdraw back to 3rd Bat's location and wait for further orders." Turning to Colonel Martin, he said, "Let's get back to 1st Bat and brief Ayres on the situation."

"Right behind you," Colonel Martin said, and both officers moved back to Lovless's jeep and directed the driver to get them to the 1st Battalion's location. Major Dunn got in his own jeep and drove to the location of the 3rd Battalion to issue the order.

"ATTENTION!" a corporal in the 1st Battalion command post yelled when Brigadier General Pearson Menoher, the assistant division commander, 24th Division, and General Church walked in.

"As you were," General Menoher responded almost immediately. Moments later, Colonel Ayres arrived in the command post.

"Sir, can I help you?" Ayres asked, surprised that the assistant division commander was there. *Well, here comes my relief of command because I did what Barth told me to do, that piece of shit*, he was thinking.

"How you doing, Ayres?" Menoher said with a smile. "I understand that Colonel Lovless is en route to this location. I need to speak with him."

"I didn't know he was heading this way. Can I get you some coffee? That's about the strongest thing we have here," Ayres said, not sure where this was going.

"No, we're good. Lay out your defensive plan if you will, please," Menoher asked as he moved closer to a map hanging on the wall in the abandoned building that Ayres had moved his command post into.

"Yes, sir," Ayres said and started explaining how he had displaced his forces. He was completing his informal presentation when Colonel Lovless and Colonel Martin walked into the command post. Both were surprised to see the two general officers.

"General Menoher, General Church," Lovless said, saluting both officers. "What brings you here, sirs?"

General Menoher approached the two colonels, handing each a piece of paper. "Colonel Lovless, by order of General Dean, you are hereby relieved of command," Menoher said, turning to Colonel Martin. "Colonel Martin, by order of General Dean, you are directed to take command of the 34th Regiment."

Lovless felt like he'd just been punched in the gut. The previous commander of the 34th had been relieved for incompetence a month before the regiment had orders to deploy to Korea. Lovless had never had time to improve a bad command.

Martin was equally shocked at this news. He slowly turned to Lovless. "I'm sorry, but I knew nothing of this. I'm as surprised as you."

"Don't worry about it. Good luck to you and I truly wish you the best," Lovless said as he extended his hand, which Martin accepted.

"Take care of the boys" were Lovless's departing words as he walked out of the command post.[2]

DURING THE CHANGE OF COMMAND, Major Dunn had been at the 3rd Battalion's location and provided the order to Lieutenant Colonel David Smith. As he did so, the I&R platoon leader drove up in his bullet-riddled jeep.[3]

"Sir, we got hit in an ambush," Lieutenant Brown said, pointing at bullet holes in the jeep, his jacket and his canteen.

"Show me," Major Dunn said, pulling his map out and spreading it on the hood of the jeep.

Scanning it quickly, Lieutenant Brown pointed to a small village about a mile up the road. "This is the village. I estimate about forty to fifty soldiers there. I have three men still in the village and cut off."

"Sir, I'll be glad to lead a company up there to get those men," Dunn said, looking at Colonel Smith.

"Love Company is the closest. Take them. Stay in contact with me on the radio if you can," Smith directed.

Almost immediately, Dunn and Lieutenant Brown were in Dunn's jeep, heading back north to Love Company's location. Upon arriving, Dunn briefed the company commander, and the unit was beginning to organize for its departure when Major Boone Seegers, the S-3 for the 3rd Battalion, drove in from the north.[4] The three soldiers that had been cut off were in his vehicle. As the company moved back to its previous positions, North Korean forces on higher ground engaged them.

---

2. Colonel Jay B. Lovless received the Distinguished Service Cross for action in World War II, during which time he served as the Assistant G-3 for the 2nd Infantry Division. He retired as a colonel.

3. I&R stands for intelligence and reconnaissance.

4. Major Daniel Boone Seegers was a 1943 graduate of West Point and was a decorated veteran of World War II.

"Shit, where the hell did they come from?" Dunn asked, diving for cover.

"Sir, that appears to be the bunch that were in the village," Lieutenant Brown said.

"I'm going back to battalion and will get the mortars on them," Seegers said, running for his jeep and departing in great haste. Love Company continued to engage the enemy at two to three hundred yards, but the accuracy of their shooting was lacking. Mortar rounds landed, almost on top of Love Company, and they were coming from behind them.

"Sir, how about you go back to battalion and tell them to either stop dropping rounds or drop them on those guys and not us?" the company commander asked Dunn.

"Will do," Dunn said before he sprinted to his jeep and departed. Arriving at the 3rd Bat CP, he found that chaos reigned supreme. The CP was being taken down!

"Colonel Smith, what's going on?" Dunn asked.

"I'm displacing back to Ch'onan," Smith said. "I've already given the order to Love to withdraw back to here."

Damn, not much I can do here. I best get back to regiment and report this to Colonel Lovless, Dunn was thinking. When he drove back to the regimental CP, he wasn't aware that there had been a change of command. Entering the regimental CP, he was looking for Colonel Lovless when the CP NCOIC informed him of the change of command. He was shocked that it had happened.

"Sir, I just came from the 3rd Battalion. They've been engaged and are withdrawing back to Ch'onan," Dunn reported to Colonel Martin.

"Major, you get back in your jeep and tell Colonel Smith to get his ass back to his previous position, now," Colonel Martin said emphatically.

"Yes, sir" was all Dunn could say. He departed immediately. Heading up the road, he came upon Colonel Smith and gave him the order. Smith was not happy but began issuing instructions for the battalion to return to their positions.

"Sir, I'll take Major Seegers and we'll conduct a recon of your old positions," Dunn offered.

"Alright, we should be back up there in an hour," Smith said with resignation. Dunn and Seegers took Dunn's jeep and departed. The trip back to the previous positions was only a mile by road. When they had almost reached the position, the ambush of thirty North Koreans opened fire.

"Ah, shit, I'm hit," Dunn yelled as the jeep went into a ditch, tossing both men out. Seegers said nothing, and from the appearance of his wound, he would say nothing ever again.

Dunn crawled away from the ditch to a small knoll and took cover. He could see Love Company coming back up the road and deploying into a combat formation. They returned fire on the enemy patrol that had ambushed Dunn and Seegers. Dunn's hopes increased as he watched Love Company firing and maneuvering forward. However, his hopes crashed when he heard someone yell, "Fall back, fall back!" and the company began retreating.[5] Two hours later, the main body of the North Korean force arrived and took him prisoner.

"What do you mean you were hit?" Colonel Martin asked Colonel Smith when the disorganized elements of the 3rd Battalion drifted south of Ch'onan.

"Sir, we attempted to return to our previous positions, but contact with the enemy was intense. I thought it best to return to here to reinforce the 1st Battalion," Smith said, hoping Martin would buy that story.

"Where's Major Dunn?" Martin asked.

"Sir, he and Major Seegers, my S-3, were both engaged and killed, I believe. We attempted to get to them, but the enemy fire was intense and increasing," Smith offered as an excuse. Colonel Martin hadn't met Smith before this, so he gave him the benefit of the doubt.

"Okay, I want you in a defensive position supporting 1st Battalion.

---

5. Major Dunn was captured and spent thirty-eight months in a North Korean POW camp.

I want your battalion along this railroad track on the northern side of the town. Any questions?"

"Ah, no, sir," Smith mumbled.

"I'm going to take some of the headquarters people and go up and have a look for myself," Martin indicated. Smith got a sick feeling about then. "Maybe I can retrieve some of the vehicles and equipment that your battalion left up there. Go get your battalion settled in. We'll talk some more when I get back." Smith found that comment rather ominous.

Colonel Martin, still in low-quarter shoes and Class B uniform, departed with a couple of vehicles and soldiers from Headquarters Company plus a security detail consisting of eighty soldiers total. By 1700 hours, they were north of Ch'onan, recovering vehicles. The 3rd Battalion moved into the position designated by Colonel Martin, reinforcing the concrete platform at the train station into a strongpoint while some mined the road leading into town. Colonel Martin returned to the regimental CP by 2000 hours.

"Sir," Lieutenant Colonel Robert L. Wadlington said, gaining Martin's attention. "Sir, I'm happy to report that a battery from the 63rd Field Artillery Battalion has moved into our sector for support and is setting up on the south side of the town. They have both HE and Willie Pete rounds and plenty of them."

"Damn, that's good news. Have they moved their FOs forward yet?" Martin asked.

"They're in the process of doing that now as well as laying wire for commo with the FOs in case the radios crap out, as usual," Wadlington reported.

"Good, I'm going to go into town and see Smith about his defense and how things are going with the FOs. Contact me at 3rd Battalion if you need to talk to me. Oh, think about who we're going to get to replace Dunn. He seemed like a good officer," Martin said.

"He was, sir, and a fine gentleman," Wadlington said with a degree of sadness not normally displayed by professional soldiers. An hour after Martin had left, Wadlington heard the distinctive sound of outgoing artillery fire. It was coming from the vicinity of the 63rd Battery.

"Why are they shooting?" Wadlington said to anyone and everyone in the command post. "Has anyone reported any enemy?" As he spoke, one of the command post sergeants was on the phone and raised his hand. Hanging up, he turned in his chair. "Sir, 3rd Battalion reports small-arms fire on the western flank. They've also spotted tanks with infantry moving down the road from P'yongt'aek. The artillery is hitting the tanks with HE and Willie Pete. Two tanks are reported burning."

"Contact 1st Bat and see what their status is," Wadlington directed.

Moments later, the NCOIC approached Wadlington. "Sir, 1st Battalion reports all quiet in their sector south of the town—3rd Battalion is the only one in contact at this time."

"Good, please contact Colonel Martin at 3rd Battalion and inform him of the status of 1st Battalion," Wadlington requested.

"Yes, sir. Sir, can I recommend you get some sleep? Everything is in hand, and it's going to be a long night, I suspect. Catch a few winks while you can," the NCOIC said pleadingly.

"Yeah, I suppose you're right. I'll be in the other room and just close my eyes for a few. Wake me if anything develops," Wadlington said, realizing he was more tired than he'd initially thought. Sleep came quickly when he lay down, keeping his boots and uniform on.

He had just closed his eyes, he thought, when a voice penetrated the silence. "Sir, sir. Wake up, sir."

"Christ, Sergeant, I just laid down. What is it?" Wadlington said in a sharp tone, opening his eyes.

"Excuse me, sir, but you've been asleep for four hours. We have a problem," the NCOIC said.

"Four hours! Oh my God, it felt like I just dozed off. My apology for being such a grouch. What's up?" Wadlington said as he sat up and the NCOIC handed him a steaming canteen cup of coffee.

"Sir, Colonel Martin is missing."

"What?" Wadlington was wide awake at this news. "What happened?" he asked, coming to his feet.

"Sir, it appears that he was at the 3rd Battalion but left. Some tanks got into town and we believe cut him off. There was a security element with him, but 3rd Bat is reporting now that some of his troops are cut off in the town as well with Martin," the NCOIC explained.

"Damn, get Colonel Smith on the line. I'll be right there after I take a piss," Wadlington said, heading out the door. Moments later he was back and the NCOIC was holding the landline with Colonel Smith.

"Smith, Wadlington here. What the hell happened?"

"We had tanks come in on the east road. We destroyed two with artillery, but some got through and are in the town. The infantry was separated from the tanks due to our engaging and the artillery fire. Martin left here and wanted to observe the tanks, so he went to my left flank company. They were penetrated by the tanks and now they have two platoons cut off in the town, and Martin is with them," Smith said. "What do you want me to do?"

"What are your options?" Wadlington asked.

"Options! I can stay here and be destroyed piecemeal, or I can maybe withdraw and join 1st Bat. We're getting low on ammo as well and need a resupply," Smith added.

"Alright, I'll see about getting a resupply of ammo up to you. Let me talk to General Dean and see what he wants us to do. I'll call you back." Handing the phone to the NCOIC, Wadlington requested, "Get General Dean's headquarters on the line. I need to speak to him."

After what seemed like hours but was actually fifteen minutes, the NCOIC handed Wadlington the phone. "General Dean's aide."

"This is Colonel Wadlington. I must speak to General Dean, now!"

"Yes, sir, I'll get him. Please hold," the lieutenant said.

Moments later, Wadlington heard, "General Dean, what's up, Wadlington?"

"Sir, we have tanks on the north edge of town and Colonel Martin is cut off in the town with two platoons from the 3rd Battalion. We need a resupply of ammo as well," Wadlington explained.

"Great! Tell Martin to E&E out of there now. And tell him to delay for as long as possible. I'll get an ammo resupply up to you right away," Dean said before he hung up.

Turning to the CP NCOIC, Wadlington said, "Get 3rd Bat on the line. Tell them to tell Martin that General Dean says for him to E&E out of town tonight under the cover of darkness and we're to delay for as long as possible. He's sending up a resupply of ammo. Understood?"

"Got it, sir." And the NCOIC was on the landline to 3rd Battalion immediately.

Two hours later, Colonel Martin strolled into the regimental CP as if nothing was happening.

"What did I miss?" he asked, moving over to the coffeepot and pouring a cup that flowed like molasses. Taking a sip, he added, "Damn, that would raise the dead."

"Sir, you're aware of the situation with 3rd Battalion on the north side of the town. The 1st Battalion on the south side has had some small-arms contact but nothing serious. General Dean is sending up a resupply of ammo. It should be arriving shortly. I'll notify General Dean that you're back and I'm sure that will relieve him," Wadlington said, looking at his watch. The time was 0230 hours.

"I'm glad the old man is so concerned about my welfare," Martin said with a small chuckle and then turned to the NCOIC. "Sergeant, can we get another pot of coffee going? This is going to keep me awake for a week."

"Yes, sir, we'll get right on it," the NCOIC indicated, tapping one of the privates on the shoulder. The private got up to make a new pot. Colonel Martin picked up a C ration meal and moved off to the adjacent room. An hour later he came back.

"I'm going to go back down to 3rd Battalion. The sun will be up soon and I want to see what the enemy is up to as soon as it's light. Did the ammo resupply arrive yet?" Martin asked.

"No, sir," the NCOIC said. "We've had no report of it coming."

"Call division and ask them when it's going to get here. I want them resupplied before daylight. I suspect this morning things are going to heat up. If 3rd Bat gets pushed back, I'm going to have them fight a delaying action back to 1st Battalion's location. Notify 1st Battalion to be ready to receive them," Martin directed and departed.

He was still in his Class B uniform and without a helmet or combat boots.

PRIVATE STEAMER HAD BEEN a deuce-and-a-half driver since he'd joined the Army. He had aspirations of being a long-haul truck driver when he returned to civilian life and figured what better way to get free training. He was having second thoughts about that line of work as he drove with blackout lights on a road that was not in the best of conditions and was full of refugees moving in the opposite direction. The blackout lights didn't provide much light to see by but had been ordered in the past couple of days. Steamer had to improvise by taking tape and placing it on the top and bottom of the truck's headlights, leaving only a small opening for the light to shine through. *I sure as hell will be glad when the sun comes up so I can see the road and not run over any of these people that don't seem to want to get off it*, he was thinking. He had been told to deliver the load of ammo to the train station in Ch'onan, and as he had made the trip several times in the previous days, he knew right where it was. As he rolled into the center of town, he noticed an absence of lights or people. "I guess I know where all the refugees are from. Place is empty," he mumbled to himself as he entered the intersection of the northeast and northwest roads. It was just growing light enough for him to see the two tanks approaching the intersection.

"Oh shit," he yelled to no one but himself and rapidly executed a U-turn before the tanks saw him. Stomping on the accelerator, he quickly departed Ch'onan without delivering the ammo.

COLONEL MARTIN WAS STANDING with Lieutenant Colonel Dave Smith when the tanks coming from the northwest were spotted on the road. Watching them approach, Smith leaned toward Martin and said in a soft voice, "They should be hitting the minefield about now. We put them in on the road when we first arrived."

"Good. When they hit, you should open up with artillery fire on them as well," Martin suggested. They continued to watch the tanks approach closer, but nothing happened. Finally Smith became concerned.

"Damn, they must have cleared the minefield during the night," Smith said and gave the order to open fire.

Immediately, the soldiers in the 3rd Battalion engaged with the 2.36-inch bazookas, only to discover that the weapon was ineffective against the T-34 tank. Even the artillery and mortars were having limited effect on the tanks, but they were separating the infantry from them, preventing them from supporting the tanks as they rolled into Ch'onan. Moving away from the tanks, the North Korean infantry in typical fashion fanned out, maneuvering around the 3rd Battalion. At 0600 hours, they were well within the town and had surrounded two companies of the 3rd Battalion. The fighting was intense.

Private Leotis E. Heater was separated from his platoon along with the rest of his squad. Sergeant Anderson, the squad leader, was bleeding profusely and out of the fight for the most part.

"Heater, I think if we can get past that tank, we can make our way back to the 1st Battalion location," Corporal Hester said, pointing at a tank that was between them and safety. They had taken refuge in a building on the north side of the intersection. The tank was freely shooting at everything and anything, with priority on American vehicles that had been parked in the intersection.

"You get Sergeant Anderson ready to move. Give me your grenades. I'm going to pay that tank a visit," Heater said, taking Hester's grenades and hanging them on his belt. Hesitating for a moment, he waited until the turret of the tank was pointing away from their position and sprinted to the side of the tank. One grenade was a thermal grenade, and he tossed that on the engine deck. Then he quickly climbed up the side of the tank, opening the turret hatch, dropping four grenades down the hatch and diving off the top. As he hit the ground, the first grenade detonated, setting off the other three. Flames blew out the top of the turret hatch as well as the driver's hatch. Hester grabbed his arm and pulled him up as the remainder of the squad sprinted past, carrying Anderson, and made it safely out of town.

Standing in a building along the northwest road above the intersection was Colonel Martin, who had just witnessed Heater's unselfish act. *I get back, I want that young man's name. He deserves a damn medal for that,* he was thinking when two more soldiers from the 3rd Battalion came through the door. They were surprised to find an American colonel standing in the room—a colonel they had not met before and who was wearing a Class B uniform.

"Sir, are you lost?" Sergeant Jerry C. Christenson asked.

"No, Sergeant, I know exactly where I am and that's right here. Is that a bazooka I see you carrying?" Martin asked.

"Yes, sir. We found it along with a couple of rounds and thought we'd bring it along. Never have fired one, though," Christenson said.

"Well, I have. Let me have it and you serve as my assistant gunner," Martin said, reaching for the weapon, which the sergeant quickly surrendered. "Let me show you how to load and prepare it for firing. As soon as it's clear, we're hauling out of here and heading south." As Martin was demonstrating the proper technique to load and fire the bazooka, the sound of a tank approaching could be heard. "It looks like show and tell is over, Sergeant. We have a tank approaching. I'll engage and then we cross the road at a dead run and get the hell out of here. Got it?"

"Got it, sir. You're ready to fire," Sergeant Christenson said, getting away from the backblast area of the weapon. Martin waited a moment and stepped into the open doorway. As he raised the weapon to his shoulder, he realized that the tank turret had stopped rotating and was pointed right at the doorway. He squeezed the trigger, the bazooka sounding off as the rocket left the tube and passed the 76mm round from the tank's main gun. Colonel Martin felt nothing as his body was cut in two when the 76mm round went through him and exploded.[6]

---

6. Sergeant Jerry Christenson was taken prisoner and related the story to Major Dunn while sharing a POW camp together. Colonel Martin was posthumously awarded the

Reports from 1st Battalion streamed into the regimental CP that stragglers from 3rd Battalion were coming through the lines. General Dean was concerned, based on the reports he was receiving from the 34th, that the situation needed his presence, especially after he was notified at 1000 hours that Colonel Martin was dead.

"Wadlington, this is General Dean. I'll be heading to your location. Meet me south of the town." Dean gave Colonel Wadlington the location's coordinates, which didn't do much good since everything on the maps was in Japanese. "Oh, hell, just meet me on the last hill south of the town," Dean finally said.

When Dean arrived, Colonel Wadlington was already there. Artillery was laying down a smokescreen in the town to cover the soldiers from 3rd Battalion that were attempting to escape and evade out of the town.

"What's the situation?" Dean asked, getting out of his jeep and approaching Wadlington.

"Sir, 3rd Battalion is withdrawing in piecemeal fashion. LTC Smith came out a half hour ago and is exhausted. I put him in an ambulance and have sent him back. I don't think he'll be returning. Only one of the company commanders has made it out. The enemy got tanks into the town and then used his infantry to flank on both sides and cut off the retreat. Several attempts to convoy through were ambushed and destroyed," Wadlington said, noting that General Dean looked exhausted as well. *The old man hasn't had much sleep either,* Wadlington thought.

Dean continued to survey the situation unfolding before him. The 1st Battalion was in its defensive position and had had little contact. Colonel Ayres was seen moving between his companies and the two companies from 1st Battalion, 21st Regiment, which was all that was left of Colonel Brad Smith's battalion. Some stragglers were still drifting in and would for the next couple of days.

Distinguished Service Cross; see Roy E. Appleman, *United States Army in the Korean War: South to the Naktong, North to the Yalu (June–November 1950)* (Washington, D.C.: United States Army Center of Military History, 1992), 87.

Turning to Wadlington, Dean said, "Alright, you're in command of the 34th Regiment. I want you to withdraw your regiment to the Kum River. Follow the Kongju Road. I'll have the 21st Regiment follow the Choch'iwon Road. The 21st arrived two days ago and aside from the 1st Battalion are in good shape. Both roads converge at Taejon, and both must be defended or we'll lose Taejon. We're reconstituting the 1st Battalion, so release those two companies from the 1st Battalion and get them over to Choch'iwon. Any idea who the enemy is?"

"Sir, we believe that there are elements of the 16th and 18th Regiments of the 4th North Korean Division, supported by tanks from the 105th Armored Division. Elements of the 3rd North Korean Division appeared and have deployed east of town," Wadlington informed him.

Chapter 25
Tropic Lightning Arrives

8 July 1950
25th Division Headquarters
Pusan, South Korea

THE 25TH INFANTRY DIVISION, known as the Tropic Lightning Division, had a long history of serving in the Pacific Theater. Serving in Schofield Barracks, Hawaii, on December 7, 1941, the division had marched across the Pacific islands and found itself as an occupation force in Japan at the conclusion of the war. Duty as an occupation force was pretty cushy for the soldiers. As for the other units in Japan, the demands of soldiering were pretty lax due to limited training areas and funds. Physical training usually took the form of intramural baseball or football competitions between units. Some of the division football teams were competitive with semipro ball teams. Most soldiers lived off the base in cheap housing apartments with a "hooch maid" who took care of most if not all of the soldiers' needs. Life was good…was.

All that changed the first week of July, when the division commander, Major General William B. Kean, received first a phone call and then written orders to deploy his division to Pusan, Korea. His advance party arrived the next morning, 9 July, with the main body debarking on 12 July and prepared for operations on 18 July. Kean had flown over with the advance party and landed in Pusan. He hadn't bothered to see the sights but immediately hopped another flight to Taejon to meet with General Dean, 24th Division commander. Dean met him at the airport.

"Bill, you're a sight for sore eyes," Dean said. From the look on his tired and drawn face, he wasn't exaggerating.

"I understand you need a bit of help in this police action," Kean said, extending his hand to his old friend.

"Police action my ass. Never seen the robbers with tanks before. Let's head over to my CP and let me give you a rundown," Dean said, leading the way to his jeep.

The ride back to the CP in Taejon was uneventful, but Kean took note of the number of refugees moving down the road as well as the ragtag look of some of the soldiers they drove past. Arriving in the town, the jeep stopped in front of what had probably at one time been a school. Dean went inside and headed straight for the large tactical map hanging on the wall.

"Bill, here's the situation. I have the 34th and the 21st Regiments along the Kum River with the 34th on the left and the 21st on the right. The ROK 2nd Division is on my right flank. The 19th minus one battalion is moving up at this time. That one battalion, the 3rd of the 19th, is over at Yongdok pulling security at the Yonil Airfield. Reports are that a sizable guerrilla force is moving down the Taebaek Range to join up with the 5th North Korean Division, which has been slowly coming down the eastern coast against the 3rd ROK Division. The 34th had been at Ch'onan until the eighth, when I had to pull them out. Had to relieve one commander and lost the next commander in the town going up against a tank. One battalion of the 21st has fallen back to Choch'iwon. I've reconstituted one provisional battalion with a senior captain in command until we find Colonel Brad Smith, if we find him. The rest of the regiment is falling back to the high ground northwest of Taejon while the 34th and the remainder of the 21st hold along the Kum River."

"What do you want us to do?" Kean asked as he understood that Dean was overall commander at this point.

"General Walker's flying over later today and I'm to meet with him. Then I can go back to being a division commander," Dean said with a slight chuckle. "For right now until he changes it, I need you to get someone up to Yonil and Yongdong to replace my unit up there so I can get him back to his parent unit."

"As soon as I have a unit ashore, I'll send them up to replace your guys. Any idea where Walker is going to stick me when he arrives?" Kean asked, attempting to plan ahead.

"There are three main avenues of approach. There's the east coast road where the 3rd ROK is fighting against the 5th Division. There's an approach on the west coast where we know the 6th North Korean Division is moving towards Ch'onon and then can peel off towards Kunsan. The 7th ROK Division has elements over there. And there's the central avenue with numerous crappy roads through the mountains, all converging on Taejon, Taegu. Your area of responsibility is going to be from Taegu on your left flank north to Yech'on at the Naktong River," Dean pointed out.

"Damn, that's a mighty big sector," Kean said, studying the map. Glancing at the scale, he exclaimed, "Shit, that's over forty miles of frontage."

"Welcome to the police action in Korea," Dean said. "Now you have an idea of what we're up against. Where are you going to put your command post?"

"Centrally located, Yonch'on. My first elements arrive on the twelfth and we should close by the eighteenth, I'm told," Kean responded. "The 27th Regiment will be the first and I'll get them moving right away."

"Not soon enough for us, but damn glad to have you," Dean said with a serious tone.

Chapter 26
Walker Visits

8 July 1950
    24th Division Headquarters
    Taejon, South Korea

GENERAL DEAN HAD BEEN RUNNING on adrenaline since his arrival in Korea on 3 July, but it was beginning to wear off. He was hoping to have a few minutes to catch some sleep when the sound of a light plane was heard passing over his command post. That could mean only one thing—General Walker, commander of the Eighth Army, was dropping in for a visit.

Thirty minutes later, "Attention!" was sounded by Lieutenant Clarke, General Dean's aide.

"As you were, men," General Walker said, coming through the doorway. He wasn't one to grandstand and wanted the people to be at ease around him.[1] Approaching General Dean, he asked, "Is there somewhere we can talk?"

"Yes, sir. I have an office if you can call it that in the back," Dean

---

1. General Walton H. Walker was a highly decorated officer for actions in World War II and Korea. He died in 1950 in a jeep accident.

said, leading the way through the command post to a back room in the building. "Can I get you a cup of coffee?"

"That would be fine. I take it black," Walker said, and Lieutenant Clarke disappeared, returning a few minutes later with two canteen cups of coffee. He then left the room and closed the door.

"How are things going for you?" Walker asked.

"Truthfully, sir, not good. Task Force Smith got the crap beat out of it. The 34th Regiment went into positions at P'youngt'aek and Ansong, only to pull out of both and fall back to Ch'onui, where Colonel Martin, the regimental commander I put in after I relieved Lovless, got cut off and killed hunting tanks. The 34th Regiment is still fighting in Ch'onui and falling back through the 21st Regiment. Lieutenant Colonel Wadlington, the regimental XO, is in command now. We've established a position just south of Ch'onui with what I'm calling the 1st Provisional Battalion, 21st Regiment, until we reconstitute TF Smith and have them rejoin. The 3rd Battalion, 21st Regiment, has moved to a position two miles behind the 1st, which is on good high ground overlooking Ch'onui. They'll hold for as long as possible and delay back to the Kum River, establishing a defensive position on the south side of the river, and will blow that bridge once they cross. As the 34th moves back through the 21st, we're moving them to reconstitute here in Taegu," Dean explained.

"And the 19th Regiment…where are they?" Walker asked.

"Sir, they just arrived in Pusan and we're moving them up as we speak, with one battalion heading to Yongdok to assist in the security of the airfield at Yonil," Dean said.

Walker didn't respond for a minute, thinking and sipping his coffee. "Dean, help is on the way. The 1st Cav and the 25th and 7th Divisions are all en route to Pusan at this time. General MacArthur has also requested that the 2nd Division at Fort Lewis and a regimental combat team of the 82nd Airborne be sent immediately as well as a regimental combat team from the Fleet Marine Force, along with its air wing, engineers and three tank battalions," Walker outlined.

"Well, sir, if you ask me they can't get here quick enough. General Kean from the 25th was here earlier and I gave him instructions to take positions from Taeju to Yech'on. He will be fully ashore by the eighteenth and his first elements arrive on the twelfth," Dean outlined and paused. "We've been getting our butts kicked with each engagement. They hit us hard in a frontal attack and then flank us and encircle, cutting off resupply and reinforcements as well as possible retreat. We were never trained against these tactics. We've been too ingrained in the orderly set piece lines of a European battlefield."

"Is that the only problem you have, tactics?" Walker asked.

"Sir, I could go on. Our equipment is lousy. Radios don't work, we don't have enough commo wire or batteries, and when we do, the rain soaks everything so it doesn't work. The 2.36 bazooka is worthless on a T-34 tank. And soldier morale and discipline don't exist. These soldiers still think they're back on the block back home and that they're getting out of here and going back to Japan. By the president himself, they've been told this is a police action. Police action my ass —this is war, but these kids don't believe it yet," Dean outlined.

"Well, I can tell you General MacArthur has a plan, but it's dependent on us stopping this southbound onslaught that we're up against."

"Sir, you can tell General MacArthur for me that I'm convinced that the North Korean Army and the North Korean soldier and his status of training and equipment have been underestimated."[2] Dean paused, then continued, "Speaking of underestimating, I think we overestimated the ROK Army."

"Let's not be too hasty there. The ROKs did a pretty good job of holding the line in the initial days. The senior leadership let them down and we let them down. We never gave them the equipment to match the enemy. The ROKs should have had tanks and a lot more artillery. They lost a lot of leaders and good soldiers in those opening days and that's hurt them. They're still in the fight for the most part. We see stragglers coming through our lines, but we're also seeing stragglers from our own forces coming through the line. The ROKs are taking a hell of a lot more casualties than us and still putting up a fight. Let's just be

---

2. T. R. Fehrenbach, *This Kind of War: The Classic Korean War History* (Dulles, Virginia: Potomac Books, 2008), 82.

thankful that they haven't collapsed, because if they do, we aren't going to be able to hold Pusan," Walker said, standing up and finishing his coffee. "Keep the faith, General."

Chapter 27
21st Regiment Moves Out

8 July 1950
21st Infantry Regiment, 24th Division
Choch'iwon, South Korea

THE REMAINDER of the 21st Infantry Regiment under the command of Colonel Stephens had arrived by ship in Pusan the previous day. Colonel Stephens had been ordered by General Dean to move to Choch'iwon and establish a defensive/delaying position there. The regiment was loaded on a train and moved through the night to Choch'iwon. What Stephens found there was chaos.

Trains were arriving with no schedule. Supplies for both the 24th Infantry Division and the 1st ROK Corps located east of Choch'iwon were mixed together and haphazardly loaded. More troubling were the train engineers. At the slightest indication of an attack, the engineers would attempt to move the trains out regardless of how much had been loaded or unloaded. Stephens finally resorted to placing armed guards on each arriving train just to keep the train engineer from bolting with the supplies. Stephens had his orders and had time on the train ride to develop his battle plan. In the train station he established his initial command post and gathered his staff and commanders, to include Captain Charles Alkire.[1]

"Captain Alkire, you're probably wondering why I asked you here," Stephens began.

"Well, yes, sir, a bit," Alkire responded.

"The reason I brought you in is because you're now in command of the 1st Provisional Battalion, 21st Infantry Regiment. Probably the youngest battalion commander in history, I would think. Until we get Colonel Smith back, if ever, you will command the reconstituted battalion. As more stragglers come in, we'll get them to you. Any questions?" Stephens asked.

Still in a state of shock over his new command, Alkire responded, "No, sir, and thank you, sir." Stephens stood and moved to the map plastered to the wall.

"We have the mission to defend this town and stop the commie advance. So here's the plan. Carl, I want you to place 3rd Battalion six miles north of the town along the highway," Stephens indicated, looking at Lieutenant Colonel Carl Jensen, the 3rd Battalion commander. "When Captain Alkire and 1st Battalion withdraw from Ch'onan, I want them to set up a blocking position at this location, just east of Ch'onui." Stephens pointed at the map. Alkire nodded, acknowledging the instruction. Colonel Jensen noted the location as he was writing notes. "This puts them a mile in front of you and should provide you warning of the enemy's approach. Hold for as long as you can and then withdraw back to this position located two miles north of Choch'iwon. Elements of 1st Battalion will prepare positions to receive you once he withdraws. Any questions?" Stephens asked.

"How long do you want me to delay them?" Jensen asked.

"For as long as you can without being cut off" was Stephens's answer. "And the same applies to you, Captain," he added, looking at Alkire.

---

1. Captain Charles Alkire was awarded the Silver Star for actions in Korea. *Military Times*, "Charles Alkire," Hall of Valor: Medal of Honor, Silver Star, U.S. Military Awards, https://valor.militarytimes.com/hero/100774.

"Yes, sir," Alkire responded.

Returning to his unit, Jensen assembled his company commanders, to include the commander of what was now the reconstituted 1st of the 21st, Captain Alkire. The position south of Ch'onui overlooked the town and was on a high ridge with a gap where the road cut through.

"Gentlemen, we've been handed the mission to defend forward of Choch'iwon. We're to delay the enemy for as long as possible north of the Kum River. When we do fall back, we'll reestablish the defense on the south side of the Kum River. Captain Alkire, as senior officer, Colonel Stephens is putting you in command of the forward position overlooking Ch'onui that you're currently occupying," Jensen indicated. Alkire gave a nod and made a note in his notepad. "The rest of us will move in the morning at first light and take up positions two miles south of Ch'onui and a position south of Alkire's position on this ridgeline," Jensen said, pointing out the position. "Alkire, when you withdraw, you'll pass through us and move to this crossing point over the river and hold the bridge until we pass through you. When we get to your position, we'll fall in on you and defend from that location. The river will afford us some assistance in defending Choch'iwon. Any questions?" Jensen asked. There were none. "We will have a battery of 155s from the 11th Field Artillery in direct support to us. My headquarters will assign the priority of fire, and, Alkire, you have it initially. Initially we'll have a company minus one platoon from A Company, 78th Heavy Tank Battalion. They have M24s." This piece of news made everyone smile. "On the downside, however, we lose the 21st Reconnaissance Company and the 3rd Engineers."

"Sir, I'll take the tanks any day over the recon company," Alkire said.

The next morning, the 3rd Battalion moved into position behind the reconstituted 1st Battalion. As soon as they were in position, forward observers began registering the artillery as well as the 4.2-inch and the 81mm mortars. As the engineers departed the area, they blew the bridge north of Ch'onui.

"Excuse me, sir," Staff Sergeant Scott Nitty said, getting Colonel Jensen's attention.

"What's up, Sergeant Nitty?" Jensen asked. Sergeant Nitty had been in the closing days of World War II and had left the service for a short time before reenlisting. He was a trained sniper and had trained several soldiers in the techniques of a sniper. Jensen was impressed and moved him up into the battalion operations section with an eye on a possible battlefield commission.

"Sir, we just got a report from regiment that tanks have been spotted north of Ch'onui," Nitty said.

"Get that to Captain Alkire, please, and tell him to notify us as soon as he sees them," Jensen instructed. He only had to wait an hour.

"Colonel, Captain Alkire reports that he has eleven tanks in sight as well as about two to three hundred infantry and is requesting an air strike," Sergeant Nitty said.

"Tell Captain Alkire that he will get his air strike and to get his FOs on the infantry," Jensen said and immediately heard the battery of 155 artillery open fire, followed by the 4.2-inch mortars. "I'm going to move up and observe this from Captain Alkire's position," he added, picking up his helmet and weapon, an M1 carbine. He also carried an M1911 .45-caliber pistol.

Moving up to Captain Alkire's position, he arrived in time to see the first of four air strikes. They were using napalm on the tanks as well as strafing and bombs, but the napalm was the most effective. Simultaneously, Alkire used his artillery to strike the infantry that was moving from building to building in the village. As Jensen and Alkire watched, a jeep pulled up to the backside of the ridge where they were standing.

"Sir, I think that's Colonel Stephens," Captain Alkire said, looking over his shoulder.

"Afternoon, Jensen, Captain. Thought I'd come have a look at how the air strike is doing," Stephens said, exchanging salutes. "Also an opportunity to firsthand see how these jokers maneuver."

"Sir, we just got a report from the flyboys that they hit a convoy of tanks and trucks north of the town. That's what that black smoke is from up there to the northwest beyond the hills," Captain Alkire said, pointing northwest. "They also reported that there are about two hundred vehicles on the road from P'yingt'aek, of which they've left about one hundred burning."

"Good for us and bad for them, but rest assured, we're going to have action in the morning. I think I'll be spending the night with you if you don't mind," Stephens said, almost in jest.

"Sir, you're the regimental commander and you can sleep wherever you like. I think we have C rations on the menu tonight. As our guest, I'll let you pick first," Captain Alkire joked. "And we'll even open the case from the top so you can see what your choices are."[2]

"Sir, if you will excuse me, I'll be getting back to my battalion," Jensen said, excusing himself and returning to his own position.

The blackness of the night was replaced with a glow to the north of the burning vehicles reported by the flyboys. Captain Alkire had about five hundred men under his command. These were composed of Companies A and D of the 1st Battalion, which hadn't arrived in time to become part of Task Force Smith, as well as stragglers that had been picked up. Their position was about three-quarters of a mile long and located on one high ridge eight hundred meters south of Ch'onui and a lower ridge that was five hundred meters from Ch'onui. Between Ch'onui and the ridges were open rice paddies. From the high ridge, one could see the road north of Ch'onui.

---

2. Frequently, cases were opened from the bottom so that soldiers couldn't pick the best C rations first, leaving the least favorite for those who came last. Least favorite were ham and lima beans as well as the ham and egg selections.

Chapter 28
Engaged

10 July 1950
   1st Provisional Battalion, 21st Infantry
   Choch'iwon, South Korea

"What time is it, Captain?" Stephens asked as he opened his eyes. He had picked a comfortable spot on the ground next to Alkire and slept pretty good considering.

"Sir, it's 0500 and we have a heavy fog over us," Alkire said, handing Stephens a canteen cup of coffee. "Sorry, but no cream this morning, sir."

"Ah, the little things we have to give up in life. I like it black anyway," Stephens responded, sitting up. "Quiet night?"

"Some probes, but Lieutenant Bixler, First Platoon of A Company, has reported hearing Korean voices this morning," Alkire said. That got Stephens's attention, as did the shrill of a whistle in the fog on the left flank. Almost immediately, small-arms fire commenced. Lieutenant Ray Bixler had positioned his platoon on the left flank of A Company, which was the left flank of the 1st Provisional Battalion. Stephens listened intently to the sounds of the firefight on the left flank. The intensity was increasing, he thought, and the 4.2-inch mortars were striking the area in front of Bixler's platoon unobserved but based on previous target reference points. This was keeping the enemy at bay. More troubling, however, to Stephens were the shifting sounds of the small-arms fire. They appeared to be moving further to the left and heading south. *Damn, they're flanking A Company*, Stephens thought.

"Sir," Alkire said, getting Stephens's attention, "I just got word from Colonel Jensen that the 4.2-inch mortars are under a ground attack and we've got the sound of tanks coming out of Ch'onui."

"We should have expected this. The damn fog was not, however, planned for," Stephens mumbled. The fighting on the left flank continued. In the morning fog, four tanks rolled through 1st Provisional Battalion lines on the highway and didn't even fire a round but just kept rolling even when hit with rounds from the 2.36-inch bazookas. For the next three hours, the fog provided concealment to the enemy.

"Sir, the fog appears to be lifting. My forward elements report being able to see into Ch'onui now," Alkire said, looking at his watch. It was 0800 hours.

"Good, now we can start placing observed fire on the enemy," Stephens said, peering into the fog in the hope of seeing something. As the fog continued to burn off, Stephens was able to observe Ch'onui and saw four tanks enter the town from the north. *Pretty soon we'll be able to get air strikes on those tanks*, Stephens was thinking when his thoughts were interrupted by the sound of tank fire to his rear. *What the—*

"Colonel, Colonel Jensen reports that tanks have joined with infantry attacking the 4.2-inch mortars," Captain Alkire reported. Soon the 4.2-inch mortars stopped firing and all communication with them went silent. Now the enemy pressed his ground attack, although the 155 artillery was providing direct support as were the 81mm mortars. The typical tactic was a frontal assault as the North Koreans began to climb the ridges.

Alkire turned to the senior FO. "Put VT fuze on them along the FPF." The order was sent to the battery, and soon black airbursts were appearing above the enemy infantry. Each airburst cut down enemy infantry as if a giant sickle had sliced through their lines. This momentarily broke the enemy assault, until tanks rolled out of Ch'onui, spraying the defenders with machine-gun fire. With no 4.2-inch mortar support, Lieutenant Bixler's position was becoming more untenable.

"Colonel Stephens," Captain Alkire said, approaching the colonel. "We have a problem. Lieutenant Bixler's platoon is reporting most of his people are wounded and wants to withdraw."

"Negative. Tell him help is on the way. Tell him to hold that position," Stephens said very quickly. He was true to his word. Five minutes later, two Air Force jets rolled in and strafed the enemy, forcing them to seek cover. They engaged the tanks as well with rockets but didn't appear to cause any damage. Bixler welcomed the pause that the jets brought to the fight, and as long as they stayed on station, the enemy infantry remained hidden. The pause lasted long enough for the survivors of the 4.2-inch mortars and the recoilless rifle teams to come up the hill and join the 1st Provisional Battalion.

"Have you spoken to Colonel Jensen lately to give him an update?" Colonel Stephens asked.

"No, sir. Our communications are down. Evidently the wires were cut and the radio batteries are dead. Even the FOs' radios have crapped out. We're sending a runner out with some commo wire to reestablish comms with Colonel Jensen," Captain Alkire said.

"Let me know—" Stephens didn't finish before he heard the sound. "Incoming!" he yelled and threw himself on the ground. The rounds were impacting on the ridge. Of more concern was that they were coming from the 155 battery in support.

"Sir! That's friendly fire," Alkire yelled.

"Stay down," Stephens responded, looking about. There was a slight pause in the incoming rounds and Stephens took advantage of it. He sprinted to his jeep, which was about one hundred meters behind and below the ridge. He did have a radio in the back capable of reaching the regimental CP.

"CP, this is Stephens. Stop the artillery fire. He's hitting us. He's hitting our own troops. Cut him off," Stephens yelled into the receiver. He understood very well how demoralizing it was to the infantry to be fired upon by their own supporting artillery. By the time the artillery ceased fire, the enemy had already started to take advantage of their good fortune and were pressing the attack on the left flank.

The TA-312 telephone rang and Alkire answered. "Alkire here."

"Sir, Lieutenant Bixler, we're surrounded and most of my people are wounded or dead. We're about to be over—" Bixler didn't finish his statement as a burst of gunfire cut him off in midsentence.[1] Captain Alkire attempted to get Bixler back on the line, but in his heart he knew it was futile.

"Colonel, I think we've lost Lieutenant Bixler's platoon on the left flank," Alkire said.

"That's not all that we're losing," Stephens said, pointing to the right flank and the retreating soldiers there. "Get those high-priced soldiers back into position! That's what they're paid for."[2]

Soon a corporal managed to gather a few of the retreating soldiers and get them back into defensive positions. As the morning wore on, it became more obvious that eventually they would be pushed off the ridge. Stephens felt that the 1st Provincial Battalion had held for as long as it could and it was time to withdraw.

"Captain Alkire, pass the word: on my signal, everyone is to get up and withdraw to the assembly area you designated back in the orchard," Stephens directed and waited while Captain Alkire passed the word. When Stephens was sure everyone had received the instructions, he yelled as loud as he could, "Withdraw!" Those closest certainly heard him, and those who didn't witnessed those nearest to Stephens leaving, which was a signal for them to do the same. Arriving at the rice paddy, which was flooded, the soldiers formed a single file and attempted to move quickly over the rice paddy on the dikes. After

---

1. Lieutenant Ray Bixler was never heard from or seen again. It is believed that most of his men died in their foxholes. Roy E. Appleman, *United States Army in the Korean War: South to the Naktong, North to the Yalu (June–November 1950)* (Washington, D.C.: United States Army Center of Military History, 1992), 93.

2. Roy E. Appleman, *United States Army in the Korean War: South to the Naktong, North to the Yalu (June–November 1950)* (Washington, D.C.: United States Army Center of Military History, 1992), 93.

the third or fourth soldier, the dikes became very slippery. To make matters worse, two US Air Force jets arrived and turned towards the fleeing US soldiers, thinking they were invading North Koreans. Everyone was forced off the dikes and into the flooded rice paddies to lie down as the jets commenced strafing runs on them. The strafing was bad enough, but not as bad as lying in the human feces that the Koreans used to fertilize their rice paddies. Once the jets departed, the 1st Provisional Battalion along with Colonel Stephens reached the 3rd Battalion location. As Colonel Jensen approached Colonel Stephens, Jensen chose to stand upwind from the senior officer.

"Carl, I want you to mount a counterattack this afternoon and retake that high ridge. Think you can do that? I'll have an air strike and the artillery support your attack as well as the heavy tank company," Stephens ordered.

"Yes, sir. Let me work up my plan and brief my commanders. We should be able to kick off at 1400," Jensen said.

"Good, now I'm going to clean up and get a fresh uniform. Let me know when you're ready to brief me and the company commanders," Stephens said, walking off towards the regimental CP.

At 1400 hours, 3rd Battalion crossed the line of departure and moved north in a combat formation. As they did so, artillery began hitting the ridge and Air Force jets began hitting forces attempting to come forward from Ch'onui. The T-24 tanks remained on the road and quickly dispatched a North Korean tank that came out to oppose them. The intense artillery fire from the 155 battery forced the North Koreans to remain in their positions until just before the 3rd Battalion rolled over them, retaking the ridge but not Lieutenant Bixler's former position.

"Colonel Jensen, sir, I found something that you should see," said Captain Baker, the A Company commander, approaching Jensen on the ridge.

"Show me," Jensen said after Captain Baker explained what he had found.

The two walked to the previous location of the 4.2-inch mortars. There lay the bodies of six American service members. Their hands were tied behind their backs and it was obvious that they had all been shot in the back of the head as they were kneeling on the ground.[3]

"How did you find this?" Jensen asked.

"A jeep driver managed to escape and witnessed it. He was hiding when we passed by him and he told me about it," Captain Baker said.

"Okay, I'll call stretcher-bearers forward and we'll get them out of here," Jensen said, turning away and walking back to the ridge.

---

3. One of the first recorded atrocities of the war, but it would not be the last. Roy E. Appleman, *United States Army in the Korean War: South to the Naktong, North to the Yalu (June–November 1950)* (Washington, D.C.: United States Army Center of Military History, 1992), 94.

Chapter 29
Train Movement

10 JULY 1950
27th Regiment, 25th Division
Pusan, South Korea

"DAMN, it feels good to get off that damn ship," Colonel John H. Michaelis said as he and Lieutenant Colonel Gilbert Check stood beside the railroad, watching the 1st Battalion, 27th Regiment, load a train.[1]

"Sir, I haven't been that damn sick in a long time. How those swabbies can eat like they do and not spend every minute puking over the side I don't know," Check said. "Hell, I'm still wobbling when I walk."

"It will wear off soon enough. I wish the hell Gordon was going with us up to Uisong. I don't like the idea of your battalion in one place and his battalion being at some airfield in Yonil as well as providing security at Yongdok."

"When I get to this Uisong, what is my mission?" Check asked as

---

1. Lieutenant Colonel Gilbert Check would be awarded the Distinguished Service Cross for his actions in Korea as battalion commander, 1st Battalion, 27th Infantry Regiment, 25th Division.

he watched his young soldiers load the train with all their equipment. The equipment had been brought over from Japan but appeared to be almost brand-new. He knew it wasn't, but as they hadn't trained much while on occupation duty in Japan, the equipment hadn't been used much. Check knew what his mission was but wanted to hear it again.

"You're to establish a blocking position north of Andong. The train will get you as far as Uisong and from there we hope to have some transportation to take you the twenty miles north to Andong. Good luck, and I'll be coming up in a day or two with the rest of the regiment," Michaelis said, extending his hand.

"Thank you, sir. I best get aboard. See you soon, I hope," Check said and climbed onto the train, which was slowly starting to move. Finding a seat next to his executive officer and operations officer, Check pulled out a map of the Andong area. The town was just on the north side of the Naktong River with two major bridges across the river. Three major roads converged from the north and northwest. Studying the map, he saw that the only flat open ground was on the immediate banks of the river, which appeared to be rice paddies. Everything else was designed for mountain goats. As Check studied, he became more concerned. *I have three major roads coming into Andong along with one major rail line from the northwest and the town is surrounded by high, steep hills. I have two major bridges almost four klicks apart with the town right in the middle. Several noticeable trails cross the mountains between the major highways.*

"What are you thinking, sir?" asked Captain Decker, his operations officer.

"I'd feel a lot better if we could establish the blocking position on the south side of the river. Makes a hell of a lot more sense. If we hold the high ground on the west side of two roads, we can control one road from the north and the road coming in from the west as well as the rail line. We can place a second company on Hill 240 north of the town and control the other road coming from the north and provide some mutual support to the company on the west side of town. The best we can do about the bridges is register artillery on them in case they get past us.

When the 2nd Battalion gets released from its mission, the colonel said it would be joining us up here as well," Check added.

"Not soon enough for me," Decker said.

"Don't be so glum. We now have the opportunity to select the best hotels for our rooms and the best restaurants for dinner. I bet I can even make a dinner reservation for us," said Major David, the battalion executive officer. Everyone got a chuckle out of that one.

"Sir, do we know who is forward of our position?" Decker asked.

"I'm told it's the 8th ROK Division and they're being pushed back towards us by the 12th North Korean Division, which reportedly has some tanks. We're going to have to put some antitank bazooka teams out and they best know how to use that new 3.5-inch tube," Check said.

"I'll get with the company commanders and make sure they've conducted training on those as soon as we're off this train," Decker said, pausing and standing. "In fact, there's no reason why they can't be doing that now. Don't have to fire the thing, just make sure their teams know the procedure to fire the weapon. I'll get them started right now, sir." Decker stood to head to where the company commanders were seated.

"Hey, tell them to be damn sure they don't blow this train up," Check said, only half joking.

Chapter 30
Delay

10 JULY 1950
 21st Infantry Regiment
 Choch'iwon, South Korea

A MAULED Task Force Smith had withdrawn to Taejon after its disastrous performance at Osan. Colonel Smith received an additional two hundred replacements that brought companies B and C up to strength as well as received new equipment to replace that which had been lost. This still didn't make 1st Battalion, 21st Regiment, a cohesive fighting force. That would take time and great effort upon the chain of command to mold the units into a fighting force.

"Brad," Colonel Stephens said over the landline from the 21st Regiment headquarters, "I want you to move your unit up to Choch'iwon and join back with Able and Dog Companies."

"Yes, sir, I can move out tonight and be there before dawn tomorrow. Be kind of nice to have my whole battalion together again," Colonel Smith indicated.

"How are the new replacements?" Stephens asked.

"Well, to tell the truth, sir, it's going to take time to pull everyone together. These new people aren't in the best of physical conditioning as most were pulled out of soft jobs in Japan. The level of proficiency isn't as high as I'd like, but I'm sure we'll get it up there in short order. The new NCOs appear to know their stuff. I guess I'll find out shortly," Colonel Smith said with some hope they would live long enough to become a cohesive force.

"When you get here, Able and Dog will be in a position two miles north of Choch'iwon where the road crosses the river. Let me know when you're close and I'll have guides to meet you. If you have no questions, I'll see you in the morning," Colonel Stephens concluded.

"In the morning, sir," Colonel Smith said, and he heard Stephens hang up.

LIGHT PROBING WAS EXPERIENCED throughout the day by the 3rd Battalion, but Colonel Jensen's soldiers were able to repel any serious attempts. He had received a tactical air control party during the day that consisted of an officer who was a pilot, a radio operator, and a radio repairman who also served as a driver for the jeep. Overhead was a T-6 Texan aircraft that was usually used as a trainer but now was providing observation and air control. The ground control party would call the T-6, which used the call sign Mosquito, and relay target locations. Mosquito would talk to the aircraft providing the close-air support and direct them on the target. For the Army this was almost a new concept, but for Marine Corps forces this was old stuff as they had always had close-air support from their own air wings. The close-air support had managed to keep the tanks and reinforcements at bay. The heavy black smoke to the north was the result of an air strike twenty-five miles north of Ch'onui.

In the early-afternoon hours, a Mosquito was working north of Ch'onui, bringing air strikes in on vehicles moving south from P'yongt'aek. Slowly the T-6 moved north, looking for more targets, until he came across a convoy of over two hundred vehicles. A mixture of trucks and tanks were all bunched together at a bridge that had been destroyed. The T-6 notified his higher headquarters, Joint Operations

Center, of the find, and the 5th Air Force quickly pulled every fighter bomber it could find, to include Marine, Navy and Australian aircraft, committing them against this lucrative target. This strike greatly reduced the pressure on the 3rd Battalion in its positions overlooking Ch'onui.

Colonel Stephens was surprised when General Dean arrived at the 21st Regimental command post. It was 2030 hours and Stephens had been contemplating lying down as the night had been quiet so far.

"Sir, what brings you to my humble headquarters?" Stephens asked, attempting to lighten the mood as Dean approached him. The men in the command post continued with their duties but cocked their ears to hear what Dean was going to say.

"What is your situation up here?" Dean asked as he approached the wall map.

"Sir, 3rd Battalion is on this high ridge overlooking Ch'onui. The 1st Provisional Battalion is withdrawing to this location two miles north of Choch'iwon and should be just about there. Task Force Smith will be arriving before dawn and fall in on this location and make 1st Battalion whole again. When 3rd Battalion withdraws, he'll come back to his previous positions here, six miles north of Choch'i-won, and conduct a delay from that location, eventually falling back to join 1st Battalion here north of Choch'iwon," Stephens explained. Dean continued to study the map without saying anything for a moment.

"Okay, I'll leave this up to you, but you should consider moving 3rd Battalion back to his original position sometime before dawn. I can't emphasis enough how important it is for us to hold Choch'iwon. It's the main supply route for the ROK forces to our west. I expect you to hold for at least a day from that location north of Choch'iwon," Dean ordered.

"Understood, sir" was all Stephens could respond as Dean was heading out the door.

"Excuse me, sir," Captain Price Marr said, breaking Stephens's train of thought. Captain Marr was what was commonly referred to as a TOC Rat, slang for staff officer. An extremely intelligent officer, he had been on the regimental staff for over a year and was looking to go to one of the battalions to take a company command.

"What?" Stephens asked, turning to face the captain.

"Sir, we just got a message from 1st Battalion. They've just left Taejon and are on their way. Colonel Smith anticipates arriving at 0430 in the morning," Marr outlined.

"Now that is some good news. Can you get Colonel Jensen on the line, please?"

Marr started putting the call through on the landline. After a minute, he handed the receiver to Stephens.

"Carl, Stephens here. I want you to move your battalion from your present position back to your last position. General Dean is a bit concerned about you being cut off so far north of everyone else," Captain Marr heard. He couldn't hear Colonel Jensen's response. "Yes, I understand you're having only light contact at this time, but we don't want you decisively engaged, so at your discretion I want you to pull out of there and get back to your previous position, but do it before dawn," Stephens said while studying the map. "Yes, Brad is bringing up his elements and will join with Able and Dog north of Choch'iwon. He's on his way now and will be in position at first light….Okay, let me know when you start to pull back and when you're in place. Stephens out here."

Stephens hung the receiver back in its cradle. "Okay, all appears quiet, so I'm going to lie down for a few. Wake me when 3rd moves and when 1st arrives. Any questions?" There were none, and Stephens departed to catch some sleep. He was a firm believer in the Army axiom that one shouldn't run when one could walk; one shouldn't walk when one could stand; one shouldn't stand when one could sit down; one shouldn't sit down when one could lie down; and one shouldn't stay awake when one could sleep. He strongly believed that leaders needed sleep to make clear decisions when under stress. An overtired leader was worthless and would make stupid mistakes. He felt so strongly about this that if a leader was sleeping, he was not to be awakened unless absolutely necessary.

Chapter 31
MacArthur Meeting

10 July 1950
MacArthur's Headquarters
Tokyo, Japan

"GENERAL, YOU CAN COME IN NOW," General Edward "Ned" Almond said, opening the door to General MacArthur's office.

"Thank you General," said General Lemuel Shepherd, USMC, standing and passing Almond to meet MacArthur. General Shepherd had met and served under MacArthur during World War II in the Pacific. Now Shepherd was the Commander, Fleet Marine Force, Pacific. Shepherd's boss, General Cates, had been given a heads-up a week before that the 1st Marine Division would be committed to the Korean campaign and was told he needed someone to talk to MacArthur. Upon entering the office, MacArthur approached his old acquaintance.

"General, it's good to see you. Looks like you and I will be working together again like old times," MacArthur said, pointing at an overstuffed chair. "Please sit. Some coffee?"

"Yes, sir, something to kick-start my heart this morning," Shepherd said, pouring some coffee for himself into a cup that sat on the coffee table between the two overstuffed chairs. MacArthur took the other.

"I'm glad that the 1st Marine Division is going to be supporting this operation, and I have just the job for them to do. The North Koreans have been rolling down the peninsula, pushing the South Koreans back to Pusan, it appears. The South Koreans and the American forces with them have got to hold a perimeter around Pusan. General Walker, who's in command of the Eighth Army, is seeing to that. Once he has a solid perimeter, I want to launch an amphibious assault and cut the North Korean supply lines. Coming in north of the main forces will accomplish that and also cut their avenues of retreat," MacArthur stated.

"Sir, I think an amphibious assault would be the right thing to do, and the 1st Marine Division is the right force to do it," Shepherd said with a smile. "You know, sir, there are those in Washington that would like to just do away with the Marine Corps or relegate it to a ceremonial unit and have Marine Corps aviation turned over to the Air Force. Some, to include General Eisenhower, feel that we duplicate the missions of the Army and the Air Force."

"I heard the nonsense. Eisenhower has never worked with the Marines, being a Europe guy, and doesn't know what he's talking about. I would think as chief of staff he'd have better sense," MacArthur said.

"Not just him, sir. General Spaatz, the chief of staff of the Air Force, feels the same as Eisenhower. Even the president thinks of us as the Navy's police force and not much more," Shepherd stated.

"Well, after what I have planned, that will all change," MacArthur said, standing and moving to a wall map of Korea. Shepherd stood and accompanied him.

"Here is the Pusan port and the Naktong River," MacArthur said, drawing his finger along the map. "Walker intends to make his perimeter along this river. Once he does and stabilizes the situation, I intend to launch an amphibious landing here, at the port of Inchon. We'll quickly seize Seoul and cut the North Korean supply lines, placing the North Korean forces between us and Walker. By this time,

Walker will have sufficient forces to start driving north, pushing the enemy into the forces that landed at Inchon. 1st Marine Division will lead the way at Inchon," MacArthur outlined.

"Sir, that's a bold plan, but executing it could bring this conflict to a rapid conclusion," Shepherd agreed.

"Well, to do it, I need two things. I need Walker to stabilize that perimeter around Pusan, and I need the 1st Marine Division. Let me ask, can a Marine brigade be in Pusan by early August and the remainder of the division here in time for a fifteen September amphibious landing?" MacArthur asked.

"Sir, if the Navy can get us there, then I can say yes and yes. We're already assembling the force at Camp Pendleton and have been since twenty-seven June," Shepherd said with a broad smile.

"Good, good, now we just have to sell the Joint Chiefs on the idea," MacArthur said, "and I think I can do that."

Chapter 32
Withdraw to Choch'iwon

11 JULY 1950
3rd Battalion, 21st Infantry
Ch'onui, South Korea

COLONEL JENSEN DECIDED to let the troops rest a bit before withdrawing. He decided that he would withdraw from the ridge overlooking Ch'onui at 0400 hours, which would give him time to move back to his next position and be in place before dawn. Throughout the night and in typical North Korean fashion, there were probes along the perimeter, but nothing serious that required soldiers to get out of their fighting positions. Jensen moved around between units and foxholes, offering words of encouragement to the soldiers and leaders. Returning to his command post, Jensen thought he would get a few minutes of sleep as well.

"Incoming!" brought him out of his sleep as a loud explosion went off.

"What the hell?" Jensen asked. As he got to his feet, the sound of small-arms fire could be clearly heard.

"Sir, we're being hit across the entire front. They're in close," the S-3, Major Mulford, said with a look of despair. "I have the mortars and artillery firing the FPF, but they're in close." The North Koreans knew that if they got in close enough before being detected, it would reduce the Americans' capability to employ close-air support or artillery fires.[1]

"Notify regiment that we're decisively engaged. Will attempt to break contact and withdraw," Jensen directed Major Mulford.

Due to the bad communications situation, reports from the companies were delivered by messenger, if they weren't killed or wounded in the attempt to reach the battalion CP. Jensen was blind staying in the CP because of the lack of communications equipment, so he took Major Mulford and they headed towards the center of the line. Much to Jensen's dismay, the firing was intense to the front. More troubling, however, were the sounds he was hearing on the right flank. When the shooting on the right flank stopped, he breathed a bit easier.

"I think the platoon on the right must have killed all the attackers," Major Mulford indicated, cocking his head to listen more intently.

"I hope you're right. Let's head over that way and see." Jensen started moving in that direction in a low crouch. As he did so, the sounds of the fight shifted more to his right rear.

"Crap, they've flanked the right side. Let's get back to the CP and see if they have commo with anyone," Jensen said with apprehension in his voice. The intensity of the fighting increased in the rear area, and as they approached the CP from the front, small-arms rounds impacted in front of the two men.

"Damn, they're behind us," Mulford exclaimed as the CP NCOIC ran out of the command post and was immediately shot in the back. Other members of the CP got out and joined Jensen and Mulford.

"We've got to counterattack these people," Jensen said to the small group surrounding him. "Major Mulford will take you three and lay down a base of fire." He pointed at the soldiers, then turned to the remaining three and added, "You three come with me and we're going to flank these guys on the right side. Understood?" Everyone nodded that they did. "Alright, let's go."

---

1. This was a practice used by the North Vietnamese fifteen years later.

And Jensen with his three companions headed for the right side of the now bullet-riddled CP tent. Mulford moved his small element to the left of the CP tent and took up prone positions. When he thought Jensen had enough time to be in position, he ordered his fire team to open fire. With only M1 rifles, they quickly went through a clip of ammo before they had to reload. The firepower they generated couldn't compare to the intensity of the North Korean burp guns, and Mulford quickly realized he was outgunned—just before he was killed.

With Mulford dead, the soldiers continued to fire, but soon they were overwhelmed by the North Koreans. Without the base of fire from Mulford's fire team, Jensen's counterattack was quickly killed. The battalion was now without a commander or senior officer.

With the coming of dawn, survivors were streaming back to join the 1st Provisional Battalion north of Choch'iwon. The survivors, less than fifty percent of the battalion, came minus boots, which were left in the muck of the rice paddies, and minus helmets or load-bearing equipment. Some didn't even have their weapons any longer. The 24th Division was in a dire situation with two regiments mauled.

Lieutenant Bartlett had placed the 34th I&R Platoon in outpost positions in the late afternoon. Their orders were to stay put throughout the night and keep quiet. Sergeant Bledsoe, Private Hanner and Corporal Perez were hunkered down in a well-prepared position covered in brush to further camouflage the position. Their position was six hundred yards north of the river adjacent to the town of Kongju. The night was as dark as they had ever seen as it was moonless with a solid overcast.

"Sarge, I hear something," Corporal Perez said in a whisper, nudging Bledsoe awake. "Sounds like someone walking very slowly and cautiously."

Bledsoe didn't move but lay listening as well. Whoever was moving about was very close. All three soldiers were now alert and peering through the brush. Slowly a figure appeared out of the darkness and it was moving straight towards them. As they watched, the figure moved right in front of them and kneeled down not three feet in front of their hide position. Bledsoe held up his hand and began to curl his fingers. As the third finger closed into the fist, all three came out of the hide position and tackled the individual, who initially attempted to resist but was quickly overpowered. Not wishing to give their position away, the quickly taped his mouth and bound his hands and feet, dragging him into the hide position with them. As first light came, they realized their guest was a North Korean soldier. What really surprised them was it was an officer.

"Let's get this guy back to regiment," Bledsoe directed and took the group back. Arriving at regiment, they turned their prisoner over to the regiment intelligence officer and went to find some chow. While eating, Lieutenant Bartlett approached them.

"Hey, Sergeant Bledsoe, nice job policing that guy up," Bartlett said, stopping in front of the group.

"Get anything good out of him, sir?" Private Hanner asked gaining the lieutenant's attention.

"I'd say. He was a reconnaissance officer coming to check out Kongju. His unit, the 16th Regiment, has that place as their objective for an upcoming attack. Nice work, guys," Bartlett said as the three soldiers exchanged broad smiles.

Chapter 33
Stand at Choch'iwon

12 July 1950
  21st Regiment
  Choch'iwon, South Korea

DURING THE EARLY-MORNING hours of the eleventh, Lieutenant Colonel Brad Smith arrived with the reconstituted 1st Battalion, 21st Infantry, and rejoined his Companies A and D. They had already started preparing positions overlooking the Kum River and the one bridge over the river. The Kum River ran parallel to the road from Ch'onui to Choch'iwon, making a sharp turn eastward about two miles north of the town, necessitating a bridge over the river. When Colonel Smith arrived, he reported to Colonel Stephens for instruction.

"Brad, am I glad to see you," Stephens said with sincere enthusiasm, shaking Colonel Smith's hand. "How are your troops?" He pointed to a folding camp chair for Colonel Smith to sit on.

"Alpha and Delta Companies are in okay shape. The replacements are green, and I question their tactical proficiency. The NCOs are okay but untested. Some have prior combat experience, some were pulled out of nice desk jobs in Japan and really don't want to be here," Colonel Smith indicated. "They don't quite understand how this is a 'police action' as the bad guys have tanks and burp guns. The officers are all green, right out of college and officer basic course."

"Well, let's hope they're up for the task. We've got to hold for as long as possible here north of Choch'iwon. Jensen with the 3rd Battalion is south of Ch'onui, but we've had no communications with him since 0300 hours yesterday. We're getting his stragglers coming through the lines now and they aren't telling a very pretty story. Typical North Korean tactics that you saw at Osan. Frontal attack with tanks leading and flanking attacks to get behind and cut off retreat," Stephens stated. "Do you need anything?"

"Yes, sir, some bazookas that can knock out tanks and some seasoned soldiers," Brad said.

"The bazookas we may be able to help with as some of the new 3.5-inch ones have been developed and are on their way over. Seasoned soldiers, I'm afraid there isn't much there, but I'll try to move some of the NCOs from 3rd Battalion to you," Stephens explained.

"We'll make do, sir," Smith said, almost not believing his own words. "Sir, if you have nothing else for me, I best get back to the battalion and see how they're doing."

"Right," Stephens said, standing up. "Brad, you take care now," he added, and the two exchanged handshakes.

"Will do, sir," Colonel Smith said and departed.

Throughout the day, stragglers from the 3rd Battalion were flowing south across the Kum River with no order to their movement to speak of. People from different companies and platoons were mixed together. For the soldiers of the 1st Battalion that were preparing defensive positions on the south side of the Kum River, the site was demoralizing, especially for the new replacements who had yet to hear the sound of the guns.

After Colonel Smith left, Colonel Stephens sat down and prepared a message to General Dean.

TO: CDR, 24 DIVISION
FROM: CDR, 21ST REGIMENT

**"AM SURROUNDED, 1ST BN, LEFT GIVING WAY. SITUA-
TION BAD ON RIGHT. HAVING NOTHING LEFT TO ESTAB-
LISH INTERMEDIATE DELAY POSITION WITH. AM
FORCED TO WITHDRAW TO KUM RIVER LINE. I HAVE
ISSUED INSTRUCTIONS TO WITHDRAW.[1]**

The order to withdraw was given, but the 3rd Battalion command post had already been wiped out for the most part and it had no commander.[2] Junior officers were attempting to organize groups of soldiers and move them back to the Kum River. Late on the afternoon of the twelfth, most were back on the south side of the Kum River. On General Dean's orders, the 19th Regiment, which had just arrived in Korea, was sent to reinforce the 21st Regiment on the Kum River.

As the 19th moved up, Captain Alex Bolding and 1st Lieutenant Robert Adams of the 24th Aviation Section were orbiting over the Kum River, directing artillery. Bolding was on the controls, with Adams adjusting artillery fire. Both were concentrating on the ground two thousand feet below.

"Hey, Captain, I do believe we have a target?" Adams stated as he watched a camouflaged truck heading towards the river.

"Yeah, but I've never seen a tree move that fast. Let's see how fast he can go with artillery impacting around him," Bolding responded. As he did, he looked up and glanced at his limited instruments. That was when he noticed the two Yak-9 enemy fighter aircraft. The Yak-9 single-engine, single-pilot multipurpose fighter was built by the Soviet Union during World War II. It could cruise at four hundred and twenty miles per hour with a range of four hundred and nineteen miles. The service ceiling was 10,500 feet. It was armed with one 20mm cannon and two 12.7mm machine guns. Compared to the L-4H, it was a formidable weapon, but it had limitations. It couldn't fly as slow as the L-4H or turn as tight as the L-4H.

---

1. T. R. Fehrenbach, *This Kind of War: The Classic Korean War History* (Dulles, Virginia: Potomac Books, 2008), 87.
2. Lieutenant Colonel Carl C. Jensen posthumously received the Distinguished Service Cross for his actions.

"We got company," Bolding said, immediately reducing his altitude in a power dive, if such a thing was possible for the L-4H. Adams immediately looked around to see who his company was.

"Ah shit, here they come!" Adams said, craning his neck to look to the right at the two aircraft. He knew they had no chance of outrunning these two aircraft and, with no weapons on board, no chance of fighting them. "What'cha gonna do?"

"Get as low and slow as I can," Bolding said as he passed through five hundred feet, below the crest of the mountains around him. His windshield filled with the mountain in front of the aircraft less than a quarter of a mile to the front.

"Watch out!" was all Adams had time to say when a burst of machine-gun fire stitched across the right wing and the first Yak-9 flashed past the slow-flying canvas-covered plane. The pilot was looking back over his left shoulder as he passed, and Bolding flipped him his middle finger. Bolding immediately made a hard diving left turn away from the Yak. The Yak pilot was more concerned with watching Bolding than with what was in front of his aircraft. When he looked up, he had about two seconds to realize he was flying into the side of a mountain before he burst into flames. The second Yak hadn't ventured to come as low as the first and departed the area.

"Holy hell, Captain…you just got the first kill by a US Army aircraft and did it without firing a shot. Congratulations…now can we return to base? Because I have to change my pants," Adams pleaded.

Chapter 34
Preparations Along the Kum River

12 July 1950
  24th Division
  Choch'iwon, South Korea

THE 21ST REGIMENT was the first to begin establishing its defensive positions overlooking the Kum River. One of the first tasks was to blow the bridge, and the engineers did an excellent job of carrying out that task. Late that evening, General Dean brought the regimental commanders and staff to his headquarters in Taejon.

"Alright, let's get started. Lieutenant Colonel Walsh, you're up," Dean said, taking a seat. Lieutenant Colonel Walsh was the division intelligence officer. He wasn't one to sit behind a desk and digest reports. He witnessed the enemy firsthand and then wrote them himself.

"Gentlemen, the Kum River is the largest river south of the Han River up north. It generally flows north, coming out of the mountains in the southwest part of Korea. East of Taejon about ten miles, there's a series of bends and curves forming an inverted U. Twelve miles northwest of Taejon, it turns to a southwesterly course terminating in the sea. The Kum forms almost a moat around the city fifteen miles to the south. Our reconnaissance company has patrolled for about thirty miles. They found and destroyed all flat-bottom boats.

"Currently we're opposed by two North Korean divisions, the 4th and 3rd Divisions according to prisoners that we've interrogated. They're a talkative bunch. They're also a hungry lot. There's a third division following these two and it's the 2nd North Korean Division. These divisions are at sixty to eighty percent strength with approximately fifty tanks between them. I think we can expect a two-prong attack or even a three-prong if the 2nd Division pushes through the ROK forces to the east," Colonel Walsh said, pointing at the map to indicate the locations where he expected the enemy to attempt to cross the river since the bridges were being blown as he spoke. "Sir, do you have any questions?" Walsh asked, but he suspected that General Dean wouldn't as he had already been briefed.

"No questions, thank you," Dean said, standing and turning to face the regimental commanders. "Gentlemen, we've got to hold the enemy at the Kum River. Elements of the 25th Division are to the east in the mountains blocking the main avenues of approach south. One battalion from the 25th is securing the port of P'ohang-dong and the airfield at Yonil on the east coast. In our sector, the 34th Regiment will be on the left and the 19th on the right. The 21st will be in reserve blocking position on the southeast side," Dean ordered, looking at each commander as he spoke. Lieutenant Colonel Wadlington was still in command of what was left of the 34th Regiment. He and Colonel Stephens both looked worse for the wear. It was obvious that Colonel Guy "Stan" Meloy Jr., who commanded the 19th and had just arrived in Korea, had had a good night's sleep. "The Kum River offers the best defensible terrain between here and the Naktong River. If we lose the Kum River, we'll lose Taejon and the road and rail connections through that city. Stan, how many soldiers do you have?"

"Sir, I have two thousand, two hundred and seventy-six," Meloy answered.

"Stephens how about you?" Dean asked.

"Sir, I have a foxhole strength of eleven hundred," Colonel Stephens answered.

Dean looked at Wadlington.

"Sir, I'm down to two thousand twenty."

"Well, we're looking at the 3rd and 4th Divisions and they're at anywhere from sixty to eighty percent strength. I'm not so concerned about superior manpower, but he has about fifty tanks and we don't have a lot of antitank support at this time. We cannot let those tanks get across the river," Dean said, emphasizing the point. "The Kum offers the best hope of stopping them. It's a wide river and deep, with defensible terrain on this south side. Okay, brief me on your plans. Colonel Wadlington, you go first."

Colonel Wadlington stood and moved the map mounted on the wall. "Sir, I'm deploying the 3rd Battalion with L, I and K Companies along the river heights. M Company, my weapons company, will be centered to the rear. My 1st Battalion is in the worst shape and I have him in an assembly area, serving as a reserve and getting some rest," Wadlington outlined.

"What concerns do you have at this point?" Dean asked.

"Commo is a problem. I have commo with the battalion headquarters, but they have no commo with the line companies, nor do the company commanders have commo with the platoons or squads. Batteries for these old radios aren't in the system. In addition, we have inexperienced leaders at almost every level. Some staff sergeants are serving as platoon leaders or company master sergeants. I had to replace the 3rd Battalion commander because he was exhausted. The battalion XO is in command now. A good major, but...," Wadlington concluded.

"Stephens, are you having similar concerns?" Dean asked, directing his attention away from Wadlington.

"Yes, sir. We're about in the same boat as 34th Regiment."

"Okay, Stan, let's hear your plan. You have the main avenue of approach into our sector," Dean pointed out.

"Sir, my plan is to have 1st Battalion overlooking the river. The 2nd Battalion will be in a reserve position behind the 1st so he can react quickly to a penetration or a flanking maneuver by the enemy.

My regimental CP will be in Palsan astride the main road and just back from the river," Colonel Meloy outlined.

"Okay, you're the main effort, so I'm going to have the artillery put six batteries in direct support to you. Wadlington, I'll put one battery in direct support to you and it'll be the 63rd Field Artillery. Where are you going to position him?" Dean offered.

"Sir, I'll get with the battery commander, but I was looking at this location two and a half miles behind the line. I believe they have ten 105 howitzers, which should be sufficient," Wadlington stated.

"Okay, sounds like we have a solid plan. Remember, we've got to hold this line. If you hear of anyone talking about getting back to Japan, tell them to forget it. Let's pray for a quiet night," Dean concluded.

Chapter 35
Defense of the Kum River

14 JULY 1950
34th Regiment
Kum River, South Korea

THE NIGHT HAD BEEN QUIET, but the monsoon rain had drenched everyone and filled most of the foxholes. The day before, temperatures had soared into the high nineties, further sapping strength from the peacetime soldiers, who were physically out of shape. The previous day, Delta Company of the 3rd Engineer Combat Battalion had blown the bridge astride the Kum River in front of Kongju. Just after it blew, it was reported that a North Korean squad had emplaced a machine-gun position on the riverbank and a tank had moved in to support it. Shortly after that, the indiscriminate shelling had commenced on the 34th's positions. The first problems showed in K Company, which had a foxhole strength of just forty men. They were in such bad shape that the entire company had to be pulled off the line and sent to Taejon for medical treatment. This left a two-mile gap between the 34th Regiment and the 19th Regiment and left only two understrength rifle companies in front of Kongju. In the dawn mist, the sound of tanks was clearly heard across the water, followed by tank fire raining on the 34th's positions.

"King of Battle, King of Battle, Little Bird, over." King of Battle was the call sign for the 63rd Field Artillery Battalion's fire direction center. Little Bird was an O-1 Bird Dog observation plane for the artillery.

"Little Bird, King of Battle, go ahead."

"King of Battle, fire mission. Troops in the open… " He read off the coordinates. In the King of Battle fire direction center, they quickly plotted the location and exchanged looks.

"Little Bird, say coordinates again, over."

Little Bird did so and waited.

"Little Bird, those coordinates are on the south side of the river. Are you sure?"

"King of Battle, I'm damn sure, now shoot."

At the same time, a runner from the leftmost platoon ran up to the L Company commander, First Lieutenant Archie L. Stith. "Sir, we have enemy on this side of the river," the soldier said, gasping for breath.

"What? Where?" Stith asked, grabbing up his map.

"They're here, sir, about two miles south of our position. I saw about five hundred and more in boats coming over," the messenger panted out.

"Alright, let me get the machine guns and mortars from Mike Company and you can take me out and show me. Wait here," Stith directed and went to get the heavy weapons. What he found was indications that Mike Company had been in the location briefed but was not there now. *Damnit, where could they be?* As Stith moved back to his CP, he heard distant small-arms fire. Arriving, he found a squad leader from the left-flank platoon.

"What are you doing here?" Stith asked as the sounds of gunfire increased.

"Sir, we have about five hundred gooks moving up on our flank from south of our location," the squad leader said. Stith was in a quandary as to what to do, but only momentarily.

"Sergeant, go back and tell your platoon leader to fall back to this location. Runner," Stith said, turning to another soldier, "you head over to Second Platoon and tell them the same thing. Go!" With no communications with battalion headquarters and no heavy weapons, Stith made the decision to pull his company out of the line. When the two platoons arrived, he gave the order to move out in a tactical formation and head towards the battalion headquarters, which was located behind the 63rd Field Artillery location three miles away. The time was 1100 hours. This left only I Company on the line. Moving to the battalion headquarters position, Stith passed the artillery.

Sergeant Wagnebreth, a platoon leader, passed an officer at the 63rd. "Hey, sir, we have enemy coming up behind us. They got across the river," Wagnebreth told him.

"Really?" the officer, Major Dressler, replied with some surprise. "Hadn't heard anything about it," he added and went on eating his cold C ration meal.

Lieutenant Stith continued moving Love Company towards the rear. Finally, to his relief, he spotted the antenna farm that usually grows up around a battalion command post at Nonsan. The higher the command level of the command post, the bigger the antenna farm.

"Master Sergeant," Stith called out to his senior NCO, "take the company and get them settled while I go up to the CP and see what the colonel wants us to do."

"Yes, sir. I'll see if I can round up some grub for them."

With that, Stith continued to walk up to the CP, which was a couple of General Purpose Medium tents. Entering, he spotted Colonel McGarity, the battalion commander, who had his back to the doorway.

"Afternoon, sir, what are your orders?" Stith asked, approaching him. McGarity looked up from the papers he was reading and immediately saw the surprised looks on those in front of him. He turned and was equally surprised to see Lieutenant Stith standing before him.

"What are you doing back here?" McGarity asked very slowly, attempting to control his temper as he quickly realized this was not good.

"Sir, we were hit on the flank and I couldn't find the weapons company, so I pulled my company off the line and here we are. What are your orders?" Stith said with a bit for frustration in his voice.

"Are you telling me your whole company is back here, now!" McGarity said with a rising voice. "Who ordered you off the line?"

"Well, no one, sir, but we had no comms with anyone," Stith stammered, "and...and we were being hit on the flank."

"Damnit, Lieutenant, you were supposed to hold and fight," McGarity yelled. He immediately turned to the operations officer, Major Mills. McGarity's blood pressure was rising and his red face showed it. "Contact India Company and see what their situation is at this time... and Mike Company also." Spinning on his heel, he had Lieutenant Stith in his sights. "Lieutenant, you're relieved of command and under arrest. For your actions, I intend to court-martial you. Now get out of my sight." Like a scolded dog, Lieutenant Stith slinked out of the CP.[1]

AT FIRST LIGHT, the 63rd Field Artillery Battalion had an O-1 Bird Dog airplane take off with an artillery spotter. The spotter had called for artillery fire on the troop concentration south of the river. Major Charles T. Barter, the battalion operations officer or S-3, studied his map as the first rounds were fired by A Battery, 11th Field Artillery, which was supporting the 63rd Artillery. *I'm still not sure about this location*, he was thinking.

"King of Battle, Little Bird, over!" came over the radio almost as a scream.

Major Barter picked up the receiver. "Little Bird, King of Battle, over."

"King of Battle, we have enemy aircraft. We're vacating the AO, over."

---

1. It appears that First Lieutenant Archie L. Stith rose to the rank of lieutenant colonel and retired from the Army in the early to mid-1970s.

"Little Bird, Little Bird, King of Battle, understood. Let me know when you're down. Over," Barter transmitted.

"King of Battle, 'down' is not a good term in this situation. How about when I land? Over," the pilot said with some agitation in his voice.

"Roger." Turning to Sergeant First Class Leonard J. Smith, the FDC chief, Barter said, "Check fire until the infantry sends in bigger targets, then a few boats cross the river. Don't want to expose our tubes to enemy aircraft." The shooting stopped. "Have we heard from any of the FOs with the infantry?" Barter asked.

"No, sir. They've reported nothing," Sergeant Smith responded. "We do have commo with the 34th Regiment CP, and they haven't reported anything."

Barter didn't know that the artillery FOs hadn't reached the infantry positions that morning. The day before, Lieutenant Colonel Robert H. Dawson, the battalion commander, had been medically evacuated for flu-like symptoms. Major William E. Dressler, the battalion executive officer, had assumed command.

Dressler walked into the CP tent. "Hey, Charlie, have we had any reports of units pulling off the river? I just had a bunch of grunts come past me saying the enemy is forcing the river," he asked almost casually.

"No. We've heard nothing. The FOs haven't reported anything. Our Bird Dog got chased off by some enemy aircraft, but that's been about it. We did fire on a couple of sampans that he reported, but nothing significant. We have commo with the regiment and they've said nothing." Barter picked up a coffeepot and poured a substance that flowed like mud into his canteen cup. He noted the time on his watch. It was 1330 hours.

Corporal Lawrence A. Ray and Private Fred M. Odie were artillerymen but had been assigned a .30-caliber machine gun and placed in an observation post five hundred meters forward of the Headquarters Battery, 63rd Field Artillery's position. At noon they had relieved the crew that was manning the machine gun, and they would be here until 1800 that night, when they would be relieved.

"Odie, why don't you get some sleep and I'll take the first watch…say I wake you at 1400?" Ray suggested. Odie immediately settled down in the foxhole, which was almost three feet deep. "When you wake up, we've got to dig this hole deeper. Lazy bastards should have dug it another two feet for sure. Damn commo guys," Ray grumbled. Odie didn't really pay attention as he was too comfortable to worry about it at this point. He didn't bother to respond to Ray but simply closed his eyes with a smile.

"Odie, wake up. Damnit, wake up, we have company," Ray said, getting Odie's attention from his slumber.

"What's the matter?" Odie asked, sitting up and noticing Ray behind the gun. That sight quickly brought him fully awake.

"We got company. Over there on the ridge. Call battalion and notify them," Ray directed. Odie reached for the EE-108 sound-powered field phone and cranked the handle to alert the Headquarters Battery that he was calling.

"Yeah, what you want?" the voice on the other end asked.

"This is OP1. We have people on the ridgeline forward of our position," Odie said, staring off into the distance movement.

"Wait one," the voice directed. After a few moments, with the group now only four hundred meters away, the voice returned. "Hold your fire. They may be friendly troops rotating off the line."

"Okay, we will," Odie said, turning to Ray and relaying the order. With that, Ray sat back from the gun and relaxed.

"Okay, let's start digging this hole deeper," Ray directed, and both soldiers turned their attention to digging, paying no attention to the approaching soldiers. Standing straight up to throw some dirt with his entrenching tool, Odie noticed that the group of soldiers were now only one hundred meters from their position, and they didn't look friendly. He slowly laid his entrenching tool down and tapped Ray on the shoulder. Ray was still bent over, digging.

"Ah, Ray,…Ray, I think you should see this, Ray," Odie said.

"Hey, never mind the scenery, just keep digging," Ray said, quickly standing and noticing Odie pointing. Ray slowly turned in the direction that Odie was looking.

"Holy shit. Friendly my ass," Ray said, dropping behind the .30-cal machine gun and firing a burst as a mortar round impacted behind them in the battery area. Odie dropped down as well and began feeding ammo into the gun. The Koreans continued to move forward. Ray realized quickly that he was not going to stop them and soon would be within hand grenade range.

"Odie, let's get the hell out of here. We can't hold them," Ray ordered. He didn't need to repeat himself as Odie had already had the same idea. The North Koreans took possession of the .30-caliber machine gun, repositioning it to point towards the Headquarters Battery five hundred meters behind OP1 as Ray and Odie ran, seeking cover and concealment from the enemy fire.

"Anything more from OP1 about those friendly troops?" Barter asked Sergeant Smith.

"Nothing, sir. Want me to call them back for an update?"

"That would be a good—" Barter didn't finish as the first mortar round slammed into the headquarters area.

"Incoming!" someone yelled, accompanied by the sound of a .30-caliber machine gun firing in the distance, but the rounds ripped through the tent.

"Stay down!" Barter screamed as a young soldier stood to run outside and was hit in the chest. He never made it to the door. Outside, Barter could hear small-arms fire from M1 rifles and carbines as artillerymen fired on the attacking North Koreans.

"Sir, I just got a report that A Battery is under attack," the sergeant said as the next mortar round impacted and it was loud.

"Shit, what did they just hit?" Barter asked, crawling to the edge of the tent and looking out. The commo truck was a smoldering heap of metal as the next round hit the medical aid station.

"Everyone out of here. This place is next on their target list. Move and stay down," Barter screamed. As he crawled out of the tent, some followed, but some remained frozen in place and weren't seen again after the next round hit the command post.

Corporal Ray and Private Odie made it back to A Battery and grabbed some discarded weapons they found. Ray picked up a BAR and Odie an M1 carbine. They moved up to one of the howitzers and joined two other soldiers who were down behind a two-foot-high sandbag ring around the gun. Between the four at that position and a few others at other positions, they were able to hold off the enemy attackers momentarily. They did notice some of the artillerymen running for the rear.

"You bastards get back here!" Ray yelled as he fired. His yelling went unheeded except by the enemy, which intensified its fire in his direction.

"Oh crap, that hurts," Ray said between clenched teeth as a round ripped through his shirt and seared his upper arm. "Son of a bitch!" he groaned and fired another well-aimed burst. His target crumpled into a ball at one hundred meters.

"Let me bandage that, Ray," Odie said, laying his weapon down and reaching for his first aid packet.

"Keep shooting or you'll be patching up bigger holes in both of us," Ray said in an elevated voice when a mortar round landed behind them and the artillery tube.

It's so quiet and peaceful here in the darkness. I should get some sleep now, Ray thought as he lay there on the ground. But a voice began to penetrate the darkness and peace. The voice was calling him. "Ray, Ray, Ray, wake up."

Damnit, Odie, can't you see I'm sleeping peacefully? Why wake me? Ray thought.

"Ray, damnit, wake up!" the voice repeated, now accompanied by the sound of gunfire, which came through loud and clear to Ray's senses. When he opened his eyes, Odie was bending over him and attempting to pull him up.

"What? What's going on?" Ray asked in a stupor, attempting to sit up as the pain shot through his gluteus maximus. "Oh shit, that hurts."

"You took a piece of shrapnel in your ass. I would suggest you not sit down, but let's get the hell out of here, *now!*" Odie said, helping Ray to his feet and pulling him back away from the approaching enemy. Running as best he could, Ray followed Odie. The two dropped down into a draw and found several other members of the battery hiding there. All were new privates that had only recently joined the unit. None had a weapon.

"What the hell?" Ray barked when he saw them. "What are you people doing here? You either fight or get the hell out of here, and since none of you have a weapon, I suggest we get the hell out of here," he said, taking charge of the group as the senior person in rank and age. "Follow me." Each step was painful as Ray led the small party down the draw and away from the enemy.

"Hey, Ray," Odie said, pointing to the top of the draw, "isn't that…?"

"Yeah, that's Captain Southerland," Ray said, moving to the body on the ground. He bent over and pulled one of the battery commander's dog tags, leaving one with the body. In a low whisper, he said, "Rest in peace, Captain." He started to turn when he saw the top of a soldier's helmet sticking out of a nearby foxhole. Crawling over to it, he saw it was another body, accompanied by a third. It was Major Dressler and Corporal McCall. Ray reached down and grabbed their dog tags as well before he crawled back to the draw and resumed the march south.[2]

Almost simultaneously, B Battery was under attack as well from the rear as the enemy had managed to get behind the battery before it commenced its assault. Fortunately, Captain Anthony F. Stahelski had positioned two .30-caliber machine guns on that side of his position.

---

2. Corporal Ray and Private Odie reached friendly lines and survived the war. Corporal Ray was awarded the Distinguished Service Cross for his actions. Major Dressler and Corporal Edward L. McCall were recovered two years later. Roy E. Appleman, *United States Army in the Korean War: South to the Naktong, North to the Yalu (June–November 1950)* (Washington, D.C.: United States Army Center of Military History, 1992), 128.

As mortar rounds impacted, Captain Stahelski made his way to the machine guns.

"Open fire and don't stop until I tell you to stop," Stahelski said, crouching down beside the two guns. *I should have separated these two and not positioned them so close to each other*, he was thinking when a mortar round landed on one of his 105mm howitzers. Gun crews on the other howitzers began falling back from their guns but had the good sense to pick up their rifles and join Captain Stahelski. The next mortar round took out a commo jeep. *Damn, they must have an FO because this is just too accurate* flashed through Stahelski's mind as a deuce-and-a-half truck exploded. *It won't be long now before they hit us with a round.* A bugle sounded from the left flank. *Here they come...oh shit!* Stahelski thought, in shock at the sight rapidly approaching. A group of ROK mounted cavalry were charging into the North Korean flank. All the Americans were stunned by a charge that appeared to come out of a Wild West cowboy movie, complete bugle, flashing sabers and pistols. This quickly broke the North Korean attack as the cavalry charge passed through the North Korean position and kept on moving south. Although the ground attack was stopped, mortars continued to rain down on B Battery, and at 1500, Captain Stahelski ordered a withdrawal back to Nonsan, fifteen miles south.[3]

"WHERE THE HELL IS LOVE COMPANY?" Lieutenant Joseph E. Hicks, Commander, I Company, asked Sergeant Justin B. Fleming. Fleming was the squad leader on the left flank of the company and had sent a runner out at noon to find Love Company, to no avail.

"Sir, my runner said he found where they'd dug in, but they were gone," Fleming offered. All day I Company had been in position and had received some artillery fire, but no ground probes or significant

---

3. Today, to find a battalion or regiment CP that far from the front would probably result in the commander being relieved.

enemy contact. Surrounding Lieutenant Hicks were his platoon leaders, all senior NCOs.

"Sir, do we have commo with battalion?" asked one of the NCOs.

"No, and we haven't been able to locate Mike Company either," Hicks said.

"Sir," another NCO spoke up, gaining the commander's attention. "We had a couple of guys from Mike Company stumble into our position and say that the gooks had set up a couple of blocking positions on the road between us and battalion. Said we shouldn't use that road."

"Great. Any more cheery news, gentlemen?" Hicks asked. The NCOs silently chucked as Hicks always referred to them as gentlemen when they knew they were anything but, especially when on pass in Japan.

"Alright, here's what we're going to do. We'll hunker down for the night. Tighten up our security. I want—" Hicks was interrupted by two soldiers.

"Is Lieutenant Hicks here?" one asked.

"Yeah, what's up?" Hicks answered.

"Sir, Lieutenant Colonel McGarity sent me to find you. He said to tell you to wait until dark and then withdraw to the battalion position at Nonsan, but not to come on the road," the young corporal said. "I'm to lead you back on the route I took cross-country." The NCOs were all watching Hicks's reaction.

"Okay, gentlemen, as I was saying…we'll assemble at 2100 hours and conduct a withdrawal from this location and conduct an overland march to Nonsan. Order of march is First Platoon, Headquarters, Second Platoon, and Third will bring up the rear. Make it as quiet as possible. No empty canteens, no loose mess kits banging around. Carry as much ammo as you can. Leave what you can't carry and quietly destroy it if possible. It's going to be a long walk, so carry two C rat meals per man. Any you leave, open the cans so the enemy can't eat them. Any questions?" Hicks asked, looking around. There were none. These NCOs had trained him well.

Lieutenant Hicks and company reached Nonsan early the following morning. They made no contact with the enemy on their overland march.

Chapter 36
Relief of the 21st

14 July 1950
  19th Regiment
  Palsan-ni, South Korea

THE WITHDRAWAL of the 34th Regiment from the banks of the Kum River left the left flank of the 19th Regiment exposed, and no one had bothered to inform Colonel Meloy or the 19th Regiment. The 19th Regiment had arrived in Pusan on 4 July and moved up to Taejon. The previous day, the thirteenth, the 19th had begun a relief in place with the 21st Regiment, which was now a shell of its former self. General Dean met with Colonel Meloy prior to the relief in place and went over the plan.

"Colonel, your regiment is to replace the 21st Regiment, which I'm pulling back," Dean said, walking over to a wall map of the area. "Your sector will be from this point eight miles north of Taejon on the south bank of the Kum River to this point here, three miles north of Kongju." As Dean spoke, he pointed at the various locations on the map. "The center of sector is Taep'yong-ni, where the Seoul-Pusan Highway crosses the Kum River. The engineers have been instructed to blow the two spans closest to the south side of the river. They'll also be dropping the railroad bridge here at Inchon. You're going to have a frontage of about thirty miles."

"Sir, you do realize that I only have two understrength battalions in the regiment, don't you? That's a lot of frontage for my size force," Meloy said as tactfully as possible.

"Colonel, I know full well the size of your regiment, but this southern bank has got to be held for as long as possible," Dean stated. "On the north side of that river is the 3rd North Korean Division, and we're the only thing between him and Taejon. If he crosses the river, he threatens to take Taejon and has an open flank on the ROK units to our north. Understood?" Dean asked as his six-foot-two-inch frame towered over Colonel Meloy.

"Yes, sir" was the only response Meloy could think of at the moment.

Dean continued, "The river will be somewhat of an obstacle to the enemy. It's two to three hundred meters wide and six to fifteen feet deep, but there are numerous sandbars that people could wade over when the river is down, which it isn't right now. The current is three to six knots. We have artillery behind you and will be in direct support to your units. The 52nd Field Artillery has two batteries of 105 howitzers, and two batteries from the 11th Field Artillery have 155 howitzers. Lieutenant Colonel Charles Stratton commands the 13th Field Artillery and he'll be the overall fire support coordinator. Any questions?"

"At this time, no, sir. I need to get out and conduct a recon. But I may have some when I get back," Meloy said, leaving the door open for him to come back with questions and requests.

"One other thing. We have some light tanks here in Taejon as well as some ADA assets that we could reinforce you with if necessary," Dean added.

"Thank you, sir, I'll keep that in mind." What Meloy was really thinking was *When I get back from my recon, I'll be asking for those tanks and quad .50-cal machine guns.*

"Okay, when you have a plan ready, send it up and we'll look it over to see how we can support you. Good luck," Dean said, extending his hand, which Meloy accepted.

Rather than drive the entire thirty miles of riverfront, Colonel Meloy went and found Lieutenant Colonel Charles Stratton, the commander of the 13th Field Artillery Battalion. Stratton had an O-1 Bird Dog observation plane at his disposal, and Meloy asked to use it for his reconnaissance. Stratton gladly obliged the colonel. As Meloy conducted his reconnaissance of the south shore, he noted several sandbars that he thought could be waded if the river depth dropped any. He knew the monsoon season was coming to a close, and with it the river would drop. How much he wasn't sure. Returning to Taejon, he formulated his defensive plan and called in Lieutenant Colonel Otho T. Winstead, commander of the 1st Battalion, and Lieutenant Colonel Thomas McGrail, along with Lieutenant Colonel Stratton and his staff.

"Gentlemen, I've had a chance to look over our assigned sector, which is a thirty-mile front," Meloy began. The commanders exchanged looks of surprise at hearing the size of the frontage. Before anyone could protest, he went on, "I know that sounds like a huge frontage, but we have a good obstacle to our front with few crossing points. The two bridges in sector will be destroyed shortly. We have good fields of fire and observation of the north shore. So my plan is as follows." Meloy moved in front of the map. "Otho, I want you positioned along the south shore. I would place one company here on this high ground to the north with this slough and streams at the base of the hills. Position one company north of Taep'yong-ni and one company south of the town along this river dike. Any questions?" Meloy asked.

"Not at this time, sir. I'll probably position Charlie Company in the north on that high ground, Hill 200, Able Company on the north side of town and Baker on the south side. My heavy mortars will be positioned with one section between Able and Charlie and one section between Able and Baker. When I've finalized the plan, I'll get it up to your headquarters. I don't mind telling you, sir, that I'm concerned with the gaps between Charlie Company's position and Able Company's, as well as a potential two-mile gap between Easy Company's positions and Charlie Company's," Otho said.

"Afraid it can't be helped," Meloy said, turning to Lieutenant Colonel McGrail. "Now, Tom, your mission is to be the reserve. Position your companies with one company screening the northern flank along the river. Your other two companies position on the high ground on both sides of the Seoul-Pusan Road south of Palsan-ni. I want one platoon from one of the companies to be under the command of Captain Montesclaros," Meloy said, turning to the captain.

"Captain Montesclaros, I want you to establish an outpost on this high ground in front of Hill 300 and overlooking the river as well as this road that comes north along the river and then heads to Kongam-ni. That's two miles south of this 1st Battalion's company position. You will be organized with one platoon from a company from 2nd Battalion, the I&R platoon, an engineer platoon and a battery of artillery. Get with Lieutenant Colonel Stratton on that. Your mission is to screen the river from your position. Any questions?" Meloy asked. The captain had none. Captain Melecio Montesclaros was probably the most experienced captain in the regiment, having seen action in the European Theater during World War II and received a battlefield commission.

"Sir, I'll give him a platoon from George Company and position George behind the company on the north side of town. I'll put my Fox Company behind the company on the south side of town. Both will be on this high ground overlooking the road south of Palsan-ni. Echo Company will be the screen force on the right flank," Lieutenant Colonel McGrail said.

"Good," Meloy replied and turned to Lieutenant Colonel Stratton. "Where are you looking at positioning the artillery?"

"I'm going to place Battery B, 13th Field Artillery, in direct support of Captain Montesclaros's force. I'll put the rest of the batteries south of 2nd Battalion's position and along the Seoul-Pusan Road. From there they'll be able to provide fire support throughout the front," Stratton said. "And as soon as your FOs have their fire support plans completed, get them up to the FDC and we'll get it all plotted."

"Alright, gentlemen, we have a lot of work ahead of us. My headquarters will be in Palsan-ni. Remember, we can't let them get across that river. Good luck," Colonel Meloy said, concluding the meeting.

As the regiment moved into positions, the soldiers watched Air

Force aircraft conduct strafing and bombing runs on enemy forces on the north side of the river opposite Taep'yong-ni. Colonel Meloy had been observing the air strikes in the late-morning hours and returned to his command post established in Palsan-ni around 1300 hours.

"Welcome back, sir. How were the air strikes?" Major Edward O. Logan asked. He had only recently taken the position of operations officer or S-3.

"Good," Meloy replied, removing his steel pot helmet and donning his soft cap. "Got any coffee?"

"Yes, sir, I'll have the master sergeant round you up a cup. Sir, we did get a report a few minutes ago from an observation aircraft. Eleven more tanks were spotted north of the river." In the distance, the faint sounds of tank fire could be heard.

"I guess the Air Force didn't get them all from the sounds of things," Meloy stated, sipping his coffee but unconcerned.

"We also were notified by division that the 34th has fallen back from Kongju," Major Logan said, waiting for a reaction. He got what he waited for. Colonel Meloy stopped sipping his coffee and lowered his cup slowly, looking at Logan, then standing and moving to the map on the wall. For a moment, he said nothing, tracing the route from Kongju to his left flank.

"Now that concerns me. Our flank is exposed with few forces in that area. An attack from Kongju combined with the river cross in that sector will roll our flank up and make it difficult for us to hold the river," Meloy said slowly and deliberately. "Get me Colonel McGrail. Have him come up here."

When McGrail arrived, Colonel Meloy briefed him on the situation and they discussed options. Meloy didn't want to make a bold decision with just the facts he had in hand, but he also wanted McGrail to have thought through options that could be executed quickly as the reserve.

Chapter 37
Contact

15 July 1950
  19th Regiment
  Palsan-ni, South Korea

THE REGIMENT HAD MOVED into position the previous day and only experienced some tank fire from the north side of the river. During the night, the typical and expected probes were experienced, but nothing serious, and the units suffered no casualties. Unbeknownst to the 19th Regiment, India Company of the 34th Regiment had pulled out during the night, thus leaving the left flank of the 19th exposed.

"Colonel Meloy, McGrail here. I just got a report from Captain Montesclaros that they're attempting to cross forward of his positions. He says they sent runners out to link up with the 34th, but no one was there."

"Alright, Tom, here's what I want you to do. Get over there with the rest of George Company. I'm attaching two light tanks and two quad .50-cals to you as well as a machine-gun platoon from How Company and a mortar section. We'll get them to you as fast as we can," Meloy stated.

"Roger, sir, I'm on my way," McGrail said.

Within the hour, McGrail had George Company loaded up and led them cross-country to Kongam-ni and up the road to Captain Montesclaros's position. When he approached Captain Montesclaros, the captain rendered the proper salute and McGrail extended his hand.

"Damn glad to see you here, sir. It appears that the 34th Regiment pulled out last night," Montesclaros said.

"Regiment was notified late yesterday that they'd pulled out. How have you got your force positioned now?" McGrail asked.

"Sir, the platoon from George is here on this high ground as was briefed to Colonel Meloy." As Captain Montesclaros spoke, he gestured with his hands, pointing to the various positions. "The I&R platoon is manning outposts along the river from here to the boundary with the 34th. They've had some light contact with the enemy coming over from the 34th sector, but nothing they couldn't handle so far."

"Good. I'm bringing the rest of George Company along with some quad .50s and two light tanks. I'll position my CP midsector behind the I&R platoon positions. We best get everyone in position before dark as I suspect things may get frosty tonight, and I don't mean the weather," McGrail said, looking north and watching movement on the far side of the river.

In the late afternoon, Colonel Meloy requested and received air strikes on the north shore of the river. This impeded the enemy's 3rd Division's attempts to prepare equipment for an anticipated attack. Psychologically, it reinforced the morale of the men of the 19th while eroding the morale of the enemy who were subjected to the air strike's effectiveness. Enemy soldiers tested the American resolve with sporadic tank fire when the aircraft were not overhead. Some enemy soldiers attempted to wade across the river and were cut down. However, each time they were, their commanders judged the strength of the American forces in that vicinity. The leadership of the 3rd NK Division was trading bodies for knowledge. This kept up throughout the evening, especially in front of Charlie Company, where the enemy attempted to cross the river under the support of mortars.

"Did you hear something?" Corporal Hanner whispered to his

foxhole partner, Private Winston. Hanner and Winston occupied the last position on the right flank of the First Platoon, Company C.

"No, but I see those bastards attempting to wade the river. They don't realize that the burning huts on their side are silhouetting them," Winston replied as a heavy machine gun off to the left opened fire, churning the water around the wading enemy soldiers. When it stopped shooting, no one was wading anymore.

"I thought I heard a plane flying down the river," Hanner said as he scanned the night sky. "Yeah, I do. He's coming this way." In the distance, the drone of a prop-driven aircraft could be heard and a red flare suddenly appeared, falling from the sky. Simultaneously, artillery batteries, mortars and tanks on the north side of the river opened fire. The shelling of the 19th Regiment was intense and very accurate. Trading bodies for knowledge had allowed the enemy commanders to pinpoint all of the 1st Battalion's positions.

"Colonel, Colonel Winstead is on the line," Major Logan said, handing off the receiver.

"Colonel Meloy here. What's your situation, Otho?"

"Sir, they're attempting to swim, wade, ferry and use the blown bridge to cross the river," Otho said.

"Use the bridge? I thought we took out the two spans closest to our side. Did they rebuild it right under our noses?" Meloy said with some confusion.

"No, sir. They're running down the existing spans and jumping into the river to swim the rest of the way. I need the artillery shooting the illumination rounds to shift one hundred meters to the south. That appears to be the concentration coming at Baker Company," Otho requested.

"Roger, I'll get them to make that shift. Keep me posted." Meloy turned to Major Logan. "Contact the artillery and have them shift the illumination rounds one hundred meters to the south."

"Yes, sir," Logan said and picked up the trans/receiver to the artillery FDC. He repeated the order. Outside, the intense battles along the river continued.

Lieutenant Henry T. McGill, commander, Charlie Company, was

concerned about the gap between him and Echo Company. South of his position, he heard the firefight intensifying in Able and Charlie Companies' sectors. Things appeared quiet in Echo Company's sector, and that worried him too. It was too quiet for his liking.

Turning to his RTO, he directed, "Get me Lieutenant Maher on the phone." Lieutenant Henry T. Maher was the First Platoon leader and the right flank of the company. To his right was Echo Company, two miles away.

"Sir, Lieutenant Maher," he heard on the receiver moments later.

"Maher, what is the situation in your area?" McGill asked.

"All fairly quiet. Had a probe earlier, but that was all. Doing fine," Maher responded.

"Okay, keep me posted," McGill said, handing the receiver back to the RTO. As he did, all hell broke loose in the vicinity of the First Platoon. Automatic weapons that sounded like communist burp guns were heard, mixed with the distinctive sounds of M1 rifles and M1 carbines along with Thompson submachine guns. This was followed by the explosive sounds of hand grenades. McGill attempted to contact Maher again, to no avail.[1] Moments later, the First Platoon sergeant dove into Lieutenant McGill's position.

"Sir, we got overrun," panted Staff Sergeant King. "They were on us so fast we hardly had time to react. The lieutenant took the first shot and was killed immediately. I think it was a company-size or larger force."

"How many did you bring out?" McGill asked, looking in the direction of where the First Platoon had been.

"Sir, I think I have a dozen with me. Sir, they were in our holes before we knew they were there. We had OPs and LPs out, but they never reported anything. And we had trip flares as well. Nothing, no warning, nothing…," Staff Sergeant King repeated.

"Okay, have your men dig in around me and we hold this position.

---

1. When Lieutenant Henry T. McGill placed his receiver back in the cradle, he was immediately shot in the head and died. Roy E. Appleman, *United States Army in the Korean War: South to the Naktong, North to the Yalu (June–November 1950)* (Washington, D.C.: United States Army Center of Military History, 1992), 135.

Understood?" McGill ordered. He believed Staff Sergeant King's tale of the experience, but he wanted these men close to make sure they didn't run when the enemy came again—and they would come again. As daylight approached and with a two-mile-wide gap between Charlie and Echo Companies, the North Koreans were taking advantage and flooding across the river unseen.

"Colonel, Otho here. Where's the illumination rounds? We had none for the past five minutes. They're across in force. I need the illumination rounds," Otho was saying in an elevated voice.

"Otho, let me check on it," Meloy said, turning to Logan, who'd clearly heard what Colonel Winstead was talking about. Logan was on the radio to the artillery FDC immediately.

"No, damnit, I said one hundred meters south…not azimuth one hundred degrees. Damnit. Get it fixed now before we lose the south shore. Shit!"

Meloy heard the exchange and almost couldn't believe it.

"Otho, the illumination will be back momentarily," Meloy said, but he knew that his one mistake would cost the regiment deeply. Little did he know that when the illumination rounds ignited, Baker Company would be staring at over a battalion-size force almost completely across the river in front of their positions. More troubling were the enemy forces that had been quietly slipping across the river between Charlie and Echo Companies. Rather than attacking the frontline units, these forces infiltrated to the rear areas. When the attack commenced, they immediately engaged the heavy mortars and combat trains. Confusion reigned supreme as reports flooded into the regimental CP of enemy forces everywhere.

"Colonel, we're being pushed back!" Otho said in an elevated voice. "Able and Baker have been penetrated and my CP and mortars are engaged. I have no reserve."

"Otho, Fox Company is pinned down right now. We've got to reconstitute a reserve. I'm sending some people to you. Get your cooks, bakers and candlestick makers together and counterattack. Major Logan will be bringing up our people to assist you. I'm sending a light tank and a quad .50-cal to support you. We've got to hold,"

Meloy said. He turned to Major Logan, who, having overheard the conversation, was already heading for the door with his rifle and a radio, leading every officer from the regimental staff to the drivers, mechanics, cooks and clerks. Two hours later, the small-arms fire had died down from the intensity that had been heard.

"How did it go?" Colonel Meloy asked when Major Logan walked back into the CP. The strain of the action showed on his face.

"We got them stopped but lost Major Cook and Captain Hacket," Logan said. Major Cook was the executive officer for the 1st Battalion and Captain Hacket was the 1st Battalion adjutant. "Some of the enemy got back across the river."[2]

"But we're holding, right?" Meloy asked, wanting a definitive answer about the situation.

"Yes, sir, we're holding," Logan responded.

"Good. I'll give General Dean a call and pass the good news on to him," Meloy said, reaching for the phone. His good news would be brief and premature.

---

2. There is a difference of opinion as to the role of Major Cook. Appleman indicates he was the 1st Battalion executive officer, while Fehrenbach indicates he was the 1st Battalion operations officer.

Chapter 38
Behind the Lines

16 JULY 1970
   19th Regiment
   Palsan-ni, South Korea

WITH A TWO-MILE GAP between Charlie and Echo Companies, the North Koreans poured through. Attention was fixed in front of Task Force McGrail and 1st Battalion. The enemy forces engaging Fox Company were thought to have been those that had initially penetrated the Alpha and Baker Company positions. Shortly after Meloy spoke with Dean, the picture changed dramatically.

"Logan, call division and find out why we have no air support this morning. They were supposed to be here at sunrise," Meloy said. Logan noticed that the lack of sleep was beginning to take a toll on the colonel as well as himself. Before he could call division, the landline phone rang and he answered.

"Major Logan, sir."

"Logan, Colonel Stratton here. We have ground forces hitting the batteries. We need assistance now," yelled Colonel Stratton, the artillery commander.

"I'll get someone to you as quick as I can, sir," Logan said. Just then, he was handed a note from the senior NCO. He looked at it in disbelief and turned to Colonel Meloy.

"Sir, the artillery batteries are under attack and requesting aid. Also, Lieutenant Nash was bringing a resupply of ammo forward to 1st Battalion and is reporting that there's a roadblock three miles behind us and the ammo trucks can't get through," Logan said.

"Shit, let's get down there and look this over," Meloy said, picking up his steel pot.

Driving south on the Seoul-Pusan Road, Meloy in the front with an M1 carbine and Logan in the back with a Thompson submachine gun acted as security guards for the sergeant driver. A second jeep followed with a .30-caliber machine gun on a pedestal and four infantry soldiers. What they saw when they arrived appalled Meloy. Sitting on the side of the road were American soldiers doing nothing. The North Koreans sat on a hill overlooking a narrow passage on the road with a forty-foot embankment on one side and a forty-foot drop into a stream on the other. Walking amongst the soldiers, Meloy was attempting to locate someone in charge and instill some spirit in the soldiers, who were shooting in the direction of the enemy but with no organization or effectiveness. Finally, he located a senior NCO, who was lying in the ditch and firing aimed shots at the enemy.

"Master Sergeant, what's your name?" Meloy asked.

"Sir, Master Sergeant Gardner," the man said, continuing to lie on the ground.

"Sergeant, I want you to—" Meloy said before he slumped over and a burst of blood exploded from his thigh. Logan was beside him immediately. Logan and the master sergeant immediately tore open Meloy's pants and applied first aid powder and a field dressing.

"Logan, notify Colonel Winstead that he's in command of the regiment now. Get word to General Dean of the situation," Meloy said through clenched teeth and with some blood trickling from the side of his mouth.

Turning to the driver and security detail, Logan directed, "Let's get him in the jeep and back to the aid station."

As soon as Meloy was delivered back to the regimental surgeon,

Logan got on the radios. First he informed Colonel Winstead that he was now in command of the regiment, then General Dean.

"Sir, Major Logan, 19th Regiment. Colonel Meloy has been badly wounded and is down. He's given command of the regiment to Colonel Winstead. We have enemy forces behind our positions…" Logan read off the coordinates of the roadblock, which was south of the 52nd Field Artillery Battalion and the remainder of the artillery. Dean patiently listened to the situation before he issued his guidance.

"Okay, Major, I'm going to send a relief force to open that roadblock. Tell Colonel Winstead that I want him to withdraw the 19th back to Taejon but bring out all of your equipment, especially the artillery, if he can. Get Meloy out of there as quick as you can. Keep me posted," General Dean said.

"Yes, sir," Logan replied and picked up the receiver to talk to Winstead. "Sir, I just spoke with General Dean. He said to tell you to withdraw the 19th back to Taejon but bring all our equipment if possible, especially the artillery. He's going to send a force to open the roadblock."

"Alright, inform Colonel McGrail and Colonel Stratton to withdraw. Tell Stratton to leave some tubes in place to support our withdrawal, but be ready to move fast once he gets the word. I'll round up my companies and begin pulling back. Have Fox Company move out and take out the roadblock," Winstead ordered. Logan relayed the order to the Fox Company commander, who responded that he couldn't move as he was taking fire from his rear northern flank and front. That was the last communications that the regiment had as an artillery round hit the regimental communications van and destroyed it.[1]

Colonel Winstead returned to his command post and began ordering the withdrawal to the regiment. Contacting each of his company commanders, he ordered them to withdraw down the Seoul-Pusan Road. Able and Baker Companies were the first to withdraw, followed by Charlie Company. Charlie Company was occupying its

---

1. Lieutenant Colonel Otho Winstead received the Distinguished Service Cross for his actions posthumously and was last seen on 16 July 1950.

original positions around Hill 200 and was under mortar fire. Soldiers were reluctant to get out of their foxholes with mortar rounds dropping all around. To add to their distress, the temperatures were now approaching 100 degrees and no one had any water as the last water resupply had been at dawn. The scorching sun was also physically sapping the strength from the unfit soldiers. Finally Second Lieutenant Augustus B. Orr was able to get the company moving towards the road. As they approached, they could see the tail end of Baker Company as it followed Able Company. Approaching Palsan-ni, Company C came under fire from six enemy machine guns located on the high ground opposite Palsan-ni. All order fell out of the company as small groups broke off and scattered to the hills, attempting to avoid prestaged ambushes.

At the roadblock, the situation was becoming critical. Communications between units were limited due to the fact that there were few radios and no chain of command to coordinate actions. Major Logan was attempting to organize an assault force when word reached him that Colonel Winstead had been killed back along the river.

"Smith," Logan yelled, getting the attention of Lieutenant Lloyd D. Smith. Smith was the mortar platoon leader in Dog Company.

"Sir," Smith responded.

"Smith, I want you to gather up fifty men and move up that hill to take out those machine-gun positions. If we can take them out, we can open this road and get everyone out. Grab another officer to assist you, but get it done," Logan ordered.

"Yes, sir," Smith said and began tagging soldiers to follow him. Soon he had his force assembled and they started up the hill. The hill was steep but offered good concealment up to the machine-gun positions. The temperature was now over one hundred degrees. Slowly the force moved upward. Three-quarters of the way up the hill, Smith signaled for a halt. Turning, he realized that his force now consisted of himself and one other soldier. The others had all slinked away on the climb up. He and his remaining force returned to the road. Logan was still determined to break the roadblock.

Gathering twenty men, Logan placed Captain Edgar R. Fenstermacher, his assistant S-3, in command at the roadblock while he took the twenty men and began to maneuver around the hill to attack from a different angle or find a bypass that could be used. Two hours later, Logan and his force came upon the 13th Field Artillery command post, which was in the process of displacing.

Although Colonel Meloy was out of the fight, Lieutenant Nash continued to carry out his orders and find Lieutenant Colonel McGrail. His jeep was riddled with bullets, but he commandeered another and went looking for Colonel McGrail's command post at Sangwang-ni on the left flank of the regiment.

"Sir, I've been told to get you back to regiment and for you to move George Company to clear the roadblock on the Seoul-Pusan Road," Nash said, approaching him.

"I know, so let's not wait around. I'm going to need trucks to haul my guys out," McGrail said, settling into the passenger seat. Nash was behind the wheel.

"Sir, I can drop you off at regiment and I know where some trucks are at Taejon that I can get," Nash said, putting the jeep in gear and tearing out to the town. Speed was of the essence, and he spared no horsepower in getting up to speed. Before he left, McGrail gave final orders to Captain Mike Barszcz, George Company commander.

"Mike, prepare your company for movement. I'll send trucks back for you. Also, tell Montesclaros to stay with the I&R platoon and have the engineers prepare the road for demolition for you to blow when you pull out. Any questions?" McGrail asked. Captain Barszcz had none. George Company mounted the trucks provided by Lieutenant Nash and proceeded south. Along the way, they encountered General Dean, who instructed Captain Barszcz to clear the roadblock. Despite the efforts of George Company, they couldn't clear the roadblock and suffered for their effort.

Colonel Meloy was still north of the roadblock. Major Logan wanted him to get through to a medical aid station and decided to put Meloy in a tank. Leading twenty vehicles, the tank started down the road, firing its main gun at anything that presented a target. Finally, it and twenty vehicles had cleared the roadblock and were rolling in relatively quiet country. The lurching motion of the tank and the sputtering engine told Meloy that they were in trouble again. Finally the tank came to a stop just off the road. None of the twenty vehicles stopped but rolled right past. Unable to fix the tank, Colonel Meloy ordered that it be destroyed, and a thermal grenade was ignited and dropped down the hatch. In no time the tank was a pile of burning metal. The first sign of encouragement appeared when Captain Barszcz and George Company came upon the burning tank. Colonel Meloy had them dig in around his position. Just after dark, a vehicle approached from the south and stopped. Colonel Meloy was transferred to this vehicle along with other wounded and taken to Taejon.

At this point the 19th Regiment existed in name only. Men had dissolved into small groups, attempting to make their way south through mountain valleys and passes. Travel at night was easiest as they knew the North Koreans would be on hilltops. Travel in the day left them exposed to plunging fire from the hilltops as well as oppressive heat now that the monsoon season was coming to a close. The only companies to arrive in relatively good shape were George and Easy, which had not been engaged while along the Kum River.

In Taejon, General Dean came briefly to the division aid station before Colonel Meloy was shipped out to Japan.

"How you feeling?" Dean asked.

"Sir, as long as the morphine holds out, I'm good to go," Meloy said with an odd grin on his face. "You know, sir, if I'd had a reserve force, my 3rd Battalion, we wouldn't have had to abandon the river. We need to get the units back to full strength," Meloy said, slightly rising up but quickly lying back down when another stab of pain shot up his leg. "A reserve would have saved the day." These were Meloy's last words before the morphine kicked in fully and he pleasantly drifted off to sleep.[2]

---

2. Colonel Guy S. Meloy recovered and continued his military career. He received the Distinguished Service Cross for his actions and had a stellar career. He received his fourth star in 1961 and became the commander in chief of the United Nations Command, Korea; Commander, United States Forces Korea; commanding general of Eighth United States Army; and commanding general of the Seventh United States Army, headquar-

tered at Stuttgart in West Germany. "Guy S. Meloy Jr.," Wikipedia, April 14, 2024, https://en.wikipedia.org/wiki/Guy_S._Meloy_Jr.

Chapter 39
Planning the Defense of Taejon

17 July 1950
   24th Division
   Taejon, South Korea

ELEMENTS OF THE 34TH REGIMENT, or what was left of it, were moving from Nonsan to take up positions northwest of the city as elements of the 19th Regiment flowed back from the Kum River. At the airfield, an assembly area was established for the stragglers to assemble, and efforts were being made to get the men back into their former units if possible. Early on the seventeenth, General Walker spoke with General Dean.

"Dean, how much of your division are you getting back?" Walker asked.

"Sir, it appears that about one-third of the division is making it back to Taejon. We'll set up a delay position here and try to hold them," Dean said in a tired and dejected voice. "If we'd just been at full strength, we could have stopped them on the Kum River, but we have no reserve forces," he added in frustration.

"Well, General, we don't, so let's make do with what we do have. We have more divisions coming over, but I need time to get them unloaded and pushed north. The 1st Cavalry Division has started landing and I'm going to push him up here, but I need you to delay at Taejon. Do you think you can do that?" Walker asked.

"Sir, I honestly don't know, but we'll give it our best. That's all I can promise at this point," Dean responded.

"That's all I'm asking for, and I know you'll do your best to make it happen. It's your decision when to pull out if you must. I'll back whatever decision you make. Please keep us posted on your progress," Walker said before he departed.

Ask for the moon, why don't you, General? Dean was thinking when he started looking at the map of Taejon. Taejon was not some straw hut village but a city of one hundred and thirty thousand civilians. Buildings were generally no higher than three stories and constructed out of cinder blocks with stucco facades. Many were wood construction. The importance of the city was the road and rail network that passed through the town. From the north was a railroad line and a highway, both crossing the Taejon River with a bridge each. The rail line passed through a tunnel three miles to the north. To the east, the Seoul-Pusan Road left the city towards Okch'on, passng through two road tunnels. This road came from Kongju-Yusong, crossing over two major bridges over the Kap-ch'on River and the Yudung River, and was probably the main avenue of approach to the city. South, a highway ran to Nangwoi-li. The Nonsan Road approached Taejon from the southwest with a bridge over both the Kap-ch'on River and the Yudung River.

Conducting a terrain analysis, Dean noted the ridgeline to the northwest along the Kap-ch'on River. This ridge was three miles long and rose about five hundred feet above the river and surrounding terrain. The north end of the ridgeline overlooked the bridge over the Kap-ch'on River as well as the road from Kongju-Yusong. The southern end overlooked the Nonsan-Taejon Road and the one bridge over the Kap-ch'on River. Between the ridge and the outskirts of town were open rice paddies full of water from the recent monsoon. Dean knew that before long, those rice paddies would be empty. He also noted that the Taejon Airport sat on a slightly lower plateau between the ridgeline and the city and just north of the Kongju -Yusong High-way. To the southeast and east of the city, the terrain was very hilly, with many ridgelines at the five-hundred-foot level. The town actually sat in a valley that ran north to south, Dean noted.

Aerial observations indicated that the 3rd and 4th North Korean Divisions were crossing the Kum River and he could expect contact within the next twenty-four to forty-eight hours. In addition, the 2nd North Korean Division was attempting to approach from the northeast but was heavily engaged by the ROK forces in that area, who were making a remarkable stand against the North Koreans. *I can expect one of two things to happen. Either both divisions will come at me from the northwest and north in a full frontal assault or one will come from the northwest in a frontal assault while the other attempts to swing to the west or southwest and get in behind us. Typical of his tactics up to now, the second option is what I believe he will attempt, and he will lead with his tanks,* Dean was thinking as he studied the map and developed a course of action.

Having conducted his terrain analysis and considered the enemy, he started looking at the forces available to him, which weren't much. All three regiments had been mauled badly in the preceding days. Instead of three battalions of infantry per regiment, the best that each regiment could muster was one battalion of infantry. Conditions were no better with the artillery either. There were no tanks available, and the flow of effective bazookas was just a trickle. The 3.5-inch bazooka had been in development since the end of World War II, but the ammunition devel-opment was the problem. The 21st Regiment had been mauled early in the previous fights and was now sitting at Okch'on. The 34th was pulling back the twenty miles from Nonsan and moving into a position along the high ridge northwest of the city. Colonel Charles E. Beauchamp was the new regimental commander and had established his command post at the Taejon airfield.[1] The 19th, mauled the most

---

1. Colonel Charles E. Beauchamp had flown over from Japan earlier in the week. He would go on to command the 1st Cavalry Division and retire at the rank of major general.

recently, was in Yongdong, twenty miles to the south, being refitted and would require time to move up. The 24th Division command post was also in Yongdong.

"The 34th is the closest to establishing a delay position along this ridge," Dean said, thinking out loud as the assistant G-3, Captain Richard Rowlands, looked over the map with him.

"Don't you mean a defensive position, sir?" Rowlands asked. Dean was tired, physically and mentally, thought the captain, and had just made a mistake.

"No, Captain, I didn't mean a defensive position," Dean said, attempting not to jump down the captain's throat. "General Walker has asked that we delay for as long as possible, and with the forces we have and the condition of the force, I fully intend to delay until tomorrow or the nineteenth. Then we're getting the hell out of here and falling back. We just don't have the force to stop two and possibly three divisions with tanks coming at us. The 34th will delay on this ridge for the next day or so and then fall back through Taejon. The best we can hope for is to bloody his nose. We have only one-third of our combat power, our troops are dog-ass tired and morale is about as low as it can go. We delay for twenty-four hours and then fall back," Dean explained, returning his attention to the map.

"How do you think they're going to come at us, sir?" Rowlands asked.

"Oh, I think the 3rd Division will probably come straight at us on the Seoul-Pusan Road in a frontal attack. The 4th Division is the question. Will he come at us in the frontal attack with the 3rd or will he try to get around to the west and come at us on the Nonsan-Taejon Road? I think option two will be what he attempts, hitting us on the west side while the 3rd comes at us on the north and northwest side. I want to give all the support we can to the 34th, so notify the artillery that I want it all consolidated at the airfield except the 11th Field Artillery with its 155 howitzers. I'll decide later where we want to position them to support," Dean outlined. He then turned to Captain Raymond Hatfield, the assistant G-4.

"Captain Hatfield, how soon will the 19th be refitted?" Dean asked.

"Sir, they should be finished with the refit in about another two hours. They're being issued ammo now and we have trucks standing by to move them. You do know, sir, that they only have about two rifle companies remaining," Hatfield said.

"Well, I want those trucks standing by to withdraw the 34th tomorrow. I intend to evacuate Taejon tomorrow. With the artillery concentrated at the airfield, the trucks can come get them quickly and get out of here. We'll displace half the artillery first, then the 34th and the remainder of the artillery with the last elements of the 34th. Any questions?" Dean asked. At this point there were none. "Good. Captain Rowlands, notify Colonel Stephens at the 21st that I want him to get the engineers and rig the railroad tunnels at Okch'on for demolition. We'll blow them as we pull out tomorrow," Dean ordered. "Okay, gents, pass this all on to the command post at Yongdong, and let's set up a TAC CP with the 21st."

Chapter 40
Maximum Effort

18 JULY 1950
Taejon Airfield
Taejon, South Korea

GENERAL DEAN HAD HOPED to get at least six hours of sleep, but Lieutenant Clarke and Captain Rowlands woke him just after he closed his eyes, or so he thought.

"Sir, sorry to wake you, but General Walker is inbound in his plane. He should be landing in thirty minutes at the Taejon airfield," Captain Rowlands said as Lieutenant Clarke held out a steaming cup of coffee, which Dean accepted as he placed his feet on the floor and continued to sit on his cot.

"What time is it?" Dean asked.

"Sir, it's 0600," Lieutenant Clarke said, looking at his watch. "You did manage to catch four hours."

Dean looked up, surprised at that announcement. "Well, I could have used another four, but duty calls. I just spoke to him yesterday. What the hell could he want today?" he mumbled.

"Sir, his aide didn't say…just that he wanted to see you when he arrived," Rowlands replied.

"Okay, let me get the hair out of my mouth and go see what he wants. I suspect this cannot be good," Dean sighed as he stood and took his shaving kit from Lieutenant Clarke. "Tell the driver to crank up the jeep."

Sergeant Bill Dowd had been awake for an hour already when Lieutenant Clarke came and alerted him that they would be going to the airfield. Dowd had been with Lieutenant Colonel Smith when they retreated from the first engagement. In reorganizing the battalion, Dowd was considered one of the "combat-experienced" soldiers and had been promoted to corporal in charge of an infantry fire team of five soldiers. After the engagements on the Kum River, he was one of the oldest "combat-experienced" soldiers left. He'd been promoted on the spot from corporal to sergeant. General Dean needed a new driver when his was wounded, and Dowd just happened to be standing in the wrong place at the wrong time.

"Morning, Sergeant. Did you get some chow?" Dean asked, jumping into the passenger seat.

"Yes, sir. The lima beans and ham was particularly good this morning…or I was just hungry," Dowd answered, and Dean chuckled.

"Okay let's head to the airfield," Dean directed. He used Dowd as a sounding board to measure the morale of the division.

The drive from the 21st Regiment CP to the airfield at Taejon was slowed by the flow of refugees moving south, on both sides of the road and in the road. As Dean's jeep and escort pulled on to the airfield, Dean could see that the artillery had assembled and the 34th Regiment CP had been established. He could also see the L-4H Grasshopper airplane, call sign Comet Six, circling the airfield in preparation for its approach. The little taildragger touched down with only a light bounce, a tribute to the quality of General Walker's pilot. Dean dismounted from his jeep and walked out on the tarmac, such as it was, to greet General Walker.

Dropping the side curtains or doors, General Walker struggled to get out of the rear seat on the small two-seat tandem airplane. Walker was a short, stocky man and not as sprightly as he had been while commanding an armored division in Europe in World War II. Some described him as bull in a china shop when he got really excited. He stood a good head shorter than Dean, but this didn't intimidate him in the least.

"Dean, we need to talk," Walker said, approaching and motioning Dean to separate himself from the horse holder staff that accompanied him, Lieutenant Clarke, Captain Rowlands and Sergeant Dowd.

As they walked for some distance, Walker turned to Dean. "Dean, I know we talked yesterday, but things have changed. The 1st Cav isn't offloading as quick as I'd hoped. I spoke with my staff yesterday and had them crunch numbers for both manpower and logistics. I need you to hold for at least two more days. Consider defending along the river and not delaying here. I've managed to get the new bazookas to come forward and they should be issued today in a good quantity. Tanks are still out of the question for now," Walker said.

"Sir, you're aware of my combat strength—" Dean started to say.

"I'm well aware of your combat strength and well aware of what's coming at you. I need you to hold for as long as you can. When you can no longer hold them, withdraw and I'll back your decision, but I need you to apply a maximum effort in holding them at the river. I need time," Walker concluded.

I think he just told me we're expendable! Dean thought without saying so. "Yes, sir, we'll do our bast to provide you the time."

"I know you will," Walker said, extending his hand, which Dean took.

Without another word, Walker turned and made a circular motion over his head, signaling for the pilot to crank the aircraft back up. Dean stood in the same spot until the aircraft lifted into the air and turned south. Then he slowly walked back to the jeep. As he approached the jeep and Captain Rowlands, Rowlands asked, "Is everything okay, sir?" He knew from the expression on Dean's face that all was not right in the world.

"Get Colonel Wadlington up here and have him meet us as the 34th Regiment's CP. Notify Colonel Beauchamp to meet us there as well if he's not there now," Dean said, turning to his aide and pulling out a map. He moved to the front of the jeep and spread the map out. Lieutenant Clarke and Captain Rowlands knew better than to interrupt his thoughts when he was this way. As Dean studied the map, they could see his lips moving, but no words were spoken as the man was in deep concentration. Finally Dean looked up and motioned for them to get in the jeep. "Dowd, let's head over to the 34th command post," Dean directed, climbing into the front passenger seat.

Arriving at the command post for the 34th Regiment, Dean found Colonel Beauchamp already there. "Colonel, what is the disposition of your forces at this time?" Dean asked without the usual pleasant salutations common back in Japan.

Moving over to the map, Beauchamp began to outline the current disposition. "Sir, the 1st Battalion is along this ridge to the west, covering the bridges over the Kap-ch'on River. He has three—"

"Here's what I want you to do," Dean interrupted. "Consolidate your 1st Battalion on the northern end of this ridge controlling the Yusong-Taejon Road and the bridge crossing. I want a platoon-size element to set up a delaying position across the railroad tracks and the road from the north. I'll attach the 24th Reconnaissance Company to you," he outlined, pointing at the map.

Beauchamp was almost dumbfounded at the change. "Sir, how long do you expect me to stay in position?" he asked.

"Colonel, I don't expect you to leave that position for two days. General Walker needs two days, he tells me, to get the 1st Cav Division in position," Dean said, looking Beauchamp dead in the eye.

Beauchamp maintained eye contact but said nothing initially. Finally, he explained, "Sir, the 1st Battalion is currently positioned on the ridge, with Able Company on the right and Charlie on the left. We'll reinforce Able with a platoon from Baker as Baker is in a reserve position between Able and Charlie. Headquarters Company is located along the road behind Able Company. Love Company is overlooking the Nonsan Road where it crosses the river."

Colonel Wadlington walked into the CP. "Sir, you wanted to see me?" he asked, accidentally interrupting Beauchamp. Since Meloy's injury and the death of Lieutenant Colonel Otho Winstead, Wadlington had been acting commander of what was left of the 19th.

Dean looked at Beauchamp. "Don't worry about the Nonsan Road. I'm giving that mission to the 19th and Colonel McGrail to you," Dean said, turning to Wadlington. "I want your regiment to block this crossing by the Nonsan Road over the river. How soon can you get McGrail up here to join the 34th?" he asked, pointing out the location on the map.

"You know McGrail only really has two rifle companies, don't you, General?" Colonel Wadlington asked, a bit surprised by Dean's order.

"I'm aware of his combat strength. Get back to me on how you're going to hold this crossing site," Dean said, looking at Beauchamp. "Gentlemen, I know this is going to be a tough fight, but we must hold here. Forget any thoughts about getting back to Japan anytime soon. The 34th reinforced with Colonel McGrail's battalion is our best chance right now. The 21st is still trying to reconstitute but won't be ready for at least another thirty-six hours and the 19th is in worse shape. The 21st has to keep the road open, and I'll be sure Stephens understands this."

"Sir, where do you want the artillery to pull back to?" Captain Rowlands asked.

"Pull the artillery back to the vicinity of the town but close to the road network, but have one battery from the 13th Field Artillery reposition to the airfield to provide support," Dean directed and paused, looking at his commanders' faces. What he saw reflected defeat and yet resolve to attempt to execute this latest mission. They all recognized the futility of attempting to defend for any period of time, but they had their orders.

Chapter 41
Defend Taejon

19 July 1950
24th Division
Taejon, South Korea

General Dean wasn't a spring chicken any longer. He'd only had interrupted sleep for the past fourteen days. His diet consisted of cold C rations and cigarettes chased by cups of thick black coffee. For a leader, lack of sleep is the major contributor to bad decisions, which Dean was about to find out. Looking at him, the staff could tell that he was in need of a lot of sleep to restore his vigor and clear thinking.

As he examined his division, he was not pleased. Instead of having three full regiments, he was down in strength to the equivalent of three battalions, one-third of the fighting strength of the division. The individual men that manned what was left of the 24th Division had been in the fight for the past fourteen days and were as physically and mentally exhausted as their commander. Throughout the previous day, soldiers had been moving into positions and preparing their foxholes for a fight they all knew was coming.

General Dean spent his time moving from unit to unit, encouraging soldiers. He felt it was important for the soldiers to see their commander on the front line as opposed to hiding twenty miles to the rear. He also wanted to know what was going on along the front as communications were nonexistent. The radios were vintage World War II and there were no replacement batteries for them if they worked. Wet from rain or being dropped in the putrid rice paddy waters, they refused to work. Wire for field phones was quickly picked up by the refugees to make harnesses for their worldly goods, which they were carrying on their backs. Communications were limited to runners, who would gladly volunteer to take a message back to division headquarters twenty miles to the rear but were reluctant to carry a message forward from division headquarters.

Dean was drinking a cup of morning coffee when Captain Rowlands approached him. *This can't be good*, he thought.

"Sir, I just got word from the division CP that an air strike just hit the railroad bridge two miles northwest of Okch'on. They also strafed the 21st Regiment CP. They said we should—"

Rowlands didn't get to finish when the sound of aircraft engines could suddenly be heard, along with machine-gun fire at the airfield. Dean immediately stood and looked towards the airfield to see four Yak fighters conducting the strafing and dropping leaflets.

"Where the hell is our Air Force this morning?" Dean asked out loud in frustration. Rowlands had no answer. "Rowlands, let's get some anti-aircraft guns up here and position them with 1st Battalion. I think we're going to see a coordinated attack with both ground and air coming at us at the same time. Let's get back to division CP and bring them up to date on what we have here." Dean tossed out the last of his coffee and headed to his jeep with Rowlands and Clarke in tow.

"We can stop at the 21st CP and check up on Stephens," Dean said as Dowd got the jeep in gear and started heading to Yongdong.

The ride from Taejon to Yongdong should have been quick, but due to the refugees, it was a slower trip than Dean would have liked. Dowd was on the gas and the horn in equal amounts, attempting to navigate between the refugees and their oxcarts.

Colonel Beauchamp had expected the 24th Reconnaissance Company to arrive sooner. It was 1000 hours and they were just arriving. The company commander reported to him upon his arrival.

"Sir, Captain John Paul Vann reporting." Captain John Paul Vann was a combat veteran from World War II, when he'd served as an Army Air Corps navigator. When the Air Force had separated from the Army, he'd seen the handwriting on the wall and realized that unless you were a pilot, only a mediocre future awaited you in the Air Force. He'd chosen to stay with the Army and become an infantry officer. Although he was infantry, he'd spent a great deal of time in supply management assignments and had done exceptionally well getting supplies and equipment out of Japan and to Korea. When offered the opportunity to take over a reconnaissance company, made up at the time of cooks, bakers and anyone else that could be policed up from the rear, he'd taken it. In a matter of a few weeks, he had them conducting reconnaissance patrols successfully.[1]

"Glad to see you. Come here," Beauchamp said, motioning the captain to follow him to the wall map. "I want your company to set up a position at this location." He pointed to the road and railroad entering the city from the north. "Do not let the enemy come down this road or use this railroad line. If you have to fall back, fall back to this side of the river and blow the bridges. I want one platoon to head west along the Nonsan Road and conduct a reconnaissance. I need to know where the enemy is along that road."

"Sir, I'll send the Second Platoon. He has thirty-nine men in jeeps and trucks. I can get them moving as soon as you say," Captain Vann announced.

"Good, I say now," Beauchamp said. "Love Company has a platoon overlooking the bridge. They can link up and conduct a

---

1. John Paul Vann would command a reconnaissance company for three months and make it one of the best. An unfortunate family emergency forced him to give up command and return to the States. He would retire from the Army at the rank of lieutenant colonel and go on to an extraordinary career in the State Department, serving in Vietnam at the equivalent rank of a two-star general. I highly recommend Neil Sheehan's *A Bright Shining Lie* (New York: Vintage Books, 1989).

passage of lines. I need that platoon to push out as far as they can until they make contact. I need to know where the enemy is."

"Yes, sir, I'll get them rolling now," Captain Vann stated.

"Any questions?" Beauchamp asked.

"No, sir. I'll get my people started. Will let you know when we're in position," Vann said, raising his arm in a salute before he departed.

"LET'S swing into the 21st CP as it's on the way to Yongdong. I want to talk to Colonel Stephens," General Dean told Sergeant Dowd. As they continued down the road in the morning traffic, elements of the 2nd Battalion, 19th Infantry, drove past them on their way to Taejon. The young soldiers didn't look happy despite the fact that the rainy season was supposedly over, and the temperature was already going past ninety degrees so early in the morning.

They look physically exhausted, with no morale, Lieutenant Clarke thought as the trucks streamed past, shuttling soldiers to Taejon. Some were walking along the side of the road, waiting for the shuttle trucks to pick them up. *Even the officers and noncoms aren't displaying encouraging leadership. There's no discipline or pride in these soldiers. They're defeated already*, Lieutenant Clarke concluded.

Arriving at the 21st Regiment CP, General Dean entered the command post and was immediately approached by Colonel Stephens. "Colonel Stephens, how did you fare in the strafing this morning?" Dean asked.

"Sir, we came through pretty good considering. People were pretty much dispersed, and what trucks we have were back in Yongdong picking up supplies. We have the tunnels wired for demolition and are reconstituting the regiment, although we're short on manpower," Stephens said.

"Guns and equipment I can replace a lot easier than manpower at this point, Colonel. What is your disposition at this time?" Dean queried.

"Sir, currently I have the defensive position on both sides for the tunnel on this ridge," Stephens said as he pointed at the map. Half of the existing regiment was on one side and the other half was across the road on the other. The tunnel was exactly in the middle of the force. As the crow flew, that was three and a half miles of twisting road from Taejon to the 21st Regiment's position. In Dean's mind that was three and a half miles of twisted undefended road that those attempting to fall back from Taejon had to negotiate to reach the 21st Regiment.

"I know we don't have the manpower to cover all this road, but damn, it bothers me to see this exposed. I'm almost positive that they'll get in behind us and set up ambushes all along those miles of road. We'll play the devil attempting to get down to you. He has us fighting his kind of war and has removed us from our kind of war," Dean said.

"Sir?" was all Stephens could say, not understanding the remark. Dean pointed at the map.

"Look—every time he's hit us with a frontal assault and peeled off small elements that get around us and block our avenues to exit with ambushes. We've been trained to fight a war with forces on both sides moving forward together. We haven't adapted to this guerrilla warfare that he's employing. We're roadbound, he's not. He goes over these mountains like a bunch of billy goats avoiding the roads. His soldiers are in much better physical condition than us. Our boys spent too much time playing sports in Japan rather than getting good physical training. And this heat we're getting now just saps what strength they have when they attempt to climb these hills with equipment. I'll bet if we had learned lessons from our grandfathers fighting across the plains against the Indians, we'd be in much better shape. Hell, if we were fighting like the Indians, this operation would be over, but we aren't. We're fighting like we fought on the plains of Europe and that's the wrong approach at this point," Dean said. Stephens didn't say anything as what the general was saying made sense and he was on a roll. Finally Dean paused and stared at the map.

"Sir, how are the ROKs doing? I understand they're to the east of us," Stephens commented.

"The ROKs lost a hell of a lot of officers and noncoms in the first week. Good men that we didn't give the equipment necessary to match their opponent's. What we see in the refugee flow is junior enlisted that are leaderless. On the east side, however, they're giving a good account of themselves. They're being pushed back but not in a mad dash for Pusan. They're making the enemy pay a price every step of the way. No doubt in my mind if we'd properly equipped them, the enemy would still be sitting north of the Han River," Dean speculated. As he did so, Lieutenant Clarke and Captain Rowlands walked in. Rowlands appeared to be anxious.

"What is it, Captain?" Dean asked. He knew this couldn't be good.

"Sir, the recon platoon that Colonel Beauchamp sent up the Nonsan Road has hit an ambush," Roland said, pulling out his map.

"Where?" Dean asked, immediately stepping up to the captain as he opened the map.

"Right here, sir. That's three miles from the bridge," Rowlands noted.

"Get Colonel Meloy on the radio or send a runner. I need that battalion to pick up the pace getting to Taejon," Dean directed, turning to Stephens. "I'm heading back to Taejon. You continue reconstituting. I think we're going to need you sooner than I'd hoped." Before Stephens could respond, Dean was out the door.

THE FIRST PLATOON, 24th Reconnaissance Company, had crossed the bridge and started up the Nonsan Road. The mission was simple…find the enemy and report. The six jeeps armed with .30-cal machine guns and two trucks with infantry seated and facing outward in the rear of the column moved down the road towards Nonsan. They kept the speed to under twenty miles an hour but didn't expect any trouble until they reached Nonsan. First Lieutenant Kevin Brown was the platoon leader and occupied the passenger seat in the second vehicle. Spacing between vehicles was approximately fifty feet. At this point, two weeks into the fight, the platoon was learning the hard way. Approaching a turn in the road, the first vehicle disappeared from Brown's view.

Suddenly, he heard, "Leader Six, Leader Five, tanks two hundred —" The transmission was abruptly stopped with the sound of an explosion. Brown immediately attempted to contact the lead vehicle but already knew what the explosion meant. As if on a signal, the enemy on the high ground overlooking the road opened fire with automatic weapons. Fortunately, only Brown's vehicle and the one behind him were in the kill zone.

"Lucky Six, Leader Six, over," Brown transmitted, hoping the radio would work. It did.

"Leader Six, Lucky Six go ahead."

"Lucky Six, Leader Six, enemy ambush three miles on Nonsan Road," Brown transmitted. His next comment, however, made the hairs on the Love Company commander's neck stand up. "Tanks!"

"Roger, Leader Six. How many?"

"One for sure but suspect more following. They're coming down the road. We're falling back to your location. Out." Immediately the Love Company commander was on the radio, calling Colonel Beauchamp.

GENERAL DEAN DROVE AS FAST at the traffic would allow back to Taejon. The 2nd Battalion, 19th Infantry Regiment, was assembling at the train station and preparing to move out when Dean pulled up. Colonel Meloy was with Lieutenant Colonel McGrail.

"Love Company is in heavy contact. Colonel McGrail, move your battalion to that location immediately. Load those trucks and get moving," Dean yelled as he jumped out of his jeep. "I have two tanks from the 1st Cav coming and will bring them there when they arrive. Get there fast."

Colonel McGrail and the battalion moved as quickly as possible to relieve Love Company. Arriving, McGrail positioned Echo Company on high ground south of the Nonsan Road and Fox Company on the north side. George Company occupied a hill one mile back in a reserve position.

Arriving at Love Company's location, Colonel McGrail noticed that the bridge had not been blown and the enemy was attempting to cross.

"Has the recon platoon crossed back yet?" McGrail asked, approaching the surprised Love Company commander, who was watching the fight and directing artillery fire on those attempting to get across the bridge.

"No, sir, and I haven't had any word from them since their first transmission!" Captain Hendricks shouted above the roar of gunfire. The other sound was the sound of a tank behind their position. McGrail and Hendricks turned to see General Dean pulling up with two light tanks from the 1st Cav Division following him.

"Colonel, can you use them, and where do you want them?" Dean asked.

"Sir, I'm going to position the tanks with one on the north side of the road and one on the south side," McGrail indicated and moved to talk to the tank commanders.

Dean turned to Captain Hendricks. "I want you to take your company, fall back to Taejon and set up a defensive position on the west side of the town. Send the recon platoon back to its parent location. Got that?" he asked.

"Yes, sir," Captain Hendricks said, glad to be pulling back away from this hill and this fight.

SINCE EARLY MORNING, Baker Company, 1st Battalion, 34th Regiment, had been in a fight west of the Kap-ch'on River. They were the westernmost company in the delay and were glad when the word came to pull back. As they did so, the sound of artillery passing over their heads traveling eastward could be heard. The impacting rounds were landing on the Taejon airfield. Colonel Ayres was consolidating his forces on the east side of the river but felt unsecure. He was aware that between his left flank and the right flank of Colonel McGrail, there was a one-mile gap between friendly forces. He just didn't have the manpower to cover the gap and suspected that McGrail didn't either.

"Colonel Beauchamp, Ayres here," he said over the EE-8 field telephone, a bit surprised that he had commo with Beauchamp's command post.

"How are you holding up?" Beauchamp asked.

"Sir, we're holding, but I recommend that we fall back. There's a one-mile gap between us and McGrail. We could very well be cut off from getting back to your location or the town," Ayres said.

"Are they forcing you to pull back at this time?" Beauchamp asked.

"Well, no, sir, but—"

"Then you stay and continue to delay them for as long as you can. Keep me posted," Beauchamp said and hung up.

Hanging up the phone, Ayres had an uneasy feeling about what was in store for the rest of the day. He looked at his watch—1400 hours.

"Leland," Ayres called out to his executive officer, Major Leland R. Dunham.

"Yes, sir," Dunham answered, coming over to where Ayres was seated.

"Leland, I want you to move all the vehicles back to the vicinity of the airfield. Leave one jeep with each of the line companies and two with the heavy weapons and mortars. I don't want those vehicles here if we start taking heavy incoming artillery. I want them to be able to get back here fast, load quickly and pull us out fast."

"Roger, sir, I'll get them moving," Major Dunham said, moving to get the vehicles organized.

McGRAIL HAD BEEN LISTENING to the sounds of a firefight on the flank of Fox Company for the past hour. Each time he spoke to the company commander, he was assured that they were holding their own. What concerned him more was the gap between Fox Company and the 3rd Battalion, 34th Regiment, to the north.

"Colonel Beauchamp, McGrail here. Sir, have you heard from

Ayres about the gap between our units? It's about a mile wide. My Fox Company is north of the road and has been in contact all afternoon. I'm concerned about a force coming through the gap and rolling up my flank," McGrail said over the EE-8 field telephone. Radio communications were spotty at best.

"Colonel Ayres has discussed it with me, but we have no force to commit to that gap at this time. If I get some reinforcements, I'll send them into that gap and make sure it's closed. That's the best we can do for now," Beauchamp said, hoping to reassure the battalion commander.

For the rest of the day only sporadic contacts were reported. Early in the evening, a light rain started, much to the displeasure of the soldiers hunkered down in their foxholes. Intermittent gunfire could be heard, but nothing sustained.

"Hey, Lieutenant," Sergeant Lester whispered to the next foxhole.

"What?" Lieutenant Warren attempted to answer in a whisper. Warren was the platoon leader on the left flank of 3rd Battalion's position.

"I hear tanks moving between us and those guys to our south," Sergeant Lester said.

"Are you sure?" Warren asked, already nervous about the exposed flank.

"Just listen, Lieutenant," Lester said.

Warren rose out of his foxhole. *Damn, that does sound like a tank,* he thought and grabbed his EE-8 field phone.

Within ten minutes, Colonel Ayres was on the phone with Colonel Beauchamp.

"Colonel, we have tanks moving between me and McGrail. They're in the gap between the two of us. We've got to get someone up there. I sent a patrol out, but they've never reported back," Ayres reported. After a brief conversation, Ayres hung up and began considering what to do if the tanks turned on his flank. Beauchamp was also considering his actions.

"XO, let's move the command post back into town," Beauchamp ordered, turning to his executive officer.

Almost immediately, the command post began loading up for the move from the airfield to the town. As the command post was displacing, reports came in that the enemy had been spotted six miles south of Taejon on the Kumsan Road.

"We need some eyes on this to verify the report," Beauchamp told Captain Vann.

"Sir, I'll send Lieutenant George Kristanoff with a nine-man detail to check it out. They should be on the road by 2300. They can take three jeeps," Captain Vann indicated and made the arrangements. Lieutenant Kristanoff loaded the three jeeps with his nine soldiers. Each jeep had a .30-caliber machine gun mounted on a pedestal. Three soldiers were in each vehicle except Kristanoff's, which had an extra soldier manning the vehicle-mounted radio. Driving with blackout lights, the small convoy made its way down the dark road. For forty-five minutes, all appeared to be going okay when Vann's radio suddenly came to life.

"Scout Six, Scout Six, Leader Five, over," said an anxious Lieutenant Kristanoff. Vann could also hear the sound of gunfire—very loud gunfire.

"Leader Five, go ahead."

"Scout Six, roadblock and ambush..." Lieutenant Kristanoff read off the coordinates. Glancing quickly at his map, Vann noted that the location was about six miles down the road.

"Leader Five, roger. Sitrep, over," Vann said. His request, repeated several times, was met with silence. *Damn*, Vann finally said to himself.

Chapter 42
1st Cavalry Division

19 JULY 1950
1st Cavalry Division CP
P'ohang-dong, South Korea

"ATTENTION!" the staff sergeant announced as General Walker entered the building, which had been taken over by the arriving 1st Cavalry Division. Major General Gay was expecting the visit and had his staff assembled to hear the commander of Eighth Army's guidance. The first thing they noticed was the tired expression General Walker was displaying.

"At ease, gentlemen," General Walker quickly stated, and everyone relaxed. General Gay took a couple of steps towards Walker, who extended his hand. "General, you have no idea how happy I am to have you and the 1st Cav here."

"Sir, we're ready to serve," Gay said, pointing to a seat in front of a podium and map. "Sir, I've had the staff put together a briefing on the status of the division."

"Good, let's get started. How are the landings going?" Walker said, taking a seat. Everyone could immediately tell he was not one for pomp and ceremony but liked to get to the facts. General Gay himself stepped behind the podium to give the briefing, which surprised Walker. He'd been expecting the chief of staff or the operations officer to conduct the brief.

"Sir, we're currently offloading ships and conducting the amphibious landings here and should complete that this evening. The 8th Cavalry and part of the 5th Regiment were off on the eighteenth. This typhoon has delayed the offload of the 7th Cavalry Regiment and the 82nd Field Artillery.[1] Once it passes, we'll get the rest offloaded. I've been assured by the shore parties that they'll get everything unloaded as soon as possible," Gay started. Walker just nodded in acknowledgment. This was the first amphibious landing of this conflict, and the Navy had assured General Walker that it would be an excellent rehearsal for a future amphibious landing, but the soldiers weren't aware of that fact.

"Currently the division is at two-thirds of our authorized strength in manpower and equipment. The tanks will be the last offloaded, and those not capable of being manned will be held in our rear motor pool. The same with the artillery. I—" He didn't finish.

"Artillery is never in reserve. If you can't man some tubes I'll get you people to do that," Walker said, and his aide immediately began writing notes. Gay flashed a look at the division artillery officer, Brigadier General Palmer, who allowed a smile to cross his face. "We've lost enough artillery tubes to supply the North Korean Army, so we have plenty of artillery soldiers around playing infantry. We'll get them to you. Your regiments are at two-thirds strength. How are they organized? Two full regiments or three undermanned regiments?"

"Sir, we're organized with three understrength regiments, each with two understrength battalions and three understrength companies per. Each regiment has two batteries of artillery and one tank company. We're also lacking key leadership at the junior officer and senior NCO levels. We had to give up seven hundred noncoms in June and earlier this month to send to the 24th and 25th Divisions. Several platoon leader positions are being filled by noncoms," Gay explained. "We did

---

1. Typhoon Helene prevented offloading until 22 July.

receive fourteen hundred replacements before we left Japan, of which one hundred came from the stockade. The rest were shaken out of sports teams, recreation centers, and other hiding places."

"That seems to be a common theme in this damn war," Walker grumbled and waved his hand for Gay to continue.

"Sir, logistically we have our basic load of ammunition and class one, three and five.[2] We don't have the new 3.5-inch bazooka but the older 2.6-inch," Gay said.

"Shitcan them! They're worthless against the enemy tanks, we're hearing. I've notified Washington and MacArthur's headquarters that we need the new, more powerful bazooka and they should be issued to you before you head out. Until they arrive, we're wasting lives against the tanks with those worthless pieces of crap," Walker said. Again his aide was taking notes. "How soon can you move up on the line?"

This question caught Gay a bit by surprise. "Sir, I'd like a couple of weeks to run some training exercises and acclimate the soldiers to the climate here," Gay said, looking over at his operations officer, who looked equally confused.

"Excuse me, sir, but on nine July I met with General MacArthur and his staff and was told we would be conducting an amphibious landing in August or early September. I—"

"You ain't got a couple of weeks. I want you moving in the morning. And forget that amphibious stuff for now. We've got to stabilize this front or there will be no amphibious landings. This will be the American version of Dunkirk. The 24th is in serious trouble up at Taejon. I want you to establish a position south of Yongdong and allow them to pass through. They're pretty beat up. General Dean is fighting for his life at this point," Walker outlined. Getting up, he moved to the map and pointed out where he wanted the division to go. "Any questions?"

"What is the enemy situation, sir?" Gay asked. "And where is Yongdong?"

"They're pouring down from the north. Yongdong is forty kilome-

---

2. Class I supply is food; Class III is medical supplies; Class V is ammunition.

up the road. Typical tactic is to fix your front lines with overwhelming infantry, artillery and armor while their additional infantry infiltrates around your flanks and sets up roadblocks and ambushes behind you. Dean is facing the 3rd and elements of the 4th North Korean Divisions. He was holding for a day at the Kim River until they got over and behind him. He then set up a defense around Taejon, where he is right now, but I need to pull them back and replace with you. Get to Yong-dong and relieve him," Walker ordered.

Stunned, General Gay glanced at his staff, who were equally dumb-founded and exchanging looks. "Sir, I could get the 5th Regiment started now to Taejon and the 8th tomorrow if we have transportation. I'll have General Palmer, my artillery commander, take them up along with a tactical CP and control the operation."

"Do it, and keep me posted," Walker said as he stood. "I'll have my G-2 get with your G-2 and give them an intel update.

After Walker left, his G-2 intelligence officer, Colonel Blankenship, sought out the 1st Cav G-2. Colonel Blankenship had studied up on the North Korean armed forces, reading all the material he could get his hands on. There wasn't much material about them. He did under-stand the tactics that they were employing, as outlined by Walker in his discussion with Gay. Colonel Harmon had served in the division in World War II in the Pacific. He was considered a legacy on the staff for all his years in the division. They had known each other from previous assignments in their Army careers. Approaching what was probably a bedroom in the Korean house that the 1st Cav staff had been given, Blankenship coughed to announce his arrival as Harmon was reading something with his back to the doorway.

"Don't tell me I have to listen to you preach to me," Harmon said without turning around.

"You do unless you want to step on your dick as usual. How the hell you doing?" Blankenship said, entering the room and removing his hat. Harmon stood and turned, extending his hand with a broad grin.

"Doing good. How's the family?" Harmon asked, shaking Blanken-ship's hand and motioning towards two empty chairs.

"Doing good. My boy is entering West Point this year. And yours?"

"Good. My daughter is getting married in the fall. I was hoping to be there but am having my doubts now," Harmon said, pausing for a moment. "What can you tell me?"

"I can tell you that I would make no plans to attend the wedding. The North Koreans are showing themselves to be tougher than we thought. First, they've been well equipped by the Soviets and have Soviet advisors with them. Their T-34 tanks are superior and our 2.36-inch bazookas bounce off them. We've got to get the new 3.5-inch bazookas over here. Second, they're in top physical condition. They run up and down these hill like a bunch of billy goats. Only their tanks will be on the roads. The infantry will be on the high ground along the roads. Third, they're experts at ambushes from those hilltops. Fourth, they mostly use burp guns with one-hundred-round drums, and at close range, that's a lot of firepower. Fifth, they're masters at infiltration. Sixth, they precede most major attacks with an intense artillery barrage. And lastly, there are a lot of them and they don't take prisoners," Blankenship outlined.

"Damn, what are their weaknesses?" Harmon asked, hoping for some good news.

"Well, they don't have any air cover. Our Air Force has pretty much controlled the sky since the opening days. But airpower alone isn't stopping them. Their logistics support appears to be a bit behind the curve as they police up any of our supplies they can get their hands on from food to medical supplies to clothing. Yeah, some of them are wearing US uniforms, which has made them effective in setting up the ambushes to some extent. They'll dress as the locals in the traditional white clothes that the farmers wear and get through your lines," Blankenship said.

"What's their disposition now across Eighth Army?" Harmon asked, moving to a map that hung from the wall. Blankenship followed.

"Okay, starting over on the eastern seaboard, the 5th North Korean Division has been moving south along the coast from the start. The 3rd ROK Division has been making them pay a price. The 5th commenced the operation with a couple of amphibious landings south of the South

Koreans, who've done a decent job of fighting and conducting a delay action, falling back in order. They're fighting around the town of Yongdok right now. Some days the South has the town; other days the North owns it. Naval gunfire is helping the South over there." Blankenship pointed out a location on the map as Harmon jotted down some notes.

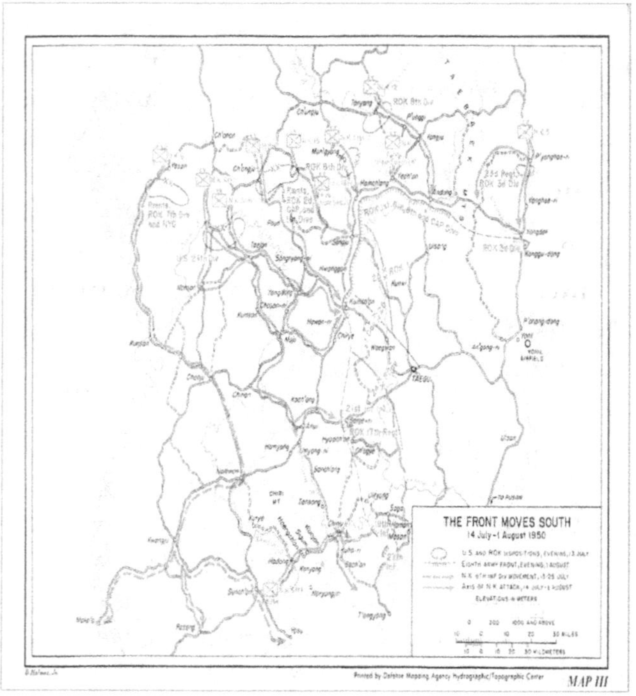

"WEST OF THE 3rd South Korean Division is the Capital Division and the 8th, 6th and 1st ROK Divisions or what's left of them on the south side of the Naktong River, all the way around to here at Kumch'on. The 25th Division's sector is on the left flank of the 1st ROK Division with their left flank just north of Kumch'on. The division CP is in Yongdong and forward elements are fighting for their lives in Taejon at this time. The North Koreans commenced a major attack this morning with elements of the 3rd and 4th Divisions," Blankenship said as he traced his finger along the river to the west and followed it south.

"That's a pretty broad front," Harmon said with a bit of surprise.

"It is, but it's also the most defensible terrain as the river is wide and deep for the most part along there. There are a few sandbars, but the water is high right now with the recent rains…another week or so and it'll be down, unfortunately."

"Okay, so who's south of Kumch'on?" Harmon asked.

"Not much. The ROK 17th Regiment is in the far south," Blankenship said, pausing for a moment. "Opposing us at this point are the 5th North Koreans back up here in the east and the 12th North Korean Division moving south towards Andong. The North Korean 8th Division is at Yech'on. The 1st North Korean is reinforced with tanks and is moving on Hamch'ang. The 13th Division and the 15th Division are driving on Sangju. The 2nd and 3rd Divisions are heading for Kumch'on. The 4th is moving towards Sanje-ri and in a very round-about way, and the 6th is heading for Kuho-ri and Sach'on," Blankenship said, reluctantly turning towards Harmon.

"Damn, that's a lot of stuff. How accurate is your intel?" Harmon asked.

"Pretty accurate. The prisoners we've been getting are pretty open about what unit they're in and where they're going. Also freely talk about supply issues and morale, which does still appear to be good. They do love eating our C rations and will sing like a bird for a meal," Blankenship added.

Harmon studied the map for a few more moments noting the road network and the mountainous terrain. "Okay, where do you think the old man is going to put us?"

"Right here," Blankenship said, pointing at a spot on the map. "In fact, since we've been talking, I'll bet your lead elements have already moved out. You'll be going in between the 25th Division and the 24th Division, and he wants your lead elements to push out to meet the enemy at Yongdong. They'll have the mission to delay for as long as possible."

"What do we know about this enemy unit—the 3rd, you said?" Harmon asked.

"Well, I know they're the unit that's going through the 24th like shit through a goose up along the Kum River at Taejon. They're about sixty percent strength at this point with plenty of our artillery that they've captured. We'll be lucky if we get many out of Taejon before it falls," Blankenship said.

"In that case, I best go brief the old man and the lead regiments," Harmon said, grabbing his helmet and map.

"Wish I had better news for you. Be careful," Blankenship said as he and Harmon walked out.

Chapter 43
Move Out

19 July 1950
5th Cav Regiment
P'ohang-dong, South Korea

COLONEL HILL STOOD next to his jeep and watched as the lead elements of the regiment obeyed the recently issued order to move towards Taejon and Yongdong to relieve the 24th Infantry Division. Most of his regiment was still coming ashore from the transport troop carrier that had delivered them to P'ohang-dong, a less-than-impressive place requiring over-the-beach offloading. Located eighty miles northeast of Pusan, it didn't have the congestion and traffic nor the dockage that Pusan had. After he was ashore, he was told movement to Yongdong could be accomplished much quicker. *Where the hell is Yongdong?* he asked himself.

Hill was an infantry officer who had started the Big War as a captain. He had served his whole time in the Pacific and was well acquainted with the Oriental mind and tactics. Despite what others were saying, he knew that this wasn't going to be easy. As he studied the 1:50,000 scale maps of the region he had been handed that morning coming ashore, he almost shuddered. Having been told they were landing at Inchon, he had only this morning received the change in plans and the maps for this new region. What he was looking at was a map written in Japanese as there were no US maps of the area. He also noted that there was no flat ground anywhere on the map. The map was a gray mass of contour lines all tightly packed together, indicating the entire area was all steep hills and mountains. *This terrain is going to kick our ass*, he was thinking. He knew his soldiers weren't in the best physical condition, and this was going to test them to the limits of their endurance. *This terrain is going to keep us pretty much roadbound, and according to the intel weenies the enemy isn't restricted to the roads. We've got to control those hilltops*, he thought as he studied the map. His thoughts were interrupted by a jeep stopping next to his vehicle as a OH-13 medevac helicopter flew over. He had heard about them but hadn't seen one before.

General Charles D. Palmer's vehicle came to a halt as the general stepped out. A tall, stocky-built man, he was the division artillery commander. Graduating from West Point, he came from a line of general officers in his family. "Colonel, are your boys ready to move?" Palmer asked.

"Sir," Hill said, coming to attention and rendering the proper salute, which Palmer casually returned. "They are, and the 1st Battalion has already started down the road. We're short vehicles, so it's a shuttle run, but I expect we'll close sometime tonight south of Yongdong."

"Good, I'll get up there and coordinate with the 24th Division CP at Okch'on and have a plan laid out when your boys start arriving. The Eighth will come up tomorrow and we'll have enough trucks and a train to get them there quick and orderly. I'll see you up there tomorrow with the rest of the 5th," Palmer said.

"Sir, when do you think the 7th will get up there?" Tom asked.

"Not sure. They haven't docked, and with this typhoon bearing down on the country, it's not clear when they can get alongside and dock. Could be a couple of days. As soon as they can, we'll get them up there with us. Until I see you tomorrow...," Palmer concluded, climbing back into his jeep and directing his driver to move out.

Arriving at the 24th Division at Och'on, General Palmer met with the acting division commander, General Pearson Menoher, the division artillery officer. They had known each other for several years and had served together in previous assignments.

"Pearson, how you doing?" Palmer asked, walking into the CP.

"A lot better now that you're here. How soon can you relieve us?" Menoher asked.

"Damn, let's cut to the chase," Palmer said with a degree of surprise. "My lead regiment is on the road as we speak and moving forward. Two regiments should be closed in by tomorrow night. My third regiment's still aboard ship until this storm passes," Palmer outlined.

"Do you have any tanks available?" Pearson asked.

"Yeah, there's a tank company with each regiment," he responded, now a bit concerned.

"Good, I need them right now to push into Taejon and escort a convoy out. It's about twenty miles and there are a couple of tough spots along the route. Can they get up there?" Pearson said, pointing at the road on the map leading up to Taejon and the positions of the 21st Regiment between Yongdong and Taejon. The 21st was on high ground four miles northwest of Yongdong, overlooking the Kum River and the main road highway bridge to Yongdong.

"Yeah, we'll get them heading that way right now," Palmer said, turning to his G-3, who was writing some notes in preparation for issuing the order. Pearson showed visible relief when the order was issued. Palmer had noticed another colonel standing off to the side during this first conversation. Finally, curiosity got the best of him.

"Who are you, Colonel?" Palmer asked.

"I'm sorry," Pearson interrupted. "I should have introduced you. This is Colonel MacLean, Eighth Army G-3."

"How do you do, sir?" MacLean said, standing up straighter.

"Fine, Colonel, and what brings you up here?" Palmer asked.

"Sir, I have your instructions for the positioning of your units around Yongdong. If you would, sir...," MacLean said, moving to the map. He pointed at the hills around Yongdong. "Sir, we want you to position one battalion on this hill four miles northwest of Yongdong on the south side of the Kum River, replacing the 21st Regiment that's there now. From here he can cover the approach on the Taejon-Taegu road. Another battalion we want placed on this hill two miles southwest of the town, which will allow him to cover the Chosan-ni–Muju–Kumsan Road," MacLean said.

Palmer initially said nothing but moved closer and studied the map. As Colonel Hill had earlier realized, everywhere there was a hilltop. After a moment, General Palmer stepped back and looked directly at Colonel MacLean.

"Let me see if I'm understanding this correctly. You're ordering me to position two battalions at these two locations. Two locations that offer no mutual support to the other due to distance and terrain. Two locations that the enemy can easily bypass and get behind, isolating both battalions. Am I understanding this correctly? Please tell me I missed something," Palmer said.

"Well, sir, these positions will deny the enemy the use of the roads," MacLean explained.

"Colonel, his tactics don't put him on the roads. He's a frickin' mountain goat and stays on the high ground. No, we'd be better served placing the division on this line of hills east of Yongdong and have the 24th withdraw through those lines," Palmer outlined.

"No, sir, that will not do. Eighth Army has already issued you the order to position your battalions on these two hills," MacLean said. "You're free to position the other battalions as you see fit, sir."

"Colonel, that's about the stupidest thing I've heard in a long time. Get Eighth Army on the line and confirm this order or I'm not executing this," Palmer said.

While they waited for a confirmation from Eighth Army, General Gay arrived. General Palmer explained the situation to him and he concurred—what Eighth Army was directing was incredibly stupid. General Palmer went over the plan he had for the division. Although everywhere was a hilltop in this mountainous terrain, a distinctive ridgeline was just east of Yongdong. He pointed out his plan that the division should occupy the ridgeline with three regiments abreast and a small reserve. The 24th could then pass through. This would allow for mutual support as well as minimize the actions of infiltrators getting into the rear area. Gay concurred.

"Excuse me, sir," MacLean said, approaching the two general officers. "Here's what I believe you're expecting." He handed a message to General Gay, who read the short message quickly.

"You've got to be shitting me. This is bullshit!" Gay said in frustration. "Someone has their head so far up their ass—"

"Sir, I'm just the messenger," MacLean said in his defense as Gay turned and looked at the map.

"Eighth Army headquarters sits in Tokyo, a thousand miles away, and looks at a one-over-the-world map and has all the answers. They're thinking European plans for maneuver warfare and not this terrain," Gay said in frustration. "Okay, let's order the 5th to take up a position on this ridgeline east of Yongdong. When the Eighth gets here tomorrow, have 1st Battalion go up on the Taejon Road and have the 2nd Battalion go in southeast of the town on this hill…until I can get General Walker in here and show him the stupidity of these positions," Gay said for MacLean's benefit.

Chapter 44
Take Up Positions

20 July 1950
  8th Cav Regiment
  Yongdong, South Korea

THE 5TH CAV Regiment minus had moved onto the ridgeline overlooking Yongdong the previous evening. Only part of the regiment had arrived, with the remainder moving up this morning. The 8th Cav Regiment had arrived as well with a combination of trucks and rail dropping off the 1st and 2nd Battalion in the town of Yongdong. General Gay arrived as the 2nd Battalion under the command of Lieutenant Colonel Eugene Field was moving towards its assigned position. Lieutenant Colonel Robert Kane, commander of the 1st Battalion, 8th Cav Regiment, was discussing their dispositions and watching the soldiers moving to their respective defensive positions. Both officers came to attention and saluted.

"Gentlemen, let's drop the formality of saluting in the field. Never know when a sniper may be lurking about," Gay said as the two junior officers dropped their salutes. "How do you feel about your assignments, truthfully?"

"Sir, truthfully, it sucks. We have no mutual defense and are stuck out on the end of the division. We have an enemy noted for hitting with a frontal attack to fix forces in place and then flanking to set up roadblocks," Kane said.

"I feel the same way, sir," Field indicated.

"Can't say I blame you, but we didn't have any control over this one. Eighth Army directed this. Field, I'm going to beef you up a bit as you're the furthest west in this situation. A Battery, 92nd Anti-Aircraft, is going to be attached to you. He's bringing quad .50 machine guns and 37mm anti-aircraft guns. That should help you some. Also, priority of fires from the 77th Field Artillery Battalion is to you, and the battalion commander should be here shortly to coordinate with you. Bob, they'll be in position to support you as well if you need it," Gay explained. "When you arrive, you will be replacing elements of the 21st Regiment. Get with the commander up there and look at how he's laid out his defense. Modify it as you see fit."

"Sir, who is the BC for the 77th?" Kane asked.

"That'd be Lieutenant Colonel William Harris. Good man. He'll give you just what you need in the way of support," Gay said, pausing. "Okay, it's paramount that we do not allow the enemy to get around and behind you. I'm going to position the 5th Cav Regiment east of Yongdong to keep them from doing that. If they do get behind you, the 5th will come up and clean them out. Your focus is to the front. If you see them maneuvering around you, I need to know about it ASAP. Understood?"

Both responded, "Understood, sir."

"Good, let me know if you need anything. We may shift things when the 7th gets up here, whenever that will be...this damn typhoon."

Having concluded their meeting with General Gay, the commanders joined their respective battalions. Lieutenant Colonel Kane had his jeep driver start up the road, which was on the southern side of the river. His assigned position was a hill mass approximately four miles northwest of Yongdong and overlooking the Kum River and a major bridge. A tributary from the Kum River to Yongdong paralleled the highway on the north side of the road. A road bridge crossed this tributary about a klick east of his position and connected with the road to

Yongdong. High ground on the north side of the river/highway domi-nated the lower hills on the south side.

As Kane surveyed his sector with his S-3 operations officer, Major Carlson, and Colonel Stephens, the 21st Regiment commander, he was concerned about the road from the north crossing the tributary, and he told them so.

"There's an ROK division on your flank. They've been putting up a pretty good fight. I wouldn't worry too much about that approach, but I would guard it," Stephens said. This would have to be watched as the enemy could cross the Kum River farther to the north and drive down into his flank. Between the tributary in this area and the main road were rice paddies offering no cover or concealment for antitank teams.

In the center of his sector overlooking the Kum River was Hill 246. It offered good observation of the river and fields of fire as well as a commanding view of the main highway bridge at Sanggo-dong. Again, permission to destroy was denied as the remaining elements of the 24th Division at Taejon still needed to get back across.

"What about the bridge of the Kum River?" Kane asked.

"I have engineers down there right now rigging that bridge to blow it. When the last of the 24th units are across, I'll have them blow it if I'm still here or turn the engineers over to you to finish the job," Stephens indicated.

The river curved around the western end of Hill 246 and turned south with a small village of Komch'on at the bend in the river. The river was wide with no fording sites to observe. The frontage for the battalion was about two kilometers. Kane positioned his three under-strength rifle companies, his headquarters company, and anti-aircraft elements. They were to reinforce the infantry, especially in the vicinity of the northern flank. Antitank teams were positioned to overwatch the main highway bridge and the road crossing the tributary. Kane's main concern was being cut off from Yongdong by enemy forces coming overland from the north.

At the same time, Lieutenant Colonel Field headed southwest for two miles down the road. As he rode, he noticed that the terrain on the west side of the road was higher than the terrain on the east side of the road. The terrain on the east side had more open ground and rice paddies between the scattered hills. Arriving in the vicinity of the village of Chon-dong, he paused his vehicle on the small road bridge. Two streams came together under the bridge, and high ground was on both sides of the road—2nd Battalion, 8th Cav, would defend here, and he began to place his companies.

Lieutenant Colonel Harris, commander of the 77th Field Artillery, had to determine where he could position his artillery to support both battalions. Both were within easy artillery range of Yongdong. The problem in both cases was not so much range as it was elevation. High-angle artillery fire would be required, and that reduced range. He finally selected a firing position that would favor the 1st Battalion but could also support the 2nd Battalion.

As the 1st Cav moved into position, the 21st Regiment was relieved of its responsibility and wasted no time departing the area. Banter was typical among soldiers from different units when one replaced another on the line, only this time, the soldiers of the 21st Regiment didn't say anything but simply stared at the cavalry troopers with dark sunken eyes and filthy faces.

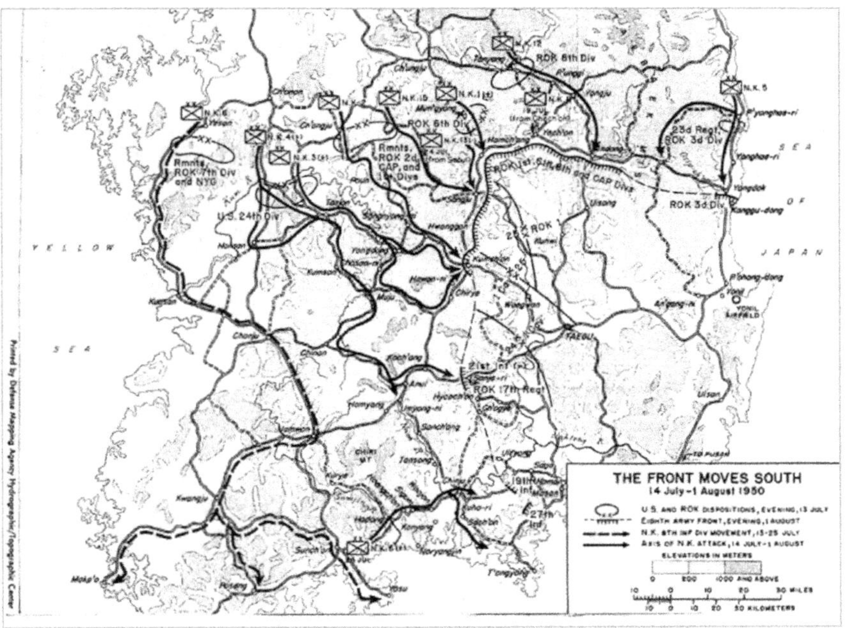

THE FRONT MOVES SOUTH
14 July–1 August 1950
U.S. AND ROK DISPOSITIONS, EVENING, 13 JULY
EIGHTH ARMY FRONT, EVENING, 1 AUGUST
N.K. 6TH INF DIV MOVEMENT, 13–25 JULY
AXIS OF N.K. ATTACK, 14 JULY–1 AUGUST
ELEVATIONS IN METERS
0   200   1000 AND ABOVE
MILES
KILOMETERS
YELLOW SEA
SEA OF JAPAN

Chapter 45
Day Two Defending Taejon

20 July 1950
24th Division
Taejon, South Korea

Coordinating for a relief force to reach Lieutenant Kristanoff's patrol took time, and it was 0300 hours before a platoon from the 24th Reconnaissance Company could depart. Vann patiently awaited word on the progress of the relief force.

"Scout Six, Leader Three, over" came an anxious call. Again Vann could hear loud gunfire in the background.

"Leader Three, go ahead."

"Scout Six, Leader Three, we're at the roadblock reported earlier. Taking heavy fire. I can see Leader Four. They're all KIA, it appears. Over." Vann had suspected this but was hoping that it wouldn't be so.[1]

---

1. Actually, First Lieutenant Kristanoff was captured and marched to North Korea, where he perished in a POW camp. He was promoted to captain and posthumously awarded the Silver Star for his actions. "Cpt. George W. Kristanoff," Korean War Project, https://www.koreanwar.org/html/16448/korean-war-project-minnesota-o-1336515-cpt-george-walter-kristanoff/.

Captain Vann's report was only one report amongst many that was coming into the 34th Regiment at this time.

"Sir, they just overran the forward outposts," the 1st Battalion S-2 yelled as he came running into the battalion command post. He had spent the night at the outpost. It was 0300. The sound of small-arms fire could be heard across the entire front of the 1st Battalion. Reports were initially coming over the field phones until the enemy found the wires and cut them. The only area that seemed quiet was on the left flank, where Charlie Company was positioned.

"Sir, Able Company is reporting the enemy is coming down the road with tanks leading and infantry on both sides for the road," Ayres's operations officer, Major Thorn, reported.

"Have they broken through his lines?" Ayres asked, fearful of the answer.

"The tanks have, but we have antitank teams along the road that should be able to stop them. They have that new 3.5-inch bazooka," Major Thorn said.

"Let's hope they do," Ayres commented. As he attempted to monitor the radio messages that were sporadically being transmitted, he noticed infantry soldiers clustering around the command post.

"Master Sergeant," Ayres called out to the command post NCOIC.

"Sir," the NCOIC responded.

"Who the hell are all these people?" Ayres asked.

"Sir, they're line dogs that have fallen back. They've been pushed back by the commies."

Crap. No wonder I can't get any of the line company commanders. They're all falling back. Shit. We can't hold here, he thought as the situation continued to deteriorate.

"Major Dunham, Major Thorn, on me." Ayres took the two majors aside. "Look, we can't hold here and the line is collapsing. Tanks will be breaking through any minute with infantry on their tail. Dunham, I want you to gather up these men, should be about two hundred, I figure, and I want you to lead them south behind the 2nd of the 19th. If the Nonsan Road to Taejon is open, head into Taejon. If it isn't, then continue on to Musu-ri. We should link up there. Got it?" Ayres directed.

"Yes, sir. I'll get them moving, but what about you?" Dunham asked.

"Major Thorn and I will wait a bit, gather up anyone else that comes in and be right behind you. I'll get a report off to Colonel Beauchamp first. Now get going," Ayres said.

Sitting in the 34th command post in Taejon, Colonel Beauchamp received the report from Colonel Ayres that tanks were approaching Taejon, but Beauchamp had his doubts, nor did Ayres mention that they were pulling out due to the enemy pressure. When he attempted to call Colonel Ayres back for some clarification, the line was dead.

"Three, let's get a commo team up to 1st Battalion and reestablish commo," Beauchamp directed. He glanced at his watch. It was approaching five o'clock. Thirty minutes later, the commo chief reported that they couldn't get up the road due to enemy action. Beauchamp wasn't convinced that they were telling the truth and thought he would go to Ayres's battalion CP himself. With his driver behind the wheel, they started heading west on the Nonsan Road to the intersection with the Yusong-Taejon Road. The sky was still dark in the east and it was a moonless night. Turning the corner at the intersection, Beauchamp's driver slammed on the brakes as his headlights suddenly lit up a tank in the middle of the road. The tank crew was as surprised as Beauchamp and his driver, which saved their lives as it took a moment for the tank crew to open fire with automatic weapons. Beauchamp dove into a ditch on his side of the road and the driver did likewise on the other side. Beauchamp's jeep took the fire from the tank's machine gun.

"Son of a bitch, that hurts," Beauchamp mumbled to himself as a bullet had grazed his arm. Slowly, he began to crawl back towards Taejon, staying in the ditch.

"Hey, buddy, can you be a little bit more quiet?" a voice said in the darkness. Beauchamp froze.

"Who's there?" Beauchamp asked.

"Who's asking?" came the answer out of the darkness.

"Colonel Beauchamp, 34th Regiment commander. Who the hell are you?"

"Oh, sorry, sir. Sergeant Jamison, Charlie Company, 3rd Engineer Combat Battalion."

"What are you doing out here, Sergeant?" Beauchamp asked.

"Sir, we're an antitank hunter-killer team. We have two teams out right now. The other team is in the ditch on the other side of the road. We haven't seen any tanks yet."

"Well, Sergeant Jamison, follow me and I'll give you a tank," Beauchamp said, crawling back toward where the tank was sitting astride the road. *Gads, I'm no longer in command of a regiment but doing a squad leader's job*, Beauchamp thought as he crawled along through the mud and muck. When he looked over the top of the ditch, the tank sat ten yards in front of him.

Motioning to the man with the bazooka to come forward, Beauchamp pointed out the tank in the darkness, which was fairly obvious. The first shot hit the tank squarely in the turret and the lower driver's hatch immediately opened, with the driver scrambling out of the tank. This was followed by two more soldiers exiting the tank. Much to everyone's surprise, a second bazooka was fired from the far side of the road and a second tank that Beauchamp hadn't noticed exploded behind the first. Satisfied with two tank kills and three prisoners, Beauchamp concluded that this road intersection was in good hands. Now he and his driver just needed to walk back to the regimental CP, a mile back in Taejon.

Arriving back at his command post, Beauchamp first grabbed a cup of coffee. "Have we had any word from Ayres?" Beauchamp asked in general.

"Sir, we heard from him a while ago and all is good in the 1st Battalion sector," Colonel Wadlington answered. "What do you want to do about the gap between Ayres and McGrail?"

"Let's send Kilo Company reinforced with a portion of Mike

Company to close the gap. Contact Ayres and notify him that Kilo will be attached to him," Beauchamp replied.

"I'll get them moving right away," Wadlington responded and began writing an order. "We've been having trouble with commo with 1st Battalion, so the first Ayres may know of this is when Kilo Company arrives. I'll notify Major Lantron to get them moving," he added. Major Lantron was the battalion commander.

Lieutenant Colonel Ayres had been moving for a couple of hours with his small band following Major Dunham's party. He was concerned that he hadn't been able to notify the regiment that he was pulling out of his position and moving south. He had hoped that a messenger he'd sent back to regiment had delivered the message. He'd told the messenger he could find the regiment CP at the airfield. It wasn't there.

SERGEANT FIRST CLASS Robert E. Dare was a platoon leader in Kilo Company. He hadn't started out as the platoon leader but as a platoon sergeant, until his lieutenant had managed to get himself killed at the Kum River. Dare felt bad for the young officer, who'd attempted to rally his men against overwhelming odds and paid a price for his action. The ultimate price. Instead of a platoon at full strength, Dare found himself with about half the platoon, twenty-five men, all exhausted and scared from retreating for the past two weeks. But he started to see some resolve in their attitudes. They were tired of retreating and were showing more enthusiasm now that they were moving forward on the offense. Having left Taejon and moved up the road to the airfield, they would then swing to the west and ideally hit the flank of an enemy breach. They passed the three disabled tanks that Colonel Beauchamp was involved with destroying, and that alone raised morale. The platoon was the lead platoon in Kilo Company and was on both sides of the road, walking in single file. As they crested a low hill, the first burst of machine-gun fire killed the first four men. Then the entire hill opened fire. They had walked into an ambush. Without being told, soldiers dove into the drainage ditches on both sides of the road. Initially Dare was down with everyone else but assessing the situation.

"Kilpatrick Six, Kilpatrick One, over," Dare yelled into his radio.

"Kilpatrick One, Six, what is your situation?" the company commander asked.

"Six, this is One. Ambush. Appears to be a battalion of infantry along this ridgeline. Over." As Dare spoke, he could hear the sound of enemy weapons engaging the company to his rear.

"Roger, One, hold your position" was the company commander's order. Dare was not impressed with the company commander and had always thought of him as a weak leader. He observed his soldiers returning fire at the muzzle flashes that appeared all along the ridgeline. He knew that he was going to have to move his soldiers back even before he heard the sound. The T-34 tank makes a distinctive sound with its tracks pounding the roadway. The sound of several could be heard moving up the backside of the hill.

"Kilpatrick Six, Kilpatrick One, over!" Dare yelled into the receiver.

"Kilpatrick One, Six, go ahead."

"Six, One, we have tanks coming down the road. I'm withdrawing. Out." Dare didn't wait for an order from the commander, nor did he want to have a discussion about them. Turning to his platoon, he yelled, "Fall back to the crossroads. Move!" He didn't need to repeat the command as the platoon immediately started crawling and jogging hunched over to the rear. Dare didn't. He stayed and continued to engage the enemy machine guns that were attempting to rake his soldiers as they retreated. Kilo Company never made it to close the gap, withdrawing to the previous location of the 3rd Battalion well east of the airfield.[2]

---

2. For his actions, SFC Robert E. Dare was posthumously awarded the Distinguished Service Cross.

"COLONEL," the young radio operator called out. When Beauchamp turned, he said, "Sir, just got word from 1st Battalion that all's quiet in their sector now."

"Thank you," Beauchamp said, turning to Wadlington. "Makes me feel a whole lot better. I guess sending Kilo Company up there solved that problem." Wadlington wasn't so sure but said nothing.

Turning back to the radio operator, Beauchamp told him to get the 3rd Battalion commander, Major Lantron, on the radio. "I think congratulations to Lantron are in order for Kilo Company's actions."

"Sir, 3rd Battalion reports that they can't locate Major Lantron," the soldier reported a moment later with a puzzled expression.

"Tell them to have him call me when he comes back," Beauchamp said dismissively.

"No, sir. They say they've been looking for him and they can't find him," the radio operator said.

"Give me the mike," Beauchamp said, reaching for it. "This is Colonel Beauchamp. Where is Major Lantron and who is this?"

"Sir, this is Captain Jack Smith, executive officer. Major Lantron got in his jeep at 0930 and we haven't seen or heard from him since." Beauchamp glanced at his watch. It read 1100 hours. *Where the hell could he have gone?*[3]

"Alright, Captain Smith, you're in command of the 3rd Battalion until you find the major, and when you do, let me know."

LIEUTENANT COLONEL MCGRAIL had been awake most of the night with scattered engagements. Easy Company was holding his side of the road with little difficulty, but Fox Company was struggling with its exposed flank. As the morning wore on, McGrail saw Fox Company slowly being pushed back from the military crest to the hill to the crest of the hill. He also noted a body of men moving behind Fox Company and became concerned until he realized they were American forces.

---

3. Major Lantron was taken prisoner.

Approaching the group, he was met by Major Dunham. "Morning, sir, Major Dunham, 1st Battalion." The group of about two hundred men paused while the lieutenant colonel and major talked. They were halted just west of the bridge over the Yudung River.

"Where are you going, Major, and where is Colonel Ayres?"

"Sir, Colonel Ayres is bringing up the rear and anyone we can find. We were overrun and are making our way here and will now take the Nonsan Road to Taejon," Major Dunham explained.

"I don't think so. There are enemy tanks between us and Taejon, reportedly at the Nonsan-Yusong intersection. I'd recommend that you head south to Kuwan-ni and Musu-ri," McGrail offered.

"Sir, do you know what the enemy situation is south of Taejon?"

"Major, I can only speculate, but if he's holding true to form, he probably has infiltrators scattered south of the town."

"Okay, thanks, sir. I'll take my people towards Kuwan-ni. When Colonel Ayres comes through, would you pass that on to him? I haven't had any commo with him since we left." Dunham requested.

"Sure will, and we probably won't be far behind you. My Fox Company has already started falling back. Good luck to you," McGrail said, extending his hand, which Dunham accepted.

An hour later, Ayres approached McGrail on the west side of the bridge, which was now under machine-gun fire.

"How much longer are you going to hold here?" Ayres asked.

"Just as soon as Fox Company gets here, we're pulling out and heading to Musu-ri. As soon as Fox clears Easy Company, they'll fall back through George. My George Company will wait until Easy is clear and then fall back to Musu-ri as well. Your XO passed through here an hour ago and is heading that way as well but first to Kuwan-ri, then into Musu-ri."

"Have you had comms with Regiment?" Ayres asked.

"No. The commies are jamming the airwaves. We haven't been able to get through at all. How about you?"

"I sent a messenger back but don't know if he got to regiment," Ayres said. "My vehicle was shot up, so my radios weren't working, I don't think, and we had to abandon a lot of equipment. I think we destroyed most of the commo gear." As the two commanders talked, the sounds of gunfire could be heard from the vicinity of the crossroads as well as smoke. "Before we pull out, I've got to get the wounded back to Taejon," McGrail said and looked around. "Lieutenant Herbert!" he called out, eyeing the young officer.

"Sir," Lieutenant Robert L. Herbert replied, jogging up to the commander.

"Lieutenant, I want you to take Second Platoon and move down the road to Taejon and open the road if you encounter any enemy. We've got to have the road open to get the wounded out. Can you do it?" McGrail asked.

"Yes, sir. I'll leave right away," Herbert answered, glad to move away from the river. Gathering his platoon, he gave a quick operations order and they moved out on both sides of the road in a tactical march formation. The distance was a little over a mile and a half. A railroad line crossed the road at the one-mile mark, and Lieutenant Herbert came upon a group of Americans. An officer with captain's bars on his collar approached him.

"Who are you, Lieutenant, and where are you going?" the captain asked.

"Sir, Lieutenant Herbert, Second Platoon, G Company. We're clearing the road to Taejon. And you are, sir…?"

"Baker Company, 1st Battalion. We're moving south to join the rest of our battalion," the captain indicated.

"Sir, I saw Colonel Ayres back at our CP less than an hour ago. He said he was moving to Kuwan-ri and then on to Musu-ri," Herbert replied.

The captain quickly withdrew his map and started looking at distance and direction. "Thank you, Lieutenant. That's most helpful," the captain said and turned to his company, who were filling canteens from a small stream. "Alright, mount up. First Platoon in the lead, followed by Second and then Third. Keep your eyes peeled. Move out, First Platoon," the captain ordered, and with heads hung low, the soldiers began the trek south into the mountains.

Lieutenant Herbert continued on the road towards Taejon.

Suddenly, his patrol came to a halt and, facing outward, took a knee. He ran forward to see why the column was stopped. Reaching the lead squad leader, he asked, "What'cha got?"

"Sir, there's someone about a hundred yards up ahead on the left side hiding behind those logs on the side of the road," the squad leader pointed out. "I just saw them briefly and couldn't tell if they were friendly or not."

"Okay, set up a base of fire and I'll take Second Squad with me to check it out," Herbert said, motioning the Second Squad leader to join him. Before the Second Squad could move up, an individual stood behind the logs and raised his weapon above his head.

"Sir, I think they're friendly," the first squad leader said.

"I'm not taking any chances until I can clearly see them. Wave him forward. Everyone stay down," Herbert ordered. Slowly, three individuals emerged from behind the log pile and began walking towards the platoon. Finally, Herbert could see they were Caucasians and not Orientals dressed in US uniforms.

Standing, Herbert approached them. "Who are you guys?"

"Sir, damn glad to see you. I'm Sergeant Little and this is Corporal King and Private Ford. We're from Charlie Company, 3rd Engineers, and have set up an ambush site with the new bazooka. We got two tanks earlier today when a Colonel Beauchamp was with us. What's the situation at the river bridge?"

"Everyone's falling back. You best join us and come along to town. We heard there were several tanks coming down the Yusong Road towards the intersection."

"Sir, it was at the intersection that we killed two tanks," Sergeant Little offered.

"How far is it?"

"Just over the rise about two hundred yards is all," King said.

"Alright, let's move out," Herbert said and gave the hand signal for everyone to follow.

Approaching the intersection, they came across the two burned-out tanks. As he was examining them, a US jeep approached on the

Nonsan Road, coming to a halt. Herbert recognized the driver and walked over to the vehicle.

"Hey, sir, Lieutenant Herbert." He didn't salute for fear a sniper might observe him and realize that the driver was a senior officer.

"Herbert, have you run into any trouble?" asked Captain Montesclaros, assistant S-3, 2nd Battalion, 19th Infantry.

"No, sir. We met and picked up an antitank team from the 3rd Engineers that killed these two earlier today," Herbert responded. "What are you doing here?"

"Battalion hasn't been able to raise regiment on the radio, so I'm taking a message to Colonel Beauchamp. When you've cleared the road, continue to the regimental CP for further instructions," Montesclaros instructed and drove off towards town.

Reaching the outskirts, he came upon a pair of jeeps and pulled up. He noticed General Dean sitting in one of the vehicles.

"Sir, Captain Montesclaros, assistant S-3, 2nd of the 19th."

"Captain, how you doing? How is the 2nd Battalion doing?"

"Sir, we're holding the bridge. What are your instructions, sir?"

"Hell, Captain, I'm not in charge. Colonel Beauchamp is running this show. You're going to need to talk to him for instructions," Dean said, almost laughing. "Follow me and we'll head over to the regimental CP," he added and gave the signal for everyone to mount up.

The drive was short, but Beauchamp wasn't present when they arrived. Wadlington took Montesclaros's report and wrote out a message for McGrail, which Montesclaros took and drove back to the battalion CP location. Except, no one was there. The site was empty except for a dead North Korean soldier. *What the—?* Montesclaros was thinking as he walked around the deserted site. Silence was all about him. No birds, no sounds of battle, just dead silence. It put a chill up his spine, and he decided to drive back to Taejon.

He had only gone a short distance when he came across elements of Easy Company. They told him they were falling back to Taejon to the new battalion location, which confused Montesclaros as he should have passed them on his return trip. He had driven almost to the edge of Taejon when he spotted a familiar face.

"Hey, Lieutenant Weigle. Where the hell is the colonel?" Montesclaros asked, stopping his vehicle. Lieutenant Tom Weigle was the battalion S-2.

"Sir, the colonel has relocated. Fox Company finally got pushed off and moved south. Easy Company was moving south behind Fox. George Company was going to pull out behind Easy. The colonel has reestablished the CP at this location," Weigle said, pointing to the new location on his map, which was spread out on the hood of his vehicle. "There's a dirt trail that you can drive partway, but then it's hoofing it to the top of this hill."

"Great. Do you have commo with him?"

"No, sir. He told me to stay here until I found you," Weigle said.

"Well, you found me, so let's get going and see if we can catch up to him." Montesclaros and Weigle started down the Nonsan Road and made the turnoff to the south on an old oxcart trail. Finally they had to stop and leave the vehicles in order to climb a hill where the CP was located, or had been located. Reaching the top, Montesclaros was surprised to find Lieutenant Lindsey from Easy Company.

"Lindsey, what are you doing here? Where the hell is the colonel?" Montesclaros asked with some frustration.

"Sir, we got chased here by some tanks and North Koreans on the road. Come here and you can see them," Lindsey said, leading Montesclaros and Weigle to the opposite side of the hilltop. Looking down, Montesclaros counted six tanks and a battalion of infantry moving towards Taejon on the Nonsan Road.

"So where is the colonel?" Montesclaros asked again.

"Sir, he moved the CP to Musu-ri. We're heading to there to join him and the rest of the battalion, or what's left of it," Lindsey explained. "Colonel Ayres and elements of the 1st of the 34th are with him and moving as well."

"So let me see if I understand this. The two and only two battalions of the 34th Regiment west of Taejon have left their defensive positions and moved south out of the enemy's way. Taejon is wide open to them. Do I have that correctly?" Montesclaros said with a raising voice.

"Sir, that's about right" was all Lindsey could say.

Throughout the morning, enemy tanks had been slipping into Taejon. Some managed to come through the rice paddy fields that weren't covered by friendly forces or forces that had the 3.5-inch bazooka. The tanks were causing chaos and destruction. One reached the field trains of the 2nd Battalion and proceeded to destroy supply trucks, mess trucks and ambulances. The cooks and supply clerks were helpless against these vehicles and could only attempt to find safety. General Dean was aware of the situation when a tank rolled past him without firing a shot. Following the tank, Dean, his aide, Lieutenant Clarke, and his driver, Sergeant Dowd, kept their distance and looked for a bazooka team, which they finally found.

"Alright, let's get into that two-story building and see if we can kill that son of a bitch," Dean said, leading the way. Taking the steps to the second floor two at a time, Dean reached the upper floor first and moved into a room overlooking the street. The tank was almost directly in front of the building with its cannon pointed right at the window that Dean was standing before. Dean motioned the bazooka team into position and they fired in the enclosed room. When the dust in the room cleared, the tank was beginning to burn, but Dean had them fire a second and a third round into the tank to make sure it was destroyed. Lieutenant Clarke and Dowd had remained on the ground floor with Molotov cocktails just in case the bazooka didn't finish the job. They saved their cocktails for later in the day. After his tank-killing expedition, Dean returned to the location of the 34th Regiment command post to confer with Colonel Beauchamp. As the two sat and ate cold C rations, they discussed the situation.

"Sir, we've seen tanks in the town, but not a large contingent of infantry. There are some snipers. The 3rd Battalion, 34th, or what's left of it, has pulled back from the airfield and is located on the north side of town now. One platoon from the 19th has a position on the west side forward of the artillery position. I'm not sure where Ayres and McGrail's battalions are at or what their strengths are. I sent messengers out to them, but they haven't returned," Beauchamp outlined.

"You know I wanted to wait until dark to withdraw from here, but I think it might be prudent to get people out while we can in daylight.

We wait until dark, it's liable to be mass confusion with vehicles going down the road to Och'on," Dean said.

"I agree, sir," Beauchamp said and motioned for Major William T. McDaniel, the regimental S-3, to come over.

"Yes, sir," McDaniel said, approaching the two officers.

"Bill, let's issue the evacuation order to all units effective 1500 today. Get that out anyway you can to all the units," Beauchamp ordered.

"Right away, sir," McDaniel replied and began issuing the order over the radio and telephone. He found two messengers and instructed them, "Find Colonel Ayres and Colonel McGrail and give these orders to them." The messengers departed in jeeps immediately. They were never seen again.

To the east of Yongdong, Colonel Hill moved the 5th Cav Regiment to a high ridgeline due south of the town of Hwang-gan. Some of the highest peaks in the area were located along this ridgeline, which ran north to south and controlled two major roads in the area both moving towards Taegu. From here, he could either reinforce Yongdong or stop any advance east by the enemy—or so he thought.

Chapter 46
Withdrawal from Taejon

20 JULY 1950
34th Regiment
Taejon, South Korea

"COLONEL, as you're running the show now, I'm going to wander around a bit," General Dean said, standing as Colonel Beauchamp oversaw McDaniel issue the withdrawal order. As Dean departed and with Lieutenant Colonel McDaniel on the radio issuing the withdrawal order, Colonel Beauchamp took another call from a forward observer on one of the remaining phone lines.

"Colonel Beauchamp here. Who's this?"

"Sir, Sergeant Waltrip, forward observer. There's a large concentration of troops moving towards Taejon from the east."

"Not to worry, Sergeant. That's the 21st Regiment moving up to cover the tunnels on that road. General Dean gave them the order this morning to cover the tunnels until we get everyone through them later today. Do not adjust fire on them. Understood?" Beauchamp asked.

"Okay, sir. Understood," the sergeant answered in a confused tone and hung up. Beauchamp had a feeling that his presence was needed elsewhere. "McDaniel, have we heard from the convoy that left earlier?" he asked.

"No, sir, I haven't, and no one has indicated that they have," McDaniel said.

"Okay, I'm going out for some air," Beauchamp said, picking up his helmet. Outside, he gave his driver the signal to crank up the jeep.

"Where to, sir?" Sergeant Winters asked. Winters was from Dickson, Tennessee, and had a great sense of humor, which he was not afraid to unload on the colonel.

"I want to look at the road the convoy went down," Beauchamp said, pointing to the east. Winters was well aware of the route through the town to get to the road to Okch'on. Beauchamp glanced at his watch. It was 1500 hours.

Lieutenant Clarke and Sergeant Dowd were sitting in the jeep when Dean walked out and started to stand.

"Keep your seats. I want to stretch my legs a bit. I'm going over to talk to the tactical air control party and see what kind of air support we're getting," Dean said, looking skyward at several aircraft orbiting at altitude. It was a short walk as the tactical air control party was located at the opposite end of a building that had been a school and was now the command post for the 34th Regimental CP.

"Afternoon, gentlemen, and how goes the air war today?" Dean said as he entered, trying to infuse his voice with some levity to raise morale. Everyone stood up, surprised to see him there.

"Sir, Lieutenant Hillery, OIC for the tactical air control party." The tactical air control party consisted of Lieutenant Hillery, two NCOs, a radio repairman and two drivers for the two jeeps. All were Air Force personnel.

"How do you do, Lieutenant? Thought I'd stop by and see how the air strikes are going," Dean stated.

"Well, sir, that's a problem. They aren't. We can't reach anyone with the 2nd of the 19th or the 1st of the 34th. We're getting requests from the 3rd of the 34th and the Recon company, but nothing from the other two. My aircraft are reporting targets moving from the north and west, but we aren't sure where the friendlies are located and there's no one to direct the strikes," Hillery explained.

"Can your planes identify enemy concentrations?"

"Yes, sir, but we're reluctant to put a strike in close to Taejon for fear of hitting one of our own units. That's happened several times in the past two weeks," Hillery explained.

"Tell your planes to give us a location that he thinks is an enemy concentration," Dean directed and began studying the map. Hillery was on the radio talking to one of the flight leaders and quickly returned.

"Sir, here's a concentration of trucks and artillery west of the Kap-ch'on River," Hillery said, handing him a slip of paper with coordinates written on it.

Without even looking at the paper, Dean directed, "If it's west of the Kap-ch'on, it's free fire. Hit anything they find west without calling in for permission. Report it for intelligence." *Here I am, a division commander directing air strikes like an artillery forward observer sergeant,* he thought. He remained in with the tactical air control party for the next hour, directing air strikes on targets reported by the circling aircraft. He was so engrossed in what he was doing that he didn't notice Lieutenant Clarke entering until Clarke tapped him on the shoulder.

"Clarke, what is it?" Dean said in surprise.

"Sir, there are two tanks from the 1st Cavalry Division outside," Clarke said with a smile.

"Damn reinforcements have arrived," Dean exclaimed, grabbing his helmet and heading for the door. Outside, his pace quickened as he moved towards the sight of two US tanks with two more moving up behind them. *Now we'll stop them with the cav arriving. Just like the old days when the besieged settlers are surrounded by the Indians and the cav arrives in the nick of time,* Dean thought with a chuckle as he approached the first tank and a lieutenant walked up to him.

"Sir, Lieutenant Paradisio," he said, rendering a salute.

"Boy, am I glad to see you, Lieutenant. Where's the rest of your unit?" Dean asked.

"Sir, this is it. The rest of my company is back by Yongsan. I was sent up here to escort your administrative vehicles back there," Lieutenant Paradisio said, a bit confused. Dean was more confused, however.

"I don't understand. Let's go into the CP and get this straightened out," Dean said, leading the way. Inside he found Colonel Wadlington, but Colonel Beauchamp wasn't present.

"Wadlington, what's with just a platoon of tanks from the cav?" Dean asked.

"Sir, Colonel Beauchamp contacted the division CP back at Okch'on and requested an armor escort to guide the vehicles back there. I guess this is all they could come up with," Wadlington responded. The disappointed look on Dean's face said volumes about his feelings.

"Okay, best get the withdrawal going. I see some vehicles are already lined up. Good luck. I'm going to stick around for a bit longer and then I'll be along," Dean said.

As he walked out into the street and examined the convoy forming up, he noted that it was mostly administrative vehicles, supply trucks, water tankers, communications vehicles and some engineer staff. He noted that there were no infantry soldiers in the convoy, which gave him some reassurance that they must be in the city, taking up positions.

"Dowd, pick us up over at the tactical air control party. I want to see what the aircraft are reporting," Dean said. As he and Clarke walked down the street, he could see the tactical air control party was breaking down some equipment but was still in contact with aircraft orbiting above. Lieutenant Hillery saw the general and approached.

"Sir, glad to see you. The flight leader's saying there's a large body of troops in twenty trucks to the south moving towards Taejon and wants to know if they should hit them," Hillery said.

"No, those are friendly. I was just at the 34th CP and they said that was the 24th Reconnaissance Company."

"Very good, sir, I'll pass that along to the aircraft," Hillery replied, puzzled why the reconnaissance company would be coming from the south when he had been talking to them on the north side of town.

LIEUTENANT COLONEL AYRES observed the large body of troops moving towards Taejon on the Kumsan Road. *Damn, that's an enemy convoy strolling up the Kumsan Road with no one putting up any resistance*, he was thinking as he watched their progress north towards Taejon. Turning to his S-3 operations officer, Major Curtis Cooper, he asked, "Coop, have we got any comms with regiment?"

"Sir, we don't have comms with anyone. Either these pathetic excuses for radios have dead batteries with no replacements or these hills are blocking any signal," Major Cooper replied.

"Have we had any word from Major Dunham and his party? They should be close to the Kumsan Road and behind this convoy," Ayres said. He had directed Major Dunham along with one hundred and fifty soldiers to head to the Kumsan Road and establish a blocking position. That was before he had seen this convoy of North Korean soldiers moving north on the Kumsan Road. Earlier, they had heard some gunfire but had no word from Major Dunham. Ayres's group consisted of Major Cooper, Captain Malcolm Spaulding, a runner, a radio operator, an interpreter and Wilson Field, *Time* magazine correspondent.

"Okay, let's move out and get down to Major Dunham and see what we have there," Ayres directed, and the small party departed the hill and headed towards the Kumsan Road, moving in single file.

Major Cooper took the point and moved with some degree of caution. Suddenly his hand went up for the column to stop and he squatted down, taking a knee. Ayres moved up alongside him in a low crouch.

"What's up?" he asked in a whisper.

"We have movement approaching. It's only one individual that I could see and he's moving fast toward us. Let's hold here and see what we got," Cooper whispered back.

While he and Ayres watched, the individual became clearer as he moved with as much speed as he could coming up the hill. It soon became obvious that it was a US soldier, who breathlessly collapsed next to the two officers when he stumbled upon them.

"Sir," the soldier said, gasping for breath. Ayres pulled out his canteen and handed it to the young man, who drank in gulps. "Thank you, sir."

"What are you doing up here? Who were you with and what's happened?" Ayres asked the young private.

"Sir, Major Dunham did as you ordered. We moved down to the Kumsan Road and started to set up a blocking position. Before we could complete it, they hit us. Major Dunham thought it was a guerrilla force. We withdrew and moved to Kuwan-ni," the private explained.

"Where the hell is Kuwan-ni?" Ayres asked, trying to recall the map.

"Sir, that's three miles south of Taejon," Major Cooper said.

"Sir, we came under fire from the surrounding hills. The Koreans were all over the hills and shooting at us in the draw. Major Dunham took a round through the neck and died. Most of the others that could took off to the west towards Masu-ri," the private indicated.

"Can you walk now, soldier?" Ayres asked the young man.

"Yes, sir," he responded.

"Okay, let's move out. I want to get across the Kumsan Road before nightfall and move on to reach the 21st Regiment," Ayres said, standing and leading the small group off the hill and eastward. The sparse vegetation on the hills didn't offer much concealment, Ayres noted, and the terrain was such that it channeled their movement off the high ground into draws. Suddenly, a burst of automatic weapons assaulted them from the hill above them. Ayres, Cooper and Spaulding along with their interpreter hit the ground in the bottom of the draw immediately. The private and radio operator were cut down, as was the runner.

"Fielder, Fielder, are you okay?" Ayres yelled but received no reply. *Damn, this isn't good*, he thought as he lay there with rounds hitting the sides of the draw, which was narrow and deep. He started low crawling with the others close behind him. *I haven't done a damn low crawl in years and I'm getting too old for this shit*, Ayres was thinking as all four remained as low to the ground as they could to avoid being seen or hit. The Koreans on the hill didn't approach them but continued to fire on the draw. Finally reaching the mouth of the draw, the party crawled into some dense bushes that offered good concealment from the hilltop. Ayres knew, however, that if the Koreans really wanted prisoners, all they had to do was come down and they would be found. But the Koreans appeared more interested in moving off towards Taejon.

LIEUTENANT HERBERT HAD ESTABLISHED a position on the west side of the town just forward of a 155mm artillery battery. Herbert had been watching an enemy unit watching him for the past hour. He had asked that the artillery swing the guns around, but the battery commander said he couldn't do that without permission from the battalion operations officer, who refused to allow that action. Herbert argued until he was blue in the face. Finally the North Koreans got tired of exchanging looks and started hitting Herbert with mortars and machine guns. A runner that Herbert had sent to the 34th CP came back with fifty soldiers led by Lieutenant William Wygal from the 2nd Battalion, 19th Infantry. They joined Herbert's forces and attempted to hold for the afternoon. General Dean observed this action from the 34th CP and sent a runner to Herbert to tell him to hold until the artillery was withdrawn.

"Major McDaniel, where is Colonel Beauchamp?" Dean asked.

"I don't know, sir. He left here two hours ago to get some air. No one has heard from him since he left," McDaniel said, looking around. Blank stares from the rest of the staff greeted him.

"Where is the XO?" Dean asked.

"Sir, I'll have someone get him. He was going over to organize the next convoy." McDaniel motioned to a sergeant to go get Colonel Wadlington. A few minutes later, Wadlington entered the command post.

"Sir, you wanted to see me?" Wadlington asked.

"Colonel Beauchamp is missing. Get the convoys organized and get them out of here. *Now!*" Dean ordered.

Chapter 47
Withdrawal

21 JULY 1950
24th Division
Taejon, South Korea

AT THIS POINT, to refer to the 24th Division as a division would be a gross overstatement. General Dean lacked communications with his division command post and could only influence that portion of the battle immediately around him. As he understood the situation, the 34th Infantry Regiment was now a scattered force around Taejon and he wasn't sure where. The 21st Infantry Regiment was somewhere between Taejon and Okch'on. The 19th Infantry Regiment was attempting to reform in Yongsan.

"General," said Colonel Wadlington as he approached, "I want your vehicle to be in the convoy as well. Your driver knows his position."

"Where are you going to be?" Dean asked.

"Sir, I'll be the lead vehicle. Major McDaniel will be tail-end Charlie in the last vehicle. Captain Smith with L Company will hold for forty-five minutes and then follow the convoy down the road. We have enemy forces engaging him at this time, but he should be able to hold." Captain Smith had brought the remnants of the 3rd Battalion, 34th Infantry, into Taejon and took up a position west of a battery of 155mm artillery. Dean wanted that artillery extracted as enough artillery had already fallen in the hands of the enemy. Lieutenant Herbert had attempted to get this same artillery unit to engage the enemy in sector, but they had refused his request. Instead of withdrawing as Colonel Wadlington had ordered, the artillerymen refused to come out of the buildings they were hiding in due to the mortar fire targeting the unit. Captain Smith was now holding a position and getting the howitzers married to trucks for extraction. Once they were connected, Wadlington gave the order to move and led the convoy of over fifty vehicles in this first part of the convoy out.

Moving through the city, which was now in flames and full of North Korean infiltrators, the convoy came under sporadic but increasing fire. Every vehicle was taking hits. Panic was setting in. Separations appeared in the convoy as some vehicles paused to engage the enemy before proceeding. Taking a wrong turn, the first elements of the convoy drove into a dead-end street. Dismounting, one hundred and twenty-five men moved south into the hills. Colonel Wadlington was one of them. The time was 1830 hours.

General Dean was in the second part of the convoy. "Dowd, try to keep up with those guys ahead of us," he directed. Dowd had the accelerator almost floored as he weaved around down telephone poles, destroyed and burning vehicles and attempting to avoid enemy fire.

As they shot through an intersection, Lieutenant Clarke yelled, "That was our turn!" But the enemy fire was too intense to turn back.

"Keep going, Dowd. We'll find a way back to the main highway," Dean ordered as the vehicle shot down the street, which now had burning buildings on both sides of the road. Lieutenant Clarke looked back quickly to see that only the escort jeep was following. The remainder of the convoy had made the correct turn at the intersection and was now heading to Okch'on.

Lieutenant Ralph C. Boyd commanded a truck platoon from the 24th Quartermaster Company and directed his driver to make the proper turn. He was dismayed to see General Dean's vehicle along with the escort heading on the wrong road, but there was nothing he could do.

Where the hell is the general going? Boyd was thinking as he watched the general's vehicle disappear into the smoke from the burning buildings. *Well, not my problem,* he concluded as he studied his map. Glancing in the side mirror, he saw that several vehicles were still following him and that was all that mattered at this point. He began to relax, knowing that the 21st Regiment was along the Okch'on Road and would provide them security. That was until the first mortar round impacted on the road. Coming around a bend in the road and only two miles from Taejon, Boyd saw a vehicle ahead blocking the road, causing his driver to come to a stop. A half-track vehicle followed Boyd and moved forward to push the damaged vehicle out of the road. A mortar round landed directly on the half-track, killing the driver and setting the vehicle on fire.

"Dismount and take cover," Boyd ordered. He didn't have to say it twice—two hundred and fifty men obeyed immediately, leaving their vehicles. Darkness was rapidly approaching. Mortar rounds continued to walk up and down the road, striking some of the vehicles and setting them on fire. Boyd made mental notes on which vehicles were still operational, paying particular attention to the artillery prime movers.

"You," Boyd said, sliding up alongside a soldier lying in the ditch next to the prime mover.

"Sir?" the wide-eyed young soldier responded.

"You know how to drive that thing?" Boyd asked.

"Yes, sir."

"Good, let's go," Boyd said, taking the soldier by the arm and heading for the vehicle. Pushing the soldier into the driver's seat, he ordered, "I want you to drive up and push any vehicles ahead of you that are inoperable off the road. While you're doing that, I'm going to start loading wounded into what vehicles we still have that are operable. Understood?" The young driver only nodded and started his engine.

"Sergeant," Boyd yelled, looking everywhere for an NCO. One finally responded.

"Over here, sir." Sergeant First Class Donaldson was with Charlie Company, 3rd Engineers. Boyd jogged over to his position, avoiding the occasional potshot that hit the ground around him.

"Sergeant, get some men and start loading the seriously wounded into any truck you can find that runs. And make it quick," Boyd directed.

As it was now getting darker, the accuracy of the enemy fire diminished greatly, and able-bodied soldiers were willing to take the chance to move from cover. Shortly, six vehicles were loaded with wounded and able-bodied soldiers and began to move. Those not in a vehicle walked along the side of the road. The word was passed to do it quietly, if a two-and-a-half-ton truck can move quietly. They weren't quiet enough and soon found themselves in another ambush.

"Damn!" Boyd yelled and his world turned black as he fell from the truck. When he woke, it was dark out and he was alone. All the trucks were gone and his head hurt like hell. Examining it with his fingers, he realized he had a new part in his hairline and a nasty gouge in his scalp, but his skull and brains were intact. He lay there for some time, getting his bearings and figuring out where he was. *If I follow this road, I should be able to get to friendly lines*, he was thinking. *But what's covering this road? Only one way to find out.*

He started down the road and had been going for some time with a voice called out, "Take another step and it'll be your last." Boyd froze and then it dawned on him—the voice had a New York accent.

"Don't shoot. I'm an American officer," Boyd called out.

"Yeah, I know, Lieutenant. We just wanted to scare the crap out of you. Come on forward," the voice said, with others chuckling. "Welcome to the 21st Regiment," the smiling young soldier added. Boyd hugged him.

Colonel Beauchamp, who had been missing in Taejon since 1500, arrived at the CP for the 21st Infantry Regiment that afternoon. Brigadier General Pearson Menoher, the assistant division commander, 24th Infantry Division, sat Beauchamp down and began an extensive back brief of the conditions in Taejon. When Beauchamp was done, Menoher told him to sit tight and wait for orders as the withdrawal from Taejon had begun. Shortly afterwards, Menoher issued new orders.

"Colonel Beauchamp," Menoher said, approaching Beauchamp, "there's a pass on the Okch'on Road that we've got to hold, and the road tunnels. I want you to take a rifle company and a platoon of tanks and head towards Taejon. Hold the pass and tunnels until the last elements from Taejon roll through. They're trying to get through from Taejon, but they need help."

Beauchamp was just glad to be doing something besides sitting and hearing what was happening. Policing up a platoon of five tanks and a rifle company, he headed north on the road. Coming towards him was I Company, 34th Regiment, and they joined his ranks to return and open the road. As they moved cautiously forward, the sound of an explosion in the forward elements grabbed Beauchamp's attention.

"Bolt Six-One, Bolt Six, over," Beauchamp called over his vehicle-mounted radio to the tank platoon leader.

"Bolt Six, Six-One, my lead tank just hit a mine. His track is off and he's off to the side of the road. Over."

"Roger, keep moving, over," Beauchamp ordered. He observed the last tank moving now, so he was sure the platoon leader had understood his orders. As the tanks moved forward, the sound of rolling explosions could be heard.

"Bolt Six-One, what the hell was that?" Beauchamp called on the radio.

"Bolt Six, they just command-detonated a string of mines. No injuries as they did it too soon. We're moving forward. Out," Bolt Six-One announced.

The sounds of small-arms fire and mortars impacting could be heard, but the column continued forward. Soon Beauchamp could see the entrance to the tunnels. The pass lay beyond the tunnels.

"Bolt Six, Six-One, over."

"Go ahead, Bolt Six-One," Beauchamp responded.

"Bolt Six, they have a cross fire set up above the tunnel. We're running out of ammo at this point. We cannot reach the tunnel. I need a resupply of ammo or withdraw, over."

Beauchamp had no resupply of ammo and could see that the enemy had strong positions overlooking the tunnels. He could request a resupply, but it wouldn't arrive until after dark, and he knew he needed to do something before dark. Reluctantly, he gave the order.

"All Bolt elements, this is Bolt Six. Withdraw at this time. I say again, withdraw at this time. Bolt Six-One, cover the withdrawal. How copy?"

"Bolt Six, I have good copy and will do. Over."

Through his binoculars, Beauchamp could see the units falling back. He could also see the bodies of the engineers that were sent earlier to blow the tunnels after those fleeing Taejon had passed through. Throughout the night, individuals and groups from Taejon passed through the lines of the 21st Regiment. The 21st Regiment was not aware of the situation in Taejon until these groups arrived. During the night of 20–21 July, North Korean forces continued to maneuver to flank the 21st Regiment positions.

"General," Colonel Stephens said, gaining General Menoher's attention, "have we heard anything from General Dean?"

"I'm afraid not. It appears his jeep missed the turn and continued into the city northbound. I suspect he's working his way this way from the north. His aide and driver are with him as well as a security jeep. He should be okay."

"Shit, we missed the turn," Lieutenant Clarke shouted as Dowd accelerated through the kill zone of the ambush. The intersection was crisscrossed with machine-gun fire. Only the smoke from the surrounding burning buildings concealed their escape.

"Dowd, I have no idea how you drove through that, but you deserve a medal," General Dean voiced.

"Sir, I'll take a friendly face at this point," Dowd said, somewhat serious and somewhat joking. They continued to barrel down the road out of town. Lieutenant Clarke monitored their progress, hoping to find a side road that would take them towards Okch'on. None appeared on the map.

"What road are we on?" asked Dean as they were a mile from the city and coming upon an overturned truck on the side of the road. Wounded soldiers lay around the vehicle.

"Sir, I believe we're on the Kumsan Road," Clarke said.

"Stop Dowd and let's load these wounded soldiers into our vehicles," Dean directed. Five people in a jeep was crowded and now there were seven in each vehicle. The tiny convoy of two vehicles continued on the road until it came upon a roadblock and took fire. Lieutenant Clarke yelled out as a bullet tore through his shoulder. Everyone immediately jumped out of the vehicles into the roadside ditch. Quickly they began to crawl out of the ditch and across agricultural fields through the night soil fertilizer common in Korea. Reaching the surrounding hills, they started the climb in darkness. After ascending to the top of one hill, everyone was exhausted and out of water.

"Lieutenant, you stay here. Dowd, you keep an eye on him. I'm going to fill some canteens in the creek we crossed. Should be back in an hour." And General Dean set off down the hill. He would not be seen for another three years.[1]

---

1. General Dean fell going down the hill and knocked himself out. Waking up, he had sustained a broken shoulder and wandered for the next thirty-six days before he was captured by the North Koreans, who did not realize for some time that they had a US general. He was awarded the Medal of Honor upon his release from the POW camp.

Chapter 48
Welcome to Korea

21 July 1950
1st Battalion, 7th Cavalry Regiment
P'ohang-dong, South Korea

"You are joking, right?" Lieutenant Colonel Peter D. Clainos said as he received his orders after finally getting off the troop transport that had been bobbing like a cork in the bay, waiting out the typhoon.

"No, sir. Our orders are to support the ROK troops here with fire only. We're serving as a security force behind the 23rd ROK regiment. Several units have pulled this ahead of us and it isn't bad duty. None have had any contact, so we should get a chance to acclimate to the area," the battalion S-3 said, handing the written order to Clainos, who read it.

"Okay, then, let's get with the 1st of the 35th and see where their positions are and take them over," Clainos said, resolved to their fate of being in the rear, which wasn't so bad, his troops thought. As he and the company commanders talked with the officers of the 1st Battalion, 35th Regiment, Clainos made assignments.

"Bob," Clainos said, addressing the Charlie Company commander,

"I want your unit to occupy Hill 181 on the southern outskirts of Yongdok."

"Sir, how long do you think we'll be here?" Bob asked.

"Your guess is as good as mine. Ours is not to question why but to do and not die," Clainos joked.

As he positioned the remainder of his companies, Delta Company being the last one, a US Army officer that he didn't recognize approached him.

"Colonel Clainos?" the officer asked. Right away, Clainos noticed the colonel insignia.

"You found him," Clainos said, extending his hand.

"Hi, I'm the advisor to the 3rd ROK Division, Emmerich. Thought I'd introduce myself and give you a rundown of the regimental commander, Colonel Kim, before you meet him."

"What is he like?" Clainos asked.

"He's a brutal, inconsiderate, ruthless, arrogant son of a bitch," Emmerich said.

"Okay, so how do you really feel about this brutal, inconsiderate son of a bitch?" Clainos mimicked.

"His self-adopted nickname is Tiger. He likes to think of himself as a disciplinarian, but he sure as shit isn't a leader I'd follow. He surrounded himself with a squad of bodyguards that follow his every order. The other day in a meeting with me and some of the other advisors, he chewed out a Korean lieutenant because his unit had been surrounded for several days in heavy contact. After he chewed him out, he had his bodyguards execute the kid. The next day he used the butt of an M1 to discipline a young private. We, the advisors, have forwarded a request to have him relieved. That's working its way up the chain and we should hear something in the next couple of days," Emmerich explained.

"Well, in that case, I don't think I need to meet him, do you?" Clainos asked.

"Not really. The enemy situation here is seesawing. One day we hold Yongdok and the next day they hold it. We have good naval gunfire support and air strikes, which has helped greatly. The flow of refugees is a problem. They're clogging the roads and we know that infiltrators are mixed in with them. We attempt to search everyone that's coming through our lines, but there are so many. Caught a pregnant woman the other day. She looked pregnant but had a field radio strapped to her belly. Baby carriages are always loaded with weapons and ammo. Tell your people that they have to watch the refugees closely. Aside from infiltrators, this has been a quiet area for you guys and those before you. I don't know how long you will be here, but enjoy it while you can. If I can help with anything, let me know," Emmerich concluded.

Chapter 49
24th Regiment into Action

18 JULY 1950
  25th Division Headquarters
  Sangju, South Korea

THE 25TH INFANTRY Division had arrived in piecemeal fashion with the 27th Infantry Regiment on 10 July but had been providing security at the airfield at Yongdok. On the thirteenth, much to their commander's pleasure, Colonel John Michaelis was able to move forward and assumed a position in the vicinity of Andong. General Walker was feeling a bit better now with two full divisions coming ashore to bolster the line on the east side. He had met early the day before with General Kean to discuss the position for the 25th Division. The finer details he left up to General Kean. After studying the map, Kean called the commander of the 24th Regiment, Colonel Horton White, to go over the plan.

"Colonel, we're taking over responsibility for a portion of the perimeter from the 24th Division. They've been beat up pretty bad over the past two weeks and are combat-ineffective at this point to say the least. Let's look at the map." Kean strode over to a wall map. "I want you to move your regiment up on the line. Your sector is along the Naktong River from Yech'on to Sangju. That's about twenty-five miles as the crow flies, but the river isn't fordable in most locations, so that's a pretty good obstacle. The high ground on the east side of the river will give your troops a commanding view of the river as well. In front of your line is the ROK 8th Division in the vicinity of Tanyong and the 6th ROK Division in the vicinity of Mun'gyong. Remnants of the ROK 2nd, 1st and Capital Divisions are in the vicinity of Ch'ongju. On top of that, you'll have stragglers from the 24th Division coming through your lines as well. Be sure your people understand that," Kean said.

"Yes, sir," White said, jotting down a note. "Sir, what is the enemy situation at present?"

"At present the 5th North Koreans are pushing along the east coast road. They're between Ulchin and P'yonghae-ri. The 23rd Regiment of the 3rd ROK is giving a good account of themselves. We believe the 12th North Korean is facing the 8th ROK and the 1st North Korean reinforced with tanks is going against the 6th ROK. The 15th North Korean is following the 1st North Korean and is located at Koesan. The 2nd North Korean is pushing at Ch'ongju. Now this is all speculation from field reports that the 24th has been able to discern. How accurate it is is questionable," Kean explained.

"And the 24th, sir?"

"Right now they're trying to give General Walker two days holding at the Kum River north of Taejon, but I wouldn't hold much hope out for them. We believe they have two divisions hitting them right now and they have no tanks to support them," Kean concluded, pausing for a moment.

"Sit down, Colonel. There's something else we need to discuss." Kean motioned to a straight-backed chair but continued to stand. "I'm hearing reports that I find disturbing about your regiment." He raised his hand to keep White from interrupting him. "I received a report that your chaplain is telling the soldiers that black soldiers shouldn't be fighting against other soldiers of color for the white man. Your regiment is a segregated regiment with mostly white officers. This talk disturbs me."[1]

"Sorry to say, sir, it's true and the chaplain has been relieved and shipped back to the States," White offered.

"Son of a bitch should be put on point for the division and shot. I suppose the rumor I'm hearing that the 1st Battalion commander was relieved because he didn't want to command white officers in combat is true also, and that your regimental executive officer faked a heart attack so he wouldn't have to go into combat with black soldiers. Are these all true rumors?" Kean fumed.

"I'm afraid they are, sir, and spread since we left Pusan. Sir, we're working to change the rumors, keeping the men informed as much as possible. Tactically we're in good shape. We've trained at the company, battalion, and regimental levels. Our equipment is old but in good order. My troops are physically fit. If we have a weakness, it's the leadership. I don't have the most sterling junior officers. The noncommissioned officers are good, but few saw combat in the last war, and if they did it was in Italy with the 92nd Division, which was also an all-black unit that performed poorly, it was reported. That reputation has tainted our unit."

"Well, Colonel, here's your opportunity to change the minds of many. I have faith that your unit will hold the line and perform with dignity and honor. They've got to. A lot is riding on them. Be sure they understand that," Kean said. Privately, however, he had his doubts. "Okay, so how are you going to position your regiment?"

"Sir, I'm looking at putting the 3rd Battalion in the vicinity of Yech'on and the 1st and 2nd Battalions at Sangju," Colonel White indicated.

"Good, the 17th ROK are operating in the Yech'on area, so let's attach the 3rd Battalion to them for this initial operation. They will take over from the ROKs in sector. The 34th Regiment is forward of Sangju

---

1. The reported performance of segregated units such as the 24th Regiment and the 92nd Infantry Division in World War II was instrumental in the desegregation of the US Army. "Black Soldier, White Army: The 24th Infantry in Korea," United States Army Center of Military History, n.d. https://www.history.army.mil/books/korea/24TH.HTM.

up at Hamch'ong. Colonel Fisher has been working with the 6th ROK Division, which is forward of his positions, and he will be forward of your positions in the vicinity of Sangju. The 27th Regiment is in the vicinity of Andong, but I'm being directed to chop them to the 3rd ROK Division to help in holding the coast road around Ch'inbo and Yongdok. You and Fisher have got to hold the roads leading into Sangju. Understood?"

"Yes, sir," Colonel White said, recognizing that the conversation was over.

Chapter 50
24th Regiment Committed

20 July 1950
   K Company
   Yech'on, South Korea

THE 3RD BATTALION had moved to Yech'on and was to move in and secure the town.

"Lieutenant Johnson, your company will be point. Move into Yech'on and secure the town. The rest of the battalion will secure the hills overlooking the town on your flanks," Lieutenant Colonel John T. Corley directed.

First Lieutenant Jasper R. Johnson had been in command for a few months of his almost-all-black company, with his junior officers being white like him. Racial tension didn't appear to be a problem, and he felt he had a good rapport with his soldiers.

"I'm going to attach the Third Platoon of the 77th Combat engineers to you as well. Any questions?" Corley asked. Corley was a West Point graduate from Brooklyn, New York. He had served with distinction in World War II in the 1st Infantry Division. His collection of Silver Star awards and his Distinguished Service Cross were impressive.

"No, sir, I'll move out at 1300 hours," Johnson said, but he had doubts about the other companies protecting his flanks.

Briefing his platoon leaders, he insisted that their respective platoon sergeants attend all the briefings so that if the platoon leader went down, the platoon sergeant would know what needed to be done. He also had confidence in the platoon sergeants as he felt he was blessed to have three that were veterans of the 92nd Infantry Division and had seen combat action in Italy in the Big War.

"Okay, gather around," Johnson called his chain of command. "We have the mission to move up this road that runs from Hamch'ang to Yech'on and clear and secure Yech'on. The 6th ROK Division is north of Yech'on, so it should be fairly quiet for us to move into. Order of march is First, Second and Third Platoons. I'll follow First Platoon. First Sergeant will follow Third Platoon and police up stragglers. Any questions?"

"What do we do when we get there?" a platoon sergeant asked.

"Secure the buildings and we'll take up defensive positions in the town. Once were in the town and we're sure it's secured, I'll assess the layout and give you assigned sectors. Let's get there first. If there are no more questions…we move out in thirty," Johnson directed.

The move up the road from Hamch'ong to Yech'on was uneventful, much to the pleasure of K Company. As they moved into the town, they found it deserted except for the refugees moving south and east, which had to some extent impeded their rapid movement to Yech'on. Johnson was expecting to become engaged and was surprised when nothing happened. In the surrounding hills, the sounds said all was not well. The town had been receiving mortar fire, from both US and enemy forces, and was burning. As Johnson attempted to position his company, he had to contend with the building that had been available suddenly catching fire and forcing his soldiers to leave. Late that afternoon, Lieutenant Johnson still had not received assurance from Colonel Corley that the ridge to the left of the town had been secured and requested permission to withdraw from the town.

That evening at the 3rd Battalion CP, Corley outlined the plans for the next day. "Alright, we're going to get back into Yech'on in the morning. Johnson, you'll lead off the same as today, and you gentlemen will take that ridge. Understood?" he said, looking at the other commanders.

The artillery and mortars began falling at 0500 hours as scheduled. As the battalion moved forward, a jeep approached Colonel Corley's position five miles from the town. It was Colonel Henry G. Fisher, commander of the 34th Regiment located in Hamch'ang.

"Colonel Corley, I got word that Yech'on had been abandoned by the North Koreans. Why the hell are you engaging the town with artillery fire? All you're doing is creating an obstacle for the ROK forced to the north," Fisher said.

"Sir, I'm sorry, but the North Koreans are still in the village…I don't—" He didn't get to finish before Fisher cut him off.

"Bullshit. I'll prove that the town is abandoned. Driver, move out." And without another word, Colonel Fisher had his driver start down the road to Yech'on. What he found was a town with several fires raging and a unit in contact with a small enemy force. He drove back to tell Colonel Corley what he'd found.

As Fisher had departed Yech'on, he'd passed another jeep approaching. The bumper markings indicated it was a vehicle from the 77th Combat Engineer Company. Captain Bussey, the company commander, was delivering mail to his platoon, which was attached to K Company. Approaching a rise in the road, Bussey noticed twelve of his two-and-a-half-ton trucks on the side of the road with the drivers taking a smoke break. He stopped.

"What are you doing here?" Bussey asked.

"Hey, sir, they in contact down there and we told to stay here," a black sergeant spoke up.

"Well, you're supposed to be down there with them, supporting the infantry company," Bussey said, climbing out of this vehicle and walking up the rise to see the town. Cresting the hill, he was stunned at what he saw. Flanking the town on the east side was a large group of what appeared to be refugees dressed in the traditional white clothing of the Korean farmers. But something didn't sit right with Bussey.

"Sergeant," Bussey yelled, getting the attention of the sergeant in charge. "Unload the two .50-cal machine guns and ammo and get them up here. Bring all your weapons. Move it!"

Initially the soldiers stood confused for a moment, but then they realized that Bussey was dead serious and began grabbing weapons. As they crested the rise, Bussey placed the two .50 cal machine guns and ordered everyone to stay down until he gave the word. The sergeant positioned a couple of additional .30-caliber machine guns.

"There's a group of people moving on the flank of the town. They're dressed like farmers and refugees, but I'm not so sure. I'm going to put a burst of machine-gun fire over their heads. If they're farmers they'll run, but if they're North Korean soldiers, they'll hit the ground," Bussey explained.

When all was ready, Bussey fired a burst of .50-caliber close over the tops of the heads of the approaching Koreans. They all immediately hit the ground and began crawling towards Bussey's position.

"Open fire," he ordered. Almost immediately, observed and adjusted mortar fire fell on Bussey's position. Some of the incoming mortar fire was airburst, showering Bussey's position with shrapnel. Small-arms fire from the group that Bussey's men had pinned down began impacting the engineers' position as well. This only infuriated Bussey, who only stopped shooting when no white-clad soldiers were moving. When the fighting in Yech'on had ceased, Bussey's engineer platoon was credited with killing two hundred and fifty-eight enemy soldiers.

Chapter 51
Troubles for the 25th

21 July 1950
2nd Battalion, 35th Regiment
Sangju, South Korea

The 35th Regiment was located at Hamch'ang with the 6th ROK north of their position. The 2nd Battalion of the 35th occupied two positions. They were on a hill northwest of Hamch'ang and south of Mun'gyong on the south side of a stream that flowed past Sangju to the Naktong River. Due to heavy rains, the stream was swollen and very swift. An ROK battalion was located on the north side of this stream and constituted the front line. Between them and the stream was a small rise.

"He wants me to do what?" Lieutenant Colonel John L. Wilkins almost screamed. Wilkins was the battalion commander for the 2nd Battalion, 35th Regiment.

"General Wilson wants you to put a company across the stream and attach them to the ROK battalion over there. He feels that having them inserted into the middle of the ROK line would bolster the morale of the ROK and add to their defense," Colonel Fisher explained. "Look,

John, I don't like this idea any more than you, but he's the assistant division commander."

"I don't give a rat's ass if he's the president. Putting an untested company in the middle of a foreign company is ludicrous. My guys don't even speak Korean," Lieutenant Colonel Wilkins offered. "If they get cut off, how am I supposed to get them back? That stream is tossing boulders downriver."

"The ROKs will get them over and back. Who you going to send over?" Fisher asked with some reservation in his voice.

"I'll have to send Fox Company."

THE RAIN HAD DECREASED in the night, but the sound of boulders being pushed along in the stream had not diminished one bit. The only sound worse to the men of Fox Company was that of small-arms fire to their front and flanks. As the morning wore on, the intensity of small-arms fire in front of the ROK units on the flanks of Fox Company grew. Some mortar and artillery fire was received as well, but not to the degree that it sounded like the ROKs were getting. Eventually it quieted down.

"Hey, Captain," Lieutenant Gorman called in a hushed voice as he approached the company CP.

"What is it, Gorman?" Captain Melvin asked, popping his head up from his foxhole.

"Sir, I sent a runner over to make contact with the ROK unit on my flank. There's no one there. They've bugged out. Have you heard anything?" Gorman asked.

"Shit no! Let me make some calls and get back with you." And Melvin was on the radio, attempting to contact his ROK higher headquarters. He also sent a runner to check on the other flank. He received a double punch: no one answered on the radio, and the runner found that the unit on the other flank had also pulled out. Fox Company was now the front line for the 25th Division and the only unit north of the swollen stream. Captain Melvin quickly gathered his key leaders.

"Okay, we're getting the hell out of here. Fall back to the stream and let's look at how we get over."

The company withdrew from its forward positions in good order, which pleased Captain Melvin to no end. The wounded, which weren't many, that were litter patients were carried out as well. Reaching the edge of the stream, the company was forced to pause. The swollen stream was deeper than the previous day when they had come across. Knee-deep had increased to waist-deep on the taller men. Short men and litter patients were going to have a time of it. Besides the swift-flowing water, the boulders being pushed along were going to be a problem. Most couldn't be seen, but they certainly could be heard rolling along under the water.

"Sir, we got an idea," Lieutenant Dawson of the First Platoon said, studying the stream.

"Well, I'm all ears. Let's hear it," Melvin said

"Sir, I'll take some commo wire and tie it to me. I'll start across the stream with Lieutenant Fuchi and the two of us should be able to make it across steadying each other. Once on the other side, we'll tie a couple of ropes to it and you bring them back and tie them off. The men then can cross and use the ropes to help steady them. We can use some air mattresses to support the litter patients across," Dawson outlined.

"That might work for everyone, but it isn't going to work for the litter patients. Those air mattresses would be carried downstream so fast you could water-ski behind them. Let's get you two tied up so you can start over," Melvin ordered.

"Sir, I think I should go with them," Sergeant First Class Reilly said. Reilly was a large black soldier that could easily have been a middle linebacker on any professional football team due to his size. "Three guys working together have a better chance. If one guy loses his footing, two guys hanging on have a better chance of keeping him than just one other."

"Alright, Reilly, tie in, but I want you in the middle. As big as you are, you'll be a hell of an anchor for these two," Melvin agreed.

A few minutes, later all three were tied together with commo wire. Across the stream, they could see other members of the battalion watching them. As Lieutenant Dawson stepped into the water, he turned to Captain Melvin. "Hey, sir, when I get across, can I tell Colonel Fisher that sending us over was a stupid idea?"

"Right after I tell General Wilson it was a stupid idea. Rank does have its privileges," Melvin said with a smile. "Now get going."

As the three entered the water, the flow immediately pulled them to walk downstream. As hard as they tried, the ferocity of the flow continued to push their path until, about one hundred yards south of where they'd started, they were against the bank on the same side of the stream.

"Damn," Melvin mumbled, realizing that they were not going to cross. Looking up at shouting from across the stream, he noticed the members of the battalion pointing past him. Turning, he didn't like what he saw. On the ridge between his old positions and the stream, North Korean soldiers were popping up.

"Everyone get down!" Melvin yelled and the unit quickly responded and faced north, taking up hasty fighting positions. To the left of his position, he could see the North Koreans positioning a machine gun, and to the right as well. *Shit, they're setting us up for a cross fire of those two guns*, Melvin was thinking when the enemy machine gun on the left suddenly exploded. "What the—"

He didn't finish his words but turned to look across the stream, where four tanks had taken up positions. The barrel on one was smoking, having just been fired. A second tank fired and the machine-gun position on the right was also eliminated. Small-arms fire from the North Korean burp guns commenced, but at that range it was not that effective. Certainly not as effective as the range of the M1 rifle in the hands of a soldier that knew how to shoot. As Melvin lay on the ground attempting to figure out how to cross the stream, the answer came soaring over his head. From the far side of the stream, four rocket-propelled grappling hooks flew over the stream. No one had to tell Melvin or the soldiers what to do.

First used in World War II, the rocket-propelled grappling hooks flew short distances, one hundred to two hundred feet, but far enough to cross the stream. Captain Bussey of the 77th Combat Engineer

Company had four with each of his platoons. These leftover relics from the Second World War had been an afterthought in his basic load when they'd left Japan. He'd really never expected to have to use them. The four lines were quickly tied off on the north side of the stream and pulled tight on the south side, creating three lanes close together. Dawson, Reilly and Fuchi were the first into the water, one on each lane. They were close enough that if one got in trouble, he had two ropes to hang on to and one individual to help him. Slowly, all three made it across the stream.

"Alright, you've seen how it's done. First Platoon followed by Second and Wounded and Third. Headquarters is last. Move it," Melvin ordered. Again, surprisingly, the company didn't panic but collapsed on the crossing point in an orderly fashion. Suppressive fire from the south side of the river kept the North Koreans at bay. When Melvin crossed, Lieutenant Colonel Wilkins met him at the stream bank.

"Welcome back, Captain," Wilkins said with a smile. "How's the water?"

"Sir, it's wet and you can tell General Wilson his idea was stupid, or I'll be glad to tell him."

"What is the butcher's bill?" Wilkins asked in a serious tone.

"Sir, six KIA, ten WIA, and twenty-one MIA," Melvin said. "If nothing else, sir, I'd like to see to my men."

Wilkins nodded, indicating permission. "Oh, let your people know that we're pulling out in the morning and moving eight miles south to Sangju."

Chapter 52

Massacre

24 July 1950
  2nd of the 7th Cavalry
  No Geun Ri, South Korea

THE 2ND of the 7th Cavalry had arrived only a few days before and part of the division still wasn't ashore due to a storm that had offloading ships in peril. The initial assignment for the battalion was securing the airfield at Yonil, five miles south of P'ohang-dong. Once the US Air Force began using it, the battalion was moved west to meet the North Korean threat. The enemy had seized Yongdong and the usual crowd of refugees were streaming east.

Sergeant Larry Edward and Corporal James Crume were in the battalion communications section when the message arrived over the AN/GRC-46 Radio Teletype system, commonly referred to as a RATT rig. Sergeant Edward read the message.

"I guess the enemy is dressing up as refugees and crossing the lines. Says here that a Korean woman that appeared to be pregnant wasn't but was concealing a radio. That's pretty damn sneaky if you ask me. I guess the higher-ups want to stop the infiltrators. Best get this over to Ops. They're going to want to get this out."

Edward handed the message to Crume, who departed right away. That evening at the commanders' meeting, the message was discussed.

Lieutenant Colonel Dobber had his company commanders present. The battalion had Easy, Fox, George and How Companies. All four had suffered losses and were hoping for replacements and reinforcements. Many of the NCOs were World War II veterans, as were several of the officers and the battalion commander. They had been pushed out of Yongdong, which was now seven miles to the west.

"Gentlemen, the last item we need to discuss. I received a message from higher today about infiltrators. It appears that some North Koreans are dressing in the traditional white clothing of the locals and slipping through our lines as refugees. Higher has issued an order that refugees are not to be allowed to cross into our lines. If this continues, we'll have no choice but to eventually load the ships and tuck tail. In the future, when you're approached by a group of refugees, do not allow them to cross your lines. Stop them. Understood?" Colonel Dobber said.

"Sir, how?" a company commander asked.

"I'll leave that up to you, Captain, just stop them," Dobber replied.

The next morning as the companies manned their defensive positions, a large body of refugees was seen approaching from Yongdong.

"Damn, Captain, that must be close to six hundred refugees," Master Sergeant Lowe said, observing the approaching crowd.

"I'll bet some are from Chu Gok Ri and some from Im Ke Ri. We're pulling back today to Ha Ga Ri, so we'll just take them that far. No further. Get everyone up and moving and keep an eye on this bunch," the company commander ordered.

Within the crowd were Yang Hae-chan, a little boy, age ten, and his friend Chun Choon-ja, a little girl, age twelve. They were walking with Park Sun-yong and her children. They had been walking from Yongdong just before the North Koreans entered. Park Sun-yong was a schoolteacher, and word had already spread that the North Koreans were executing schoolteachers. Her husband, Chung Eun-yong, a policeman, and children were with her. The other two children appeared to be parentless and had tagged on to his family. As the group moved east, they were glad when they began to see the American soldiers again. The Americans had been kind, giving candy to the children and some food in cans that could be eaten cold, though it wasn't really appealing to the Koreans. All day they walked with the American soldiers until late afternoon, when they approached the village of Ha Ga Ri.

"It appears we're stopping here for the night," Park Sun-yong said to her family. "Let us find a place to sleep off the road. There's a well over there where we can get some water." As the sun set, the refugees bedded down for the night under a star-filled sky. Thankfully the heat of the day dropped, so sleep came quickly.

"Mother, wake up," one of Park Sun-yong's children said, shaking her. Opening her eyes, she could see it was daylight and people were up, some walking to the road. She didn't see any American soldiers.

"Come, children, get up. We need to be moving soon. Get some water and your things," Chung Eun-yong directed them, turning to his wife. "Where are the American soldiers?"

"I saw them leave in the night. They headed towards the east at midnight. We should follow them," she said, confident that the way was clear as she heard no shooting.

Soon the flow of refugees was on the road heading east. They had gone about three miles when they came to an American roadblock. The soldiers were directing everyone off the road and onto a railroad track that ran parallel with the road. Once on the railroad track, each person was being searched before they were allowed to go past the soldiers and were then held at a stream bed that flowed under a concrete railroad bridge that had two tunnels for the water to flow through. Being summer and very hot, there was little water flowing.

"Why are we sitting here?" Park Sun-yong asked.

"I don't know. Maybe they want us to stay together while they check everyone. Just be patient," Chung Eun-yong said as he sat next to her and gave her a hug. As the afternoon wore on, the Americans continued to search everyone and then left, moving east again as a couple of American planes could be seen off in the distance. The longer the people watched the planes, the larger they became, flying lower. As the twinkling lights on the wings began to flash, people began to die.

"Father, they are shooting at us!" Park Sun-yong's son yelled before the bullet pierced his chest.

"Run, children, into the tunnels!" Park Sun-yong yelled as the second plane dipped his nose and began his approach with guns flashing. More people dropped to the ground, never to get up again. Reaching the tunnel, Park Sun-yong pushed the children to the middle of the tunnel and had them face the walls as she didn't want them to see the carnage outside that they had just run from. The sounds of the planes were replaced with the moans of those wounded but still alive and children's cries as they didn't comprehend what was happening to their world. More people crowded into the tunnel, compressing Park Sun-yong's group closer together in the interior. Park Sun-yong lost track of time.

Chun Choon-ja was the first to hear the voices. "I hear American voices. The Americans are coming to get us out of here," she exclaimed in hope. Park Sun-yong was not so sure.

"Everyone stay down. Wait until they call us before we get up and move out of here. Let the others go first," Chung Eun-yong said quietly to the children and his wife. To Chung Eun-yong, his instructions made sense, but not to his wife. She panicked and stood, pushing her way to the tunnel opening. A shot was heard and she fell. Almost immediately, a machine gun opened fire at one end of the tunnel, with rifle fire at the other end. The refugees were caught in a cross fire. Those closest to the opening were killed instantly. Those in the center of the mass of people were initially more fortunate as those on the outside absorbed the bullets ripping through the tunnel. Screams almost drowned out the sounds of the gunfire as the civilians were shot.

Finally the shooting stopped, leaving only the sounds of the dying. Chung Eun-young was in shock, holding the lifeless body of his wife and attempting to console his remaining son and daughter. No one could comprehend what had just happened. Throughout the night, some survivors attempted to leave the tunnel, only to be shot as they stepped outside. The soldiers were still there. The stream offered no relief from the thirst as the water flowed red with the blood of those who had been shot.

"Children, just be still and in the morning when the soldiers leave we will leave the tunnel," Chung Eun-yong told his son and the others. But when the sun came up, the American soldiers had not left and the shooting began again. Those that had been wounded the day before and were still alive received the brunt of the shooting. Finally, the shooting stopped and the soldiers could be heard leaving. At least they could be heard by those who were still alive. Slowly, Chung Eun-yong, Chun Choon-ja and Yang Hae-chan made their way out of the tunnel, climbing over the bodies of those that did not survive. None of Chung Eun-yong's children exited the tunnel. Three hundred other souls couldn't hear the Americans depart as those souls had already departed this world.[1]

---

1. The massacre at No Geun Ri is well documented in official reports and several books on the subject. This was the first of two major stains on the history of the US Army in the twentieth century, the second being the My Lai massacre in Vietnam in 1968. Events like this happen when anger, poor leadership and a lack of discipline are present on the battlefield. We are better today than this. All the American names in this chapter except Levin and Crume are fictitious. The Korean names are those of survivors.

Chapter 53
Hadong

25 July 1950
  19th Regiment
  Chinju, South Korea

THE 19TH REGIMENT was licking its wounds from the fight along the Kum River when word came to move out and establish a defensive position on the southwest side of the developing Pusan Perimeter at Chinju. Intelligence had identified a division-size force moving south of the Kum River along the western road. General Walker had no choice at this point but to order the 24th Division to shore up this side of the perimeter even though the division hadn't had time to refit, rearm and reorganize. General Church had been placed in command of the division the day before as General Dean was still missing and presumed dead.

The day before, some relief had come to the 19th. Two battalions of the 29th Infantry Regiment had been brought over from Okinawa and attached to the 19th. The 1st Battalion and 3rd Battalions of the 29th had been given many promises about stopping in Japan for some additional training and equipment issue as well as a chance to run through weapons qualifications and small-unit tactics. As happened in the early days, promises were made and broken. As soon as the elements of the 29th were ashore, they were rushed to join the 19th at Chinju.

Colonel Moore, commander of the 19th Regiment, arrived in Chinju early in the morning and was joined by the 2nd Battalion of the 19th later in the day. The 1st of the 19th remained in Kumch'on, north of Chinju. Moore was at his newly established command post when the commanders of the 29th Regiment battalions arrived.

"Sir, Lieutenant Colonel Wesley Wilson and Lieutenant Colonel Harold Mott are outside," the 19th Regiment adjutant announced. Wilson commanded the 1st Battalion, 29th Regiment, while Mott commanded the 3rd Battalion.

"Show them in, Major," Moore said, happy to have the reinforcements. Standing, he greeted both officers and offered them seats.

"It goes without saying that I'm glad to have you with us. I know you would rather have been sent here with your own regimental headquarters, and for the life of me I can't explain why you were not, but that's in pay grades higher than yours or mine, so let's not dwell on the fact. What's your status?" Moore asked, cutting directly to the chase.

"Sir, we're both at full strength manpower-wise. However, we need to get weapons zeroed and distribute ammo. We'd also like to test-fire the new .50-caliber machine guns we were issued in Pusan," Lieutenant Colonel Wilson said.

"Well, you have today to do that as I have to send one of you out tomorrow to seize Hadong, which is north of here. The other will maintain a defensive position here at Chinju," Moore said. The two commanders exchanged looks. "Colonel Mott, how about you take Hadong?"

"Okay, sir, what can you tell me about it?" Mott asked.

Moore walked over to the wall map and had both officers join him. "Hadong is a major crossroads thirty-five miles north of here. We have indications that the North Koreans are moving to the southwest in an attempt to flank us by using the west coast roads. Two major roads come into Chinju, one from the north and one from the west. We need to block this intersection at Hadong. There's a pass just south of the town, which is nothing more than a few wood structures. The road north to the pass is a twisting road, not in the best condition, with hills on the north side and rice paddies on the south. I have trucks standing by to run you up there, and you leave at 2330 hours," Moore outlined.

"And the enemy situation?" Mott asked.

"We don't believe they've gotten there yet. It has been reported and Eighth Army believes that it's elements of the 6th North Korean Division, but we aren't sure. We want to get you there before them. You are to establish a defensive position when you do arrive. You will have an Air Force tactical air control party in support of you as you will initially be out of artillery range. 5th Air Force has moved their advance headquarters to Korea now and you can have F-86 jets over you in about fifteen minutes from the time you call," Moore informed him. "Oh, one more thing. Major General Chae Byong Duk, chief of staff of the South Korean Army, wants to accompany you up there. He will serve as an interpreter and guide but has no command authority over you. I want you to be sure and understand that."

"Gee, thanks, sir, just what I always wanted...a major general straphanger," Mott said with some disgust in his voice. Moore ignored the tone, in part as he sympathized with Mott.

For the remainder of the day, Mott discussed the mission with his company commanders and his executive officer, Major Tony Raibl.

"Okay, the order is for us to motor convoy up to Hadong and establish a blocking position. The road is twisting and has high hills on the north side and lowland rice paddies on the south side. We leave at 2330 hours tonight and hope to be there by daybreak. It's only thirty-five miles, so that shouldn't be a problem. Captain Sharra, I want Love Company to take the lead. You'll be followed by battalion headquarters, then Kilo Company," Mott said, looking at Captain Joseph Donahue, the K Company commander, "followed by India Company, Lieutenant Makarounis." Makarounis was the I Company commander. Mott had chosen Captain George F. Sharra to lead as he had combat experience in the Second World War in North Africa and Italy as well as Germany. "Tony, you'll bring the battalion trains up. For right now, just class three, five and medical. Once we're established, you can send back to have the rest sent up."

"Very good, sir," Tony replied, jotting down notes.

At 2330 hours, the battalion commenced loading the trucks, and just after midnight they departed Chinju. However, the road was not what Colonel Mott was expecting and movement was slow. By first light, they were only halfway to Hadong in the settlement of Wonjon. Driving up to the lead vehicle for Love Company, Mott motioned for Sharra to pull over.

"Hey, George, let's stop here and get the boys fed," Mott suggested. As he did so, Sharra's attention was fixed on the road ahead. Turning to see what Sharra was looking at, Mott saw a group of about fifteen men that appeared to be soldiers approaching from the north. General Chae came up and addressed the group. For a few moments, a conversation was carried on in Korean. Finally, Chae turned to Mott.

"They are garrison soldiers at Hadong. They say North Korea soldiers are there now, but not many. They go Chinju now."

"Sir, I need to let Colonel Moore know this," Mott said and called for Major Raibl. Moments later, Raibl pulled up in his jeep.

"Tony, I still don't have comms with Colonel Moore. Run back to the regimental HQ and explain to him that the garrison at Hadong has pulled out and reports the North Koreans are already there. In light of this, I don't think it wise for us to continue with this mission—we should return to Chinju," Mott said.

"Sir, I'll get back as quick as I can," Major Raibl said and turned his vehicle around.

"Colonel, we should continue to move forward," General Chae prodded. "Hadong is important crossroads and we must get it before the enemy does. We can move forward until we receive word from Colonel Moore and return if he so directs."

Just what I need…the chief of staff of the entire South Korean Army telling me to move forward when he has no command authority but can still bring the world down upon me and the battalion if I ignore the bastard, Mott was thinking. "I suppose we can move up some more until I hear from Colonel Moore, sir. We'll do so right after my troops get something to eat and service the vehicles, say one hour," Mott said, hoping to stall long enough for Raibl to get word back to him to return to Chinju. After an hour, Raibl had not returned and Chae was growing impatient. Mott made the decision to continue north. Finally Raibl returned, but the news was not what Mott was hoping for.

"Sir, Colonel Moore said to continue the mission. I tried to explain things to him, but he said to get up there and let him know the situation," Raibl said.

"Did you tell him we have no commo with his headquarters?" Mott said in frustration.

"Yes, sir, but it didn't seem to make a difference," Raibl said in almost an apologetic voice.

"This is exactly why they've been getting their ass kicked since they got in-country…piecemeal commitment of forces with no support, no tanks, no artillery. Their people just don't learn. Military tactics and common sense have been left in Japan with these people," Mott fumed. "Alright, we'll be coming up on the town at Hoengh'on soon and will stop there for the night. Pass that on to Captain Sharra if you would, please."

The battalion halted for the night as Mott didn't want to approach Hadong after dark, believing that the enemy had established itself there already, especially as he had no artillery. He did seek out his Tactical Air Control party, however. Captain Flynn, USAF, was assigned to provide the battalion with close-air support. He had a jeep with radio equipment that allowed him to talk to the close-air support aircraft.

"Captain Flynn, I suspect we're going to get into it tomorrow. What's our close-air support status?" Mott asked.

"Sir, 5th Air Force moved their advance headquarters to Taegu, and I have good comms with them. Once I call, I can have fast movers over us in about fifteen minutes. In addition, 5th Air Force is keeping a MiG cap up during daylight hours, which if we really are in deep trouble, we can get them in about five minutes. There's also Navy aircraft available that 5th Air can call upon," Captain Flynn outlined.

"Good, I suspect I'm going to be counting on you come morning," Mott said, walking off to his jeep.

At first light, the battalion stood to for an hour. No contact was made and the order to move out was given. The order of march didn't change, with Love Company in the lead. Approaching the Hadong Pass, Captain Sharra had the unit dismount and move on foot towards the summit. First Platoon was on the right, with Second followed by Third Platoon on the left. A platoon from heavy weapons followed Third Platoon. At 0930 hours, Love Company reached the summit of the pass. Captain Sharra deployed along the ridge with the First Platoon under the command of Second Lieutenant J. Morrissey on the right side and the others on the left side of the road. The right side was higher than the left side, and even higher ground overlooked the right side of the road and Lieutenant Morrissey's platoon's location. As Captain Sharra was positioning his weapons, he noticed men on the very high ground to the right of Lieutenant Morrissey's location. Colonel Mott and the battalion staff had just moved up and Sharra asked about those individuals.

"That's Captain Donahue and K Company. I ordered them to take that hill," Mott explained and turned to look at Hadong with his field glasses. Sharra, satisfied with the explanation, moved off and joined his platoon on the south side of the road and took up a position next to one of the .30-caliber machine guns.

"Sir, are those friendlies coming up the road?" the machine gunner asked, directing Sharra's attention towards Hadong. A group of about thirty men were slowly walking up both sides of the road towards the company's position. Sharra couldn't make out their appearance— peasants, garrison troops, North Koreans, he couldn't tell until he heard the shouting. Looking to his right, he found General Chae standing in the middle of the road, yelling at the group approaching. They were only about one hundred yards away when the bullet struck Chae in the head and he dropped. Sharra's machine gunner didn't need an invitation and immediately opened fire at the group, dropping several where they stood. Almost simultaneously, mortar rounds landed on the road and the First Platoon's position. One round landed close to the battalion staff, wounding several of them. Machine-gun fire and small-arms fire came from the hilltop to the right overlooking

Morrissey's position, a round slicing across Colonel Mott's back but not penetrating.

"Captain Flynn, get me an air strike," Mott yelled. Flynn was already calling 5th Air Force when two rounds penetrated his radio, rendering it inoperative. Suddenly Flynn had nothing to do. Picking up his M2 carbine, he moved up to Colonel Mott's position and told him what had happened. He noticed blood across Mott's back and torn shirt.

"Sir, are you okay?" Flynn asked.

"Yeah, I'm fine. Can you go back down and get India Company? Tell the company commander to come up and fill the gap between Love and Kilo companies. Can you do that for me?" Mott asked.

"Will do, sir," Flynn said and scurried away, helping a wounded soldier down the road as he did so. Major Raibl was one of those wounded when the mortar round hit the battalion staff. It was obvious that his left arm was broken, and his face was pitted with dirt and metal.

"Tony, get your ass down the hill and to the medics," Mott said. "I'll be right behind you and help the S-3 down as well. If you can get one of the RTOs…"

"Yes, sir, I'll help him," Major Raibl said, helping the wounded radio operator. His radio was destroyed by shrapnel, which had probably saved the soldier's life. Slowly, Mott and those capable of walking or being helped by the staff moved down the hill.

Finding Lieutenant Makarounis, Flynn pointed up towards the pass. "Lieutenant, Colonel Mott wants you to move your company up the pass and go on line between Love Company and Kilo Company. Kilo is attempting to take the top of that hill, and Love has a platoon on the north side of the road and the remainder on the south side. The enemy has the top of that hill that Kilo is attempting to go up and pretty much has Love pinned down."

"Sir, if I try to take the company straight up to the gap, I'll be subject to enfilade fire from the hilltop. It would be best if I swing around to the south, cross the rice paddy, which will give me concealment from the hilltop, and come up over Love Company. I'll coordinate my approach with Sharra as we close," Makarounis said, referring to his map and comparing it with the terrain he was seeing.

"Okay, I guess I'll fall in on you and head back with you," Flynn said, picking up a steel pot helmet he found. Air Force pilots doing double duty as tactical air control parties weren't issued combat helmets.

Lieutenant Makarounis moved the company to the left side of the road and brought the company across the rice paddies, which were full of water. The mud sucked at the soldiers' boots, but they were outside of small-arms fire from the enemy on the high ground. The stench wasn't as noticeable at the moment due to the adrenaline rush caused by the enemy small-arms fire. Makarounis was pleased that the company was moving in good order and with confidence, especially as this was their first time in contact with the enemy.

"Sir," a runner from First Platoon gasped, sliding into Captain Sharra's position.

"What is the situation over there, Mahankn?" Sharra asked. He had known most of the messengers from the platoons for some time as they also doubled as radio operators when the radios weren't working, which everyone was finding happened often in Korea.

"Sir, Lieutenant Morrissey told me to tell you that he's exposed to fire from that hilltop. We've had a few of those guys rush our positions and we've had some hand-to-hand fighting. He requests permission to pull back to the south side of the road," Mahankn announced.

Sharra thought for a moment. He had to consider that Kilo Company and Captain Donahue were attempting to climb that hill and needed whatever support Love Company could provide, even if it was just to keep the enemy focused on Love Company and away from Kilo. "Tell Lieutenant Morrissey that I need him to hold. Dig in and get some overhead cover if he can, but he has got to hold until Kilo Company take the top."

"Alright, sir, I'll tell him, but he ain't going to be happy," Mahankn added.

"Well, if he's too disappointed tell him I'll see that he gets a cupcake for dinner tonight," Sharra said with a smile.

"Really, sir?" Mahankn asked in a surprised voice. When he realized it was a bad joke, he slinked out of Sharra's position and started back up the hill.

Having gotten the wounded to the battalion aid station, Colonel Mott turned around and headed back up the road to Sharra's position. On the way he came across soldiers unloading boxes of ammo from a trailer and decided to assist as he could carry some extra ammo up as he went.

"Sir, be careful," a soldier yelled as Mott pulled a box of ammo off the back of the trailer. A second case of ammo tumbled out and landed on his foot, and the sound of breaking bones was noticeable. Instantly, Mott was on the ground, in pain. One of the soldiers came over and immediately began looking at the foot.

"Sir, I believe you have a broken foot. You aren't going to be able to walk on that. Best we keep your boot laced up," the young private suggested. Mott was in too much pain to object.

"Sir, when we get this trailer emptied, we'll go back to the battalion trains and get a vehicle to come up and get you. Would that be okay?" the soldier asked. Mott could only nod his head in agreement. "Okay, sir, here's your weapon and a canteen of water. We'll get back as soon as possible." And the two soldiers took off at a run towards the south.

Raibl at this point was being attended to at the aid station when a runner from Kilo Company came looking for him. "Sir, where's Colonel Mott? I have a message from Captain Donahue."

"The colonel is up with Love Company. What's the message?" Raibl asked.

"Sir, Captain Donahue says he has fifty percent casualties and can't reach the top. It appears that the enemy is reinforcing their position and their strength appears to have increased to a full battalion. He requests permission to withdraw," the messenger stated.

Damn, the colonel should be here or in communication with his company commanders to make these decisions, Raibl was thinking. "Okay, tell Donahue to withdraw to the south side of the pass. Go!"

Looking around, Raibl saw plenty of wounded soldiers but few able-bodied soldiers. Finally two soldiers came in carrying a buddy who had been wounded.

"You," Raibl yelled and pointed at one of the soldiers.

Startled, the soldier looked around before pointing at his own chest. "Me, sir?"

"Yeah, you…come here." Unsure of what was happening, the soldier approached. "What unit are you with?" Raibl asked.

"Ah, Love Company, sir," the soldier responded.

"Good. I want you to hightail it back to Captain Sharra and tell him to pull out. Kilo cannot take the hilltop and is pulling back. I want Love Company to do the same. If you see Colonel Mott, tell him what I've ordered and why. Can you do that?" Raibl asked.

"Yes, sir. I'll head back right away. I have a jeep and should be there in ten minutes."

"Good, now get." Raibl had done all he could at this point. The morphine was beginning to work as the doctor was about to set the broken arm.

"Captain Sharra," a voice called out from behind his position. Looking around, he caught sight of Lieutenant Ernest Philips approaching his position with a soldier over his shoulder. Sharra quickly recognized Colonel Mott as the soldier being carried.

"Sir, what happened?" Sharra asked as Philips laid Mott on the ground.

"Order a withdrawal," Mott blurted out. "Kilo isn't going to take that hill and the North Koreans are reinforcing from what I could see. Broke my damn foot. Send a runner back to the CP and tell them to tell Kilo to withdraw back to the pass. Get everyone loaded up and we're heading back to Chinju."

"Will do, sir," Sharra said and began issuing orders to runners to get the order out to withdraw.

"Here they come!" yelled Staff Sergeant Morris to his platoon leader, Lieutenant Morrissey. From his position, Morris could see the North Koreans moving down the hill towards their position. First Platoon's position had not been chosen to withstand a flank attack, as this was developing into. Morrissey never got the order to withdraw from Sharra—it came from Captain Flynn, who had moved up with India Company and found that Love Company, except for Morrissey, had withdrawn.

"Lieutenant Morrissey, move your platoon down to the road. There are some vehicles there that we can get you out on. The rest of your company has already withdrawn. Didn't you get the word?" Flynn asked.

"No, sir, but I'll take your word for it," Morrissey said and passed the word to withdraw. Flynn was shocked to see only twelve men rise from the foxholes and move back to the road. Commandeering abandoned vehicles on the side of the road, Flynn loaded the platoon up and sent them on their way. When he got into his own vehicle, he found it wouldn't start, and a close examination showed bullet holes in the engine. *Great, I guess I get to walk out with India Company now.*

"Lieutenant Makarounis, I suggest we pull out as we're the only ones on the south side of the pass. In fact, we're the only ones on the pass and I think those guys coming down the hill want it," Flynn said, returning to the previous positions held by Love Company and pointing up the hill, which now appeared to be covered in downward-scurrying ants.

Makarounis gave the order for the company to move out and retrace their steps across the rice paddy. As the company moved, soldiers attempted to pick up the pace as they all knew the enemy was closing in on them. The faster they attempted to move in the mud and water, the more tired they became. The mud sucked at their boots. Some fell in the muck and had to struggle to stand as they attempted to push up with their arms, only to sink into the mud. Soon soldiers began to drop their equipment, their rifles, their jackets. In their panic, they missed where they had entered the rice paddy and found themselves suddenly confronted with a deep ditch twenty feet across and filled with water. Stripping off their uniforms, some swam the ditch. Some drowned in the ditch. Some were shot attempting to cross as the North Koreans had now caught up with them and stood on the road, firing down on the panicked soldiers.[1]

It would be three days before a count of the combat losses could be compiled. The largest group of stragglers arrived in Pusan by boat. Sergeant Applegate, I Company, guided ninety-seven men to the seacoast five miles west of Hadong and convinced a Korean fisherman to take them all. They motored west until they met a South Korean naval vessel and transferred over. Within the battalion, Colonel Mott, Major Raibl, the adjutant, the intelligence officer and the assistant operations officer were wounded. The company commanders of Headquarters, India, Kilo and Mike Companies were lost. Lieutenant Makarounis was taken prisoner but managed to escape three months later. Only four hundred and eight officers and men were accounted for, with three hundred and forty-nine missing. Equipment losses were equally dismal, with thirty vehicles destroyed or captured along with all crew-served weapons, commo equipment, and most individual weapons.

---

1. Several weeks later when the regiment swept through this same area, the bodies of 312 soldiers were found around the ditch. Roy E. Appleman, *United States Army in the Korean War: South to the Naktong, North to the Yalu (June–November 1950)* (Washington, D.C.: United States Army Center of Military History, 1992), 221.

Chapter 54
Command Decisions

24 July 1950
    Far East Command (FECOM) HQ
    Tokyo, Japan

The Joint Strategic Plans and Operations Group had been created after the plans for Operation Bluehearts, the original plan for an amphibious landing behind enemy lines, were scrapped by 10 July. General Almond, the chief of staff for FECOM, realized that a more detailed planning group headed up by a general officer was necessary to pull together the sort of amphibious operation General MacArthur wanted to execute. Tagging Major General Wright, the deputy G-3, to head up the group, Wright pulled in staff officers from all branches of service and started over again. The plan was now ready to brief to General MacArthur.

Once everyone had filed into the conference room, General MacArthur entered and everyone came to attention, as is military custom when a senior officer enters the room.

"Take your seats, gentlemen, and let's get started," MacArthur said, nodding at General Wright, who was standing behind a podium.

"Good morning, sir. The purpose of this brief is to receive your final approval of the plan we developed for the amphibious assault on the Korean Peninsula. We'll start with an intelligence brief, then some topography issues and then the operations plan. General Willoughby," Wright said, stepping aside while the FECOM intelligence officer approached the podium. General Charles Willoughby was German born and had migrated to the US prior to World War I, during which he'd served in the US Army, first as an infantry officer, then as a pilot. He'd remained in the service and had come to MacArthur's staff prior to World War II. He had been with MacArthur ever since and was deeply loyal, to a fault, some said.

"Sir, the current intelligence picture is as follows: the bulk of the North Korean Army is pushing south against the Eighth Army, which is falling back towards Pusan. The North Korean Army is approximately one hundred and fourty thousand strong and equipped mostly with World War II equipment that the Soviets had discarded. They have a small air force of mostly Yak-9 aircraft. Their naval forces consist of approximately twenty patrol boats. They have no submarines or anything to compare to, say, a destroyer-class ship. Initially they took advantage of the road network and rail system, which had been degraded significantly by the US Air Force interdiction campaign.

"Movement now is becoming a nighttime operation. They're excellent at camouflaging equipment and personnel. The average soldier is illiterate but well disciplined for the most part. Senior officers and noncommissioned officers served in the Chinese Army during World War II and in the Chinese Civil War, so they do have combat experience. They have very limited artillery but do have an armored division, which has been primarily supporting the advance down the western side of the country. We've identified the following divisions," Willoughby said, picking up a pointer and moving to a wall map.

"Starting in the east, the North Korean 5th Division is pushing south and is currently at Yongdok on the east coast. The 12th Division is driving on Andong and the 8th Division is at Yech'on. The First Division reinforced with tanks is at Hamch'ang with the 13th and 15th

Divisions at Sangju. The 2nd and 3rd Divisions are at Kumch'on. The 4th Division is at Sanje-ri and the 6th Division is moving on the west coast and is at Sunch'on at this time. All have paused at the Naktong River except the 6th, which is attempting to cross the Samjin River and the Kum River. We estimate his strength at this time to be about eighty percent or less," Willoughby stated. As he read off each division, he pointed at its location, although they were all clearly marked on the map in red, indicating the division location.

"What is the status of his reserves?" MacArthur asked. This caught Willoughby by surprise.

"Sir, he has very little in reserves with only scattered guerrilla elements in the mountains. Everything he has is committed against Eighth Army," Willoughby explained.

"Any indication that the Chinese are poised to support this action, or the Soviets?" MacArthur asked.

"Sir, we have no indications of Chinese or Soviet movement aside from resupply activities from Vladivostok. Chinese forces in Manchuria are doing nothing unusual or moving. I doubt if they will jump into this fray, sir," Willoughby stated confidently. "If you have no questions at this time, I'll be followed by General Wright." And Willoughby moved back to his seat as General Wright came forward. As he did so, a new overlay was placed on the map, showing friendly objectives, landing zones and axes of advance.

"Sir, based on your guidance, we developed three courses of action. The overall operation is Operation Chromite. Those three courses of action are as follows. Course of action one is OPLAN 100-B, calling for a landing at Inchon." As General Wright spoke, a sergeant pointed at each of the objectives and areas for the landings. "Course of action two is OPLAN 100-C, calling for an amphibious landing at Kunsan on the east coast. And course of action three is OPLAN 100-D, calling for a landing at Chumunjin-up on the west coast south of Inchon." Wright paused for a moment.

"Each course of action has pros and cons that we've considered in formulating our recommendation. OPLAN 100-B allows for a deep strike behind enemy lines, quickly severing his lines of communications, allows for the quickest liberation of Seoul and provides us with the only ice-free port in Korea before winter sets in. In addition, the enemy forces in the area are insufficient to oppose us and this would be a surprise to the enemy. The cons to this course of action are the approach and beaches at Inchon, which is a fifty-mile approach up two channels in drastic tides, resulting in landings only possible at early-morning hours and very late afternoons. There's really no beach but a sixteen-foot seawall and wharfs at Inchon that would have to be scaled," Wright said, referring to his notes to make sure he covered the points.

"OPLAN 100-C calls for a landing on the east coast of Korea. This course of action offers low tide changes and good over-the-beach topography. Enemy forces are almost nonexistent in this area. On the negative side, it doesn't provide a year-round port and doesn't interdict the enemy main supply lines to the south. It doesn't offer easy lateral access across the country to Seoul," Wright said, pausing for a moment to see if MacArthur had a comment. He did not.

"OPLAN 100-D is also on the west coast but further south than Inchon. It has the drastic high and low tides of Inchon but better approaches to the beach area and beaches to land the force upon. Enemy forces are closer, as this approach is closest to the enemy forces pushing on Pusan. It doesn't quickly cut the enemy's supply lines and could force us to fight in two directions—counterattack from forces opposed to the Eighth Army and forces moving down from Inchon and Seoul," Wright stated.

"Sir, these are the three courses of action, and the staff recommends OPLAN 100-B. What are your questions?" Wright asked, knowing full well there would be none as they had already given MacArthur a rundown.

"Alright, gentlemen, it appears that you've covered the bases very well. I see no reason for further delay. Let's get this to the people in Washington. Start working on the details and be able to give me a detailed plan by 1 September. Plan on using the 1st Marine Division and the 7th Infantry Division for the force, which will be under the command of the X Corps. We'll activate the X Corps on twenty-six July, and it will serve as GHQ reserve initially," MacArthur said, standing and looking around the room. Everyone was expecting a lecture, but he left almost immediately with General Almond in tow.

Chapter 55
Walker's Ultimatum

29 July 1950
Eighth Army HQ
Taegu, South Korea

GENERAL MACARTHUR'S pronouncement that everyone would be home by Christmas grated on General Walker. *How dare the man make a statement like that when we're fighting for our lives all along this perimeter? If we don't hold them on the Naktong River, there's almost no other natural obstacles that we can use. Our best hope is along the Naktong,* he was thinking. *As I visit the troops, they keep asking when they're going back to Japan. Hell, even some commanders are thinking that they're going back to Japan in a few weeks. How naive can they be?*

"Colonel Landrum, come to my office," Walker said to his chief of staff as he walked by the door.

"Yes, sir?" Landrum said in a questioning voice.

"What have you been hearing about going home by Christmas?" Walker asked.

"Sir, that was Mac making pronouncements before he realized how this situation was unfolding. I think he's changed his mind about that but doesn't want to admit he was wrong," Landrum offered.

"Well, the troops have it in their heads that it was a promise and is true. I've got to put out something to Eighth Army to wake them up to the fact that they're in a fight for their lives. I'm going to write something up, and I want it out to every command and read to every soldier in the Eighth Army. I'll have it for you in an hour," Walker said, picking up a pen and a yellow pad of paper. For the next hour he locked himself in his office, thinking, writing, scratching out what he had just written and rewriting. Finally he called his aide, handing the yellow pages to him. "Please get this typed up and back to me ASAP."

Twenty minutes later, Colonel Landrum came in with a typed page. "Sir, are you sure you want this read to the troops? This is giving reality to them with both barrels," Landrum said, looking at the typed words.

"Damn straight I do. It's time to wake these people up. Let me see it," Walker said, extending his hand and leaning forward over his desk. He began to read the words out loud.

"There will be no more retreating, withdrawal or adjustment of the lines, or any other term you may choose. There is no line behind us to which we can retreat. Every unit must counterattack to keep the enemy in confusion and off-balance. There will be no Dunkirk; there will be no Bataan. A retreat to Pusan would be one of the greatest butcheries in history. We must fight to the end. Capture by these people is worse than death itself. We will fight as a team. If some of us must die, we will die fighting together. Any man who gives ground may be responsible for the death of thousands of his comrades."[1]

"Yep, that's exactly what I want to say. Let's get this out to all commanders with instructions that this is to be read at every command level down to squad. These kids have got to realize the situation we're in. There can be no more retreats," Walker said, handing the typed page back to Colonel Landrum.

---

1. Dario Politella, *Operation Grasshopper: Army Aviation in the Korean War* (Burtyrki Books, 2020), 45.

Chapter 56
We Need Help

1 AUGUST 1950
   Eighth Army Headquarters
   Pusan, South Korea

GENERAL WALKER STUDIED the map and the decreasing perimeter around Pusan. The situation was becoming critical as forces attempted to withdraw south to the Naktong River, the last major natural obstacle between Pusan and the advancing North Koreans. As he studied the units, he recognized that he had problems. The 24th was a shell of its former self, having been decimated at the Kum River and around Taejon. Even its reinforcement with two battalions from the 29th Regiment didn't appear to help the situation any. General Dean, the division commander was still missing and presumed dead. The 25th Division was no better, but its wounds were self-inflicted, many felt.

Seated with General Walker for the briefing were General Almond from General MacArthur's headquarters and General Craig, USMC, commander of the 1st Provisional Marine Brigade. General Craig had flown over to Japan a few days before in preparation for the brigade's arrival by ship as the original plan was for them to train in Japan before conducting an amphibious operation at Inchon. However, the current situation placed an amphibious operation on hold until the perimeter around Pusan could hold the North Koreans. General Almond, although only a major general, approached both Walker and Craig in his usual condescending manner, thinking he was wearing General MacArthur's stars. There was no love lost between him and General Walker.

"Walt," Almond said, addressing the senior officer as if they were the best of friends. "Good to see you." He didn't offer his hand, nor did Walker. "I've brought General Craig with me," he added, turning slightly toward the Marine general.

"General Walker, General Craig, sir. Very glad to meet you," Craig said with all the formality of a junior officer addressing a senior officer and accepted the hand offered by Walker.

"Very glad to have your fire brigade joining us, General. I understand your ships will start offloading in the morning," Walker said, motioning to three chairs in front of a wall map. The Eighth Army chief of staff, Colonel Landrum, stood next to the map. Colonel Landrum had held the temporary rank of a major general during World War II but after the war had been reduced to his permanent rank of colonel.[1]

"Yes, sir. I've issued orders that the Marines will come off ready to move out," Craig reported.

"Good, and we'll need them. The South Koreans initially made a good effort and it cost them most of their most capable officers and NCOs, but they were never given the equipment they needed to stop tanks and this onslaught. We were forced to commit the 24th piecemeal and it proved to be a disaster with untrained and physically unfit soldiers," Walker explained, flashing a glance at Almond. "The 25th Division comes in and they've been backpedaling, especially the 24th Regiment as it's untrained and unfit for combat. This damn segregation policy for all Negro units does not work. It didn't work in the Second

---

1. Colonel Landrum was restored to his rank of major general before his retirement from the Army. It was common after World War II for officers to be returned to their permanent rank from the temporary ranks they had received in combat. That policy has not been followed since World War II.

World War with the 92nd Division and it isn't working now," he went on, adding a barb at Almond, who had commanded the 92nd Infantry Division in the World War II. "The 1st Cavalry Division was supposed to have offloaded at Inchon, but that was canceled and it was sent to P'ohang-dong as Pusan is already too crowded. Their offloading was delayed in part by that damn storm that blew through last week. It wasn't until twenty-two July, and it caused us to be down to a one-day supply for the entire Army."

"Sir," Colonel Landrum said, "in all honesty the 1st Cavalry has been exercising a delay operation along the eastern coast with some success. They're slowing down the advance there."

"Yes, but they haven't stopped it," Walker pointed out and emphasized his point by putting his finger on the map. "And now we have indications that the North Koreans are going to attempt a major push here on the Naktong Bulge." The Naktong Bulge was located on the west-northwest side of the river that reached westward into territory held by the North Koreans. "Okay, I'm going to shut up and let Colonel Landrum take over," Walker said, taking a seat.

"General Craig, the enemy situation is as follows. The North Korean 5th Division is on the east coast at Yongdok. Between Yongdok and Andong are the 12th and 8th Divisions. The 13th Division is between Andong and Naktong-ni, where the Naktong River turns south. The 15th Division is south of Naktong-ni and Waegwan. At Sangju is the 3rd North Korean Division, with the 4th Division at Ch'ogye. The 6th Division is the southernmost division, reinforced with a tank regiment, and it's located in the vicinity of Masong-ni. These are their frontline units. Backing them up are the 2nd Division in the vicinity of Kumch'on and the 1st Division in the north in the vicinity of Hamch'ang. They have almost no air support but do have artillery with each of the divisions. We estimate that they must be low on supply with their extended lines, harassment by our own Air Force and reports of them pilfering off the land," Landrum outlined, pausing to check his notes.

"What are his usual tactics?" Craig asked.

"Sir, from what we've seen, he fixes our forces with frontal pressure but maneuvers to the flanks or even well behind to establish road-blocks and encircle our forces. He will always go for the high ground. He's a night fighter and seldom launches attacks in the daylight. His soldiers are tenacious, tough and physically fit. They're also ruthless as we've found they don't take prisoners. We've come across many of our men with their hands tied behind their backs and executed," Landrum stated. Craig had no comment.

"Sir, I'd like to now cover the friendly situation if I may," Landrum requested, and Craig nodded for him to continue. "In the north along the east coast we have the 3rd ROK Division. The Capital, 9th and 6th ROK Divisions are arrayed along the Naktong River in the north. We're in the process of realigning our forces on the west side of the Naktong River with the ROK 1st Division taking over the area previously held by the 25th Division. The 1st Cav will be assuming responsibility for the area on the east side of the Naktong River from Waegwan south to Koryong, where the 24th Division assumes responsibility south to the Nubtong River, where the 25th is moving to and assumes responsibility to the coast," Landrum concluded. "As you can see, sir, we have no depth, and a penetration anywhere could be fatal to our defense."

"So where do you want my brigade?" Craig asked.

"General," Walker interrupted before Landrum could answer, "I intend to use your brigade as a fire brigade. You are my reserve. Wherever we see a penetration, I'm going to rush your unit there to plug the hole. I suspect that it will be in the Naktong Bulge area for the start. We'll initially centrally locate your brigade and then see where you go from there. How does that sound?"

"Sir, that sounds like my boys are going to be busy and that's fine by us," Craig stated.

"Now we can attach your air wing to 5th Air Force...," Almond began.

"That ain't happening, General. My air wing supports my brigade and stays under my command," Craig said, slowly turning his head to stare directly at Almond. "We train extensively with our air wing in close-air support operations. They understand how we operate on the ground and we understand what they need to support our ground opera-tions. There's no need for us to have to relinquish that relationship so we can derogate our operations to train 5th Air Force pilots in close-air support operations. No, I'll retain control over my air wing." Almond started to say something, but the words never left his mouth. "If you would like to take this up with the Secretary of the Navy, be my guest." Ned Almond closed his mouth and remained quiet. Walker just silently and internally chuckled to himself.

"Sir, what are your immediate orders for the brigade?" Craig asked, turning from Almond and directing his question to Landrum.

"Once you offload, we'll have you moved to a bivouac site. Where I'm not sure right now and will discuss it with General Walker. Before you're ashore, we'll get the word to you. The location is going to be situation-dependent, you understand," Landrum said apologetically.

"Yes, sir, I do. If there's nothing else, then"—he turned to General Walker—"I'd like to get to the harbor and meet the ships when they come," Craig said, ignoring Almond and standing.

Walker followed suit and extended his hand. "Again, General, it's rather reassuring having you here with us."

"Thank you, sir," Craig responded with only a nod in recognition of Almond as he departed.

Chapter 57
Ashore at Last

2 August 1950
1st Provisional Marine Brigade
Pusan Harbor, South Korea

PEOPLE of all ages had assembled at the docks in Pusan. The harbor was filled with small boats, most crowded with people and flying flags of South Korea and the US. Their attention was focused on three ships painted in the gray color of the US Navy. Aboard the ships, men lined the rails and decks, looking out over the harbor. Some returned waves of people in the small boats. The lead ship was the USS *George Clymer* (APA-27). The ship was an *Arthur Middleton* attack transport ship commissioned on 15 June 1942 and had seen service in World War II and other actions prior to the Korean War. The members of the 1st Provisional Marine Brigade had been at sea since 14 July, and they were very pleased to finally be in a port with the prospect of getting off the ship soon.

Standing on the dock to greet the ship was a welcoming committee along with a Korean band attempting to play the Marine Corps Hymn...attempting. Sergeant Major John Runch was present along with Sergeant Augustus Siefkin, both from the embassy guard contingent. "What the hell took you so long?" and "We thought you would never get here!" could be heard yelled by other members of the embassy guard contingent. Another Marine was present, but not in a jovial mood. General Craig had forwarded specific orders as to the attire and appearance of the arriving Marines, and it was obvious that those orders had not been carried out. The men manning the rails were dressed for the most part in their utility uniforms, but some were in white T-shirts. Some had hats and many did not. None wore load-bearing equipment, or 782 gear as the Marines called it.

Standing on the deck and looking at the crowd, Lieutenant Colonel Robert Taplett, commander of the 3rd Battalion, 5th Marines, saw and felt the despair of the people. "They're cheering, but I wonder if it's for our arrival or the possibility of their boarding the ships and getting out here," he said to Colonel Edward Snedeker, chief of staff for 5th Marine Brigade.

"Probably both," Snedeker replied. "Let's move to the gangplank and greet the general when he comes aboard." The two men moved off and headed to the gangway. As General Craig came aboard, he stopped short of stepping on the ship, turned and saluted the colors on the stern, then turned to the side board officer and requested permission to come aboard, exchanging a salute. Both Snedeker and Taplett were present and rendered salutes with smiling faces, which quickly disappeared.

"Which battalion is the advance guard?" Craig asked, catching both officers off guard.

"Sir?" was all Snedeker would say.

Colonel Raymond Murray, commander of the 5th Marine Brigade, appeared suddenly with an equal smile, which he quickly removed when Craig asked, "Didn't you get my orders?"

"No, sir. What orders?" was Murray's response. At this point Colonel Taplett entered the conversation.

"Sir, we haven't heard anything about your orders or what's going on over here. We're aware that there's a conflict, but aside from that, nothing. Nothing about troop dispositions, tactics or support. We've been adrift in darkness since we left the States," Taplett said.

This seemed to calm Craig a bit, realizing that his orders hadn't been ignored but had never been received. As the small command group discussed the next twenty-four hours, they noticed the USS *Pickaway* (APA-222), a *Haskell*-class attack transport, pulling into an adjacent dock with more of the 5th Marines aboard. She had been commissioned in 12 December 1944 and served in the Pacific in World War II.

"Alright, gentlemen, I want all commanders to include company commanders in the ship's wardroom in one hour," Craig ordered.

Once everyone had arrived, including those aboard the *Pickaway*, Craig began. "You men have been kept in the dark for the past two weeks and I'm not sure why, but we're all together now and it's time to get to work. First order of business is an intelligence update for you. I'll turn this over to Lieutenant Colonel Van Orman. Colonel," Craig said as he took a seat. Lieutenant Colonel Ellsworth G. Van Orman was the brigade intelligence officer.

Approaching a wall map, Colonel Van Orman commenced his briefing. "This map shows you the disposition of the North Korean forces around Pusan. As you can see, they're on the north and west side of the Naktong River, the only natural obstacle between them and Pusan. On the east coast they're in a fight with ROK forces north of P'ohang-dong, a second port in southern Korea. In the southwest, they're driving on the town of Masan, which is only thirty-five miles or so from Pusan. At their current rate of march, they could be in Pusan by the fifteenth of the month." This last revelation brought low murmurs and looks exchanged.

Colonel Van Orman was followed by the brigade operations officer, who outlined the disposition of friendly forces. Again looks were exchanged as those present wondered what sixty-five hundred Marines were going to be able to do against an enemy force of between ninety and one hundred and twenty thousand screaming North Koreans. When the operations officer was done, Craig took the stand.

"I don't have to tell you that this is a serious situation. With the forces available, it's obvious that the perimeter can't be held in strength. Eighth Army has adopted a plan of holding thinly and counterattacking enemy penetrations to keep them off-balance and prevent them from launching a coordinated effort. General Walker considers us as a fire brigade. When a penetration occurs, we're the ones who will counterattack. This is going to be intense fighting against a numerically superior force that has had nothing but success so far. Well, that ends when he meets us. Marines have never lost a fight in our history and we'll not lose this fight. Most of our movement will be on foot, so we take only what's essential. Two days' rations and enough ammo for two days, and extra socks. Everything else will stay in warehouses here in Pusan. We start unloading immediately. We move out at 0600 tomorrow morning."[1]

Almost immediately, the unloading process commenced. Marines on both ships began hauling the cargo needed to support the brigade, followed by their own equipment. Throughout the night, the Marines worked in the hot holds of the ship, loading crates into nets to be hauled out and placed on the dock, where others moved the crates and equipment into warehouses. As the night wore on, tempers became thin and harsh words could be heard, but everyone still pulled together to get the ships unloaded. By 0600, tired Marines lined the docks in full combat gear, ready to move out to what awaited them.

The 1st Battalion, 5th Marines, was designated as the lead battalion and departed at 0600 on trucks provided by the Army. In addition, the Army provided communications vehicles, reconnaissance jeeps with .50-cal machine guns. Their destination was Changwon, where they were to go into a bivouac area.

Moving down the road, the lead vehicle came to a halt as a helicopter, which the Army driver had never seen before, landed in the road ahead of him.

"What the…?" the young man mumbled, not sure what it was in front of him. He did notice, however, the words "US Marine Corps" on the side of the machine. The 1st Battalion commander riding in the

---

1. Bill Sloan, *The Darkest Summer: Pusan and Inchon 1950: The Battles That Saved South Korea—and the Marines—from Extinction* (New York: Simon & Schuster, 2009), 91–92. I have taken the liberty of both quoting and paraphrasing Sloan's passage.

second vehicle immediately recognized the passenger who exited the helicopter.

"General Craig, good morning, sir," Lieutenant Colonel George Newton said, approaching the front of the convoy.

"Morning, how goes it so far?" General Craig asked.

"So far no problems, sir, except the refugees moving in the opposite direction. They don't seem to understand that they have to get out of the way of the vehicles. We even had a few wait till the last minute and jump in front of the vehicle. Lucky we haven't killed one or two," Lieutenant Colonel Newton explained.

"Yeah, it's a cultural thing, doing that. Old Koreans believe if they step in front of an onrushing vehicle, the evil spirits that follow them won't be quick enough to get by the vehicle and it will hit those spirits and kill them," Craig said with a straight face.

"Sir, are you bullshitting me?" Colonel Newton asked with a slanted eye.

"Nope, straight truth. Changing the subject, when you get to Changwon, I want you to hold off going into a bivouac site. Conduct a recon for a tactical dispersal in a defense oriented north." Craig pulled out his map and spread it over the hood of a jeep. "I want you to look specifically at these areas, so when the rest of the brigade arrives, you can brief them on what you find. They're coming by train and won't be there until late this afternoon. Any questions?"

"No questions, sir. I'll have it checked out before they arrive," Colonel Newton assured General Craig.

Aboard the train, the Marines hunkered down and got to business. They demonstrated little interest in the Korean countryside but focused on weapon maintenance, eating and sleeping. Members of the 1st Battalion were riding in the back of two-and-a-half-ton trucks with canvas covers, so there was nothing to see except for the truck behind them. Most of the Marines elected to sleep if they could while the dust swirled around them from the road. The new M26 tanks were loaded on the train to reduce wear and tear on them.

Reaching Changwon, Lieutenant Colonel Newton eyed the town before electing to approach it. Halting a mile west of the town, Newton set up a defensive position on a ridge overlooking the Changwon-Masan road. As the train arrived in Changwon, Newton went to meet with Colonel Murray and Lieutenant Colonel Taplett.

"I take it you had a comfortable ride up here, sir," Newton said, approaching both officers.

"Well, it sure wasn't Amtrak. No beverage car and no dining car. Thing must have been left over from the Japanese days. What have you got for us?" Murray asked.

"Sir, General Craig stopped me on the road and told me to pick a location outside the town the dominates the main highway. There's a ridgeline a mile to the west that accomplishes that and I've positioned my battalion there. There's more than enough room to position the entire brigade there in good defensive posture," Newton outlined, drawing his finger across his map, which he had pulled out. Murray studied it for a few minutes along with Taplett.

"Okay, that's where we'll spend the night in a defensive posture. Let's set up a hasty defense and I want fifty percent standing throughout the night. Don't let them sneak in on us. Set out your night LPs.[2] Let's get wire communications established between CPs," Murray ordered. "My CP will be located here," he added, pointing at the map. "Any questions?" There were none as everyone understood what had to be done.

Throughout the late afternoon and early evening, the Marines executed setting up a hasty defense position. Foxholes were dug, fields of fire determined, LPs sent out and established. As good as these Marines were, this was their first night in a combat zone. Two men were positioned in each foxhole and foxholes were generally fifteen feet apart. The night was extremely dark and full of new sounds unfamiliar to the Marines.

"What time is it?" Little asked.

"Why, you have a hot date?" Lance Corporal Bridges asked,

---

2. LP stands for listening post. These were generally used at night and positioned forward of the unit defensive position in order so that the enemy could be heard approaching. In daylight it might be referred to as an OP or observation post, but these were typically farther away and intended to see the enemy and render early warning.

looking at his luminescent watch. "It's 2200 hours. I have two more hours before I relieve you. Wake me one more time and it'll be three hours."

"Damnit, I can't even see my hand in front of my face," Private Dave Little complained.

"Just keep looking and you'll find it. Now shut up so I can sleep. Wake me in two hours," Lance Corporal Bridges said.

"Well, just don't you snore and give our position away," Little responded.

"Hey, if you both don't shut up you'll give the entire battalion's position away," Sergeant Duffy said in a loud whisper from the adjacent foxhole. "Now shut up!"

While Bridges attempted to get some sleep, Little stared into the night darkness. *I wonder if I can even see the end of my barrel and sights in this darkness*, Little thought, raising his weapon to his shoulder. *Damn, I can't even see the front sight.* Suddenly there was movement to his front, announced by the sound of a rock rolling across the ground—or was that a grenade! Immediately Little opened fire on the movement and was blinded by the muzzle flash amid the intense darkness. Bridges was up and opened fire with his BAR, and soon the entire platoon was shooting into the night, followed by the entire ridge. For the next four hours, the brigade was placing devastating fire on ghosts.

"Cease fire!" someone yelled down the line, and everyone slowly complied. Word was passed down the line that unless a North Korean shook their hand, they were not to shoot. For the rest of the night, things remained relatively quiet. In the morning, General Craig let it be known that he was not having any more of that undisciplined conduct. He had the worst-offending commanders before him, only to discover that his own headquarters were the worst of the worst. They were out of ammo.

Chapter 58
Welcome to the 25th Division

5 August 1950
  25th Division CP
  Masan, South Korea

GENERAL WALKER CALLED a meeting for that morning with General
Craig and General Kean. Arriving at the 25th CP, General Walker was
surprised to see an HO3S-1 Marine Corps helicopter already there.
Inside he found General Craig sipping coffee with General Kean and
Colonel Goodwin Ordway, commander of the 5th Regimental Combat
Team, which Craig had just met. The 5th Regimental Combat Team
had arrived on 31 July from Hawaii, which was its home station.
Colonel Ordway had flown over five days prior at the request of
General Walker. The 5th RCT was attached to the 25th Division when
it flowed into Korea.

"Good, I see you've met Colonel Ordway, Craig," Walker said,
extending his hand to each individual. "Tell me, where did you get that
thing, Craig?" Walker asked, accepting a cup of joe from a soldier.

"Sir, I have four assigned to the 1st Provisional Marine Brigade.
They're part of VMO-6, which has four helicopters and four OY-2
light aircraft. Two of the HO3S are at my CP every morning. Surprised

you don't have a helicopter here supporting you," Craig said, hoping to discourage Walker from asking for one of his.

"What do you use them for anyway?" Kean asked.

"I use it to stay off the crappy roads here and get around much faster than if I was roadbound. We also use them to deliver supplies, water, and ammo to surrounded locations as well as extract wounded if need be—at least, that's the plan and what we train for back home," Craig said.

"I thought about requesting some, but the Army only has fifty-three at this time and they're mostly located on the east coast. What do you use the light aircraft for?" Walker asked.

"Sir, they have a two-hour flight time, so we put one up and they work with the pilots of the close-air support aircraft, marking and spotting targets. They rotate with the pilots of VMF Two-One-Four and Three-Two-Three, so they all know each other. They understand each other's needs and how best to support the ground commanders. They also serve in radio relay if necessary and do courier duty as well as reconnaissance work," Craig explained.

Turning to his aide, Walker directed that he look into acquiring some helicopters to support Eighth Army headquarters.

"Sorry for being late, sir," Colonel White, commander of the 24th Regiment, said, entering the room. He was accompanied by Colonel Henry G. Fisher, commander of the 35th Regiment.

"No problem," General Kean said and made introductions to General Walker and General Craig.

Changing the subject, Walker walked over to the map. "I think it's time for us to take the fight to the enemy for once. Five days ago, my headquarters issued the plan to pull everyone across the Naktong River and blow the bridges. The 24th Division has withdrawn from Gechong County to Changnyong. The 1st Cav is now in Waegwan. General Gay had to order the cav to blow one bridge with refugees on it as they couldn't stop them from attempting to cross. He had no choice. Our lines of communications are consolidated now, so I can resupply easily enough and reinforce by shifting forces. The 2nd Infantry Division and the British 27th Commonwealth Brigade are preparing to join us." Pausing, he tapped the map at Wonsan in North Korea.

"The Air Force has been active in bombing the enemy supply bases. Wonsan is the main port that receives supplies from the Soviet Union as it's close to Vladivostok and it gets those supplies by both sea and rail. The port and rail yard have been pounded into the stone age since the twenty-seventh of July. They've also been taking out the few bridges, specifically the railroad bridge at Pyongyang as well as Hamhung and the marshaling yards at those locations. The bombing campaign has reduced his resupply movements to night operations and using oxcarts and pack animals. He's eating one meal a day and scrounging off the locals for anything he can get," Walker concluded and returned to a chair.

"There are four possible axes of advance for the enemy. He can come through here at Masan; he can hit us at the Naktong Bulge and head for the railroad yards at Miryang; he can continue to beat on Taegu and force his way; or he can come down the east coast through Kyongju. If he hits us on all four simultaneously, we're in big trouble. General Kean, I understand the 5th Regimental Combat team has been in heavy contact here at Chindong-ni."

"That's correct, sir. Right now Dog Company is sitting on Hill 342," Kean indicated, "our westernmost position. The 27th fought off the attack by the 6th North Korean Division last week as they attempted to take Chindong-ni and we were able to retain Hill 342."

"This hill must be held as it controls the road north," Walker pointed out. "There are other surrounding hills, but this one hill controls that road and must be held if we're to move up to seize Chinju Pass. My staff is putting together an attack plan right now to take Chinju. You will move west to seize the Chinju Pass and move to the Nam River. When the 2nd Infantry Division is ready, I'll push them up to support you and join your attack. General Kean, I'm attaching General Craig's 1st Provisional Marine Brigade to you. This will give you four regiments, the 24th, the 35th, the 5th RCT, and the 1st Marine. Any objections, Craig?" Walker asked.

"No, sir. Makes sense with us all operating in this area," Craig stated.

"We call this Task Force Kean. General Kean, my staff will issue you the operational order later today. I want this operation to launch on the morning of the seventh. Craig, you should move your brigade up to Chindong-ni starting in the morning. This has got to be a decisive victory for us. Any questions?"

"Sir, one item if I may," Craig asked.

"Sure, ask away," Walker said.

"Sir, we're pretty light in strength. The ROK have recruited a lot of young men. What would be the possibility that I could get about a thousand to serve as interpreters, guides, rear area security guards and POW guards? That would keep my boys free to do the fighting," Craig asked.

"Not a bad idea, General," Walker commented and nodded to his aide, who was making a note. "I'll see what we can do and how soon we can do it. Anything else?"

"No, sir," Craig said, feeling good that he had raised that flag. He turned to address Kean. "General Kean, if you have nothing for me at this time, I'd like to get back and get my brigade moving. It's about a twelve-klick hump to Chindong-ni, so this will be good for the boys' legs," Craig explained. "And with the heat today, it will help acclimate them to the weather here. I understand we're moving out of the monsoon season and into the warm days of summer now."

Walker interrupted General Kean's response. "That may be an understatement. July and August are the hottest months in Korea and you can expect temperatures to reach into the high nineties and low one hundreds."

"No problem. I'll get word to you when we're ready to brief you on the operation. Have a good flight back. How long will it take you?" Kean asked.

"About fifteen minutes," Craig said with a broad smile. It was a two-hour ride by jeep.

The flight was pleasant and quick, but Craig took a detour and flew on to Chindong-ni to conduct a short reconnaissance. He could see elements of the 5th Regimental Combat Team as he flew over and had a chance to examine the road that they would have to follow. Nothing looked challenging for his Marines. That evening the order from the 25th Division came down. Craig and Murray were not happy when they read it.

"I can't believe that they're attaching my battalions to their regiments. So I command what in this upcoming fight, with a battalion attached to the 24th Regiment and the other attached to the 35th Regiment? I have one battalion. How stupid is this?" Colonel Murray fumed.

"It's just for the move up to Chindong-ni. Once everyone's there, you'll be rejoined with your battalions," Craig said, trying to calm Murray down and play nice with the Army. "Who are you chopping to the 5th RCT?"

"It'll be Taplett and the 3rd Battalion. I'll get the word to him, but I know he's not going to be happy," Murray said reluctantly. "We have to fight the North Koreans, the environment in this godforsaken country, and now the stupidity of the US Army. What more can we expect?"

Chapter 59
Naktong River Bulge

5 AUGUST 1950
34th Regiment, 24th Division
Yongsan, South Korea

THE 34TH REGIMENT was positioned along the Naktong River in the southern portion of the 24th Division. In the northern portion was the 17th ROK Regiment, with the 21st Regiment in the center. Three avenues of approach came into the 24th Division sector, two in the north and one in the 34th sector at the Ohang Village ferry crossing. In his estimatation of the situation, General Church felt that the two northern approaches were the most likely avenue of approach for the enemy division opposed to him, the 4th NK Division in the 21st Regiment sector.

The river meandered from the northeast mountains very close to the coast, westward for several miles and then made an abrupt turn to the south. The river varied from a quarter to a half mile wide and about six feet deep depending on the rainfall in the mountains. Hills surrounded the sides of the river, with many coming right down to the river's edge. Those hills were five to six hundred feet high along the river, with much higher hilltops further back from the river. The division had a river frontage of thirty-four miles. Within the 34th sector were two major dominating areas—Hill 165, north of the road from the ferry crossing to Yongsan, and a long ridgeline that ran north to south and was topped with several small hills down the spine. This ridge was known as the Obong-ni Ridge. Hill 165 was shaped like a four-leaf clover with the stem on the northern side.

To cover this amount of ground, General Church established positions along the river, none of which were really intended to defend but to report enemy activity and, in the event of an attack, provide time for the reserve to come forward. Some of the outposts were separated by a couple of miles and manned by only a squad of eight to ten soldiers. Jeep patrols ran the river road between these positions. The 34th Regiment had positioned the 3rd Battalion along the river with I Company in the north, L Company in the center and K Company in the south. The gap between I and L Companies was two miles wide, with a three-mile gap between L and K Companies. In the gap between I and L Companies was the Ohang ferry crossing. Battalion 4.2-inch mortars were located 1.4 miles up a valley that extended from the vicinity of the Ohang ferry crossing to Yongsan with the 3rd Battalion CP a half mile further up the valley in the village of Soesel. The 34th Regiment CP was located in Yongsan. The reserve battalion was 1st Battalion located in the vicinity of Yongsan, nine miles from the river as well. The 3rd Battalion commander was Lieutenant Colonel Gines Perez, who had just reported for duty from the States a few days before. Behind I Company's position and north of the road was Hill 165.

"What the hell...?" Captain Bullock mumbled as he watched red and yellow flares light up the night sky west of the Naktong River. Captain Bullock commanded I Company, 1st Battalion, 34th Regiment. As he stared at the colored flares, his attention was drawn to the west bank of the river. What first appeared to be ants entering the water soon registered as North Korean soldiers. They were stripped almost naked and swimming across the river. A few rafts could be seen as well, but most were swimming. Turning to his radioman, he said, "Get battalion on the horn and tell them the North Koreans are crossing the river between us and Love Company."

"Hey, Colonel Perez, sir," the battalion operations officer said gently, waking the sleeping battalion commander.

"Yeah, what is it?" Perez asked, not really awake.

"Sir, Captain Bullock just reported the North Koreans are crossing the river between him and Love Company."

"Shit, what time is it?" Perez said, sitting up straight on his cot. "Have you reported to regiment yet? What strength are they coming at? Is he engaging?" Perez asked hurriedly, pulling on his boots.

"Sir, I haven't yet and he didn't say. Just said they're coming across. It's 0230 hours."

"Get some more information and have him adjust artillery on them, *now!*" Perez said with some excitement. Once he was dressed, he went into the battalion CP. "Get Colonel Beauchamp on the horn," he directed.

"Colonel, Perez here," he transmitted when Beauchamp answered. "The North Koreans are crossing the Naktong, my India Company is reporting—" Perez suddenly got cut off when three men from the heavy mortars came running past the CP, yelling that the enemy was right behind them. Small-arms fire broke out accompanying them. Immediately the staff and headquarters soldiers of the 1st Battalion were in headlong retreat.

Captain Agather commanded Love Company and had been the commander from the start. He'd also observed the flares over the river but was unable to raise the battalion on the radio.

Agather called Bullock on the SCR-300 radio, a leftover from World War II. "Iroquois Six, this is Lakota Six, over."

"Lakota Six, go ahead."

"Roger, do you have movement across the river from you? Over."

"Lakota Six, I have people crossing the river between your location and mine. I've had negative contact, however. Am adjusting artillery now. Over."

"What are you going to do? Over," Agather asked.

"Going to sit tight for now. I got no orders to move and they aren't coming my way. Maybe they don't know we're here," Bullock responded.

"Roger, I'll do the same. Lakota Six out."

"Fire mission, enemy personnel in the open…" The forward observer provided the coordinates to the fire direction center at Baker Battery, 13th Field Artillery. The battery, consisting of five 105mm howitzers, was located east of the 1st Battalion CP and opened fire.

Perez was out of breath when he ran into the 3rd Battalion command post. Lieutenant Colonel Ayres was just pouring a cup of coffee when Perez came through the door. "Ayres, we're being overrun!" Perez yelled.

"What the hell are you talking about? What's happened?" Ayres asked, approaching Perez, who in gasping breaths told him about the situation.

As he did so, the phone in the CP rang and an NCO answered it. "Yes, sir, wait one," he said and held the phone out to Colonel Ayres. "Colonel Beauchamp for you, sir."

"Colonel Ayres, sir." Perez could only hear one side of the conversation from where he sat, but that was enough for him to fully understand what was being said. Ayres kept looking at him as he spoke. At one point, he covered the receiver and told the assistant S-3 to fetch the battalion executive officer.

"Sir, I'll keep you posted and move out immediately," Ayres said, hanging up the phone and turning to Perez. "Where are the rest of your soldiers?"

"As far as I know, India, Love and Kilo are still in their positions… I don't know," Perez said in surrender as Major Charles Payne, Ayres's executive officer, came in.

"Charlie, mount up Charlie Company and get them moving on the road to the river. I'll be along shortly," Ayres directed. After a moment, however, he said, "Hold that. Get Charlie Company mounted, I'll lead them out. You get Able, Baker and Weapons Company and follow on foot." As he headed for the door, he turned and looked with some disappointment at Perez. Perez noticed the look and averted his eyes.

Mounting his jeep, Ayres, his operations officer and the assistant operations officer joined him and headed on the road to the front.

Charlie Company loaded trucks and followed. Reaching the location of the 3rd Battalion CP, everyone dismounted.

"Captain Akridge, set a perimeter," Ayres ordered the Charlie Company commander. *CRACK, CRACK!* penetrated the morning hours as small-arms fire commenced from the dominant hill on the north side of the road. Captain Akridge began positioning two reinforced platoons facing the immediate threat but was concerned about the south side of the road as well, being familiar with the North Korean tactics, and left a squad to cover the back door. As Captain Akridge maneuvered in the lead of his two platoons, he was hit.

Ayres moved to a position next to the weapons platoon leader, who had two 60mm mortars. "Lay in on the crest of the hill," Ayres ordered and watched as the first rounds hit the crest.

"Need to drop twenty and right ten," the mortar platoon sergeant said, standing to observe the rounds. As he started to get back down, machine-gun fire stitched his chest, killing him instantly.

"Damn, that was a .30-cal, one of ours. They must have captured it when they overran the 4.2-inch mortar position," the weapons platoon leader said in surprise.

"Stay here and keep hitting that hilltop. I'm going to bring the rest of the battalion up," Ayres said, getting into a low crouch and moving as fast as he could towards the rear. He hadn't gone far when he met Payne and the rest of the battalion. Leading the battalion were a couple of anti-aircraft vehicles with quad .50-caliber machine guns.

"They're on the top of that hill on the north side of the road. That hill dominates the road and the entire valley. Right now Charlie Company is pinned down in a stream bed at the base of the hill and is taking heavy casualties. Clyde Akridge has been hit three times, and we need to evacuate him and the others. Me and Lieutenant Martin are the only officers left and Martin has been hit," Lieutenant Payne said.

As Ayres was talking to Payne, Captain A.F. Alfonso, Able Company commander, and Captain Pannachea, Baker Company, joined them along with Colonel Beauchamp, leading a tank.

Spreading his map on the hood of a vehicle, Ayres briefed his plan. "Al, I want you to take A Company on the south side of the road.

Pannachea, you take Baker and head along the north side and clear that hill that has Charlie pinned down."

"Coming up, I saw that four of the 105 howitzers were abandoned back there. Surprised the Koreans didn't take them," Beauchamp said, surprising Ayres, who hadn't noticed him as yet.

"I don't think they have any heavy equipment across the river, sir. Machine-gun fire is from what appears to be captured .30-cals that someone left behind, either the mortars or that battery," Ayres offered.

Lieutenant Payne and Martin decided that staying in the stream bed was a death sentence. Looking south of the road, they could see a grist mill made of stone that could offer more coverage than where they were. Gathering up those who could still move, they moved rapidly to the grist mill and entered to find it empty. Looking to the east, they couldn't see that help was approaching.

Alfonso deployed Company A on the south side of the road and had a tank join his force, and he scrambled up to stand next to the tank commander. They met only light resistance as they approached a stone building. From the windows, Alfonso noticed some small-arms fire being directed across the road to the north and tapped the tank commander on the shoulder.

"Put a round into that building. It appears that whoever is in there is firing on those guys on the north side of the road," Alfonso ordered. Slowly the main gun on the M26 tank rotated and leveled on the building. The aim was true and it blew a hole in the side of the building. The shooting stopped. Infantry from Able Company ran forward to secure the building and were horrified to see only friendly forces inside. Most were wounded. Lieutenant Payne was thought to be dead.[1]

"Big Chief Six, Apache Six, over," Alfonso transmitted.

"Apache Six, go ahead," Ayres responded.

"Big Chief Six, meeting light resistance. Continuing to move to Lakota Six position, over."

---

1. Lieutenant Payne was loaded on a truck taking out deceased soldiers later in the day. As they loaded him, he regained consciousness, to the surprise of the loading detail. He was rushed to an aid station and survived.

"Roger, move to and join Lakota Six. Lakota Six, did you monitor?" Ayres asked.

"Big Chief Six, Lakota Six monitored."

Over on the north side, things were not going as well. The quad .50 anti-aircraft vehicle supporting Pannachea and Baker Company was hit by an antitank rocket and destroyed. The increasing heat of the day, the steepness of the hill and the lack of water were taking their toll on Baker Company as well as what appeared to be an increasing strength of the enemy forces on the hill. Ayres decided that it was time to get India Company involved.

"Iroquois Six, Big Chief Six, over." No response was received.

"Iroquois Six, Big Chief Six, over." After several attempts, Ayres concluded that India Company must have been overrun, until news of their situation reached him.

"Colonel Ayres," Beauchamp yelled, approaching Ayres in the middle of the fight. He didn't sound happy. "Ayres, I just got a call from division. Who the hell told India Company to pull out? They were just seen along with the air-defense company, moving through the 21st Regiment's sector."

"Sir, I got no idea. They aren't one of my units and I've been attempting to contact them with no response. Love Company appears to be in position still and is in contact with Able Company."

"Well, I have Colonel Wadlington looking to find India Company and get them back to their position…and relieve that company commander," Beauchamp ordered.[2]

While Wadlington was moving India Company back to its original position, General Church became very concerned about this open flank. He ordered the 24th Reconnaissance Company to move and occupy a hill on the boundary between the 21st and 34th Regiment. Not satisfied and with intelligence reports from the 24th Reconnaissance Company, he ordered the 19th Regiment to counterattack along the boundary between the 21st and the 34th. A mile from the river, they

---

2. It was never determined who gave the order to India Company to withdraw, but they did return to reoccupy their position. The company commander was relieved.

engaged a battalion-size force of North Koreans and overwhelmed them.

As night fell, Able Company was collocated with Love Company and a total foxhole strength of ninety-seven soldiers. Baker Company held one arm of the Hill 165, or the Cloverleaf as it was being called. Item and King were in their respective positions, retaining the high ground overlooking the river. Artillery fires and close-air support prevented the enemy from reinforcing forces during the day across the river, and artillery concentration that night aided as well during the night. The first day of the Battle of Naktong Bulge was over. It would not be the last.

Chapter 60
Expect the Worst

6 August 1950
3rd Battalion, 5th Marine Regiment
Chindong-ni, South Korea

At 0600, the 3rd Battalion moved out, heading for Chindong-ni. A battalion of artillery, a platoon of 75-mm recoilless guns and an engineer platoon accompanied the battalion. The march was about twelve miles and relatively easy with a dirt road that wasn't hard to follow. The flow of refugees maintained the sides of the roads, allowing the center of the road to the Marines moving north, which made way for any vehicles on the road as well. The refugees understood quickly to get out of the way of the Marines. The young Marines were a bit curious about the local population, but good discipline reinforced by strong NCO leadership prevented any fraternization.

"Hey, Sarge, why are all these guys dressed in the same white outfits? Is this some sort of club or organization?" Private Dawson called out.

"These guys all dressed in white are Korean farmers. The white outfit is the traditional garb for farmers in these warm summer months. The white color reflects the sun's heat better than darker colors,"

Sergeant Jack Macy, a platoon sergeant for the First Platoon, George Company.

"What about the little black hats? They're so small, they don't offer any relief from the sun," Private Cassidy asked.

"That hat is called a hanbok. It's a sign of high social status and draws respect to the wearer, just like I deserve some respect for these stripes from you Devil Dogs," Macy said. He was greeted with a loud "oorah" from the Marines. He was impressed that their spirits were high even as the sun rose and the temperature was climbing. He noticed a change, however, when they began to pass by numerous rice paddies that were partially filled with water from the recent monsoon rains.

"Hey, Lieutenant Cahill, what's that stench?" one of the Marines called out. Second Lieutenant John "Blackie" Cahill was the First Platoon leader in George Company.

"What do you think it smells like?" Cahill responded.

"Sir, it smells like shit," a voice came back.

"Well, then, there's nothing wrong with your sense of smell because that's what it is. The Koreans fertilize their rice paddies with human shit. Before long today as it gets warmer, the whole place is going to stink to high heaven. This should be a lesson to you all. Don't drink the water without using your iodine tablets, and even at that, don't drink from a rice paddy," Cahill instructed.

"Jesus, sir, if the enemy doesn't kill us, this damn country will," another voice rose from the platoon.

Lieutenant Colonel Taplett pushed on ahead of his battalion, reaching Chindong-ni about 1230 hours. His first stop was at the location of the regimental CP. A battery of artillery was located adjacent to the regimental CP. From the amount of discarded expended shell casings, it was obvious that they had been actively supporting forward-deployed units. The CP was located in what appeared to have been a schoolhouse at one time. Pockmarks on the exterior walls indicated that at some point, small-arms fire had been directed at the building. Entering, he witnessed a lot of soldiers doing nothing. Spotting a major, he approached, hoping to gain an interview with Colonel Ordway.

"Major," Taplett said, attempting to get the major's attention, "can you point me to Colonel Ordway?"

"Sir," the major responded, turning with a look of surprise at seeing a Marine in the command post, "sir, he isn't here right now. Why do you need to see him?" the major asked, appearing a bit confused.

"My battalion has been attached to this regiment until the attack kicks off, I thought, and it's traditional in the Corps for an attached commander to meet with his superior. When will he be back?" Taplett asked, his patience wearing thin.

"I don't know, sir."

"Well, can you tell me where he is so I can go to his location?"

"Sir, we don't know where he is right now."

"Well, can you tell me where he wants my battalion to set up at?" Now Taplett was attempting to hold his anxiety in place.

"Sir, I don't know where he wanted your unit to go. I was never told that you were joining us," the major responded. He turned to face the center of the command post and in a loud voice called out, "Anybody know anything about a Marine battalion being attached to us?" In response, he got only stares.

"I'm sorry, sir, but we can't help you. If you go into the town, there's a battalion there and they may have some information for you. I can send a guide with you if you like," the major offered.

"No, Major, I'm sure I can find my way to the town. Please tell the colonel I stopped by." And Taplett departed, not waiting for a response. Getting into his jeep, he told the driver to head to the center of town.

Finding the command post for the battalion wasn't difficult as it was set up in the middle of the main street. Although he didn't see any bodies, it was obvious that there had been some recent fighting in the town. Pulling up to the building, Taplett exited his vehicle in front of a young soldier who was sitting next to the front door. His weapon lay across his lap.

As Taplett approached, he asked, "Is this battalion headquarters?"

He really expected to see the soldier stand and salute. That didn't happen.

"Yeah, but the colonel isn't here," the soldier said.

"Well, do you know where he is?" Taplett asked, coming to a stop in front of the soldier.

"No. Maybe the captain inside might. Just go on in." *No wonder these guys are getting their ass kicked. No discipline, and no military bearing. What the hell has the Army come to?* Taplett was thinking when he entered and spotted a captain standing with his back to the door.

"Hey, Captain, where is the battalion commander?" Taplett said loudly from the doorway.

"I don't know, not my day to watch him," the captain responded without turning around.

Taplett had had all he could take. "Attention!" he shouted. Everyone immediately came to attention and turned to face the doorway. "When a senior officer enters a room, the first person to see him calls the room to attention—or is that not how it's done in the Army… well, Captain?"

"Sir, that's the way it's done, sir."

"Good. Now that I have your attention, the rest of you can get back to whatever it was you were doing. You, Captain…where is the battalion commander?"

"Sir, I don't know. He left about an hour ago and didn't say where he was going."

"Alright, show me where your units are and then I'll decide where I'm going to put my battalion," Taplett said, pulling out his map. As the captain talked, Taplett plotted positions and studied the map. When the captain was done, Taplett had decided where he was going to position his battalion and left. The captain began to breathe much easier.

Taplett chose to position the battalion on high ground on both sides of the main road to Masan. Later that day or evening, he was expecting to be joined by a second battalion from the 1st Marine Brigade. He hoped that the situation would be much better when another Marine battalion arrived.

WHILE TAPLETT WAS MOVING FORWARD, General Kean was issuing the order for the attack on the following day. The 25th Division had developed the plan for the attack to Chinju. The 1st Marine Brigade would attack on the left on a road that bowed around to come into Chinju from the south. The 5th RCT would attack up the center highway to Chinju Pass and the 35th Regiment, would attack on the right flank on another road. The 35th would join the 5th RCT about halfway to Chinju and continue the attack north together. The 24th Regiment was assigned the task to advance into the hill country between the center highway that the 5RCT was to attack along and the roadway that the 35th was to travel. This action would help secure the trains and resupply of the 5th and the division as it moved north to Chinju.

Chapter 61
First to Fight

7 August 1950

Company G, 3rd Battalion, 5th Marines
Hill 342, South Korea

"Colonel…Colonel, wake up, sir," said a voice, penetrating the darkness that had enveloped Taplett's mind. Before he opened his eyes, he heard the words again and knew it was no longer a dream.

"Okay, I'm awake. What is it and what time is it?" Taplett said, attempting to sit up.

"Sir, it's 0130 hours and Colonel Michaelis is on the phone for you. He wants to speak to you," the sergeant said, handing a cup of coffee to Taplett, who gladly accepted and thanked the sergeant. Walking into the command post, Taplett picked up the phone.

"Colonel, Lieutenant Colonel Taplett here."

"Colonel Taplett, I need you to send one rifle platoon to reinforce the company on Hill 342," Colonel Ordway said. "This is coming from the division headquarters. I can't afford to send anyone before we kick off the attack this morning, so you have to do it."

"Sir, I need every Marine I've got for my own attack in the morning. I can't afford to send a platoon, not now," Taplett stated.

"Colonel, division headquarters says that hill must be held. Now you have the order, carry it out. I'll send you a guide to get that platoon there," Ordway said and hung up.

"Son of a bitch," Taplett whispered under his breath, turning to his operations officer, who was now awake and had eavesdropped on the conversation.

"What company are we handing this one to, sir?" he asked Taplett.

"Get Lieutenant Bohn in here. He's going to love me for this," Taplett joked and waited. When First Lieutenant Robert "Dewey" Bohn arrived, Taplett handed him a cup of coffee.

"Sir, I know you didn't invite me here for morning coffee," Dewey said.

"No, but I figured that would help swallow the pill better," Taplett said, taking a sip of his own coffee. "I need one of your platoons. They're going to go to Hill 342 and reinforce an Army company that's been having a rough time of it. Division wants that hill held. Who's it going to be?"

"Sir, why doesn't the Army send one of their own platoons? Why us?" Bohn objected.

"We're attached to them until 0700, so they can order us as they please. I don't like it either, but not much we can do about it. So, who you sending?" Taplett asked again.

"Lieutenant Cahill is my strongest platoon leader. I'll get him up," Dewey said reluctantly.

"Have him report here to me. We'll have a guide here to lead his platoon up to this hill. The guide should be here shortly, so get them moving."

"Yes, sir" was all Dewey could say as he left to get Cahill.

After Cahill received his brief from Taplett and met the guide, he assembled his platoon and briefed them. He made it a point to tell them to have full canteens before they moved out. At 0215 hours, they set off accompanied by a machine gun with crew and a radio operator carrying the fifty-pound radio. The guide led the platoon through what was thought to be friendly lines when small-arms fire started. *Crack,*

Crack, Crack! Everyone dove to the ground but didn't return fire as the shooting was coming from the friendly lines.

"Hey, assholes, cease fire!" Cahill yelled, and the shooting stopped with no apology.

"I'm hit," a voice cried out as a Marine fell to the ground, grasping his leg.

"Medic," another voice was heard calling out as people were moving quickly to their fallen buddy.

"We have two men down, Lieutenant." Cahill recognized the voice of Gunny Macy.

"How bad?" Cahill asked, walking towards Macy.

"Not bad, sir. I'll get them sent back to the aid station. One is a shoulder wound and the other a leg wound. Dumbass Army," Macy finished.

"Alright, let's move out," Cahill directed when the wounded were removed. Finally they reached the bottom of a steep hill and the guide started up. The more they climbed, the steeper the hill became. The sun had come up a half hour before the climb started, and the temperature slowly rose with the sun.

"Gunny, this is too steep to maintain a tactical formation. Let's get everyone in single file and move up," Cahill directed. Marines had to grab bushes and trees to help pull themselves up. Canteens were being drained as the men started feeling the combined effect of the steep hill and the rising temperature. Finally they reached the crest of the hill, only to find no one there nor any sign that someone had been there. Cahill turned at the guide, who was looking around frantically.

"Oh shit, I screwed up, sir. This is the wrong hill. I must have taken a wrong turn before dawn. We'll have to go back down. We need to be on that hill over there," the guide said, pointing to the west.

Threats to his longevity could be heard as the platoon worked its way down the hill they had just climbed. When they reached the bottom, they traveled another thirty minutes before the guide came to the base of another hill located next to the main highway.

"For your sake, you best be right this time, young man," Cahill said as they started to climb again. As they slowly made the ascent, men began to drop from heat exhaustion. Canteens were mostly empty now, having been drained assaulting the wrong hill. They hadn't gone far when the sound of gunfire from above could be heard. A little further up, small-arms fire impacted around the platoon, who dropped and began crawling up the remainder of the hill. As Cahill crested the hill, he saw US helmets peering over the edge of the crest.

"Don't shoot. We're Marines," Cahill shouted.

"Oh, good, we can all go home now. The Marines are here, boys" was heard as a burst of machine-gun fire walked across the crest.

"Over here, Lieutenant," another voice cried out, and Cahill crawled in that direction. Reaching the foxhole, he came face-to-face with an Army captain. Captain Parker looked worse for the wear. Dark rings under his eyes highlighted the fatigue that he was experiencing.

"Boy, am I glad to see you guys. We've been under pressure all night and all this morning. We're low on ammo and out of water. Did you bring any?" Captain Parker, the Dog Company commander, asked.

"Lieutenant Cahill, sir," Cahill said, accepting Parker's outstretched hand. "No, sir, I was going to ask you about water. The guide took us up the wrong hill, which pretty well drained our canteens," Cahill responded.

"Well, when we get back to battalion, I'll have them send some up to you."

"Sir, when are you leaving here? I'm here to reinforce you, not relieve you," Cahill said, a bit surprised.

With shock, Parker exclaimed, "What? I was told you would relieve me."

"Sir, I only have a platoon, not a whole company. I was told this hill had to be held and we were to reinforce you. Sir, please get on the radio and get this cleared up. If you're having trouble holding with a company, there's no way I can hold with just a platoon," Cahill insisted. "While you do that, sir, I'm going to position my men with one of my men in a foxhole with one of your men if that's alright."

"Yeah, that will work, but stay down. You stand up, you will be shot. They have pretty good coverage of this hilltop from those surrounding hilltops. They've been building up ever since late last night. Their snipers manage to keep us pinned down while they crawl up close and attempt to overrun us. We've had some hand-to-hand. How many men did you bring?"

"I started out with fifty-seven. Only thirty-two are here now. We took some fire coming up the backside," Cahill said, adding, "and some heat casualties."

"In that case, they've managed to surround us. We aren't going anywhere, then. Damn."

"Sir, let me get on the radio with my CO and see if I can get us an airdrop of water and ammo," Cahill offered, which the captain accepted. Cahill crawled to his radio operator's position and contacted Lieutenant Bohn, requesting an airdrop of water and ammo.

Gunny Macy was positioning men in foxholes. He couldn't stand up due to the enemy fire raking the hilltop and had to do it while crawling. With him were Private First Class William Tome and Private First Class Melvin Brooks.

"Keep your heads down," Macy instructed. Just then, a machine gun opened fire and ripped through Tome.

Brooks crawled to his buddy. "It's no use, Gunny, he's dead." Those were his last words as the same machine gun found him. Private First Class Lonso Barnett lay to the left of Macy. Flipping to his back, he unclipped the grenade on his 782 gear and threw it as best he could. The machine gun was silenced and Macy continued on positioning men.

Crawling back to Captain Parker's location, Cahill brought some good news. "Sir, I got in contact with my company commander and put the request in for a resupply drop. Also he told me that our 2nd Battalion is coming to relieve us."

"Did he say when?" Parker responded with enthusiasm.

"No, sir, just that they were."

"Well, let's hope they find someone here to relieve the lieutenant." As the morning pressed on, the intensity continued. Enemy riflemen would snipe at any movement on the hilltop while others attempted to crawl in close and rush the defenders. Occasional hand-to-hand fights would occur. Although no foxhole was taken, several soldiers and Marines were wounded in these hand-to-hand exchanges.

"Do you hear a plane?" Parker asked Cahill, and they both started scanning the sky. "There," he said, pointing to the south. A C-47 cargo plane was coming straight for their hilltop at low altitude. As it approached, small-arms fire from enemy positions commenced targeting the aircraft, but it pressed on. As it passed over Cahill and Parker, parachutes blossomed, bringing water and ammo. Most of it drifted down into the enemy's hands. Only two bundles remained within the unit's grasp.

"Damn," explained Parker when Macy crawled over and told them that the bundles contained rations, no ammo and no water. The bundles remained where they'd landed as no one was thinking of eating and no one wanted to take a chance of being shot attempting to unpack the bundles.

Cahill put another call in for water. An hour later, the drone of a small plane could be heard approaching Hill 342. Cahill recognized the small aircraft right away as it passed low over the hilltop, dropping ammo and water bags. Unfortunately when the water bags hit the ground, they burst open, spilling a good deal of their contents. Enough was saved that each man received about four ounces of water. Throughout the day, the sounds of battle could be heard from Hill 342 and elsewhere. It was going to be a long day.

"Sir, we've got to get some water. We're going to lose people to heat stroke before the enemy ever gets to us," Macy said. "Let me take some volunteers and go down the backside and see if I can find some. I think I see a stream down there." Cahill and Parker exchanged looks and Parker finally nodded approval. Macy crawled off, retrieving water bags that hadn't burst and policing up three volunteers. Cahill watched and said a small prayer as Macy and team crawled over the crest of the hill.

Going down the hill was much easier than attempting to come up. Macy had spotted a stream at the base of the hill and reached it unscathed. Plunging into the water, the small band of Marines drank their fill before they filled their own canteens. All thought of using their iodine tablets was lost as they drank. When the water bags were full, the foursome started the long climb back to the top. It seemed a bit easier now that they had drunk some water before starting up.

AT APPROXIMATELY 0700, the division commenced its attack with a twenty-minute artillery barrage. The planned air strikes didn't happen due to fog and low ceilings. As the artillery lifted, the ground assault commenced. The 2nd Battalion, 35th Regiment, was the first to step off and immediately ran into a firefight, but within five hours it fought its way through the enemy and reached its assigned first night objective at Much'on-ne. The 35th was ordered to hold until it linked up with the 5th RCT the next day. The first unit to step off was the 5th RCT, which was destined to move up the center on the road north past Hill 342. However, at the first crossroads, the lead battalion took a left turn onto the road designated for the 1st Marines. The battalion moved three miles and ran straight into an enemy roadblock and stalled.

Unknown to the 25th Division or Eighth Army was the fact that the 6th North Korean Division had planned to launch its own attack this morning. The 1st of the 5th Marines was stuck in Chindong-ni, unable to move because of the 5th RCT's mistake. The 24th Regiment was in positions west of Chindong-ni on the morning of the sixth when enemy forces struck at Love Company as it moved forward with Item Company. Both companies ran, as had been the case with the 24th in the past.

A day later, the battalion commander found the two companies four miles to the rear. Colonel White was relieved and Colonel Arthur S. Champney was placed in command. The 3rd of the 5th Marines was supposed to move back to a reserve position but was ambushed by an enemy force that had negotiated its way east around the 24th Regiment frontline forces. The 2nd of the 5th started towards Hill 342 and was heavily engaged while other units of the 5th RCT ran headlong into an attack by the 6th North Korean Division. By early afternoon, General Kean recognized that he had a problem.

Arriving at 1st Provisional Marine Brigade headquarters, Kean found General Craig.

"Craig, you understand the situation we have here?" Kean asked.

"Yes, sir. I think it's best described as chaos," Craig said, not really wanting to use the unprofessional words he was thinking.

"We've got to get this sorted out. I'm putting you in charge now. The 5th RCT is under your command along with the Marine brigade. I'll notify Colonel Ordway," Kean directed, much to Craig's surprise.

Why the hell don't you sort this out? This is your division and your command, Craig was thinking. As soon as Kean departed, Craig took off in his helicopter and visited the front to observe exactly what was happening. His first stop was the 5th RCT CP, where Colonel Ordway was residing, not having been to the front to observe the situation first-hand but relying on reports. Despite what Craig considered to be light resistance, Ordway couldn't move the 5th RCT. The heaviest fighting was around Hill 342.

Chapter 62
Load Out

8 AUGUST 1950
1st Marine Division
San Diego, California

THE HARBOR in San Diego was teeming with ships. Not unusual for this Navy town, but it had been several years since the community had witnessed the number of ships and activity at the port. The docks were occupied by troop transports, civilian cargo ships, military fuel tankers, and aircraft carriers. That morning, trains arrived with military vehicles, artillery tubes, and tanks. All had to be loaded on the waiting ships.

Major General O. P. Smith sat in his office at Camp Pendleton. He had taken command of the 1st Marine Division only two weeks before on 26 July 1950. At that time the 1st Marine Division consisted of 3,459 personnel, which was about half the strength of a Marine regiment. The knock on his door got his attention. "Come in," General Smith responded.

"Morning, sir. Everyone is here for this morning's update," Lieutenant Colonel Godbold said.

"Okay, send them in and let's get started. I want to head into San Diego later and see how the loadout is going," General Smith said, clearing off the papers on his desk. General Cates and members of the G-staff filed in along with Lieutenant Colonel Godbold. General Smith moved to the conference table, and once he was seated, each officer took a seat.

"Gentlemen, let's review where we've come from and what's ahead of us. Colonel Godbold, how about covering our personnel situation?" Smith requested.

"Yes, sir. On the day you took command, sir, the 1st Marine Division had a total of strength of three thousand, four hundred and fifty-nine personnel. As a result of the president's call-up on July nineteenth, we received on thirty-one July the first of the reserve units: the 12th Amphibian Tractor Company from San Francisco, the 13th Infantry Company from Los Angeles and the 3rd Engineer Company from Phoenix. The units of the 2nd Marine Division are at less than fifty percent strength at this time and are heading this way by train from Camp Lejeune. Those units will be redesignated 1st Marine Division. To fill out the ranks, the Marine Organized Reserve of thirty-three thousand has been activated. Marines in post throughout the US have been arriving daily now and we're processing them into the units as fillers. The Volunteer Marine Corps Reserve is also being called up, and selected individuals can be expected in the weeks to come, probably as replacements once we're deployed," Godbold outlined.

"How many are we talking about in the Volunteer Marine Corps Reserve?" Colonel Alpha L. Bowser, the G-3 operations officer, asked.

"Sir, there approximately ninety thousand souls in that force, but these people have had no military training since they left active duty versus the Organized Reserve, who've had weekend drills and two weeks each summer," Godbold explained. "As of yesterday, our division strength is seventeen thousand, one hundred and sixty-two. We're approaching full strength at this time."

"Good, let's get these people in-processed and assigned to units as quickly as possible," General Smith directed. Looking at Colonel

Bowser, he asked, "Alpha, how are we expanding the units with this new manpower?"

"Sir, we're able to expand from two companies per battalion of one hundred men to three companies of two hundred men. This will give each rifle company a third platoon now. We've also expanded the heavy weapons companies from two machine-gun sections to three sections and the same for the antitank sections and the eighty-one mortar sections. Our air wing is almost at full strength as we've had several reserve units arrive both in flight units and aviation ground units, all of which are at El Toro now," Colonel Bowser replied.

"When those elements from the 2nd Division arrive, what's the plan for them?" Smith asked.

"Sir, they'll be reactivated as the 7th Marine Brigade on seventeen August. Colonel Homer L. Litzenberg, the current commander, will assume command of the 7th, which is forming out of what was the 6th Marine. These guys just completed a six-month Med cruise and barely had time to change uniforms before they boarded the trains to get here. They're scheduled to sail on the first of September," Bowser said.

"When are we looking at the 1st Marine deploying?" Smith asked.

"The 1st Marine is schedule to board ships on the fourteenth of this month, only ten days after they were activated. That's pretty good and attributed to a lot of hard work to get ready," Bowser offered.

Looking at Colonel Francis McAlister, the G-4, Smith asked about the equipment loadout. "Having scrounged up equipment left all over the Pacific after the war has been a godsend to us. The equipment is old, but the folks at the Barstow Depot have done a great job of bringing it all up to standards. Old, yes, but functional and operating just fine. We've received the new tanks and they're on flat cars as we speak and rolling into the port today. We're attempting to combat-load the ships to minimize the cross-loading that will be required in Japan," McAlister stated.

"Are the tanks being loaded on LSTs?" Smith asked.

"Sir, that's a problem. It seems we gave a lot of our LST fleet to the Japanese after the war to make up for what we sank. The Japanese are allowing us to use those ships manned with Japanese crews as well, but they will be loaded in Kobe, Japan, when the tanks arrive there," McAlister explained. Smith just shook his head in disbelief.

"Okay, good rundown. I'll be flying to Japan on the sixteenth and some of you will be going with me. I'll talk to you later about who's going early. Any questions?" Smith asked. There were none and the meeting adjourned.

Chapter 63
Hill 342

8 August 1950
  Company D, 2nd of the 5th Marines
  Hill 342, South Korea

Captain John Finn Jr. had been leading his company slowly towards Hill 342. The battalion had stepped off the day before with orders to relieve the Army unit on the hilltop but had been engaging enemy resistance the whole time. Resupply of water had been lacking, with only small amounts coming forward to fill canteens. As the sun came up, Dog Company was just beginning to climb the hill. As they moved up, they experienced the same difficulties as Cahill's platoon had undergone, but worse with the increased sniper fire. Reaching the summit, Finn held the company back until he could talk with Captain Parker.

"John Finn, Dog Company, 2nd Marine Battalion," John said, rolling into Parker's foxhole.[1]

"Nice to meet you there, John. Robert Parker, Dog Company, 5th

---

1. There are discrepancies between Army sources and Marine sources as to which company this was that relieved Hill 342. I have used Marine sources in this instance.

RCT. Welcome to hell's half acre as that's about all we hold on this hilltop."

"Yeah I noticed it is a bit warm, action-wise and temperature-wise. Gads, it's hot and only 0900. What's the situation up here?" Finn inquired, and Parker gave him an in-depth brief on the importance of holding the hill and the enemy locations as well as tactics that he had experienced.

"Well, I have a lieutenant that can help with one of those problems. Lieutenant Wirth!" Finn yelled out.

"Sir?" was sounded from the far crest of the hill.

"Get your ass over here, young man," Finn responded. A few minutes later a baby-faced young officer peered over the edge of Finn and Parker's position.

"You called, sir?" Second Lieutenant LeRoy Wirth asked.

"Crawl in here, Wirth, and get your map out," Finn directed. Once Wirth had his map out, Captain Parker commenced to explain the location of the most dangerous enemy positions. Wirth took copious notes. When Parker was done, Wirth looked at Captain Finn.

"Okay, Wirth, you have your targets, now go do your thing," Finn directed. Wirth crawled out and moved to the RTO who'd accompanied him in the climb. Immediately Wirth was on the radio, making a call. Shortly, Corsair aircraft in flight could be heard and seen along with a Grasshopper observation plane. The Grasshopper was at about a thousand feet when it suddenly rolled into a steep dive and fired a rocket at the adjacent hill. When the rocket impacted, a cloud of white smoke drifted up but no explosion.

Captain Parker had been watching but plopped back in the foxhole and with disgust and disappointment stated, "Well, that was a damn dud. Some support we're getting from this exercise."

"Just wait," Finn responded, looking skyward. He could no longer see the F4U Corsair fighters, but his attention was immediately drawn to the hill that had received the smoke rocket when the first explosion was heard. Parker jumped up and likewise directed his attention when the second fighter passed over the hilltop and incinerated the hilltop with a load of napalm. Parker had never seen such close-air support before. Each one of the four fighters made a bombing run over the hilltop with a mixture of two-hundred-and-fifty-pound bombs and napalm. When they were done dropping, they returned to strafe what was left on the hilltop.

"My God, I've never seen anything like that before. There may be hope up here yet," Parker exclaimed, just before mortar rounds impacted on their positions.

"It appears we have more work to do today," Finn said as a burst of fire erupted close to the position and four enemy soldiers jumped up fifty feet away, firing their burp guns. Three were cut down before they reach the neighboring foxhole, where the fourth jumped in with an empty weapon swinging. The soldier and Marine in the foxhole made short work of subduing the attacker and tossed his body out of the hole.

The rest of the day was spent adjusting artillery and air strikes while holding off close-in attacks by the enemy. It wasn't long before Second Lieutenant Wallace Reid and Second Lieutenant Arthur Oakley were killed and Second Lieutenant Edward Emmelman was wounded and had to be carried down the hill. The only commissioned officers left were Wirth and Captain Finn, who in the early afternoon was hit in the head and had to be carried down as well.

On the trek down, Finn met his executive officer, First Lieutenant Robert Hanifin. "Bob, take command. The bastards nailed me," Finn said from his stretcher.

Lieutenant Hanifin was moving up the hill with a 60mm mortar crew. Like everyone else, the heat was taking its toll on those coming up the hill. *Damn, it has got to be over a hundred degrees*, thought Hanifin as he watched another mortarman drop with heat exhaustion. Removing his canteen, he soaked a bandanna and laid it over the Marine's face and then dragged him to some shade under a bush. Leaving him, Hanifin picked up the mortar and began moving up the hill. He finally reached the crest and was met by Master Sergeant Harold Reeves. Master Sergeant Reeves was an "old Marine" with thirty years of service already under his belt. He was supposed to be entering retirement but was held for the duration, which he didn't object to. At forty-six, he was still in great shape and had a wealth of combat experience beginning on Guadalcanal in 1942. He had also served in China in his very early days.

"Sir, Colonel Rosie is on the horn and wants to talk to you. I told him that all the platoon leaders are gone and only Lieutenant Wirth is here with you."

"Thanks, Master Sergeant," Hanifin said, crawling next to Reeves and taking a seat next to him in the foxhole. It was still unsafe to stand too long as the snipers were still active even with air strikes and artillery pounding the surrounding hills. Accepting the mike/receiver, Hanifin depressed the switch. "Anger Six, Dog Five, over."

"Dog Five, Anger Six, what is your situation? Over," Colonel Reeves responded. Hanifin never heard him as he keeled over.

"Anger Six, Dog Six India, Dog Five just went down with heat exhaustion, over."

"Dog Five India, you said Dog Five is down now. You're in command, then. Get back to me when you've assessed the situation. Over."

"Roger, Anger Six," Reeves responded. He felt he was up to the task, and he commanded the company with Wirth directing the air strikes and artillery. Between the two, they held the hill until ordered to withdraw.

By late morning, Captain Parker received word to vacate the property and bring Lieutenant Cahill's platoon with him. What water was left by the soldiers was given to the Marines remaining on the hill. Cahill rounded up his platoon. He had started the operation with fifty-seven Marines, and he was coming off the hill with eighteen.

Chapter 64

It's Over

9 August 1950
  1st Provisional Marine Brigade HQ
  Chindong-ni, South Korea

HAVING BEEN HANDED command of the 5th RCT as well as the 1st Provisional Marine Brigade, General Craig took immediate steps to sort the chaos out and get the attack moving. The first order of business was to get the 1st Battalion, 5th RCT, off the southern road.

"Colonel Newton," General Craig said, walking directly into Newton's command post, much to the surprise of everyone. No one had heard a helicopter land. Craig headed straight to the map. Someone immediately yelled "Attention!" in response to Craig's announcement.

"As you were. Newton, come here," Craig said, heading for the map board.

"Yes, sir," Newton said, still surprised to see Craig there.

"The 1st Battalion, 5th RCT, has itself stuck at a roadblock three miles up the road and is causing this cluster mess. Get your battalion up there and relieve those dog faces, politely. Get the road open so we can get the brigade rolling. Any questions?" Craig asked.

"No, sir. We'll move out shortly."

"Good. The 3rd Battalion will follow you, and once I get the 2nd Battalion back he will follow as well. I want you guys leapfrogging as you go up. Now open this road," Craig said. "I know you can do it."

Colonel Newton had to first clear the road enough to move his battalion forward. Setting up a vehicle control point at the road intersection, his Marines began turning the Army vehicles around and having them return to Chindong-ni as his Marines walked the three miles to the front. Slowly replacing the soldiers of the 1st Battalion, 5th RCT, the Marines assumed the fight, which included calling upon an asset that the Army didn't have readily available—Corsair fighters. As the Marines pounded the elements of the 6th NK Division, they still had more casualties from heat than enemy action.

Over the next two days, the 1st Provisional Marine Brigade moved forward, exercising the tactics of leapfrogging one battalion over the other, which allowed Marines to replenish water and rest somewhat as they moved forward. Approaching the village of Kosong, 3rd Battalion, 5th Marine, was in the lead and came upon elements of the 83rd Motorized Regiment of the 105th North Korean Armored Division. Immediately, artillery fire was called for along with close-air support.

"Eagle One, Knight Three, do you see what I see down there?" Captain Howard Burbank said as he led his flight of four Corsairs.

"Knight Three, Eagle One, I sure do. I guess the grunts have found the mother lode for us. I believe that's about two hundred vehicles on the road. Over."

"Eagle One, let's hit the north end first and close the road. Then we can swing around and hit the southern end and work north. Over."

"Sounds good, Knight Three. Let me tell Switchblade Four what our plan is. QSY at time," Captain Bob Witt said, switching from his VHF radio to the FM radio that allowed communications with the forward observer on the ground.

"Switchblade Four, Eagle One, over."

Switchblade Four, Lieutenant Waldrop, was standing next to

Colonel Taplett and acknowledged the call. Taplett listened as Eagle One outlined the plan of attack and nodded in approval, which Waldrop relayed. Standing on a rise overlooking the valley and road that the vehicles were lined up on, he raised his binoculars to observe the strike. After a moment, he could see the rising cloud of destruction in the distance, followed a moment later by the sound. He also noticed the streaks of green tracers arcing skyward at the twisting and turning Corsairs. He didn't notice the flight of four aircraft approaching his position from the south until they passed over his head at about one hundred feet and unleashed small objects. When those objects impacted, the fireball created by the exploding napalm engulfed the vehicles closest to his Marines. A second flight came in, strafing the surrounded grounds along the sides of the road as enemy soldiers attempted to hide, having abandoned their vehicles. The Marines could only watch at this point and wait until the close-air support had finished their work. When it was done, the Marines continued to advance through the carnage of burned vehicles and bodies. The road to Chinju was open for some time, it appeared, and the Marine Brigade moved forward.

Chapter 65
1st Cav Tastes Battle

9 AUGUST 1950
1st Cav CP
Taegu, South Korea

"WHY AM I just hearing about this now?" General Gay almost yelled. "So what exactly is going on?"

"During the evening hours last night, the enemy moved two regiments across the Naktong between Indong and Waegwan in the 1st ROK sector. This alerted 5th Regiment to possible action. At 0300 hours, the 5th detected movement on the river and called for illumination. It caught an approximate regiment attempting to cross. They engaged with direct fire, mortars and indirect fire. This crossing occurred at Noch'on, two miles south of Waegwan," the Ops officer explained. "Sir, we were hoping for confirmation before bringing this to your attention. First Lieutenant Harry Buckley, acting S-2 for the 5th Cav, observed this action. Let me have him come in and explain to you."

Gay nodded and Lieutenant Buckley was summoned.

"Sir, Lieutenant Buckley reporting as ordered," Buckley said, coming to attention and saluting General Gay, who returned the salute.

"Report, Lieutenant, and stand at ease."

"Thank you, sir," Buckley responded and did so. "Sir, just prior to daylight this morning, I, with a small group of men from the I&R platoon, was on reconnaissance. Approximately forty-five minutes prior to daylight, I observed enemy forces moving up the ridgeline just northwest of Hill 268. The enemy were moving at a dog trot in groups of four. Every fourth man carried an automatic weapon, either a light machine gun or a burp gun. I watched them until they had all disappeared into the brush on Hill 268. In my opinion, and I counted them carefully, the enemy was in strength of a reinforced battalion, approximately seven hundred and fifty men," Buckley said, pausing for a moment. "General, I'm not a very excitable person and I know what I saw, when I saw it, where I was when I saw it, and where the enemy is going."[1]

General Gay studied the young man for a moment. "I believe you, Lieutenant. Good report and thank you," he said. "Dismissed." Buckley came to attention and saluted, which Gay returned. Then Gay began studying the map, thinking to himself, *We just have too damn big of a front to hold. The 5th Regiment in the north has a fourteen-thousand-yard front; 8th Regiment with his two battalions has a twenty-thousand-yard front. The 7th is the only one with a reasonable front. Artillery is so scattered they can't mass fires except two batteries at a time. And being seven thousand yards from the front lines doesn't help much. The river is an obstacle, but not a great one if they're wading across in our sectors. I'll bet there's an underwater bridge as well. Hill 268 controls the railroad line from Pusan to Seoul to Manchuria and to the highway. Cannot let them control that hill.*

Gay's thoughts were interrupted by Colonel Houser. "Sir, I spoke with the Ops officer at the 5th Regiment. The illum rounds revealed possibly two regiments attempting to wade across the river. The 5th hit

---

1. Roy E. Appleman, *United States Army in the Korean War: South to the Naktong, North to the Yalu (June–November 1950)* (Washington, D.C.: United States Army Center of Military History, 1992), 340.

them with both direct and indirect fire. They're sure some got across the river as Lieutenant Buckley reported."

Turning to his operations officer, Gay said, "We need to clean those people out and pronto. Get Lieutenant Colonel Pete Clainos, commander of the 1st of the 7th. He's bivouacked outside of here. I want his battalion uploaded in trucks. Attach a tank platoon to him and have him attack to seize and secure Hill 268 and continue the attack to seize and secure Hill 154. Place 61st Field Artillery Battalion in direct support and start prepping Hill 268."

"Yes, sir, I'll hand-carry the order to Colonel Clainos myself," Houser replied.

"What's the weather forecast for today?" Gay asked.

"Sir, clear skies and high temperature, I'm afraid."

"Be sure Clainos understands his people are going to need water as much as ammo going up that hill," Gay said over his shoulder as he was still examining the map. *Don't need to lose this fight to heat-exhausted soldiers*, he was thinking.

Chapter 66
It Only Gets Worse

10 August 1950
   Task Force Hill
   Yongsan, South Korea

THE SITUATION for the past five days had only gotten worse. The North Korean 4th Division had managed, despite artillery and close-air support, to build an underwater bridge across the Naktong River and was pouring men and heavy equipment across the river. In addition, the bridge across the Naktong well south of Kilo Company was still intact and the US soldiers from Kilo Company defending the bridge had been overwhelmed. The bridge was now in North Korean hands. With two bridges in place, the 4th North Korean Division was almost completely across.

Needing assistance, the 9th Regiment of the 2nd Division was attached to the 24th Division and commanded by Colonel John Hill. Hill arrived on the morning of the eighth and went into the attack at 1600 hours, relieving Company B, 1st Battalion, 34th Regiment, on Hill 165 as well as the Heavy Weapons Company on Obong-ni Ridge to the south of the road. By nightfall, the 2nd Battalion had taken part of Hill 165 and the 1st Battalion had taken and lost Obong-ni Ridge.

Pusan Perimeter

The previous day had been a day of only small success for the 24th Division, with the 2nd Battalion, 19th Regiment, seizing a couple of hills overlooking the Naktong River. The North Koreans attacked off Hill 165 and hit the 2nd Battalion hard; the result was that only one company had more than one officer. The rest of the day was a standstill. General Church needed to make some decisions and called a meeting with Hill, Beauchamp, and Moore, commander of the 19th Regiment, as well as his staff.

"We have too many units all working, but not in unison. The 34th and the 19th have been in the fight since the beginning. Their soldiers are tired—hell, they're exhausted, and the units are understrength. The 9th Regiment, however, is fresh from the States and at a much higher strength level. I'm placing Colonel Hill and the 9th Regiment in charge of all forces in the Bulge area. We'll call this Task Force Hill. Anyone object?" Church asked. No one did.

"Okay, then, Colonel Hill, I want to see your plan for cleaning this mess up and driving the enemy back across the river. Can you have that in the morning for me?"

"Can do, sir" was Hill's response. "We'll start working on it right away." As soon as Church left, he and Beauchamp began putting a plan together. Working through the night, they had a plan ready by morning.

"Sir, as you designated, TF Hill will consist of the 9th Regiment minus 2nd Battalion, the 34th Regiment, the 19th Regiment and the 1st Battalion, 21st Regiment. The 9th and 19th Regiments will counterattack southwest to seize Hill 165 and Obong-ni Ridge. 1st Battalion, 21st, will attack south to the south end of the Obong-ni Ridge. The 34th Regiment protects the left flank. We'll kick off at 0800," Hill briefed.

"Do it and good luck" was all Church said.

Unfortunately for TF Hill, the North Koreans had reinforced throughout the night and now had several artillery pieces across the river along with other heavy weapons, to include mortars and a few tanks. Exercising their usual tactics, the North Koreans slipped behind TF Hill and established roadblocks, cutting off supplies to the frontline forces. Yongsan began receiving incoming artillery fire. For the next five days, the situation ebbed and flowed, with neither side gaining ground. By day, US forces seized their objectives on Hill 165 and Obong-ni Ridge, and by night they were driven off those positions, only to have to go back the next day with fewer men. Over the course of the five days, one battalion of the 34th was down to less than a rifle company in strength. Many companies were being commanded by noncommissioned officers because of officer casualties. By the fifteenth, General Church ordered everyone to hold their present positions.

Things weren't much better for the 4th North Korean Division. Prisoner reports indicated that the 4th Division were on its last legs in terms of logistics and manpower. There was a shortage of food and ammunition. There was no medical support. Replacements were untrained, and over half didn't arrive with weapons. US Air Force bombing campaigns had severely reduced the flow of goods to the front lines, which could only be moved at night and mostly in animal-drawn carts or by porters.

Chapter 67
New Orders

12 AUGUST 1950
1st Provisional Marine Brigade
Chindong-ni, South Korea

"CRAIG, I need you to meet me at my headquarters. Ordway will be there as well as Fisher and Champney," Kean ordered over the field phone. "Be here at 1100 hours."

Craig looked at the wall clock next to an old faded calendar on the wall. It was 0900 hours and 12 August. *I wonder what this is about.* He had more important things on his mind right now. Turning to Lieutenant Colonel Ray Murray, commander of the 5th Marine Regiment, he asked, "What is the situation now?"[1]

"Sir, the 1st Battalion conducted a passage of line with 3rd Battalion and had an ambush sprung on them. Fortunately the North Koreans sprung it early and close-air support is making them pay dearly. We've moved eleven miles unopposed since the air strikes had

---

1. Lieutenant Colonel Raymond L. Murray was highly decorated in his Marine Corps career, with multiple Distinguished Service Crosses, Navy Crosses and Silver Stars. He rose to the rank of major general before retirement in 1968. He died in 2004.

decimated the retreating enemy convoy the other day. We're only three miles east of Sach'on. Now 1st Battalion is in the process of taking Hill 301 and Hill 250 on the right side of the road, and 3rd Battalion is on Hill 202 on the left side of the road. The fight on Hill 202 has been tough and we lost the entire third platoon up there and another platoon has been badly chewed up."

"Okay, keep at it. I have to run over to Kean's headquarters and check on the 5th RCT to see how they're doing. I'm controlling two regiments in the fight and division is controlling two regiments barely in the fight. Working for the Army sure is different," Craig said as he grabbed his hat and left for his helicopter.

Arriving at Kean's headquarters, he had stopped to pick up both Colonel Fisher and Colonel Ordway. Neither said much on the flight, and Craig chalked it up to the noise of the helicopter as he was the only passenger with a headset to muffle the sounds.

Walking into Kean's CP, Craig noticed that Kean didn't look happy.

"Sit down, gentlemen. Ordway, what is going on up there?" Kean growled.

"Sir, we've run headlong into what I believe is an attack by the 6th. We got to Pongam-ni and established positions around the town on the high ground. They attacked on the night of the tenth, morning of the eleventh and overran our artillery positions. Colonel Jones was seriously wounded and Colonel Daley, the artillery battalion commander, took command of the 1st Battalion. We had to pull out of the town and had an ambush hit us down the road. If the 24th would have kept the road clear—" Ordway began.

"Enough!" Kean said loudly, not wanting to hear complaints. "Pull back to Chindong-ni. Colonel Fisher, do the same. I don't want your regiment out there alone. It appears that the 6th North Korean Division has launched a major attack and we're both at a stalemate. I'd expected the 2nd Infantry Division to be here by now as General Walker briefed us, but it appears they're bound for someplace else," Kean said, sounding rather disheartened. He then looked at General Craig.

"Effective 1200 today, the 1st Provisional Marine Brigade is detached from the division. General Walker needs you someplace else. Losing you cuts my combat power significantly and we cannot continue this attack. Orders will be waiting for you from Eighth Army when you get back to your headquarters. Good luck and thanks for your help," Kean said, standing and extending his hand to Craig.

"Best to you too, sir" was all Craig could say.

When he arrived back at his headquarters, the orders had been received to move the 1st Provisional Marine Brigade to Miryang and bivouac in Army reserve. Nice thought, but that was not what happened.

Chapter 68
Mopping Up

12 August 1950
  1st Cav Division CP
  Taegu, South Korea

"Attention," someone yelled as General Walker walked into the 1st Cavalry Division command post.

Walker immediately responded, "At ease," putting everyone back to work instead of standing at attention. General Gay came out of his office, surprised by Walker's visit. He was visibly limping. "Understand I have to put you in for another Purple Heart, General," Walker said, eyeing Gay's leg. "How bad is it?"

"Sir, it's nothing," Gay said with a wave of his hand. "But let's sit down. Coffee?"

"Yeah, I'll take a cup and then you can tell me exactly why one of my division commanders is out getting a Purple Heart," Walker commented, partly in jest but partially scolding.

When Gay returned to his office with coffee in hand, he began to explain.

"Our attack on the ninth failed to take Hill 268. The enemy was in strength on that piece of ground, more so than we expected, and the heat got to the troops. I blame the heat more than the enemy. The next morning, yesterday, the ADC, the chief of staff and my G-2 with an MP escort drove over to look at Hill 268 and got ambushed. No one killed, but a few wounded MPs. Yesterday afternoon my aide and I drove out to have a word with the battalion fixing to take the hill when a mortar round landed right in the middle of us as we were holding a powwow. I got this piece of shrapnel in my leg, but I came out pretty good compared to some of the others," Gay explained, pausing long enough to take a sip of coffee. "Pissed me off, so while I'm getting patched up a platoon of tanks came rolling up. I called for an artillery prep on the hill and had the tanks take the Pusan-Seoul Road around Hill 268 and engage the reverse slope with tank fire. By 1600 we secured Hill 268."

"Well, that's good," Walker said. "At least I don't have to worry about this now."

"We found one group of about two hundred dead that were caught by artillery fire. The battalion counted three to four hundred dead on the hill," Gay added.

"What were your losses?"

"The 1st Battalion suffered fourteen men killed and forty-eight wounded over the two days. But that's not the worst of it. They came across twenty-six bodies of US soldiers that had their hands tied behind their backs, no boots, and all were shot in the back. They were executed," Gay said, his anger obvious in his voice.

"Well, this isn't the first I've heard of these atrocities. We've come across executions in almost every village along the Naktong. It appears that the enemy is attempting to wipe out the middle class, educators, government officials, police, anyone except peasants. These people were under Japanese rule for some fifty years and the brutality they experienced under that regime left a permanent imprint on these people. Life means little to them, and cruelty is common. Certainly not in line with Western standards," Walker explained. "What info are you getting out of the prisoners?" he asked. "You did take prisoners, didn't you?"

Gay chuckled. "Yes, sir. We still aren't barbarians. The prisoners are telling us they were part of the 7th Regiment of the 3rd Division and crossed the Naktong with about a thousand. They say the artillery and mortars were the biggest casualty producer. They were out of food, ammo and medical supplies. This is the same bunch that beat up the 19th Regiment at the Kum River and tangled with us at Yongdong. Payback is a mother," Gay added with a smile.

"Well, don't get cocky on me. We have reports that the 10th North Korean Division arrived across the river from you. We believe they will attempt to cross the river around Tuksong-dong and drive east to cut the Taegu-Pusan Road. We think they will attempt to use the partially destroyed bridge. Night before last, a battalion from the 10th waded across four miles west of Hyongp'ung and took Hills 265 and 409 in the 24th sector. Ambushed a patrol from the I&R Company of the 21st Regiment. Took most of the day to drive them off and back across the river," Walker outlined.

"We have action this morning in the 2nd of the 7th sector. Enemy crossed at Tuksong-dong and got into it with the 2nd. They penetrated to Wich'on-dong, where an intense fight broke out with H Company. The 2nd Battalion counterattacked at that point and ran their asses back across the river," Gay said.

"Think they'll attempt that again?" Walker asked, looking up at the map hanging on the wall.

"I hope they do. We have preplanned fires registered on the approaches on both sides of the river. The 2nd of the 7th Battalion is positioned there and should be able to handle anything they throw at them. My concern, however, is how are they able to wade the damn river?"

"Simple—this hot weather with little rain has dropped the water table three feet. That's allowing them to wade across, at least most of the little buggers," Walker pointed out, standing.

"Have we heard anything from the 1st ROK Division on my right flank?" Gay asked as he stood.

"No, their sector has been fairly quiet…and that concerns me.

Think I'll head over there and talk to them. You have a good day," Walker said, departing the command post.

As long as the bastards stay on the west side of the river, I will, Gay was thinking as he watched Walker depart.

Chapter 69
Cross the Naktong

14 August 1950
2nd Battalion, 5th Cavalry
Waegwan, South Korea

"Did you hear that, Sarge?" Corporal Moralis asked almost in a whisper. Moralis and Sergeant Welch had been manning an outpost along the river on the boundary with the 1st ROK Division. In the early-morning darkness, they could barely see fifty yards to their front but looked forward to the sun coming up.

"Yeah, I heard it. Either we have company or the ROK soldiers have gotten lost. We best call this in to the CP." Sergeant Welch picked up the receiver of the TA-1 field telephone and cranked the handle. "CP, this is OP1. Hey, we're hearing voices to the north along the boundary with the 1st ROK," Welch reported. He listened for a moment and then responded, "No, I don't know what they're saying. It sounds Korean, and I don't speak Korean." He paused again. "Alright, I reported. What you do with it is your business. Jesus!" Welch slammed the receiver back into the cradle.

"What'd they say, Sarge?" Moralis asked.

"They wanted to know what to do with the information. They can shove it up their ass for all I care. Let's get out a sterno can and fire up some coffee," Welch instructed Moralis.

At the company CP, Captain Everheart was handed a note by the master sergeant along with a cup of coffee. "Hey, sir, this just came in from OP1. Thought you might like to see it. Careful, the coffee is hot."

"Thanks, Master Sergeant. What time is it?"

"Sir, it's 0645. Sun should be up in a few more minutes. Seems OP1 is hearing voices along the boundary with the 1st ROK Division."

Captain Everheart sipped his coffee and read the note. After he finished, he started to get up. "I best call this in to battalion. Let them know we're doing more than just sitting out here taking in Korean culture," he said, putting down his coffee and reaching for the TA-312 field telephone. "Hello, Battalion? Hey, Captain Everheart, George Company here. Our OP1 is reporting Korean voices along the boundary with the 1st ROK," Everheart said, pausing while someone on the other end spoke. "No, they don't know what the Koreans were talking about. My guys don't speak Korean. Just tell the colonel. Everheart out." He hung up the phone, picking up his coffee cup and looking at the master sergeant.

"I sometimes wonder what idiots we have working the CP," Everheart said, standing. "I suppose I should take a trip out to OP1 and see for myself. Be back in an hour." Before he could leave, all hell broke loose to the north in the 1st ROK Division sector north of Waegwan.

George Company, the right flank company for the 1st Cavalry Division, occupied Hill 303. Nine hundred and fifty feet in elevation above the river, it offered great observation of the river, as well as Waegwan, the road and railroad arteries. An elongated oval terrain feature, it was over a mile long with the town of Waegwan sitting at the end of the southern slope. For several days, Captain Everheart and the men of George Company had observed gunfire and explosions in the 1st ROK sector, but their own sector had been relatively quiet, until today.

"Hey, Sergeant Welch! What the hell is going on in the 1st ROK sector?" Everheart asked as he approached OP1.

"Sir, it appears that they have a full-blown attack on their positions in progress and it's creeping towards our position now. Instead of flowing east, it appears to be coming south towards us," Welch said.

"Get the artillery folks prepared. If that attack crosses into our sector, I want artillery on it immediately. I'm going back to my CP and call battalion," Everheart ordered as he headed for his jeep.

Reaching battalion, he informed the battalion commander of the situation. Artillery fire was already being adjusted for OP1. Finally OP1 was in small-arms fire with the attacking North Koreans. By 1200 hours, the entire company was in contact.

"Sir, Everheart here. We're in heavy contact. So far it's just infantry, but we can hear tanks moving at the base of the hill. Haven't seen them."

"Are you able to hold?" Colonel Jewels asked.

"For now…yeah. We need a resupply of ammo if we can get it, however."

"I'll have some run up to you later today. Keep using the artillery and battalion mortars as much as you can. I expect that their main attack will come tonight."

"I believe you, sir. It's going to be a long night." And it was. Although a major assault didn't occur, there were probes all night along the perimeter, which kept the soldiers of G Company awake and vigilant. All were glad to see sunrise approach as it meant that they had all made it through the night alive. When it became light enough to see, their hopes sank.

"Sir, Everheart here."

"Good to hear your voice, Captain. How did it go last night?"

"We had only probes during the night with no casualties. However, right now I'm looking at about fifty North Koreans and two tanks at the base of Hill 303 moving on the road. That's what I can see, but I suspect there are a lot more."

"Roger, Fox Company got hit hard and I'm pulling Fox Company back and sending Baker to reinforce you with a platoon of tanks. They should reach you by 1200 hours."

"I'll be looking for them. I'll contact the Baker commander on the SC-300 and coordinate his arrival," Everheart said.

"Sounds good. I'll monitor your transmissions. Good luck."

Good luck? That's the best you can do? Everheart was thinking as he placed the receiver back in the cradle. He turned to his RTO. "Get me Baker Company on the radio."

A few minutes later, Everheart transmitted, "Sabre Bravo, Sabre Golf, over."

"Sabre Golf, Sabre Bravo, sounds like you got yourself into another pickle that I have to bail you out of," the Baker commander said with a chuckle. He and Everheart were good friends and rival commanders.

"Sabre Bravo, actually, I know you're just sitting on your ass, so I thought I'd make an excuse for you to get into the fight. When are you getting here? Anytime soon would be nice. Over."

"Sabre Golf, we're loading up now and should be on the hill by 1200 hours. What's the situation? Over."

"Sabre Bravo, I see about fifty bad guys and two tanks on the road moving east. There's also a lot of movement around the hill. Waegwan appears to be deserted. Over."

"Roger, Sabre Golf. Keep me posted. Sabre Bravo out."

Baker moved out to reinforce George Company. By 1200 hours, George was undergoing a full-blown attack and totally surrounded. They hoped that Baker would arrive soon. As the sun began to set, Everheart received a call from Baker.

"Sabre Golf, Sabre Bravo, over."

"Sabre Bravo, Sabre Golf. Anytime you want to get here would be appreciated. I think we have a full battalion hitting us, over."

"Sabre Golf, we've been trying but can't seem to break through. They're hitting us with mortars and have dug in just outside of Waegwan. It will be dark soon. I'll hold here until dawn and then make another stab at it. Can you hold? Over."

"Sabre Bravo, I don't think so. We have an E and E plan. I'll let you know when we execute and where we're going. Over."

"Has Sabre Six approved that? Over."

"Sabre Bravo, I haven't heard a word from him since this morning. Don't know if it's my radios or what. Over."

"Sabre Golf, I have you five by five and I've spoken with him earlier today, over."

"Roger, well, I'm about to get busy, so I'll talk later. Sabre Golf out."

Throughout the night, enemy forces pushed against George Company. Finally Captain Everheart made a command decision and under the cover of an artillery barrage moved his company, to include the wounded, out of their position and off the hill. It was now in the hands of a North Korean battalion.

"Sabre Six, Sabre Bravo, over."

"Sabre Bravo, Sabre Six India, over."

"Sabre Six India, let me speak to Sabre Six Actual, over."

"Sabre Bravo, he's with Gary Owen Six, over." Garry Owen Six was Colonel Marcel B. Crombez, the 5th Regiment commander.

"Colonel, what is the disposition of your forces at the time?" Colonel Crombez asked, looking at the map of the battalion's positions. What he was seeing didn't please him as the information posted on the map was a day old.

"Well, sir, right now George Company has withdrawn off the hill and is moving," Lieutenant Colonel Hoss said.

"Where are they moving to?" Crombez asked. "They came off the hill when?"

"I'm not sure when they came off the hill or where they are right now," Hoss indicated.

"You don't know where one of your companies is at?" Crombez said, a bit surprised. "When did you last have commo with them?"

"Sir, I spoke to Captain Everheart yesterday morning. Baker—" Hoss started to explain before he was cut off by Crombez.

"You have no commo with them since yesterday," Crombez said, his voice slightly elevated. "Where are the rest of your companies?"

"Well, sir, Baker is in Waegwan and holding his position. Fox withdrew yesterday from his position and—"

Again, Crombez interrupted him. "So where is Fox now?"

"Sir, I'm not sure. Last word I had, he was withdrawing," Hoss said, avoiding eye contact with the regimental commander.

"Hoss, you're telling me that you don't know where two of your companies are at right now. Am I hearing you correctly?" Crombez said with a hard stare.

"Well, sir, we're attempting to locate them at this time," Hoss offered.

"Unsat, Colonel. You're relieved!" Crombez said, turning to his operations officer. "Get the XO up here to take command of this battalion." Addressing the 2nd Battalion operations officer, he added, "Notify Easy and Fox Company to move to Waegwan now. Get the 70th Tank Battalion command to attach a company to Easy Company. I want an air strike on Hill 303 scheduled for 1500 along with an artillery prep. This shit stops now."

At 1530, Air Force aircraft used napalm on Hill 303, followed by an artillery prep. Easy and Fox companies moved up the hill at 1600 and secured it by 1630 virtually unopposed. What they found, however, disturbed everyone. The bodies of twenty soldiers lay side by side, all with their hands tied behind their backs and shot in the back of the head. It was obvious that the North Koreans were not taking prisoners.

Chapter 70
Counterattack

15 August 1950
   24th Division CP
   Yongsan, South Korea

THE SITUATION across Eighth Army was terrible. The entire perimeter was under attack. General Kean and the 24th Division were barely holding the same ground that they'd held at the beginning of the month, having given up on their push to Chinju. General Gay with the 1st Cavalry Division to the north of the 25th had his hands full with a major penetration in the vicinity of Hill 409 by Hyongp'ung. The ROK forces on the east coast were being pushed back and lost P'ohang-dong. General Walker had already committed the bulk of his forces with only one unit in reserve at the moment. "Get General Craig on the horn. Tell him to move now to Yongsan, and be quick about it," Walker ordered. "I'll meet him there."

Arriving in his helicopter, Craig entered the command post for the 25th Division. Colonel Murray accompanied him. The atmosphere was oppressive. Besides General Walker and General Church, Colonel Hill and Colonel Beauchamp were present as well as Colonel Ned Moore of the 19th Regiment. Everyone looked haggard and tired, especially

General Walker. Craig could only imagine the strain the man was under with the entire perimeter under attack. Looking at Church and his experience with Kean, Craig could understand why things might not be going so well for the Army. *Church looks much like Kean, old, lacking stamina and energy. These two should have been put out to pasture some time ago, not be division commanders*, Craig was thinking, and he wasn't far off the mark. Church had come to Korea to observe the situation, not take a division into combat. He had fought in the First World War with distinction and as an assistant division commander had been wounded in the Netherlands during the Second World War. He was fifty-nine years old and looked every bit of it.

"Alright, now that everyone is here, let's get started. General," Walker said, glaring at General Church, "I'm attaching the Marine brigade to you and now I want this mess cleaned up and damn quick. Is that clear enough?"

Almost in a whisper, Church replied, "Yes, sir."

"Good, so what's the plan for how you're going to do that?" Walker asked.

Church moved to a map spread on a table. As he did so, his operations officer covered the map with a piece of acetate that had the plan sketched in grease pencil. Lieutenant Colonel Hall, the division intelligence officer, moved to the map.

"Gentlemen, the intelligence picture as of 1600 hours yesterday was as follows: The enemy continues to hold the initiative. He launched a series of low-level attacks against the 9th Regiment and 34th Regiment and attempted one against the 19th Regiment, which was stopped by artillery fire. There's actually little change in positions from the period of last report. The 19th Regiment bore the brunt of the enemy activity, which it repulsed with artillery at this morning at 0500. A small-scale attack was reported as well. A heavy attack was stopped by an air strike as reported by the 9th Regiment. In the 34th sector, an attack supported by six automatic weapons and what's believed to be an SP gun successfully dislodged Baker and Charlie Companies from this hill at 1600 yesterday evening," Colonel Hall said, pointing at the map. "The 19th Regiment reported an attack at 1521 last night, which was dispersed by artillery fire. The 21st and 3rd Engineer Battalions reported increased enemy activity in sector. If there are no questions, I'll be followed by Colonel Hyzer, the operations officer."[1]

Lieutenant Colonel Peter Hyzer stepped forward and picked up a pointer. "Sir, the division will attack at 0700 on August seventeenth to destroy enemy forces in sector and establish defensive positions on the high ground overlooking the Naktong River. The 19th Regiment attacks from present position to seize Obong Hill and continues the attack to secure Hill 223 on the right flank. The 34th Regiment attacks to seize Hill 240 and establish defensive positions on the high ground overlooking the Naktong River. The 9th Regiment attacks to seize and secure Hill 165. The 5th Marine Brigade attacks to secure Hills 102, 109, 117, 13, and 153, continues the attack to seize Hill 311 and establish defensive positions along the Naktong River. The 1st Battalion, 21st Regiment, will protect the left flank of 1st Provisional Marine Brigade from present positions," Colonel Hyzer outlined.

"Why wait until the seventeenth? Why not tomorrow?" Walker asked with frustration.

"Sir, 1st Provisional Marine Brigade is going to need some time to get here from Masan, where they're currently located," Craig offered. "I've already issued the order to break the bivouac and get ready to move out."

"General Craig, that sounds like a tall order for the brigade," Walker noted.

"We'll be in position by the morning of the seventeenth. And those hills are all part of this ridge that runs north–south. If we take the northernmost hill, then it will be possible to come south across the others, hitting the enemy in his flanks. I'll get some air support to soften up the target before we get there," Craig said with confidence.

"What about your artillery support, General?" Walker asked, directing his attention to Church.

"Sir, we have two battalions of artillery along with the battalion

---

1. "24th Infantry Division Records: Korean War Project," Korean War Project, n.d., https://www.koreanwar.org/html/2018-jpac-24div.html.

that the 5th Marines have. We'll concentrate fires on Hill 165 and Obong Hill. General Craig will utilize his to support his plan," Church explained.

"Alright, then—get it done this time," Walker said and paused. "Look, I don't mean to be a son of a bitch, but right now I have problems in two other places as well. The east coast forces of the ROK divisions are being pushed back. Hell, we had to relieve the 3rd ROK Division commander two weeks ago for cowardice. The Air Force has pulled their aircraft out of Yonil Airfield. We had to throw together a task force and send it up there to defend the airfield, which was getting small-arms fire from the surrounding hills. The 1st Cav and the ROK forces in the Taegu area are barely hanging on now that the commies crossed the Naktong at the beginning of the month and stand a good chance of taking Taegu. I need reserves and have none at this point," Walker said, his level of frustration clearly evident.

After he left, the group continued to discuss the plan. Church's intent was to have the 9th Regiment and the 5th Marines step off together.

"I request that the 9th hold until I've secured Obong-ni. The north end of our objective and Hill 165 are fairly close and I wouldn't want to have a fratricide situation," Murray requested. Church looked at Hill.

"I consider them to be one long terrain feature," Church said. "This town between the two hill masses, Tugok, along the road may pose a problem on your flank, although I suspect his main line of defense is this ridgeline three miles to the rear of Obong-ni as it's higher."

"Our intel doesn't show any large force on Obong-ni, more of a screen line. We should be able to get up and secure it with little difficulty and then Colonel Hill and the 9th can take Hill 165 with flanking fire support from us," Murray argued.

"I don't have a problem with that, General," Colonel Hill responded, so the decision was made that the 5th Marine would step off first and the 9th would hold until the north end of the ridge was secured.

"What is the fire support plan?" Church asked, looking at the commanders. "We have fifty-four tubes of 105 artillery and a battalion of 155 howitzers."

Murray looked at the other commanders before he spoke. "I'd rather not use an artillery prep on Obong-ni. I can get eighteen sorties of Corsairs to hit it before we go up. That should be sufficient to do the job. Concentrate the artillery on the other regimental objectives," Murray offered. No one argued with him as they were grateful for all the artillery support they could get.

"Alright, but throughout the night, we'll be firing on known and suspected enemy locations to the rear of Hill 165 and Obong-ni," Church stated. "Gentlemen, let's get some rest. The next couple of days are going to be busy."

Chapter 71
The Plan That Did Not Work

17 August 1950
   5th Marine Brigade
   Obong-ni Ridge, South Korea

DURING THE NIGHT, the 5th Marine Brigade moved into position one thousand yards east of Obong-ni Ridge. The 2nd Battalion had the honors of leading the attack, with 1st and then 3rd Battalions following. Colonel Rosie positioned Easy Company on the left and Dog Company on the right. The objective for each was the two northern hilltops on the ridge. As they stood with Colonel Rosie in the early-morning light, they reviewed the plan.

"What time is the air strike going in, sir?" asked Captain Andy Zimmer, commander, Dog Company.

"It's scheduled for 0730, Andy," Rosie answered. "Now you see that landslide area in the saddle between those two northern hilltops? I want that to be the boundary between your company and Bill's. Got that, Bill?" First Lieutenant Bill Sweeney commanded Easy Company.

"Yes, sir. There are enough erosion ditches between the hilltops that they should provide some cover and concealment for our move up the hill," Sweeney pointed out.

"How are you going to tackle your objective, Andy?" Rosie asked.

"Lieutenant Shinka is going to take the Third Platoon around to the road and cross the three rice paddies at the foot of Hill 109. First Platoon will follow with the rocket teams setting up along the road. I thought it best to lead with Third Platoon as Staff Sergeant Al Crowson is leading First Platoon now. Good man, but—" Zimmer said before he was interrupted by Major Morgan.

"Sir, I hear the aircraft now," said Major Morgan McNeeley, the battalion operations officer. Everyone looked skyward, finally spotting the flight of Corsairs as they commenced their bomb runs.

"Are they using napalm?" Zimmer asked.

"No, there's a shortage of drop tanks, so no napalm on this run," McNeeley replied. The look of disappointment didn't go unnoticed by Colonel Rosie.

"This should be sufficient to do the job," McNeeley added. As the Marines stood watching, their confidence level increased, knowing the enemy was getting the worst of it and that the hill would be easy to take. Finally 0800 hours registered and the order to move out was given. As Delta Company moved out, Zimmer took a position behind the Third Platoon. He had the Second Platoon in reserve but felt they wouldn't be needed until they had crossed the crest and were moving on the next ridgeline. Progress across the three rice paddies was slow because of the sucking mud. The stench was noticeable as well. The sun was rising and so was the temperature. By 0900 they had reached the foot of the hill and were about halfway up. Due to the steepness, the going was slow, but things had been quiet.

"Hey, sir, do you think the air strike took them all out?" Sergeant Taggart asked, huffing alongside Lieutenant Shinka.

"It would appear—" Shinka didn't finish when the rounds for a machine-gun position across the road in Tugok village opened fire.

"Medic!" was immediately heard, and more than once. Shinka's platoon was totally exposed to Tugok, and more machine guns hidden on Hills 117 and 143, fingers of Hill 165, joined the suppression. Whatever enemy was at the top had not been killed by the air strike as hand grenades now descended from the summit. *How in the hell could anyone be alive up there after that bombing?* Zimmer was thinking as he watched the platoon continue to inch its way up Hill 109 with the Third Platoon following. Looking around, he noticed the worst of the suppressive fire was coming not only from Hills 111 and 143 but from Hill 125 as well. All three hills were objectives for the 9th Regiment. *Where the hell is the 9th?* Zimmer was thinking, not realizing that Colonel Murray had negotiated for the 9th to delay its assault. Delta Company was paying for that decision.

Reaching the crest, Zimmer quickly surmised why the enemy was able to lob hand grenades on them. They had set up a reverse slope defense whereas the air strikes had gone in on the forward slope military crest, the usual place a defender on a hill sets up. Now he understood why, when they'd observed the forward slope and seen so few enemy, they'd thought this would be easy.

Easy Company was moving up as well, stepping off at 0800 hours. As they approached the village of Obong-ni, they came under intense machine-gun fire. For an hour they fought through the village before they reached the foot of Hills 143 and 147. The casualties were so high that they could go no further.

"Colonel, we've got to get the 9th moving to take Hill 125. It's murdering Dog Company," Colonel Rosie said over the field telephone.

"I'll call the 9th and see if they'll get moving," Murray said, looking at his radio telephone operator, who immediately and without instructions rang up the 9th CP.

"Is Colonel Hill there?" Murray asked impatiently. After a moment, his question was answered.

"Murray, Hill here. Do you want me to attack now?" Hill asked, having been watching the situation across the road.

"Please do. Hill 125 is killing us," Murray said.

"We will launch now" was all Hill said before he hung up.

Immediately, artillery fire began landing on Hill 125. Murray could see soldiers of the 9th moving forward towards the base of the hill. As they moved, they came under mortar fire as well, which was tearing through the ranks. Looking back at Delta Company, he could see that they were attempting to bring their wounded down the hill.

Lieutenant Shinka had withdrawn from the crest under pressure from the enemy as he had too few men left to attempt to hold it. Those that could walk dragged those that couldn't back down the hill. Shinka wasn't convinced that they'd removed all the wounded. Reaching the First Platoon coming up the hill, Shinka grabbed Staff Sergeant Crowson.

"Forget about getting up there. Help get my men down. I'm going back up to see if we left anyone behind," Shinka stated.

"Lieutenant, don't be a fool. They have us pinned down now. Wait until someone clears Hill 125 before you try that," Crowson yelled, to no avail. Shinka headed back up the hill. Almost reaching the crest, he came across a wounded Marine. As he lifted the Marine out of his foxhole, Shinka was hit in the jaw, which dropped him like a rock. At first he didn't realize what had happened, but as the blood flowed down his throat, he became aware very fast. Again he pulled on the wounded Marine, getting him out of the foxhole, and started to head back down, dragging the young man, when a bullet passed through his arm and spun him around and down the hill he rolled.

Sergeant Crowson watched as Shinka moved up the hill. *Son of a bitch, we've got to help him.* Searching the hill, Crowson spotted a machine-gun position that was raking the slope. Moments later, he spotted a second machine-gun position close to the first.

"Follow me," Crowson said, and First Platoon did so despite taking fire. Crawling up and to the side of the enemy positions, Crowson had the platoon open fire and suppress the machine guns while he crawled forward and lobbed a grenade into each position. Those guns didn't bother the Marines again.[1]

General Craig had been observing the actions and decided that the 1st Battalion was going to have to relieve 2nd Battalion, which in four hours had acquired over sixty percent casualties. Colonel Newton

---

1. For their actions, Lieutenant Shinka received a Bronze Star and Staff Sergeant Al Crowson received the Distinguished Service Cross.

received the order at 1230 hours and prepared to move out. This time his attack was coordinated with the attack by the 9th Regiment, which had a preplanned artillery strike on the Cloverleaf, Hill 165. In the interim time, another flight of Corsairs delivered another load of bombs on the reverse slope positions. The relief was completed at 1600 and the assault on Hill 165 and Hills 109 and 107 on Obong-ni Ridge commenced. Baker Company, 1st of the 5th Marines, was on the right flank with Able Company on the left. As Baker started up, heavy fire came from Tugok as before. Captain Tobin, Baker commander, was notified that his rightmost platoon was taking heavy casualties.

"Big Dog, Big Dog, Pointer, over," Captain Tobin transmitted, trying to reach Colonel Newton, the 1st Battalion commander.

"Pointer, Big Dog, go ahead," Newton responded.

"Big Dog, taking heavy fire from Tugok, over."

"Pointer, I'll take care of that."

Moments later, an artillery barrage pounded the village. When it was completed, there was no more fire drawn from the town.

Captain Tobin was very happy to report at 1700 hours that Hill 107 was secured. He had been talking to Captain John R. Stevens, the Able Company commander, who had secured his objective as well. Both Hill 107 and Hill 109 were now in American hands. Tobin was making his rounds, checking on his men, when movement along the road to the west caught his eye.

"Big Dog, Pointer, over."

"Go ahead, Pointer."

"Big Dog, we have three Tango Thirty-Fours moving eastward on the road. Over."

This got everyone's attention. Craig had monitored the call and was immediately taking action along with Colonel Newton. Newton had positioned a 75mm recoilless team along the road, and now he rushed two 3.5-inch bazooka teams to back them up. Craig ordered that three M26 Pershing tanks deploy to back up the infantry teams.

"Okay, we have three T-34s coming up the road," Gunny Tobin said as he stood in the open top turret hatch. "Jamie, take up a position short of the bend in the road and on the inside of the curve," he directed the tank driver. Tobin commanded the lead tank of a three-tank element. The other tanks took up overwatch positions along the road as well.

"Inside? Why inside?" Jamie questioned.

"That way we'll see him before he sees us. If he gets past the grunts, then we take him," Tobin instructed.

Pulling off the road, the tank took up a firing position overwatching the bazooka teams and the 75mm recoilless rifle team. The muzzle of the first tank came into view and was immediately hit with a bazooka round in the track at one hundred yards. The track separated, but the tank continued forward. The 75mm recoilless rifle opened fire, stopping the tank but not silencing its guns as it continued to hose the surrounding terrain, looking for targets. Tobin had already dropped down inside his tank and had his sight for the main gun fixed on the enemy tank.

"Fire!" Tobin yelled, and the Pershing belched a loud roar and raised a cloud of dust. Satisfaction registered on Tobin's face as the enemy tank burst into flames and the shooting ceased. Two more enemy tanks attempted to bypass their disabled brethren, only to meet a similar fate at the hands of the other two tanks. A round of cheers could be heard from Hills 165 and 109 as Marines and soldiers cheered at the destruction of the enemy tanks.

While the Marines and soldiers were joining hands, they weren't aware that the 1st Battalion, 27th Infantry, reinforced with a platoon from the heavy mortar company, a tank company, and supported by the 8th Field Artillery Battalion minus one battery, had received orders to move to the village of Ch'ilgok as part of Eighth Army reserve. They would arrive the next day.

Chapter 72
Situational Update

18 AUGUST 1950
24th Division HQ
Yongsan, South Korea

GENERAL CHURCH WAS as nervous as a whore in a convent. The previous day had started with hope and had quickly deteriorated by noon. The late-afternoon news restored some of his hope, especially when he learned that the enemy tanks had been destroyed and Hill 165 and Hills 109 and 107 were secured. Throughout the night, the sounds of artillery, machine-gun fire and mortars along with North Korean burp guns could be heard. As he walked into the command post for the morning update brief, his stomach was in turmoil.

"Attention," an NCO yelled, and everyone stood when Church walked in. General Craig, General Cushman, the Marine Air Group commander, and the staff and regimental commanders all stood upon the command.

"Keep your seats, gentlemen. Let's get this dog and pony show started. Who's on first?" Church asked, mimicking a popular Abbott and Costello skit. The division intelligence officer stepped forward to the map.

"Morning, sir. In the last twenty-four hours, the situation is as follows—"

"Just give me the last twelve hours. I was awake for the first twelve and don't care to relive that time," Church said, looking around the room. Most commanders didn't make eye contact with him.

"Yes, sir. In the last twelve hours we've seen the enemy holding in place. We did intercept a radio transmission that his frontline troops are low on ammo and food and requesting to withdraw west. The request was denied. Indications are that he may be at the limit of his resupply capability," the intelligence officer said.

"Now that is good news," Church exclaimed with a smile.

"We have reports from aerial observers that the enemy is withdrawing to the west. The underwater bridge appears to be the exit route, but there have been reports of swimmers as well," the G-2 stated.

Turning to his operations officer, Church said, "I want that bridge destroyed any way we can do it. Get air strikes on it." The operations officer nodded and made a note.

"We've identified the 4th North Korean Division as opposing us. Prisoner reports indicate that their regiments are probably only three to four hundred soldiers now. They're out of medical supplies. Indications are that there are pockets of resistance, but they're more interested in getting back across the river than staying and fighting. Sir, that concludes my brief. Any questions?"

"No, no questions," Church responded.

Immediately the operations officer stood and walked up to the map.

"Sir, today's operations planned are as follows." As he spoke, he used a pointer to indicate the locations of the various objectives on the map. "The 1st of the 5th is attacking south along Obong-ni Ridge to seize Hills 143, 147 and 153. They've been reorganized from last night's fight with Able Company. The 3rd of the 5th attacks west to seize Hill 206, the next ridgeline west of Obong-ni Ridge. The 9th Infantry will support by fire from Hill 165. They will then continue to attack west to seize Hill 311, which is the last hill before the Naktong River. The 34th and 19th Regiments on our right flank are attacking south and southwest to clear any remaining pockets. The 34th's final objective is Hill 240, and the final objective for the 19th is Hill 223. These are the final hills overlooking the river. We planned artillery fires to support each regiment as well as air strikes on selected targets and the river. An aerial observer will be on station all day, directing air strikes on targets and anyone attempting to cross the river. Any questions, sir?"

Turning to look at Craig, Church asked, "How confident are you that your boys can do this today?"

"Sir, if I didn't think they could do it, I wouldn't have planned it," Craig responded.

"If that ain't putting your money where your mouth is, I don't know what is," Church said with skeptical confidence. "Alright, gentlemen, let's clean this mess up today." With that, he stood—this meeting was over.

Throughout the day events unfolded as planned. Resistance was light for the most part as the North Korean forces were fleeing back across the river. Air Force and Marine Air were on station supporting the ground forces and striking enemy troops attempting to cross the river. Delay fused artillery was most effective in killing swimmers, as were strafing runs by supporting aircraft. During the night, there were no enemy attacks reported as the enemy was taking advantage of the darkness to cross the river. On the morning of August 19, elements of the 34th and 19th Regiments joined hands with members of the 5th Marine Brigade.

Chapter 73
27th Brigade Notified

21 AUGUST 1950
1st Argyll Battalion
Hong Kong

THE WEEKEND HAD BEEN the usual, with games at the Portuguese Club, drinking at the Fleet Club and shopping at the unlimited places in Hong Kong where a British soldier was rich. The only oddity in the weekend was Lieutenant Colonel Leslie Neilson being called out of the party at the Portuguese Club for an hour on Saturday night, although the soldiers did notice the commander and others in the conference room on Sunday. Colonel Neilson had called a meeting for 0800 hours. Among those present were Major Kerry Muir, executive officer; Major Alastair Gordon-Ingram, Baker Company commander; Captain Colin Mitchell; Lieutenant Robin Fairrey, mortar platoon leader; Captain Andrew "Dodger" Brown, quartermaster; Lieutenant Douglas Haldane, medical officer; Lieutenant Sandy Boswell, intelligence officer; and Regimental Sergeant Major Paddy Boyd.

"Gentlemen, last evening I was notified that the 27th Brigade will be dispatched on the twenty-fifth to Korea to join UN forces there,"

Colonel Neilson said. Murmurs were immediately heard around the room. Raising his hand, he continued, "I know you have lots of questions, and they will all be answered in good time. Deploying will be the brigade headquarters as well as the 1st Middlesex Battalion. The troops are being notified as we speak and rounded up in town and sent back to their barracks. All leaves and passes are canceled. We have a great deal to do before the twenty-fifth. Fortunately, we've recently completed a deployment exercise, so most activities will be by standard operating procedures," Neilson said, pausing for a moment. "Sergeant Major, we need to dirty down our kit as it appears to be white for the parade grounds. That will not do."

"I'll see to it, sir," Sergeant Major Paddy Boyd responded.

"Now you know all that I know. What are your questions?" Neilson asked.

"Sir, our infantry companies are understrength. Are we getting replacements?" an officer asked.

"We'll merge the fourth company into the first three. That will bring us up to strength in those three companies but leave us short for the battalion. We'll have twenty-eight officers and six hundred eighteen in the ranks. Instead of three battalions for the brigade, we'll only have two until the Australians join us—if they do."

"Sir?"

"Yes, Andrew?" Neilson responded, recognizing Captain Brown.

"Sir, who will we be under when we reach Korea? Who provides our logistic support?"

"The 27th Brigade will initially be under the command of US Eighth Army, whose headquarters are in Taegu. They will provide not only our logistic support but also artillery and tank support as we won't be taking any," Neilson explained and then looked at Dr. Haldane. "Doc, medical support will be provided by the Eighth Army as well."

"Sir, how soon can we get needles from them? I have about three thousand inoculations to give and only have twenty needles on hand. I'll be sterilizing them, but they're going to get really dull towards the end of the line," Haldane stated.

"I'll see what we can do and maybe get some from the Navy. I'll be at the head of the line, of course," Neilson said with a smile. Everyone laughed, knowing his style would put him at the back of the line. "If there are no more questions, then let's plan on an evening update and a morning update. Certainly, gentlemen, if you have a question during the day, ask. My wife will be in contact with the ladies and keep them abreast of the situation."

Over at the 1st Middlesex Battalion, Lieutenant Colonel Andrew Man was conducting a similar briefing to his officers. Many of the same questions were asked and answered. Major John Shipster approached the colonel after the meeting broke up.

"Excuse me, sir, but do you think I should take my golf clubs and tennis racket?" Shipster asked. He was very serious.

"I'd think that would be a capital idea. We should be able to get a round or two in after we arrive. You will be in the advance party flying over, so take them on the plane. The key people in the Argylls will accompany us and maybe we can get a match together."

"Very good, sir," Shipster replied and moved off to pack his kit. Turning, Colonel Man spotted two of his company commanders in a huddle—Major John Willoughby, Company D commander, and Major Dennis Rendell, commander of Company A.

"Gentlemen," Man said, approaching the two and gaining their attention.

"Sir," they replied in unison.

"How do you think the lads are going to take this?" Man asked.

"Sir, I think they will be quite keen on the adventure. Some are probably wondering where Korea even is," Rendell replied.

"Sir, since they've been here, they've been running up the damn hills fortifying positions for a Chinese invasion that has never come. They're in excellent physical condition and this will be an excellent break from the day-to-day activities. Will do them some good to get out a bit. The Yanks will probably have the North Koreans tucking tail by the time we get there and the lads will merely be hiking across Korea," Willoughby said.

"I wouldn't be so sure about that, Major. The Koreans have been steadily pushing the Yanks back down the cost towards Pusan. Appears that they have a perimeter established along some river but are still under a great deal of pressure. This could be the Yanks' Dunkirk."

Chapter 74
27th UK Brigade Deploys

25 August 1950
27th Brigade
Kowloon, South Korea

"Oh, bloody hell, we're supposed to put all of us on that bloody cruiser?" Corporal Bob Yerby exclaimed. The Middlesex Battalion was lining the dock next to the HMS *Ceylon*, a heavy cruiser. "There no sleeping berths on that ship for us. We'll be sleeping on deck, in hallways and the good Lord only knows where." The soldiers of the Argyll Battalion gazed upon the HMS *Unicorn*, a fleet support carrier that had ample room for the entire battalion. As the soldiers were loading the ships for their four-day sail to Pusan, the leadership was boarding an aircraft to fly to Korea via Japan.

As the ships departed Pusan Harbor, wives, families and those members of the brigade left behind stood dockside and saw them off. The King's Own Scottish Borderers played and were answered by the Royal Marine Band while the pipes from the Argylls competed from the deck of the HMS *Ceylon*. The song was "Will Ye Nae Come Back Again," a very popular tune. As the ships got underway, the commander of HMS *Ceylon* hoisted the Argyll regimental flag alongside his battle ensign, much to the pride of the soldiers.

To pass the time and reduce the boredom of shipboard life for the soldiers, aggressive marksmanship was undertaken. Anything that could float became a target, with no limit on the expenditure of ammo. Empty milk cartons, egg crates, wood pallets, all were targets for the small arms aboard ship. When they weren't engaged in marksmanship training, lectures were held on the current situation in Korea. Engagements lost by the Americans dominated the discussions. Reality struck home when soldiers were directed to fill out next-of-kin forms. Even some of the combat-experienced old soldiers from World War II, Malaysia or Palestine got misty-eyed completing the form.

The troop carriers were joined the next morning by two Australian destroyers. "Hey, boys, looks like we have company," Private Roy Vincent said as the HMAS *Warramunga* and HMAS *Bataan* came into view, approaching fast.

"Yeah, we'll have an escort now as we're off the coast of Formosa and there may be Chinese subs in the area. Be sure you close all porthole hatches at night. The captain wants total ship blackout and that means no smoking on deck after dark," Sergeant Major Boyd explained.

Major General Basil Coad commanded the 27th Infantry Brigade. General Coad had a distinguished career commanding in World War II at battalion and brigade level. He was twice awarded the Distinguished Service Order for his leadership under fire. The 27th Infantry Brigade was considered to be the United Kingdom's Strategic Reserve, commonly referred to as Britain's Fire Brigade. They spent their first night in Japan at a US Air Force base and formed their first impression of Yanks—Air Force Yanks.

"Sir, am I wrong or does the bunch seem a bit casual?" Major Shipster asked Colonel Man.

"They do seem that way," Man replied with slight disapproval. "But they're flying over in Korea every day, and I suspect our RAF lads were the same in the Battle of Britain. I shouldn't worry about it," Man replied.

The next morning, the advance party flew to Taegu, Korea. As the aircraft came to a halt on the tarmac, the flight engineer yelled, "Get out!," just as the first artillery shell exploded on the ground between the tarmac and the runway.

"Incoming," someone yelled as everyone bolted to the door. As Man and Shipster lay in the grass waiting for the shelling to stop, Mann noticed Shipster didn't have his golf clubs or tennis racket.

"Major, did you misplace your golf clubs?" Man asked.

"No, sir, I placed them in that ditch. I really don't think I'm going to have an opportunity to play," Shipster said. And he never saw his golf clubs again.

Chapter 75
Welcome to Pusan

29 August 1950
  27th Infantry Brigade
  Pusan, South Korea

ACTIVITY at the docks in Pusan was always lively, with ships of all types delivering much-needed logistical supplies and troops. The HMS *Ceylon* eased into its berth. The HMS *Unicorn* had a less-than-stellar docking, initially having run aground and required a tug to pull him off, which allowed HMS *Unicorn* to pull in behind HMS *Ceylon*. The soldiers on HMS *Unicorn* didn't have much of an opportunity to witness their arrival as they had been told this was going to be a contested landing and they should be prepared to fight their way off the ship. They were down below getting their kit on when the gangplank was put in place. When they came on deck, instead of machine-gun bullets greeting them were a group of dignitaries, a Korean reception committee and an American band playing "Colonel Bogey March" and "God Save the King." Instead of being tossed grenades, young girls tossed flowers to the debarking soldiers. They were not impressed with the rear-echelon US Army folks standing to the side with weapons, sidearms and knives on their ankles. It was determined that these were the forklift drivers and stevedores working the docks.

"What is it about those working in the rear area attempting to look like the gents on the line?" Corporal Roy Vincent asked of Corporal Yerby.

"Methinks these people want to be like John Wayne. It's the same with our lads too," Yerby responded.

"Alright, stop your jabbering and get ready to step off," the sergeant major said, walking past the couple.

Final instructions were issued and the Argylls fell into a four-man front and marched off to the railroad station. As they moved down the streets in a smart formation with kilts on and bagpipes playing, a crowd lined the street and cheered them on. As the soldiers marched, however, they began to notice Pusan. The streets were covered in litter and the stench was immediately apparent. The city was packed with refugees, and as there were no public toilets, human waste in street gutters was plentiful. Some of the cheering crowd looked as they hadn't eaten in days, and children ran alongside the formation begging for anything and everything—cigarettes, gum, candy, C rations. All the soldiers could do was maintain eyes forward and keep marching, ignoring the pleas from the children.

Arriving, they found a train already positioned for them. Nothing like the trains in Great Britain. These were left over from the Japanese occupation. Inside they found hard wooden benches for seats along with chicken and duck feathers and droppings from the birds as well as from goats and pigs. Their legs were immediately attacked by the numerous fleas inside each car. Garbage from refugees that had arrived on the train was still in the cars, and it all had to be cleaned out before the soldiers could load.

"Doc, have you seen the condition of these cars?" Colonel Man asked.

"I have, sir, and I'd recommend that we attempt to disinfect them," Doc Haldane recommended. "I'll contact the Navy and see if they can send over a disinfection team before we board."

"Doc, if somebody had said bubonic plague was rife, I wouldn't have been a bit surprised," Colonel Man said. "Pusan is a filthy hole."[1]

As the men loaded, another train arrived. What the men saw sobered many right away. The train was carrying hundreds of wounded American soldiers. The reality of the situation was beginning to set in.

The train ride was mostly at night, which the soldiers didn't mind. What they did see pulling out of Pusan didn't impress them. Refugees had taken up residence in the open fields on the outskirts of the city. They could see tents and cardboard box houses. What looked like cooking pots over open fires were actually US Army steel helmets. Some helmets were used as receptacles for human waste, which was then carried into the rice fields and used as fertilizer. The street corners were usually occupied by one or two maimed soldiers competing with kids for any food the Brits would give them. The British soldiers had been issued US C rations as they boarded the train, and the ham and lima beans meal was quickly being discarded out the train windows.

The train finally came to a stop twenty miles southwest of Taegu. General Coad was there to meet the commanders as they stepped off.

"Gentlemen, I hope you had an enjoyable ride," he said, welcoming them.

"Sir, the best part of that train ride was the fact that we didn't have to walk from Pusan. Although in hindsight, walking may have been better," Colonel Man said, bending down to pick a flea off his leg.

"Well, we'll set up in that stand of willows by the stream bed. The American 24th Infantry Division command post is over that small rise, and I've met their commander, Major General Church. Rather odd fellow. Told me he was glad we were here as we're experienced in retreating. I guess they're just learning how to do it."[2]

Despite the arrogant remark by General Church, the 27th was supplied as adequately as any American unit. Doc Haldane was equipped with the bare minimum of blankets, stretchers and aspirins

---

1. Andrew Salmon, *Scorched Earth, Black Snow: Britain and Australia in the Korean War, 1950* (London: Aurum Press), 65.
2. Andrew Salmon, *Scorched Earth, Black Snow: Britain and Australia in the Korean War, 1950* (London: Aurum Press, 65).

when he arrived. The next day, he was handed a complete medical kit sufficient to perform surgery in the field. Field kitchens provided hot meals twice a day, breakfast and supper and plenty of it. Ice water was available to anyone who wanted some. Training classes were held when the new 3.5-inch rocket launchers were issued. One per platoon with six rockets was the standard issue. Training the soldiers in other battlefield techniques was a concern for the leadership. Many of the young soldiers were National Servicemen. They were only half trained before they were sent to Hong Kong. The NCOs had their work cut out for them to get these men trained before they were sent to the front. They would come to realize they only had a couple of days to make it happen.

Chapter 76
Naktong Bulge, Again

1 September 1950
  G Company, 9th Regiment
  West of Yongsan, South Korea

COMPANY G, 9th Regiment, was commanded by First Lieutenant Frank Munoz. A few days before, he had moved in to replace the 3rd Battalion, 19th Infantry, which was covering a frontage of seven thousand yards. His undermanned company now had responsibility for the same frontage. Fortunately, since arriving, George Company had received about three hundred replacements, mostly men who'd been lightly wounded and returned to duty. In addition, they had acquired some additional weapons, such as an M16 quad .50-cal half-track and an M19 40mm self-propelled anti-aircraft gun as well as a platoon of tanks. On his right flank was Fox Company, which was to the left flank of the 23rd Regiment. Also assigned, over his objections, were two hundred KATUSAs—Korean Augmentation to the US Army troops. Munoz didn't speak Korean and they didn't speak English, so they were only good to serve as laborers and porters. Payday for the KATUSAs was always on the first of the month, but on the previous morning they'd insisted on being paid and by early afternoon were all gone. This raised Frank's anticipation level.[1]

George Company was in a good position on the high ground except for the Third Platoon, which was on a finger by itself. At 2100 hours, the first of the incoming mortars and artillery rounds fell on George Company's position. From what Frank could observe all along the Naktong River, red, green and white star clusters were being fired into the night sky on the west side of the river. Frank pulled in his platoon leaders and told them to be ready for a ground attack.

On the right flank of George Company, Fox Company was holding a position on the south side of the Yongsan-Naktong Road. The main assault in the Bulge came down this road and overran Fox Company. The gap between George Company and the 23rd Regiment opened and widened.

Sergeant Ernest Kouma commanded two tanks at Agok overlooking the Naktong River. A heavy fog was over the river for the early part of the evening. Sergeant First Class Barry commanded the second tank and both were collocated with the quad .50-cal and the M19 anti-aircraft gun. The rising star clusters gained Kouma's attention. As he looked over the fog-covered river, the fog dissipated, and to his amazement, a bridge had been constructed across two-thirds of the river. He and Barry opened fire immediately on the bridge. As they engaged, they were approached by a group of soldiers in GI uniforms.

"Hold fire! Hold fire!" one of the group yelled, and both tanks stopped shooting, allowing the soldiers to approach. Suddenly, hand grenades were hurled at the quad .50-cal, killing the crew. The soldiers were North Koreans dressed in US uniforms. Kouma and Barry both engaged and killed the attackers, but not before the Koreans would engage the 40mm gun crew and destroy the weapon.

"Barry, let's move to a more open area and stop these guys as they come off the river," Kouma suggested.

---

1. In Vietnam, the hooch maids and Vietnamese civilians working on base would leave some days at 1300 hours. When that happened, there was an excellent possibility we were going to get hit hard with ground attacks that night.

"I'm with you," Barry replied, and both tanks moved into an open field that covered the Naktong-Yongsan Road. Repeatedly they engaged groups of soldiers attempting to attack down the road to Yongsan. After an hour, Barry's tank became overheated and he withdrew, but only for a mile before the tank caught fire and had to be abandoned. Kouma remained for the night, turning back several attacks before withdrawing at first light.

To the north of George Company sat Baker Company, 9th Regiment. They were on Hill 209, preparing to kick off Operation Manchu. Operation Manchu was a bold plan by the 2nd Division to have one company cross the Naktong River to the west side and conduct a raid of the North Korean positions. Easy Company, the division reserve, would make the actual crossing supported by a platoon from 2nd Engineer Battalion. The attack would be supported by Dog and How Companies from Hill 209, which were heavy weapons companies.

At 2100 hours, First Lieutenant Ed Schmitt, How Company commander, and First Lieutenant Caldwell, Dog Company commander, moved up Hill 209, conducting a leader's recon to show the respective NCOs where to position their guns to support the attack. As they did so, they were hit with a surprise attack from the North Koreans, which inflicted serious casualties on both companies. Consolidating their forces, they continued through the night to move to the top of the hill, expecting to link up with Baker Company. When they reached the summit, Baker Company was nowhere to be found as they had withdrawn in the night. Schmitt and Caldwell found themselves surrounded. Easy Company attempted to reach them but was turned back before they could reach Hill 209.

"Alright, dig in," Schmitt ordered. "We're holding this hilltop." Turning to Caldwell, he directed, "Get on the radio and tell battalion to send help."

At first light, Master Sergeant Travis Watkins approached Schmitt. "Sir, we have a couple of people from Easy Company coming in. They say that most of the company was hit bad and will not be making it up here."

"Alright, put them into positions, and if they need weapons, issue them what we have laying about," Schmitt ordered.

While Schmitt and Caldwell are holding on by a thread on Hill 209, Munoz had established a solid position west of Yongsan but had lost his Third Platoon. The enemy for the most part had bypassed his position as they flowed through the gap between his location and the 23rd Regiment. He was surprised that he still had landline commo with battalion headquarters in Yongsan.

"Battalion, this is Munoz. Let me speak the colonel," Munoz said.

"Sir, no officers are here at present. I've been told to tell you to withdraw back to Yongsan," the voice on the other end said.

"What! Hell no. We have a good position here. There's no reason for us to withdraw and give this up," Schmitt argued.

"Hey, sir, I was told to tell you to withdraw and I've done that. Out!" And the line went dead.

I swear to God if I get back and find that guy I'll personally shoot him, Schmitt was thinking when the first ground attack commenced. The North Koreans had managed to attack out of the Third Platoon location, and in typical fashion the first wave had crawled in close to Munoz positions and initiated the attack with hand grenades. The second wave came on, firing their burp guns. The firefight was intense, with hand-to-hand fighting at the height of engagement. Artillery support broke the back of the attack, but not without casualties. Master Sergeant Watkins was severely wounded, being paralyzed from the waist down.

"Master Sergeant, we need to get you off this hill," Munoz said, kneeling beside the old soldier.

"Sir, you can't afford to have four able-bodied men carry me off this hill. I can still fire a weapon, so I can contribute to the defense," Watkins said. Munoz noticed that he wasn't in pain.

"Watkins, I've been ordered off this hill and to take the company back to Yongsan," Munoz told him.

"In that case, sir, leave a BAR here with me and plenty of ammo. I'll cover your withdrawal. They won't get past me very easily," he said, pausing for a moment and noticing the look on the young officer's face. "Now, sir, you do what you need to do and that's to command this company and move it to fight another day. I need to do what I need to do and that's cover your withdrawal. So let's not dillydally."

Watkins looked the young officer in the eye. All Munoz could do was pat the old soldier on the shoulder and stand. At 1600, Munoz ordered the company to move off the hill in a column of twos. Several soldiers walked past Watkins and dropped off cigarettes and ammo to him. When the company had moved about five hundred meters, they heard a BAR firing rapidly from the hilltop. The sound of burp guns could be heard for a few minutes, and then silence.[2]

"General Kaiser, we have a situation developing between the 9th and the 23rd Regiments," said Colonel Hill, commander of the 9th Regiment, entering the division command post at 0800.

"What do you understand the situation to be? Because we have no contact with the 23rd Regiment or the 19th," Kaiser said. General Kaiser was commander of the 2nd Division.

"Right now, there's a gap between my regiment and the 23rd that's about four miles wide and six miles deep. I've ordered my people to move to Yongsan and defend," Hill said, pointing at the map.

"The only reserve we have right now is Easy Company minus, the 2nd Engineer Battalion, division recon and 72nd Tank Battalion minus. I'll hold the tanks in reserve as a mobile counterattack force. The engineers will set up positions around Yongsan. Where is George Company now…and Fox?" Kaiser asked.

"Sir, Fox has been overrun and stragglers are flowing into Yongsan. George is holding his position on this high ground west of Yongsan," Hill pointed out.

"Have George withdraw back to Yongsan. He's out on a limb there and will be cut off soon, I'm afraid," Kaiser ordered. "Once he's here, we'll develop a plan for tomorrow. I have to call General Walker. He

---

2. Master Sergeant Travis E. Watkins was posthumously awarded the Medal of Honor for his sacrifice.

isn't going to be happy," he added, walking to his office to make the call.

General Walker was not the least bit happy at hearing the news. All morning, reports had been flowing, and now it was apparent that the North Koreans had crossed the Naktong in seventeen places. The biggest dangers were in the 24th Division sector, the 2nd Division sector, and a penetration on the east coast in the ROK sector. It had been many years since an American general had faced such a dire situation. As he studied the map, he thought, *I've got to hold this line along the Naktong. I cannot let them get a major corridor to Pusan. Right now he's throwing at least six divisions at the perimeter in those three areas. Each of those areas has high ground to the sides but a natural corridor to Pusan. Right now I have the 5th Marine Brigade, the 27th Infantry Regiment and the 19th Regiment being reconstituted. I hadn't attached the British brigade to the 1st Cav, but Gay may be needing them before this is over. Time is running out. I've got to counterattack by the 3rd, if they haven't gotten too far. Kaiser has got to hold them in front of Yongsan.*

Chapter 77
The Plan

2 SEPTEMBER 1950
  Eighth Army Headquarters
  Taegu, South Korea

GENERAL WALKER HAD CALLED a meeting with Brigadier General Craig and Major General Kaiser.

"Kaiser, what is the situation in your sector?" Walker asked, almost fearful of what he was going to hear. General Kaiser opened a map that he held and spread it over a table. The others gathered around.

"Sir, in the north, the 23rd Regiment has Able, Baker and Charlie Companies along the river from Pugong-ni north. It appears that the enemy is forcing his way between Able and Baker and a second breach through Pugong-ni. Between Able and Baker Companies is the 1st Battalion CP and George Company, which are holding at this time. Behind Charlie Company is Fox Company of the 23rd at Ponch'o-ri and they're holding the enemy there," Kaiser indicated.

"Good, so we don't have a major problem there," Walker said, looking to Kaiser for reassurance. "What about the 9th Regiment sector?"

"In the north, George Company had heavy contact initially, but it quieted down and he was ordered to withdraw back to Yongsan. Baker Company is sitting on Hill 209, which controls the Paekchin ferry site. Fox Company is on his right flank and is under pressure. On Baker's left is Charlie Company with some pressure and Alpha Company controls the Kihang ferry site. Dog and How companies were moving to Hill 209 when they were hit at the base of the hill and are now attempting to reach Baker Company. Easy Company was moving forward to execute Operation Manchu when they ran into a force that penetrated between Baker and Charlie Companies. They took heavy casualties, to include the company commander and my aide, who was accompanying them. That force is now heading for Yongsan and is being engaged by the 2nd Engineer Battalion, Division Recon Company and the 72nd Tank minus. Those units are located on the south and east side of Yongsan. This morning, George and what's left of Fox Company attacked into Yongsan with tanks. At 1600 hours we were notified that the town was cleared of enemy forces, who have withdrawn and regrouped on Cloverleaf and Obong-ni Ridge," Kaiser concluded.

Walker said nothing but continued to stare at the map. Finally, he asked, "Okay, what's happening in the 38th sector?"

"The 10th North Korean Division got across the Naktong, but the 38th has them bottled up there. They haven't been able to break out and are congregated around Hill 409. The 38th has good defensive positions on good terrain and is well supplied. They're holding just fine," Kaiser said with some pride.

"Alright, here's what I want. It certainly appears that the situation in the 9th Regiment sector is the most troublesome. General Craig, I'm attaching you to the 2nd Division. General Kaiser, I want an attack down the Naktong-Yongsan Road to clear the enemy out of the Bulge. Any questions?" Walker asked.

"No, sir. We'll launch the attack with the 5th Marine on the left and a supporting attack on the right by the 2nd Battalion, 9th Regiment," Kaiser said, looking at Craig and Colonel Hill. Both said nothing but nodded that they understood. "We launch in the morning, gentlemen," Kaiser directed.

Before he left, General Walker took General Craig aside. "General, Far East Command is screaming to get you back and released from me. I told them if they took you now, I wouldn't be responsible for the collapse of the Pusan Perimeter," Walker said. "Lay the responsibility for that disaster at the feet of others and their demands back down real quick. But I can tell you, as soon as this operation is over, I've got to release you back to Far East Command. They're planning a major amphibious operation and you will return to the 1st Marine Division, which is on ships and heading this way as we speak."

"Can you tell me anything about this operation, sir?" Craig asked.

"All I know is that MacArthur wants to do one of his famous behind-the-lines amphibious assaults somewhere north to cut the supply lines to the North Koreans. Several places have been talked about, but I don't have a final word on where or when it's going to take place. But it will be as soon as they get you back. You will be part of the newly enacted X Corps, which will be the 1st Marine Division and the 7th US Army Infantry Division. Might be a couple of others as well, but I'm not aware an anyone else in the organization," Walker said.

"And who is the commander for X Corps?" Craig asked.

"General Ned Almond, MacArthur's chief of staff," Walker said, turning and walking off in disgust.

At first light, Corsair aircraft from the Marine wing streaked across the landscape, dropping a combination of bombs and napalm on Obong-ni Ridge and the Cloverleaf. This was followed by an artillery barrage, which commenced as the Marines and soldiers stepped off. The 1st and 2nd Marine Battalions led the attack, which continued into the night with the 3rd Battalion conducting a passage of lines through the 2nd Battalion and pushing on to the Naktong River. It became obvious early on that the enemy was out of supplies and could no longer fight.

Chapter 78
Garry Owens

THE 1ST CAVALRY Division was positioned on the north and northwest side of Taegu. Taegu, being a strategic location, had to be held at all costs or the enemy could easily roll on to Pusan. On the right flank of the cav was the 1st ROK Division. The 1st Cav sector was thirty-seven miles of frontage, with the Naktong River forming the left boundary and flank of the division. The division was positioned with the 5th Cav Regiment on the left, the 7th Cav Regiment in the center and the 8th Cav Regiment on the right flank. The day before, General Walker had directed that the division was to conduct a spoiling attack in the northwest to cause the enemy to divert forces from other locations against this attack. He was hoping that this would relieve pressure in other sectors along the perimeter.

The morning started off with the 7th Cavalry Regiment attacking to seize Hill 518, which was a large mountain that dominated the area. Simultaneously, the 8th Cavalry Regiment would conduct a supporting attack to seize Hill 490. Artillery and aircraft softened up the hills for the respective attacks.

"Colonel McGarrett, I'm telling you that even with the air strike and artillery prep, taking Hill 518 is going to be difficult. The approach to the summit is narrow and steep and it's the only way to get up there," Lieutenant Colonel Hancock attempted to explain. Hancock commanded the 1st Battalion, 7th Cavalry.

"If it was easy, we would have already been on top. Get your people moving as soon as that prep is completed. I want to report to General Gay that we have it by close of business today," McGarrett said. McGarrett had been given the moniker "the Senator" by those within and outside his command. He had served for a time in the Pentagon and was always compromising on decisions. Tactically, he was no genius. Hancock knew he was getting nowhere, so he returned to his command post and met with his company commanders.

"Sir, did you get him to change the order?" Captain Stein asked. Stein commanded Company A.

"No. The order stands. The order of march is Company A, followed by Baker, then Charlie and then Dog. I want you to stay abreast, at least you"—he pointed at Stein and Mulford, the Baker Company commander—"for as long as you can. That's a narrow approach, so we cannot get the whole battalion on line. In fact, at some point I suspect it will be such a narrow approach that hopefully we can at least keep a company on line with supporting fires from those following," Hancock voiced. "Captain Mulford, when you can no long stay abreast with Stein, drop back and support him by fire. Understood?"

"Yes, sir" was all Mulford said, making notes.

"Sir, may I ask, if this is a regimental attack, why are we the only ones going up the hill? What are 2nd Battalion and 3rd Battalion doing?" asked Captain Gurbich, the Charlie Company commander.

"The 2nd Battalion is setting up a blocking position west of Hill 518, and 3rd Battalion is in reserve behind 2nd Battalion as they just arrived in-country this week," Hancock said. "Look, I don't like this any more than you, but we have orders, so let's get on with it. I'll follow Able. Alright, gentlemen, get back to your units. The prep will end in thirty minutes and we want to step off right away." Hancock didn't have a good feeling about this operation.

As the companies moved out in the proper order, it wasn't long before the approach narrowed and Baker Company had to pause and let Able take the lead. For the first quarter of the way up the mountain, companies were abreast. Now it was one company in the lead with the others following. And the climb was becoming steeper and narrower.

"Hey, Captain," Master Sergeant Lyle said, gaining Stein's attention.

"Yeah, Master Sergeant," Stein responded between deep breaths.

"Sir, we're starting to bunch up. We aren't going to be able to keep the platoons on line much longer and it's going to be difficult to position machine guns to support the forward elements if this approach is any narrower." Stein was thankful at this point that they still hadn't had any enemy contact. *Maybe the air strikes and artillery prep really did their jobs*, he was thinking.

"Alright, let's pause for a moment. Have First Platoon take the lead with Second and Third following," Stein said. He quickened his pace to reach the First Platoon, ordering him to continue and have Second and Third Platoons hold and fall in behind. *Shit, a regimental attack with one platoon—this is madness*, Stein was thinking when he caught up with the First Platoon leader, First Lieutenant Flack.

"Flack," Stein called out, getting the lieutenant's attention.

"Sir," Flack responded.

"This avenue is getting too narrow to keep platoons abreast. Take the lead and the others will follow you. Move cautiously as I don't know what's up there. The air strikes and artillery may have knocked their socks off, but they may just be playing possum. Understood?" Stein asked.

"Understood, sir," Flack said. He was one of the battalion super lieutenants and Stein as well as Hancock held him in high regard. While the rest of Able Company paused, Flack continued to move up the hill, which was not becoming any easier to ascend. The approach path was continuing to narrow with steep drop-offs along the sides.

"Lieutenant, Lieutenant," Staff Sergeant Bectold called out. Bectold was the platoon sergeant and a father figure to the young officer. He had seen action in World War II and was a career soldier, not married as few below the rank of master sergeant were married soldiers. The word was, "If the Army wanted you to have a wife, they would have issued you one."

Gaining Flack's attention, Bectold pointed up the hill. "Sir, we can't go much further with the platoon on line. This is getting too narrow and we're going to have guys dropping over the side pretty soon. What do you want to do?"

"Sergeant, about the only thing we can do is lead with a squad and have the others follow. We haven't had any enemy fire, so maybe there's no one left up there. It's, what, another five hundred meters to the crest?" Flack speculated.

"About that. I'll move up behind the First Squad and why don't you follow the Second Squad, sir?" Bectold suggested.

"Okay, but no hero shit. We start taking fire, I want you to pull back. Conducting a regimental attack with one squad is plain stupid," Flack said.

Staff Sergeant Bectold moved up to the side of the First Squad leader, Sergeant Manning.

"I'm going forward with you. You're point for this one," Bectold said, placing his arm over Manning's shoulder.

"Nice having you with me" was all Manning said before the first machine gun cut him down. At once, First Squad lost over half the squad to machine-gun fire. Bectold was hit in the arm. Thankfully it was a through-and-through with no broken bones. Everyone was on the ground as they began to crawl up the hill. Behind them, Second Squad was now firing, but at this range, their fire was ineffective.

Stein had been afraid this was going to happen and immediately ordered the company machine guns to open fire over the heads of the leading platoons. The machine guns were at their maximum effective range but were able to suppress the enemy machine guns to some extent as the First and Second Squad members that were capable crawled up the hill. The call for medics could be heard several times over, even from the medics themselves, who with their red crosses on their helmets were a target for the enemy.

Turning to his forward observer, Stein directed, "Get me mortars on those machine-gun positions." Moments later, the first of the heavy mortars from battalion fell on the enemy machine-gun positions, which allowed the leading elements to move up the hill. As the lead elements approached within one hundred meters of the first of the enemy's positions, a shower of hand grenades came down the hill along with a multitude of automatic weapons fire. Bectold looked to his right and left. Most of the First Squad was wounded or dead. Second Squad wasn't in much better shape, and Lieutenant Flack was approaching with the Third Squad.

"Sir, this is madness. We just don't have the combat power to take this hill. Not one squad at a time. At this rate the other platoons aren't going to make it up here because our bodies will be blocking the trail. We need to pull back!" Bectold stated emphatically.

Flack looked to his right and left. He had already come to the same conclusion but was trying to determine how to pull back with the least amount of exposure. "Have everyone that can do so crawl backwards down the hill. No one is to stand and run. Pass the word," Flack ordered. Both he and Bectold began crawling to individual soldiers and told them what to do. None had to be told twice as the squads and then the platoon slowly crawled back down the hill.

By early afternoon, the attack on Hill 518 had failed, and it would do so the next day as well. The 8th Cavalry wasn't having any better luck in securing its objective on Hill 490. For the next several days, the regiments of the 1st Cav division would conduct a delay to a new defensive line north of Taegu. The enemy advance would finally be stopped seven miles north of Taegu.

Chapter 79
27th Moves to the Front

3 SEPTEMBER 1950
   27th British Brigade CP
   Taegu, South Korea

THE BRIGADE WAS SETTLED in for the night in the willow tree grove. The distant sounds of artillery could be heard, but nothing close. General Coad was in his tent and had just finished a letter to his wife when his aide requested to enter.

"Sir, I think you need to come to the CP. Message traffic from Eighth Army is coming in that the staff thinks you should see immediately," Captain Mallory reported.

"I'll be right over. What is it about, do you know?" Coad asked, sealing his envelope and standing.

"I think it's orders, sir" was all the aide could say. Both walked the short distance to the CP together, and when General Coad entered, the aide announced, "Attention!" This was quickly followed by an "As you were" from the general. His operations officer approached him immediately and handed him a message. Coad read it, looked up and read it again.

"Well, gentlemen, I was hoping that we could have time to acclimate the lads to the country before we went on the line, but I guess the Yanks need us right away. Let's get Colonel Man and Colonel Neilson and inform them of this," Coad ordered. "Have we any tea? I think it's going to be a long night."

When the battalion commanders arrived, they immediately noticed the flurry of activity in the command post. General Coad spotted them and waved them over to his seat, pointing at two empty chairs. "How are your lads doing?" he asked.

"They appear to be doing fine, sir. The Americans are meeting all our requirements for supplies. They look like a ragtag bunch, but they do know how to resupply the troops," Colonel Man replied, accepting a cup of tea.

General Coad paused for a moment, looking at the message in his hand before he spoke. "I called you here to give you the latest from Eighth Army. Appears they have problems all along the perimeter with penetrations at seventeen locations along the Naktong. Effective at 2350 hours yesterday, we were attached to the 1st Cavalry Division and will be moving into positions that they're sending to us after dark tonight. It will be a night move by trucks. We should be receiving an operations order from the 1st Cav sometime this morning and you will be briefed then. Suffice it to say your immediate concern is preparing your lads for the move tomorrow night. I'll be going over to the 1st Cav Division CP in at first light to meet Major General Gay, their division commander."

That morning, General Coad took a jeep and went to visit with Major General Gay. During the night, a warning order had been received by the 27th and Coad wanted to discuss it with Gay to be sure he understood the mission.

"General Gay, General Coad is here," Gay's adjutant announced.

"Show him in," Gay said, approaching the door to his makeshift office in the abandoned schoolhouse. "General Coad, am I glad to meet you and have you join us. The professional caliber of your soldiers has preceded you."

"Thank you, and we've certainly heard of the 1st Cavalry Division and its colorful history. I think we'll work well together," Coad said, accepting Gay's extended hand and taking a seat in one of the folding chairs in Gay's meager office. The aide appeared with a couple of cups and a pot of coffee.

"Sorry, sir, we don't have any tea," the aide said.

"Coffee is just fine, young man, and thank you," Coad replied graciously as the aide poured.

"General Coad, I'll get right to the point. I need your brigade to go on the line tonight. We have pressure in several locations along the Naktong and the enemy has gotten across. I'll attempt to put you in a relatively quiet sector so you can get acclimated to this place and start dealing with the enemy. I'm afraid that where we're putting you is a bit larger frontage than what any of us would like, but it's good defensible terrain about fifteen hundred meters east of the river."

"How large is our frontage?" Coad asked, taking a sip of his coffee.

"Sixteen thousand meters, maybe a bit more," Gay answered. Coad nearly spat his coffee out.

"Did you say sixteen thousand meters! My God, that's three times the normal frontage for a brigade," Coad said.

"Oh, the good news, however, is that there's an eight-thousand-meter gap between you and your left flank unit, the 2nd Infantry Division," Gay said.

Coad said nothing for a moment. "Well, I suppose we'll just have to make do, won't we? My lads will be ready to move as soon as the trucks arrive to move us. That will be after dark, I understand. I want to bring the commanders forward and conduct a recon of our position before the soldiers arrive if that would be alright. Is the position occupied at this time?" Coad asked.

"It is, and the 7th Cavalry Regiment is there. I'll have guides standing by to get out in positions after dark. If you and your commander want to go up there today, I'll provide a security detail to go with you," Gay offered.

"Most appreciated, sir. I'll go back and bring the commanders forward and contact your CP when we do so. I understand the operations order has been issued to my command post. When I get back, I'll finalize our plans and bring a copy back to you," Coad said, standing. "If there's nothing else, sir, I want to get back and get things moving."

Standing, Gay extended his hand. "General, I'm sincere when I say we're glad to have you join us."

Returning to the 27th Brigade command post, Coad was pleased that the order had been received and the brigade order was being completed. It outlined the order of march and initial positions on a ridgetop. He rounded up Colonels Neilson and Man and the three returned with a security detail to the 1st Cavalry Division sector, where they were provided a ground guide to their assigned sector. The position was currently occupied by the 3rd Battalion, 23rd Infantry, which was returning to its parent division. Coad decided that the brigade would set up a perimeter defense on this hilltop with even his headquarters responsible for a portion of the perimeter. Returning to the 1st Cavalry command post, they were surprised by the excitement being displayed.

"General Gay, what has happened?" Coad asked, seeing Gay studying the map.

"Oh, good, I'm glad you're here. One of the line units policed up a deserter from the 19th Regiment, 13th Division. He's a major and the S-3 for the regiment. He's telling us that a major ground attack can be expected tonight and the 13th Division just got four thousand replacements, most untrained and only half have weapons," Gay outlined. "Right now we have the 8th Cav northwest and north of Taegu. The 5th Cav Regiment is around Waegwan and the 7th Cav is covering this mountainous area in the center of sector. You will be positioned at the southern end of the line, but it appears that he's not attacking in your sector. According to Major Kim Song Jun, they're going to attack with 3rd Division attacking in the Waegwan area; the 13th attacks these mountain ridges north of Taegu and the Sangju-Taegu Road; and the 1st Division attacks along the mountain ridges east of the Sangju-Taegu Road. The 8th Engineer Battalion is going to be positioned on your right flank. I may have to pull you out of the line for a reserve force," Gay concluded.

"Sir, wherever you need us, we'll serve," Coad responded and excused himself, returning to his command post.

That night the trucks arrived, and with them the monsoon rains. The road was like a mud field as the trucks maneuvered their way to the base of the hill that was to be occupied by the brigade. The soldiers did their best, weighted down with equipment and ammo and with mud sucking at their feet as they trudged up the hill. When they arrived, the members of the 3rd Battalion, 23rd Infantry, displayed an uncalled-for lack of discipline in vacating their positions. The soldiers of the brigade would spend the rest of the night digging new positions.

Chapter 80
Enough Is Enough

12 SEPTEMBER 1950
 Eighth Army Command Post
 Taegu, South Korea

IT WAS obvious that the last two weeks had taken their toll on General Walker as well as the division commanders who sat in Walker's office. Each officer held a glass with ice and scotch, a rare treat. Already in the US, some religious groups were clamoring for the US Army to stop the beer ration to the soldiers. It was felt that young men under twenty-one shouldn't be encouraged to drink, but it was okay for them to fight, kill and be killed.[1]

Seated in the room were General Walker, General Kaiser, General Gay, and General Kean as well as General Church and General Coad. "Gentlemen, I've called you together first to commend you all on the job you've done in these past two weeks. Amazingly, we've held the

---

1. In Vietnam there was no beer ration either, but soldiers could use their ration cards to purchase beer. In Desert Storm, service members could not even purchase beer, and an attempt was made to cut off cigarettes and other tobacco products to the soldiers. I and other battalion commanders told our high commanders if they did that, they would have a mutiny on their hands.

Pusan Perimeter

Pusan Perimeter along with our ROK counterparts and it has not been an easy task. I have a stack of recommendations for Medals of Honor on my desk and each will get my approval and be forwarded. We've also, however, had some disappointments. In too many cases our troops have been untrained, undisciplined and poorly led. This has got to change and quick," Walker said, looking at General Kean, who had the 24th Regiment in his command, and in every case this regiment had broken and run from the enemy.

"The best offer I can make on the 24th is if we could integrate that unit...," Kean said, recognizing where the comment was directed.

"It's not just the 24th but other units as well. We'll get there," Walker said, taking a sip of his drink. "I've spoken with Ned Almond about Operation Chromite. The launch date has been set and we'll launch our offensive the day after the initiation of Chromite. We've bled the North Koreans dry. They're running at less than fifty percent strength in manpower. We've destroyed most of their tanks. Their supply lines are almost nonexistent and thus they're out of food, ammo and medical supplies. I suspect their morale is equally low at this point.

"We on the other hand are in pretty good shape. Before we launch our offensive, you will each be brought up to full strength in equipment. We have a good supply base of food, ammo and, with a full-blown field hospital now in Pusan, good medical support and adequate aircraft flying wounded back to Japan," Walker pointed out. He paused to take another sip of his drink. "I wish I could say we can bring you up to full strength, but I can't. We're about fifty percent strength as well, but that will have to do.

"I can tell you gentlemen that this upcoming operation, the amphibious landing has not been without controversy. Seems the idea was born about a week after the North Koreans attacked. MacArthur put together a working group to develop the plan. They wanted to launch long before now but couldn't until we stabilized the perimeter and released the 5th Marines. I told them that if they took the 5th Marine, I wouldn't guarantee holding the perimeter. They backed off until two weeks ago and demanded that I release them," Walker explained.

"So, sir, what is the plan now, for the amphibious landing?" Gay asked.

"They had three plans. Option one was Plan 100-B, calling for a landing at Inchon. Plan 100-C was for a landing at Kunsan south of Inchon, and Plan 100-D was for a landing on the east coast at Chumunjin-up. They finally settled on Plan B, to a lot of consternation from the Navy. Seems that Inchon has one of the most drastic tide changes in the world as well as a narrow channel approaching the city. In addition, there really isn't a beach but a seawall that they're going to have to come alongside. Not the best of locations for an amphibious operation," Walker stated.

"So why are they going there?" Kaiser asked.

"Seems after the plans were briefed and the Navy's objections were voiced, MacArthur went into a forty-five-minute dissertation, educating the participants on why it had to be Inchon. It really boiled down to the fact that he wanted to seize the city of Seoul as quickly as possible so he could have a parade…I didn't say that," Walker quickly added.

"So who is going in on the landing, may I ask?" Coad said.

"It appears that the 1st Marine Division has been reconstituted and will be going in with the 7th Infantry Division, all under X Corps, commanded by Ned Almond. To get the 1st Marine Division up to strength, they had to have the 5th Marine from us; they reactivated the 7th Marine Brigade and one other brigade, forgot the designation on that one. I know that to man them they've pulled Marines out of every other assignment across the country, recalled reservists, even stripped the Fleet Marines out of the Med and have them heading over," Walker exclaimed.

"Just so I understand this correctly, we aren't falling under X Corps, correct?" Gay asked.

"No, Eighth Army will remain as we are and attack north on the sixteenth. I will, however, be activating the IX Corps and the I Corps in the days ahead. The operations order will be in your hands tomorrow, outlining axes of advance and objectives. The main avenue of approach will be the Taegu-Kumch'on-Suwon axis. Do you want to work under X Corps, General Gay?" Walker asked, curious about the question.

"God, no, sir. I've had to serve with Ned before and have no desire to have to serve under that pompous ass. I'm sure he has his nose so far up MacArthur's ass that he only breathes when Mac farts," Gay said with disdain in every word. Walker held a similar opinion of Ned Almond but refrained from any comment in the negative.

"Well, you needn't worry. We've done well together and we're all going forward together. Gentlemen, a toast," Walker said, standing and raising his glass. "May God be with us...to success!"

Keep reading for a look inside Book Two, INCH'ON TO THE YALU

I hope you enjoyed this first novel, ***Pusan Perimeter*** from my new series, **The Forgotten War**. If you did, I ask you to please leave a review. Reviews from readers are so important to the success of independent writers. Certainly any review is helpful, even if it is painful for me to read. I thank you for any review I am given.

INCH'ON TO THE YALU

Hope to release in the second quarter of 2025.

Operation Chromite
23 July 1950

FECOM HQ
  Tokyo, Japan

The Joint Chiefs of Staff had doubts about MacArthur's plan for the amphibious landings in Korea slated for September. MacArthur had been holding the cards close to his chest and sharing little with the senior leadership which was typical and earned MacArthur the nick name The Emperor. Seldom if ever did the joint chiefs challenge him. This time however as his plan was a multi-service operation, they wanted to understand it and approve of it completely. The meeting was scheduled for 1700 and right on time MacArthur entered the room. Not a minute before typical of his style.

"Attention," a master sergeant standing at the door announced when MacArthur was halfway through the door. Everyone in the room came to attention as is the custom in the military when a senior officer enters. Even though General J. Lawton Collins, Chief of Staff of the United States Army was present and wore four stars, MacArthur wore five stars and therefore was of a higher rank. MacArthur made it into the room before he said, "Please take your seats Gentlemen."

After he was seated, MacArthur looked over the faces around the table. General Collins was seated to the right of MacArthur who was seated at the head of the table. Admiral Forrest B. Sherman, Chief of

Naval Operations was seated to the left of MacArthur. Vice Admiral Turner Joy, Commander Naval Forces, Far East, and Vice Admiral Arther D. Struble, Commander US Seventh Fleet, Pacific, were next to Sherman as well as Rear Admiral James H. Doyle, Commander Amphibious Group ONE. On the other side of the table next to General Collins was Major General Ned Almond, Chief of Staff, Far East Command, Brigadier General Doyle O. Hickey, Deputy Chief of Staff, FECOM, and then Brigadier General Ed Wright, Assistant Chief of Staff G-3 and head of the Joint Project and Planning Staff. For some weeks based on what the JCS had been hearing they had reservations about an amphibious landing at Inchon.

"Gentlemen I am glad that you have come to sit down with us and go over OPERATION CHROMITE which proposes an amphibious landing behind the Korea front lines. I will have General Wright, head of the Joint Project and Planning Staff, and the man responsible for this plan to brief you," MacArthur said and nodded to General Wright who stood and moved to a podium with a map of Korea behind him.

"Good Evening Gentlemen, first slide please," General Wright called for as a slide with three operation plans listed appeared on a screen to the right of a wall map of Korea. "We have developed three operational plans that reflect the three courses of action that we have considered. The overall operation is Operation Chromite. Under Operation Chromite, we have OPLAN 100-B, OPLAN 100-C and OPLAN 100-D. I will now discuss each in more detail. OPLAN 100-B calls for an amphibious landing in the vicinity of Inchon," Wright said. Right away he could tell that Admiral Doyle was not in agreement but refrained from asking Wright any questions. OPLAN-C calls for an amphibious landing at Kunsan, one hundred miles south of Inchon on the west coast and PLAN-D which is a landing on the east coast at Chumunjin-up." As Wright spoke an aide used a pointer to point to each location on the large wall map to the right side of the slide. "In each case, 8th Army will conduct a simultaneous attack to the north to fix and destroy enemy forces opposing them. In the case of OPLAN B and C, a deception attack will be launched on the east coast consisting of South Korean forces. Next slide please," Wright called for and the slide changed. The slide indicated the organization of ground forces. "In each course of action, the same organization of ground forces will be as indicated. The X Corps under the command of General Almond will have overall command of the amphibious operation. They will have the 1st Marine Division and the 7th Infantry Division for the operation." As he spoke, he covered all three proposed courses of action and thoughtfully presented the pros and cons of each course of action. MacArthur said nothing during the brief. When Wright had finished, MacArthur took the floor.

"Gentlemen I believe that OPLAN 100-B offers the best hope for success for several reasons. The enemy has an exposed rear. He has moved the majority of his combat power south and is up against, or will be shortly, the Eighth Army along the Naktong River surrounding Pusan. The North Korean forces have no reserve forces in the vicinity of Inchon, the closest forces being in Suwon to the south. Inchon is the port for Seoul, only eighteen miles from Seoul and the quickest route. This port is an ice-free port in the winter months which will be coming in the not-too-distant future. The rapid seizure of Seoul will have a military affect as well as a political and psychological impact on the enemy and the world stage. The main supply routes to the south are through Seoul with rail and highway connections. Cut them and the enemy will rapidly run out of the ability to fight thus relieving pressure on the Eighth Army which will be able to counterattack. Inchon and Seoul are the anvil; Eighth Army is the hammer. Lastly the enemy would not expect an attack this deep in their rear at a location not perfect for an amphibious landing," MacArthur concluded and surveyed the room. He paused at the expression on Admiral Doyle's face. "You have a question, Admiral?" MacArthur asked.

"No Sir, not a question, but I do have concerns. We are facing a drastic tide change every twelve hours of 31 feet. The only times suitable for the landings is early morning and very late afternoon. There is no real beach but mud flats which the heavy equipment cannot be brought over nor the LTS off load over. In Inchon proper there is a sixteen-foot concrete seawall that the landing craft are going to have to come up to and the troops use scaling ladders to climb up the wall.

There are wharfs that follow on shipping could use if they are not destroyed. The approach is a fifty-mile narrow, twisting channel and only usable at a rising tide and the ships must be out on the ebb tide which does not leave much time for off-loading the forces. I honestly cannot think of a worse place to execute an amphibious assault, "The operation is not impossible but I do not recommend it."[1]" Doyle concluded.

"Thank you and I hope we have addressed your concerns and will do so in the final plans," MacArthur said being gracious despite the criticism.

"What additional troops are you planning to use for this operation?" General Collins asked.

"I will use the First Marine Division and the Seventh Infantry Division stationed here in Japan as General Wright outlined. We will have to beef up the Seventh as we stripped them to bring the Twenty-Fourth and Twenty-Fifth Divisions up to strength especially in infantry and artillery soldiers," MacArthur responded no longer having General Wright taking any arrows.

"What do you estimate at the number of ships needed for this operation?" asked Admiral Sherman looking at Admiral Joy.

"Sir a rough estimate at this point is two hundred and thirty ships not including submarines are going to be required to support this operation. That includes carriers, cruisers, destroyers, battleship, troop carriers, and supply vessels," Admiral Joy said exchanging looks with Admiral Struble.

After a long pause, MacArthur broke the silence. "Well Gentlemen if there are no more questions, let's move to the dining room for drinks and dinner," he said standing and leading the way. *They are here to listen, not to question or approve,* MacArthur was thinking as he passed through the doors.

---

1. Appleman, Roy E, LTC, USA (ret), *East of Chosen, Entrapment and Breakout in Korea,* A&M University Press, College Station, 1987. Pg 493*1950,* Texas

Appendix A

UN Resolution 82 (1950) Resolution of 25 June 1950 (S/1501)

The Security Council,

Recalling the finding of the General Assembly in its Resolution 293 (IV) of 21 October 1949 that the Government of the Republic of Korea is a lawfully established government having effective control and jurisdiction over that part of Korea where the United Nations Temporary Commission on Korea was able to observe and consult and in which the great majority of the people of Korea reside; that this government is based on elections which were a valid expression of the free will of the electorate of that part of Korea and which were observed by the Temporary Commission; and that this is the only such government in Korea,

Mindful of the concern expressed by the General Assembly in its resolutions 195 (III) of 12 December 1948 and 293 (IV) of 21 October 1949 about the consequences which might follow unless Member States refrained from acts derogatory to the results sought to be achieved by the United Nations in bringing about the complete independence and unity of Korea; and the concern expressed that the situation described by the United Nations Commission on Korea in its report menaces the safety and well-being of the Republic of Korea and of the people of Korea and might lead to open military conflict there,

Appendix A

Noting with grave concern the armed attack on the Republic of Korea by forces from North Korea,

Determines that this action constitutes a breach of the peace; and

I

Calls for the immediate cessation of hostilities;
Calls upon the authorities in North Korea to withdraw forthwith their armed forces to the 38th parallel;

II

Requests the United Nations Commission on Korea:
(a) To communicate its fully considered recommendations on the situation with the least possible delay;
(b) To observe the withdrawal of North Korean forces to the 38th parallel;
(c) To keep the Security Council informed on the execution of this resolution:

III

Calls upon all Member States to render every assistance to the United Nations in the execution of this resolution and to refrain from giving assistance to the North Korean authorities.[1]

---

1. United Nations Security Council, "Resolution 82 (1950): Complaint of Aggression Upon the Republic of Korea," June 25, 1950, https://digitallibrary.un.org/record/112025?ln=en.

Disclaimer

I have attempted to recount the events of this battle from a primary and secondary sources. Names of individuals in the events are actual names except in a few cases. Conversations are what was said or would have been said under those combat conditions.

Bibliography

"1st Lt. Jansen Calvin Cox, Service Member Personnel Profile." Defense POW/MIA Accounting Agency: n.d., https://dpaamil.sites.crmforce.mil/dpaaProfile?id=a0Jt000000x894YEAQ.

"24th Infantry Division Records." Korean War Project, n.d. https://www.koreanwar.org/html/2018-jpac-24div.html.

Appleman, Roy E. *East of Chosin: Entrapment and Breakout in Korea, 1950.* College Station: Texas A&M University Press, 1987.

Appleman, Roy E. *United States Army in the Korean War: South to the Naktong, North to the Yalu (June–November 1950).* Washington, D.C.: United States Army Center of Military History, 1992.

"Battle of Sangju (1950)." Wikipedia, February 24, 2023. https://en.wikipedia.org/wiki/Battle_of_Sangju_(1950).

"Battle of the Pusan Perimeter." Wikipedia, September 24, 2024. https://en.wikipedia.org/wiki/Battle_of_the_Pusan_Perimeter.

"Black Soldier, White Army: The 24th Infantry in Korea." United States Army Center of Military History, n.d. https://www.history.army.mil/books/korea/24TH.HTM.

"Bodo League Massacre." Wikipedia, October 25, 2024. https://en.wikipedia.org/wiki/Bodo_League_massacre.

"Cpt. George W. Kristanoff." Korean War Project. https://www.koreanwar.org/html/16448/korean-war-project-minnesota-o-1336515-cpt-george-walter-kristanoff/.

"Charles Bradford Smith." Wikipedia, July 9, 2024. https://en.wikipedia.org/wiki/Charles_Bradford_Smith.

"Col. Carl Franklin Bernard." Military Hall of Honor. https://www.militaryhallofhonor.com/honoree-record.php?id=309299.

"Dean Acheson." Wikipedia, September 19, 2024. https://en.wikipedia.org/wiki/Dean_Acheson.

Bibliography

"Edward Almond." Wikipedia, November 2, 2024. https://en.wikipedia.org/wiki/Edward_Almond.

Fehrenbach, T. R. *This Kind of War: The Classic Korean War History*. Dulles, Virginia: Potomac Books, 2008.

French, Howard W. "John J. Muccio, 89; Was U.S. Diplomat in Several Countries." *The New York Times*, May 22, 1989. https://www.nytimes.com/1989/05/22/obituaries/john-j-muccio-89-was-us-diplomat-in-several-countries.html.

Gady, Franz-Stefan. "Is This the Worst Intelligence Chief in the US Army's History?" *The Diplomat*, January 27, 2019. https://thediplomat.com/2019/01/is-this-the-worst-intelligence-chief-in-the-us-armys-history/.

"Guy S. Meloy Jr." Wikipedia, April 14, 2024. https://en.wikipedia.org/wiki/Guy_S._Meloy_Jr.

Halberstam, David. *The Coldest Winter: America and the Korean War*. New York: Hachette, 2007.

Military Times. "Charles Alkire." Hall of Valor: Medal of Honor, Silver Star, U.S. Military Awards. https://valor.militarytimes.com/hero/100774.

Military Times. "Miller Perry." Hall of Valor: Medal of Honor, Silver Star, U.S. Military Awards. https://valor.militarytimes.com/hero/7062.

Millett, Allan R. "Captain James H. Hausman and the Formation of the Korean Army, 1945-1950." *Armed Forces & Society* 23, no. 4 (Summer 1997): 503–39. https://doi.org/10.1177/0095327x9702300401.

"No Gun Ri Massacre." Wikipedia, September 26, 2024. https://en.wikipedia.org/wiki/No_Gun_Ri_massacre.

Pocock, James. "Task Force Smith: Artillery Commander." HistoryNet, March 10, 2020. https://www.historynet.com/task-force-smith-artillery-commander/.

Politella, Dario. *Operation Grasshopper: Army Aviation in the Korean War*. Burtyrki Books, 2020.

Press Release, Statement by the President; 6/27/1950; June 1950; White House Press Releases, 4/1945—1/1953; Collection HST-WHPRF: White House Press Release Files (Truman Administration); Harry S. Truman Library, Independence, Missouri.

Reference Data: Infantry Regiment, May 1951. Fort Benning, Georgia: Infantry School, 1951.

Salmon, Andrew. *Scorched Earth, Black Snow: Britain and Australia in the Korean War, 1950.* London: Aurum Press, 2011.

Sawyer, Robert K. *Military Advisors in Korea: KMAG in Peace and War.* Washington, D.C.: United States Army Center of Military History, 1988.

Sides, Hampton. *On Desperate Ground: The Marines at the Reservoir, the Korean War's Greatest Battle.* New York: Doubleday, 2018.

Sloan, Bill. *The Darkest Summer: Pusan and Inchon 1950: The Battles That Saved South Korea—and the Marines—from Extinction.* New York: Simon & Schuster, 2009.

Smith, Charles R., ed. *U.S. Marines in the Korean War.* Washington, DC: History Division, U.S. Marine Corps, 2007.

Stokesbury, James L. *A Short History of the Korean War.* New York: William Morrow, 1988.

United Nations General Assembly Fifth Session Official Records for the 282nd Plenary Meeting. September 25, 1950. https://documents.un.org/doc/undoc/gen/nl5/012/54/pdf/nl501254.pdf.

United Nations Security Council. "Resolution 82 (1950): Complaint of Aggression Upon the Republic of Korea." June 25, 1950. https://digitallibrary.un.org/record/112025?ln=en.

Wiersema, Richard E. *No More Bad Force Myths: A Tactical Study of Regimental Combat in Korea, July 1950.* Fort Leavenworth, KS: United States Army Command and General Staff College, School of Advanced Military Studies, 1997. https://apps.dtic.mil/sti/pdfs/ADA340611.pdf

Y'Blood, William T. *MiG Alley: The Fight for Air Superiority.* Washington, D.C.: Air Force History and Museums Program, 2000.

Acknowledgments

Writing any historical account that attempts to put accuracy into the story requires research. Unfortunately, there are only a few around who lived through these days. Those few that I was able to contact, I thank you for your time and input, especially Mr. David Shepherd.

I would be remiss not to thank my editor, Ms. Eliza Dee of Clio Editing, for putting up with me. As always, give Momir Borocki an idea and within an hour he presents you with a great cover. My newest member of the team and one who has freed my time to pursue my research is Mrs. Margaret Daly of Rukia Publishing US, for formatting and so much more.

The one other person that deserves a major thanks is my wife of fifty-four years, who has put up with my constant time on the computer.

The author enlisted in the US Army in 1968 and served on active duty until 1993, when he retired as a colonel. In the course of his career, he commanded two infantry companies, one being an airborne company in Alaska, and commanded an air assault infantry battalion during Operation Desert Shield/Storm. When not with troop assignments, he was generally found teaching tactics at the United States Army Infantry Center or the United States Army Command and General Staff College, with a follow-on assignment as an exchange tactics instructor at the German Army Tactics Center. His last assignment was Director, Readiness and Mobilization, J-5, Forces Command, and Special Advisor, Vice President of the United States. His badges include the Combat Infantrymans Badge, Expert Infantrymans Badge, Master Aviator Wings, Senior Parachutist Wings and Air Assault Badge. His awards include the Silver Star, Legion of Merit, Distinguished Flying Cross, Bronze Star with oak Leafs and Air Medal with "V". Upon retiring from the US Army, he went into private business. He and his wife have been married for the past fifty-two years and have two sons, both Army officers.

www.MattJacksonBooks.com

amazon.com/stores/Matt-Jackson/author/B09HP4L2WY

bookbub.com/authors/matt-jackson-e002f7c1-7f90-4681-9d93-1dd281a27c68

youtube.com/@mattjackson654

Also by Matt Jackson

Books by Matt Jackson can be found on Amazon in print paperback, print hardback, and kindle formats.

Undaunted Valor Series: Follow a young man from the time he joins the military in 1968 after two worthless years in college and watch his progression from a private to an accomplished combat instructor pilot over the course of two years. All events are true, and most of the characters are people he flew with.

Undaunted Valor: An Assault Helicopter Unit in Vietnam 1969–1970

Undaunted Valor: Medal of Honor

Undaunted Valor: Lam Son 1971

Battle of Quang Tri, 1972

Battle for An Loc, 1972

Battle of Kontum, 1972

Crisis in the Desert Series (coauthored with James Rosone): How much different would Desert Shield and Storm have been if Saddam had carried his attack through Saudi Arabia and into the UAE? This series examines the difficulties and challenges that would have faced the allied forces if Saddam had carried the attack as well as received assistance from the crumbling Soviet Union at the time.

Project 19

Desert Shield

Desert Storm

The Cost of Valor: A screenplay based on *Undaunted Valor: Lam Son 1971* and currently being offered to studios. Please visit *Undaunted Valor* on Facebook for updates on the status of this effort.

Copyright